LEFT TO THEMSELVES

RANDOM HOUSE
NEW YORK

LEFT TO THEMSELVES

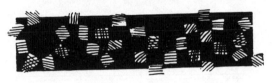

MARY GRIMM

Library of Congress Cataloging-in-Publication Data
Grimm, Mary.
Left to themselves / Mary Grimm.—1st ed.
p. cm.
ISBN 0-679-40101-6:
I. Title.
PS3557.R4933L8 1993
813'.54—dc20   92-24611

Manufactured in the United States of America
98765432
First Edition

Book design by Lilly Langotsky

FOR DAVID AUGUSTUS GRIMM
AND JOSEPHINE BERNADETTE MORROW GRIMM

LEFT TO THEMSELVES

Lucette closes the door of her mother's house with both hands, fitting it carefully against the jamb. She pushes until she feels it sucked into place and then stands with the flat of her hand against the wood.

On the other side of the door the kitchen is dark. The table is swept clean of breakfast crumbs, with a bowl, a spoon, a cup, a glass—cereal in the bowl, tea bag in the cup, orange juice glowing in the glass, all sitting there in the dark where the clock ticks. It is dark outside, too, a dark Friday morning, January. The familiar bad feeling comes over Lucette: She has forgotten something, maybe has left the keys on the counter just the other side of the door, a foot away from her hand but unreachable now it is locked. She cups her coat pocket for the lumpy feel of the metal keys, puts the other hand in her purse. Keys wallet cigarettes—all there—these are the important things. She goes down the steps to the sidewalk, letting her feet slide on the icy patches, as if she were dancing.

She looks west, toward the alley, but there is no sign of Bev's car yet. She walks up and down the sidewalk and thinks of lighting a cigarette to make something happen. She kicks the little piles of snow and turns to look at the prints left by her high heels. She walks to where the street ends at the alley, looks down it, walks back to her mother's house and leans against the maple on the tree lawn. She takes out her cigarettes and lights one, and as she draws the smoke of the first puff in, Bev's car comes around the corner from the alley, the tires quiet on the snow.

"You want to go out after work tonight?" Bev says as she gets in.

"I guess." Lucette arranges her coat and cracks the window so she can tap her cigarette ash off.

"You want to go to the Maple Leaf?"

"I don't care."

"I want to go see that guy, the drummer."

"Okay." Lucette looks out the car windows at the white and black of the streets, the scarred, gray buildings, the traffic lights the only color in the early morning air. She watches the black iron points of the Riverside Cemetery fence tick past, and the great blank white face of the Christian Science church on the other side of West Twenty-fifth Street. "Why don't you ever take the free-way?"

"We don't have to stay long if you don't want to," Bev says. "I just want to see if he shows up."

"There's a lot of old people at that place."

Bev snorts. "This time be a little more cold, why don't you? Let them look and that's it."

"All I did was dance with him once."

"Well, why did you? He was drunk."

"Not very," Lucette says.

"Like I can't tell." Bev looks over at her. "You liked him?"

Lucette sighs, taps her cigarette on the window edge.

"You didn't like him, did you?"

"Come on, Bev."

When they ride over the Cuyahoga River, Lucette looks first to the left where the dark water channel twists between the piles of brick and concrete and then right to the lake and its flat gray-white horizon. The gulls are rising and wheeling over the river, silent as a cloud.

Bev pulls the car over across the street from the drugstore where Lucette works, cutting off a bus. "Call me about tonight."

"See you." Lucette slams the car door and walks in front of the bus, hurrying to catch up with the last of the crowd crossing at the light.

At the cash register, she lets her fingers rest on the keys in between customers. They've been told they're supposed to look busy when they are not ringing things up, rearranging the cartons of cigarettes or changing the prices on sale items or wiping the counter and the glass of the cases that hold watches and cameras, but Lucette never does this. When a customer comes up to her she taps in the prices as rapidly as possible. She is very fast. She moves her hands and body in regular patterns, touching the keys, slapping the button that opens the drawer, sliding the jars and bottles and boxes into the bag, presenting the customer with the change. She likes to add small lists of purchases up in her head and ring just the total. The manager doesn't like this, though, so she does it only when he's in the back having a toke. The customers never notice. They barely look at their change.

Lucette is thinking about the man at the bar last night. He wasn't so old, she thinks. She saw him on the other side of the bar. The smoke made a haze, like something burning on a cold day. They were all old men in that bar, sitting over their beer, no one dancing except these two fat girls wearing long dresses. The band was playing those old slow songs where everybody leaves everybody else, country songs, totally uncool, not even the Eagles.

This might be a story Lucette is telling someone, and she pauses, as if there was someone across the counter from her, as if this person might have asked a question. He was probably thirty, she calculates. He got up from his seat at the other side of the bar and walked all the way around to where she and Bev were sitting. She felt him stopping behind her. The old guy sitting next to her had said, "Hey, Harry." And he said back, "How are you, Tase?" and he just stood there about an inch away from her.

Lucette thinks herself back to the bar, the dim golden smoky light, the clinking, the buzz of talk, the noise of the band, the bass chords booming in her chest. He said what a lousy dancer he was, like a lot of older guys do. He was wearing these big boots, all beat up, he shuffled them around the dance floor. But he had a nice way of holding on while they danced, with one hand folded over Lucette's, keeping it against his chest, the other flat on the middle of her back. His shirt was soft from washing. He kept a little space between them, but his face would brush up against Lucette's and she could feel the scratch of his beard growing out.

The phone rings. "Gray Drugs, can I help you?" Lucette says.

"Lucette? Honey?"

Lucette turns her body away from the rest of the store. "Yes," she says.

"Lucette honey, I think we're out of milk. Did you notice?"

"Yes."

"I'd go out and get some, but I have this headache."

"That's okay."

"The mailman came." A pause. "There wasn't anything, though. I don't know why he bothers. It was pretty cold out, didn't you think?"

"Pretty cold."

"Well, you're probably busy, I better go. Lucy—"

Lucette holds the phone, pressing the tips of her fingers against the circle of the mouthpiece, listening to the faint sound of her mother's breath.

"Are you coming right home after work?"

"Yes."

"I just wondered, because of the milk."

"Okay."

"Well, I'll go now."

"Good-bye."

"Good-bye honey. I'll see you later, okay?"

Lucette hangs up the phone. The manager, Mr. Abruzzi, is coming up front, eyes wide, floating up the aisle. He gives her a little salute as he passes her register. She pouts her lips at him and lets the tip of her tongue protrude. He shakes his finger at her and comes around behind the counter. He grips her elbows and leans up against her, raising his eyebrows.

"In your dreams," she tells him.

He puts his mouth to her ear and whispers, "Fix the cigarette display or die."

Lucette pushes him off and he floats away. She resumes her position, fingers resting lightly on the keys of the cash register.

At three o'clock, Cynthia lets herself in the back door. The house is empty, Derek has already gone to work. Joey is not home from school yet. She dumps the bags of groceries on the floor and starts to unpack them. When she finds the coffee, she abandons the rest and pulls the silverware drawer out, searching for the can opener. She opens the coffee, runs water, testing it with her finger for coldness, and holds the coffee pot under it. When the coffeemaker begins to drip, she picks up her purse and runs upstairs. In the bathroom, she pulls the chain of the overhead light and looks at herself in the mirror. She combs her hair so that it stands away from her face like wings. When she turns away from the mirror, her hair falls back to hang on either side of her face as it always does. She looks down at her shirt, pulls it over her head. Hugging herself, rubbing her arms, she goes into the bedroom and pulls out the bureau drawer.

Looking into it, she stands still and thoughtful. One lock of her hair drops forward and she twists it around her finger and then smooths it flat against the knob of her collarbone as she bends over the drawer. In the gray afternoon light her skin has no color. Her hair is cool, like water falling over her shoulders and down her back. She slides her hands in among the piles of shirts and blouses, remembering them with her fingers—too dressy, too tight, a button off, faded, too young. She takes out a red turtleneck and pulls it over her head, twitching it down over her breasts and ribs, turning to the mirror to look at it. She takes it off. She puts on a blue T-shirt, but already there are goosebumps on her long thin arms, and she takes this off, too. She goes to the window and looks out, her arms crossed over her chest.

There is the noise of a car in the driveway, and immediately Cynthia seizes a man's white shirt from the doorknob of the closet and pulls it on, buttoning it as she runs down the stairs. She looks through the stained-glass window on the landing. Through one of the long red panes, which is like a slab of cherry candy worn thin and translucent by licking, she can see the car. She runs down to the mirror by the front door. She pushes her hair back and buttons the top button of the shirt. In the kitchen she begins to put the groceries away, carefully, competently. Deliberately she divides the things she has bought into three groups: cupboard, refrigerator, freezer. She is balancing a net bag of apples in one hand when she hears a key in the back door.

She goes to the door, still holding the bag of apples, and opens it before the key has turned all the way.

"Harry," she says.

"Any coffee?" he asks.

"I just made some," she says, handing him two cups. "Pour me some too, while I put the rest of this away."

Her cousin Harry sits at the big round table. "Where's Joey? I've got something for him in the car."

"It's his day for trumpet."

"It'll wait, I guess."

Harry sits holding the cup in both hands. He looks out the window at the frozen branches of the climbing roses as they bend and claw with the wind. Cynthia puts the cereal boxes in the cupboard and goes to stand next to Harry. She picks up a box of crackers and a bag of chocolate-chip cookies.

"Did you work today?" Cynthia opens the bag of cookies and holds it out to him.

Harry takes a cookie. "Only a couple hours. Too cold to work on the foundation. The ground's frozen."

Cynthia sits down with her coffee. The house is entirely still. Outside, snow has begun to fall. She holds the cup in both hands as Harry does. She feels the emptiness of all the rooms around and above them. The steam from their cups rises and disappears. Cynthia lowers her face to feel the warmth. Harry clears his throat. The square of the window shows the world outside to be blue, as if the house and yard and the neighbors' houses and yards were all under water, the long branches of the roses waving and reaching like seaweed. Cynthia puts her hand on top of Harry's, and they sit there, unmoving for a minute.

Then Harry lifts his cup, swallows the rest of the coffee, and gets up.

"Will you be here for dinner, Harry?"

"Not tonight." He takes his coat from the hook by the basement door.

"You're going out, I suppose." Cynthia picks up both their cups and takes them to the sink.

"Over to Al's."

"Well, then."

"See you tomorrow, Cyn."

Cynthia turns the kitchen light on, so that all the objects in the kitchen turn from gray to green/red/yellow/blue. Outside it is dark. From the front window, if she wants to look, she would see Harry's red taillights getting smaller and smaller in the snowy street.

Now that Harry is gone, Cynthia pours herself another cup of coffee. She sits down in the rocking chair, turning it so that she can put her feet up. She looks at the ceiling. The house seems noisier now the light is on, and she listens to the tap of the furnace and the small rattle of the storm windows. This is the house that belonged to her grandmother. She crawled on this floor and kicked her feet at the stooping figures who picked her up, her old uncles and aunts. When she and Harry were babies, the aunts used to put them both in the rocking chair and coo at them and say how cute they were. Harry would bat at Cynthia's ear and Cynthia would grip his finger and the old uncles and aunts would laugh and say, look how they love each other. Cynthia doesn't really remember this, although she has tried.

Now it is Cynthia's house, Cynthia who looks out the kitchen window while she washes the dishes, Cynthia who roots around in the back room for old papers or rubber boots, Cynthia who worries over a crack in the kitchen ceiling. No sense in asking Derek to do anything about it. Harry can take a look at it over the weekend.

She has a little time before Joey comes home, and she wonders what to do. She could start dinner, although this is not really necessary, because they are having fish sticks, one of Joey's favorite meals. She could go down and do some of the week's pile of laundry. She could read the magazine she bought at the grocery store. She could call someone—who? This is the time of day when a lot of women might call their mothers, a time when no one is around to accuse them of dependence. They would call and talk about this and that, what Joey did in school this week or what they both were making for dinner or the weather or what some relative had or had not done. Her mother is dead, though, and Cynthia allows the bitterness of this to fill her, thicken her tongue, block her throat. Other women's mothers are not dead, she is only thirty-seven and her mother should not be dead. She tilts her head back against the rocker's head rest, swallowing, dizzy. No mother, no father, useless though he was. Why do I have to do everything by myself? she thinks. Why does everything have to be on me? Why don't I have any help?

Cynthia grips the armrests of the rocker. She thinks about what she has. I have Harry, she thinks. I have Joey. I have this house. I have a husband. I'm healthy. If she opens her eyes, she knows she will not see the room falling away from her, its bright-colored contents tiny like a kaleidoscope kitchen at the end of a tunnel. Her throat burns but she doesn't cry. She opens her eyes.

She pushes herself up from the chair and goes to the sink. She runs water on her hands and then in a glass. She looks out of the window and sees Joey, hears him hitting his lunchbox against the gate.

"I hear you banging that lunchbox," she yells through the window.

At Al's Maple Leaf, Harry sits at the bar and watches Al set up. The bar is empty, except for one old man at the end by the door who is singing to himself. Harry follows Al with his eyes, watching carefully while he wipes glasses, sets them up in rows, checks the levels in the bottles, runs a wet rag over the taps. He sets out a small chipped dish of lemon wedges and another of maraschino cherries.

"Geneva," Al calls.

"What do you want now?" she yells from the other room, where the small stage is already set up with the band's equipment.

"You want some help with those tables?" he says, winking at Harry.

"I suppose you and Harry are going to get off your butts and do something."

"I thought we'd send old Penfield here," he says.

The man at the end of the bar looks up.

"You go to hell," Geneva yells.

The old man laughs, wheezing each gasp out, and then holds up his finger for another beer. Al opens the beer cooler.

Harry goes in the other room. The lights are not turned on in here. Geneva is a dim figure toward the back, overturning chairs with a quick fierceness. He goes over and starts pulling the tables out from the wall and arranging them in rows, leaving space to walk between them. When he is finished they make a pattern, the small round tables lined up along the walls, the square ones in two more rows in the middle. He goes to the back of the room and turns the light on in the stuffed-animal machine.

"It's too early for that," Geneva says.

"It's almost eight."

"Nobody'll be in for an hour, Harry. You don't pay for the electric."

Harry starts to turn it off.

"Oh, leave it alone." Geneva goes up and down the rows with a rag, swiping at the tables.

Harry leans against the back wall and watches her. He likes the way the glow from the machine lights up this one corner, and how it looks different from the way it will look later, when the room is full of people and smoke and the stage lights are on as well as the Christmas lights Al has strung up near the ceiling.

"You work today?" Geneva asks, wiping her way down the tables.

"Yep. The Billings job. Got paid and went right out to buy you a diamond bracelet."

Geneva slings the rag at him. "You're a bum, Harry."

Harry doesn't answer. He reaches behind the door by the stuffed-animal machine and flicks a switch. The faceted silver ball hanging from the middle of the ceiling starts to turn, throwing back ghost lights that it gathers from the room next door.

Geneva comes to the end of the row in front of Harry. "When are you going to get serious, Harry? When are you going to buckle down?"

"It's the lack of a good woman like you, Geneva," Harry says, bowing his head. "When you picked Al, well—"

"I'm not kidding, Harry. Al would tell you the same if he wasn't such a cream puff."

"I've got to go out for a little while," Harry says, and slides out from between Geneva and the stuffed-animal machine.

"Right." Geneva turns back to the next row of tables.

"Got to go out for a while," Harry says to Al as he walks past him at the bar.

"See you later," Al says.

Outside, Harry starts his truck and backs it out of the bar's parking lot. He is going to see his mother, which is something that he does two or three nights a week, although not usually on Fridays. The heater doesn't work right, and his breath steams like fog in the truck. He grips the steering wheel and drives fast, a little over the speed limit, partly to get away, partly to get there before 8:30. Visitors are allowed only until 8:00, but Harry has been coming so long and so regularly that the nurses let him in to say good night to his mother. She goes to sleep better if he is there, doesn't thrash and mutter as much. Harry hunches over the wheel. When he pulls into the nursing-home driveway, he is sweating. He leans his forehead against the wheel for a minute. He ought to have had another drink before he came, he thinks.

The nurse at the desk sits behind a fortification of counters, file cabinets, piles of papers, potted plants. Harry looks at her through the glass of the door before he opens it. She is serene, her head bent, the light glinting off her glasses, surrounded by white and pale colors. When he comes in, she looks up and smiles.

"Hello, Mr. Walker," she says.

"Hello." Harry is not close enough to read her name, and he cannot remember it, although her face, her voice, the way she puts her hand up to adjust her glasses are as familiar to him as a lover's.

"Is it snowing yet?" she asks.

Harry half turns around to look back outside. "No," he says. "Not yet."

"I hate it when it snows after Christmas, don't you?" she says, putting her finger in the book she is reading.

"It's bad on a job," Harry says. He moves closer and rests his elbows on the smooth blue Formica of the counter. Her hair is a very nice color, sort of brown with red in it, he thinks, although she isn't pretty. This is something he has noticed, that a lot of women, most women even, have beautiful hair.

The nurse reaches up to tuck a piece of her hair behind her ear, as if she has felt his thought. She is not wearing a cap, although she has one, he sees. It is behind her on one of the shelves, sitting up white and stiff.

"Your hair looks different," he tells her.

Both of her hands go up to it, and she looks pleased and con-fused. "I didn't do anything new," she says. "Maybe I combed it different when you were here last time." She smooths it back from her face and then drops her hands into her lap. "Well," she says, "I guess your mother will be waiting for you."

"Yeah," he says.

Walking along the bright empty corridors, he has forgotten her already, only her hair, maybe, an afterglow in his mind. At the door of his mother's room he knocks, although the door is open, although she never answers, and waits a minute before he walks in. His mother is propped in her bed so that she is half lying, half sitting. Her long, dark, graying hair is rumpled, as if it was brushed earlier and then messed up. Probably she has been tossing her head from side to side as she does sometimes.

Harry kisses her and sits down. "Hello, Ma," he says.

She looks at him with her good eye, which is dark and shiny under the hood of its lid. Her mouth moves a little, the twist in its left corner deepening, but she doesn't make any noise. She doesn't like even trying to speak.

"I saw Cynthia today," he tells her. Her mouth twists further. "I had a present for Joey, but he wasn't there." He says this in a conversational tone, and waits as if for her answer. "I'm going over to Al's tonight."

His mother makes no sound, but she doesn't look away from him, so they are having a conversation. Even before her stroke, she was a silent person. When Harry visited her then, they would sometimes sit saying nothing for a while, and then she would ask a question, and he would answer, and then nothing again. But the silence of her room is not complete. There is the noise of her roommate's breathing, raspy and thick, the small tick of her clock, the same one that she had in her bedroom in her own house. There is the sound of heated air coming through the registers, a thin whispery sound. Her bad hand moves restlessly on the covers of the bed, a raspy scratch that makes Harry's fingers tingle unpleasantly.

She raises her good hand and with difficulty holds one finger, the fourth one, separate from the others.

"Not yet, Ma."

She grunts.

"Maybe I'll meet someone tonight," he says. "What do you think?"

She grunts again, her mouth twisting.

"Maybe Cynthia will fix me up with someone. Eh?"

She bats this away with her hand. Then she takes his hand in hers and looks at him hard.

"What is it? What do you want?" Harry looks around the room for something she might want.

She shakes her head no.

"About getting married?"

No.

"About Cynthia?"

She squeezes his hand, still looking at him.

"What about her?" This has come up before, but he has never found out what she wants to ask him about Cynthia.

"I'll tell her to come visit you," he says.

No. She shakes her head, and drops his hand.

"What?" he says. He reaches for her hand again and she bats it away, a slap that is stronger than he expects.

"It's time for bed, Mrs. Walker," the attendant says, coming in without knocking.

His mother shakes her head again.

"We haven't been getting upset, have we?" he says, looking at Harry.

Harry looks at his mother, but she is disgusted with him and turns her bright dark eye toward the window. He stands there a minute, and then leans to kiss her cheek. "Good night, Ma," he says.

She waves her hand, a queen dismissing her favorite. She is disappointed in him, but it's not final.

On the way out, he thinks of asking the desk nurse when she gets off. They could have a drink together. He thinks of holding her head in his hands, gathering a handful of her glinting hair, and of how calm she looks when he sees her through the glass before he comes in. But when he gets to the lobby, she is not there. A red light on the phone is blinking. Her cup of coffee is there, half full, her cap still on the shelf, her book open facedown.

"Do you want to wear the purple blouse?" Bev asks. She throws it over to Lucette, who is lying on Bev's bed in her underwear.

"I don't care," Lucette says. She runs her hand over the lumps and tangles of the bedclothes Bev has pulled the spread over.

"Well, get dressed. I want to go," Bev says. She is putting on earrings, bending over her dresser to look in the mirror. Bev's clothes are tangled on the floor, clean and dirty. The clean ones are still half folded, slipping from their stacks. Bev's stereo is playing and Bev hums along and moves her hips.

Lucette sits up on the bed and holds the purple blouse against her chest. She can see herself in the mirror behind Bev, another room behind Bev's room.

"Or would you rather wear the black knit thing?" Bev asks.

"I don't care," says Lucette.

"Wear the black. It makes your hair look blonder."

Lucette picks the black top off the floor and pulls it over her head. "Do you wear the shoulders on or off?"

"Depends on how I feel. If I feel hot I wear them off." Bev laughs and shakes her head so that the earrings she has just put on jump. "You better wear them on or you'll have old men all over you again." She turns to look at Lucette. "Maybe you better wear the purple. You look too hot in the black, whatever way you wear it."

Lucette stretches her arms and examines her torso in the mirror. It is narrow, soft, curving up to her raised arms, held in by overlapping bands of black spandex. "This is okay." She starts going through the boxes of earrings on Bev's dresser and the ones lying loose on the dresser top. She holds them up, one at a time, to her ears, tilting her head to see herself in three-quarter profile.

"Wear the silver hoops," Bev says. "What about your mom?"

Lucette holds up the silver earrings, which chime—they have small bells attached to the bottom of the hoops. "What about her?"

"Do you have to go home?"

"Yes," Lucette says. She hooks the hoops in her ears, peering carefully to find the holes.

"We better get going then."

Downstairs they linger in the kitchen while Bev gives her mother a hard time about the old housedress she is wearing.

"Nobody cares how I look. I'm an old woman."

"Come on, Mom," Bev says, holding the material of the dress out with her pinched finger and thumb. "Look at this. Ex-nuns dress better than this."

"I could be dressed up like in the movies and your father wouldn't notice. He'd just come in and say, 'Dinner ready yet?' "

"Well, then, come out with us. I bet there's a lot of guys would be willing to say how nice you looked." Bev puts her arm around her mother's shoulders and pretends to be dancing with her.

"Get out of here, you two." She pushes them toward the door.

At the door, Lucette pauses to wind her scarf around her neck. "Good-bye, Mrs. Archacki," she says. "Thanks for dinner."

Out in the car Bev makes revving noises to match the engine. Their breath is visible in the air and on the windows, and Bev hands Lucette a rag to wipe her half of the windshield. "Do the back, okay?" she says.

Lucette crawls between the bucket seats and stretches awkwardly to wipe the rear window. She can see the hard cold moon through it and the yellow light glowing from the windows of Bev's house.

"I've got to go to the store before I go home," she says.

"Damn," Bev says. "Why didn't you say so before?"

"I've got to get milk."

"Hell. Let's go then."

Ten minutes later, holding a bag with two milk cartons in it, Lucette approaches her house. It is dark except for the bathroom light that is left on all the time, and a watery blue glow from an upstairs room.

Lucette's boots make no sound on the snow or on the uncleared sidewalk. She unlocks the side door quietly, goes up the steps to the inside door, and goes through it into the kitchen. Although the first floor is dark, the moon is shining on the great white bulk of the old refrigerator and the kitchen is filled with its reflected light. She sets the bag down on the table next to the bowl, the cup, the glass, the spoon. There is no other plate or knife, no boxes of crackers left out, no jars of peanut butter, no pans on the stove, no dishes left in the sink. She stands still, listening, and can hear the whisper of the TV upstairs and the rushing noise of the toilet running. In the dining room she can see the long ghostly shapes of plants, reaching for the windows. She goes out, closing and locking the doors behind her.

Bev flicks the lights on as Lucette gets in, and puts her foot on the gas as soon as the door is shut. "What time is it?" she asks Lucette.

"A little after nine."

"Good. They don't start playing until nine-thirty, so we can hang around for a while." She looks over at Lucette. "We can go some other places after that. I don't care as long as we end up at the Maple Leaf."

The main streets are clear, but when Bev cuts down side streets, as she likes to do, the car is running on packed-down snow that squeaks when the tires go over it. The night is full of light. Lucette pulls her jacket closer around her throat.

"How was your mother?"

"She was watching TV," Lucette says. "How was work today?"

"It was crazy. We got in a shipment of stuff for the junior department and it was the wrong stuff, or part of it was, and Marcia ran around like a chicken and yelled at everybody because we'd already started to rack things. So we had to repack everything. Was

I glad to leave. I found this really cute purple-and-pink striped dress—short, sort of a V-neck, but in the back? I put it in layaway."

"Did they have any black jean miniskirts?"

"We're getting jean stuff in two weeks. I'll look for your size and hide something, but you've got to come in as soon as you can. We're not supposed to stockpile. Come between one and two, when Marcia's at lunch, the bitch."

"Maybe Marcia's just lonely. Maybe you should invite Marcia out with us sometime," Lucette says.

"Are you nuts?" Bev turns a corner, fast.

"You could fix her up with someone at the Empire, with that guy Tommy."

"The one who sweeps up?" Bev is laughing, pounding the wheel. "The one with the glass eye?"

"I'm sure they'd have something in common." Lucette adjusts her bracelet, pulling it out of her jacket sleeve. "It would be an act of Christian charity. Feed the hungry, visit the sick, fix up the desperate."

"You're sick, you know that?" Bev peers out through the windshield, looking for a parking place. "It's getting crowded already. Good thing we got here early."

When they come in, the men at the bar turn their heads to check them out. Bev walks past them with her head tilted, swishing her hips a little extra. She looks as if she is thinking, "I know you're looking, and too bad for you." She sits down at the end of the bar next to the drummer.

Lucette stands behind Bev. She drinks some of her beer when it comes and listens to Bev and the drummer talking. She picks up her glass and walks over to look at the jukebox. There is nothing on it she wants to hear. She walks slowly around the back of the room, stopping to look at the bowling machine and the pinball game and the game that is supposed to be like racing in the Indy 500. She moves to the arch between the bar's two rooms and looks through it. The stage is lit and the band's equipment set up, but the rest of the room is dark, except the light from a stuffed-animal game in the back corner, and empty. She goes back to stand behind Bev.

"You looking for somebody?" the drummer asks her.

"No," she says.

"Did you meet Jimmy?" Bev asks her.

"Yeah," Lucette says.

"Oh right, you met last week," Bev says. "So, do you ever get to dance?" she asks the drummer.

The other three guys in the band are bent over a sloppy pile of sheet music, arguing, stabbing with pencils. Lucette is thirsty, too thirsty for beer. She looks for the barmaid, who is down at the other end of the bar. Lucette stands behind an empty stool, waiting to be noticed. The barmaid is setting up beer mugs. She is old, Lucette thinks. She is wearing dark glasses. When she is finished with the mugs, she turns around and sees Lucette.

"What'll it be?"

"Just some water," Lucette says. She watches her scoop up some ice and pull down the tap. She goes over in her head what she wants to say, but says nothing. The barmaid is starting to turn away.

"I was wondering—" Lucette says.

The barmaid turns back, looking at Lucette through the dark lenses of her glasses.

Lucette forces the words out of her mouth. "That guy, with the red bandanna—"

The woman behind the bar laughs. "Harry?" She looks at Lucette with her head cocked to the side.

"Does he ever come in with a girl?" Lucette says. She holds the ice water carefully, feeling her fingers separately on the glass.

"Him? Never." The woman laughs again. She leans forward and looks at Lucette more closely. "Leaving with them, now that's another thing. He leaves with girls. Never the same one, though."

"Oh, I just thought. I thought he might be going out with a girl I used to know. Someone I knew in school—"

The woman turns away. Lucette looks around to see if anyone

has been listening. The old men on either side of her are not interested. Bev is laughing at something the drummer has said. Lucette drinks some of her water and then puts her hand, cold from the glass, against her cheek. She walks back to where Bev is sitting, very conscious of how she places her feet, as if someone is criticizing how she moves.

The jukebox has been turned off and the guys in the band are getting up. "They're starting," Bev says. "Let's just listen to the first song and then we'll go, okay?"

Lucette nods, then sits where the drummer was sitting, feeling safer to be down, out of sight. Bev stands in the arch between the two rooms, leans against the wall, and looks toward the stage, sipping her drink. Lucette gulps her water so fast that she feels an ache in her throat that spreads, a core of cold in her body wrapped in its still-hot skin. Her face especially feels hot and she brings her cold hands up to her cheeks again, and sits like that, elbows on the bar, until Bev waves good-bye to the drummer and comes to get her and they leave.

They go to the A & K over on Fulton. They go to the Ivy League because someone Bev works with said he might be there. They go to the Arrow, which is a rough bar, but the guys there all know them and treat them like their little sisters. They go to the dance place where they just look in through the door while the bouncer looks at their fake IDs, and then they decide to leave because it's full of kids, Bev says. Kids with haircuts, kids with white shirts, she says, flicking her hair.

"They all looked, oh, you know what I mean. Not my type," she says to Lucette in the car. "Let's just drive around for a while."

Lucette knows what Bev likes. She likes guys who look a little dark, a little dangerous, but who will submit their dark danger to Bev when she falls in love with them.

What kind is Lucette's type? She doesn't know. She has slept with three guys, whom she counts silently on her fingers. Index finger, Jim Arends, when she was sixteen and he was twenty-one, a job in insurance, his own car, talked fast, liked pizza. They had pizza every time they went out, which was four times. Middle finger, Mr. O'Keefe, she was still sixteen, after she baby-sat for his kids, divorced, a policeman. He kept calling her to come and baby-sit again but she never did. Ring finger, Bob Dolicetti at the drugstore, she was eighteen, he was nineteen, going to college in marketing, combed his hair all the time, even more often than Bev, for five months, but that was last spring, almost a year ago. He has a new job now and when he comes in to buy something or just say hello she always thinks of how he looked naked. She hopes he can't tell.

"So what about this drummer?" she asks Bev.

"Jimmy? He's hot, don't you think?"

"He's not my type."

"Oh, you. We've got to find you somebody really cool."

"I'm not looking."

"Everybody's looking. You want to go to McDonald's?"

"It'll be full of kids."

"We can go to the drive-through. You can't go around all the time looking like you do and expect to meet anybody really cool."

"Looking like what?"

Bev pulls into McDonald's parking lot and up by the drive-through speaker. "A large Coke and large fries. What do you want?"

"Large fries and ice water."

Bev edges around to the pickup window. "You look too serious."

"I can't help it." Lucette drums her fingers on the dashboard.

"Sure you could." Their order is ready. Bev pulls into a space and hands Lucette her fries and water. "Everybody's got problems, you know."

"What do you mean?"

"Bad stuff happens to everybody. Nobody's parents are perfect." She looks at Lucette, who says nothing. "You know what I mean?"

"Just shut up." Lucette pokes a hole in the top of her cup with a pen and pushes her straw through.

"Don't get mad, I just meant—"

"I'm not mad. Just shut up, is all."

They sit without talking, eating their fries and drinking. There are the small sounds of chewing, the squeak of their straws in the plastic tops, the gush of ketchup being squeezed out, the metallic ticks the car is making, like a clock winding down. They both look straight ahead toward where there is another parking lot, the one for Burger King. Bev sighs. Lucette takes the top off her cup and tilts it back so that the ice cubes slide into her mouth.

"Look," Bev says, sitting forward. "Is that someone we know?"

There is a car blinking its lights at them from the Burger King parking lot. One of the people in the car leans out the driver's side window and yells at them, waving.

"What'd he say?"

"I don't know," Lucette says, although she is pretty sure that he asked if they wanted to party.

Another guy leans from the passenger-side window and yells, clearly this time, "Hey, how about it?"

"They're kids," Bev says with disgust. She pulls her lipstick out and outlines her lips without looking in the mirror. She runs her hands through her hair. She gathers their napkins and cups into the big paper bag and opens the door. Lucette watches her walk across the parking lot to the garbage can, stepping with great precision and disdain, her whole body indicating to the hooting boys in the car opposite that she is desirable, mobile, hot, what they are all dreaming about in their kid dreams, but too bad. She thrusts the bag into the can and walks back, giving her hips a little more grind. She drops into the car. "Ready to go?"

"Okay," Lucette says.

Driving down Pearl, Bev speeds up to make all the lights. "Look at that," she says. "They're following us."

Lucette looks back, there is a car behind them. "How can you tell it's them?"

"I saw them pull out behind us. Let's see how far they stick. You keep an eye on them."

Lucette turns halfway around and leans her chin on her arm. The car takes the bumps harder as Bev presses her foot to the accelerator, aiming straight as an arrow toward the light at Wetzel but at the last minute veering left onto Fulton through the red light. "They still there?" she asks.

Lucette, watching, sees their headlights, two each side, set on a spreading diagonal, a block behind them. "Yes," she says.

There is construction on Fulton, where they are putting in new sewers, and the road is down to two lanes, and in a couple of places, only one lane. But Bev drives this way every Sunday when she takes her mother to visit her grandmother and she threads her way through the barrels and flashing yellow lights at forty-five miles an hour. The slewing sound the tires make on the wet pavement, the air rushing in through the cracks, fill Lucette's head and make her breathless, wishless. She turns on the radio and opens the window an inch.

Bev is making for the bridge over the zoo, which is the way back to the real Cleveland, the Cleveland where they live. Lucette, watching the slanting headlights behind them, thinks that perhaps they are faltering, hanging back now that they are approaching this land of bad pavement, broken streetlights, old cars. They are Parma boys, probably, with sharp-edged suburban haircuts.

Bev takes the corner onto the bridge almost without slowing down, fishtailing a little at the point of her turn, grinning. "Turn that radio up," she yells to Lucette, so Lucette does and they go over the bridge streaming music from the open window, bouncing over the holes where the cold patch has worn away. At Denison, Bev takes a hard right and pulls up in front of a bar a block up. They both turn around and look for the lights, and there they are, coming along more slowly now.

"Come on," Bev says, and opens the door. They get out and stand in the doorway of the bar. Bev opens her coat, puts her hands on her hips, and stands there grinning. When the car comes abreast, she waves. They slow down and inspect the girls, the bar, the motorcycles parked in slanting rows in the street. It is a biker bar; Lucette and Bev have never been there, although they have heard about it. Through the door comes the heavy bass thumping of the music, the stomping of boots against the floor, the sound of mugs being slammed on the bar. Lucette can feel the doorknob against her spine. She has an urgent desire to open it so that they fall into the bar. She imagines the bikers lined up, all in black leather, with eye patches and with blue-green snakes tattooed on their arms, imagines them all turning to look at what has fallen through the door, the two of them in a tangle on the floor. She hooks her fingers around the cold metal of the knob. One of the boys yells something at them, but almost immediately the car speeds up and goes down Denison.

Lucette laughs. "They'll probably get lost." They laugh, holding on to each other. "My God, if your father saw you driving that car—"

"Come on, we've got to get out of here," Bev says, pulling on her, still laughing. "I'm not up to being a biker chick. I don't want a tattoo. Come on."

They drive in silence toward the Maple Leaf. Lucette leans her head against the seat. Bev sings along with the radio. "What if someone had been coming out? I'd have died. Some big old biker with a beard and mean little eyes?"

"It might have been a nice biker." Lucette closes her eyes.

Harry is leaning against the wall between the two rooms of the Maple Leaf. He takes the shot from Al, nods his head to the boy, Charlie, and knocks it back.

"You want another, Harry?" Charlie asks.

"No thanks."

"I didn't see you last Saturday. I was in here for a while with some of the guys and we shot some pool. I looked for you around nine."

"I stopped in later."

"Well, that's why, I guess. We left about eleven and went to the Top Choice, over on Brookpark. Beaner met this girl, see, and she was supposed to be over there, so we decided to go along with him and check it out."

"So how was it?" Harry holds up his empty bottle of beer and Al pulls another one from the ice drawer under the bar.

"Don't know. They got this rule you can't come in if you're wearing colors. This old broad stops us at the door and says no jackets with no colors, this ain't a biker bar, she says, so we said forget it. Beaner tried to talk her into it, you know, saying we weren't looking for trouble or anything. We didn't even have our bikes, we went in Beaner's car. So then she says we can come in if we leave our jackets in the car. But what's the point of having colors if you don't wear them when you're out, so we said no way. Beaner was pissed."

"So Beaner's out a girl."

"She wasn't so great. I mean, what's the point of colors if you can't wear them when you party, you know?"

Harry nods. He looks up and down the bar. A girl waves at him from over by the pinball machines. He doesn't know who she is, but he smiles at her. She pokes the girl she is with and she waves too, and he remembers them, their faces anyway. They are from the neighborhood, a little older than Charlie, maybe around twenty-five, the daughters of the man who owns the gas station just up Broadview. He turns back to Charlie, who is looking down into his glass. Charlie sighs.

"This band's not so hot, you know?" Charlie says, jerking his head in the direction of the stage in the other room.

Harry is aware that a girl Charlie had his eye on has started hanging out at the band table between sets. She is sitting at the bar now, ignoring Charlie. "I thought you liked rock 'n' roll," Harry says.

"Well, country goes over better here, right? I don't care if they play rock, but all these old guys don't like it. You know," he says to Geneva, who is rinsing a rag at the sink at the end of the bar, "if I was you I'd stick to country. That's what the regulars like. Old Penfield, he's not going to go for rock 'n' roll."

"Shut the fuck up, Charlie," Geneva says. "And next time you think about telling me what to do, think again, because the last thing that I will put up with is a barely twenty-one-year-old just-started-shaving jerk giving me advice." She wrings the rag with a quick mean twist and walks away.

"Well, Jeez," Charlie says.

Harry laughs.

"Try and tell some people anything," Charlie says, nervously gulping his beer.

"Don't worry about Geneva," Harry says.

"I'm not worried, not to say worried, but why a guy can't express an opinion if he happens to have one, I mean what's the point?"

Al appears. "Anything wrong?"

"Not a thing," Harry says, "except that Geneva's chewing up and spitting out the customers again."

"Well, you know how she is," Al says to Charlie.

"Don't you buy that idiot a beer," Geneva yells from the other end of the bar. "Don't you do it, Al."

Al slides a beer to Charlie. "I'm putting it on his tab," he yells back. "Don't worry about it," he says to Charlie.

Charlie takes the beer and drinks some. "Try to say one thing to some people and all you get is your head bit off."

"Come on, Harry," Al says, drawing him toward the back of the bar.

"Don't you go off and leave me up here alone," Geneva yells.

"Be right back, honey," he says, pulling Harry with him. "Let's just step into the office a minute." He switches the light on as they go into the crowded little room. Al sits down in the rocking chair behind the desk. Harry drops into the old leather recliner jammed between a file cabinet and a card table piled with register tapes and folders spilling papers. Al brings out his pipe, fills it, tamps it. He holds it unlit, looking at Harry, who is reclining the chair as far as it will go and then jerking it back.

"Did you see your mother?" Al asks.

"I did," Harry says.

"Doing okay?"

"She's doing all right. The same."

"You say hello to that good-looking nurse for me?"

Harry laughs. "I'm going to bring her by one night and introduce her to Geneva."

"Oh no, oh no you don't." Al lights his pipe, grinning. "That'd put me in some deep trouble. Some deep shit."

" 'Geneva, this is Nurse'—what was her name?—'Nurse Nancy.' "

"Diane, her name was. Diane Renfrew."

" 'Nurse Diane, then, whose name Al remembers so well, who he talked to in the hall at the nursing home for a full twenty minutes.' "

"Cut it out now." Al relights his pipe. "There wouldn't be enough time in the world for all the explaining I'd have to do."

"You should come by with me again, Al. Say hello yourself."

"I wouldn't mind seeing your mother again. She's a fine woman."

"Kill two birds with one stone. You know what they say about nurses."

"I could never understand that, you know? Why should nurses be hot, do you think? It's not so sexy—dealing with bedpans and blood."

"You could ask her."

"Cut it out." Al's pipe has gone dead, and he taps the ash out in the battered coffee can on his desk. "Well," he says.

Harry looks at him. "Probably ought to be getting back before Geneva comes looking." He starts to get up.

"Wait," Al says. "I been meaning to talk to you, Harry."

Harry sinks down again.

"I've got a chance to buy the old Sandman Lounge, what used to belong to old man Tomchek, remember? On Fulton?"

"Good price?"

"Great price. His son don't want it, and his daughter wants her share of what they'll get, so they're in a hurry." Al twists the heavy ring he wears on his little finger, taps it against his pipe. "They've been closed a while, and it's got run down some."

"That's okay then," Harry says, watching Al light his match, suck and puff, suck and puff.

"I was thinking, what if we went in together?"

"Well, now," Harry says. A thought comes to him. The shape of his future is like a box. He's in the box, and Geneva is advising him what he should do. Every glass, every chair, every rag to wipe the bar with would hold him in place like the length of chain they string between your legs at the county jail if they think you're violent.

"I haven't got the kind of money it would take," he says to Al.

"I don't see that as a problem," Al says. He is watching Harry, his hands still on his pipe.

"There's no way I'd go in with no money," Harry says, "and that's final."

"Harry—"

"No charity loans, Al." Harry thinks how he will help Al out when he buys this bar, to make up. There will be things to build and fix. Maybe there will be a place for the revolving liquor rack they had tried to talk Geneva into for the Maple Leaf.

"But I got it figured where the money could come from, Harry." Al is smiling. He sets the pipe, out again, on the desk on a pile of papers. "What about your money from the house? What about that?"

"The house?"

"Your grandmother's house. Cynthia can buy you out. You said her husband wants to do that, right?" He leans toward Harry, his palms flat on the paper-covered surface.

"Derek? He said something about it."

"Well, that's it, then. All you have to do is start things in motion, right? Cynthia should be happy to do it for you—they'll have the house free and clear, you'll have a business you're set up in." He sits back, still watching Harry.

"I don't know." Harry smooths his hands down the length of his thighs, feeling the bunched-up muscle under the cloth. "I don't know if Derek can get that kind of money together in time. You know. The accounting business can get slow."

"What are you saying, Harry? It'll be tax time in a couple of months."

"You know, Al, I kind of had that money figured to be for Mom. Something to fall back on if I didn't have any jobs. Her savings won't hold out forever."

"You got to think of Louisa, sure, but better to have a steady income, right? After we get it fixed up, that bar will bring in a profit almost right away, and then between us we'd have a good sum every month, free and clear."

Harry moves uneasily in the recliner. "You know how I am, though. I like working with my hands. I don't know if I can see myself being an owner. A manager."

"It'd be just like what you do around here. You put as much work in here as I do now, without a dime going in your pocket."

"You know that doesn't worry me."

Al waves his hands. "I know it doesn't. But all I'm saying is it wouldn't be much different. You think about it, Harry. I won't press you for an answer now. Talk to Cynthia and Derek."

"What's Geneva say about this?"

"Don't worry about Geneva. You think about it. Everything's held up for six weeks, anyway, until the estate is settled."

They come back into the colors and darkness and music of the bar and Harry is steadied. Everything here is the same. Charlie is still sitting at the end of the bar. Geneva is shaking her finger in a customer's face. The black light that he helped Al install under the bar is reflected in Geneva's dark glasses, making her white blouse shine with an unearthly glow, whiter than white. Stray beams from the revolving silver ball in the other room move over the bottles on the top shelf, highlighting them one by one: Yukon, Black Jack, Wild Turkey.

Harry goes behind the bar and pours himself a shot. He is aware of Geneva's eye on him. Al is watching him, too. He settles on a bar stool and tilts his head back for the shot, then holds his glass up for another. He stares steadily at the wall at the other end of the bar, where there is nothing to distract him. Onto this screen he projects images from his possible future: A bar, not like this one, different people, Harry behind the bar talking to customers, the beer supplier, the people from the city. Dealing with paper, bending over a desk, not the desk in Al's office. He sees himself wearing glasses.

He would be doing what he did with Al, hardly more than that. Fixing things. Being there. Making things work. The difference would be that if anything went wrong, it would be his fault. That is bad, of course. But worse, he would have Al to think of. He imagines this future Al, this disappointed Al, putting his hand on Harry's shoulder, Geneva standing thin-lipped in the background, arms folded.

Harry holds up his glass. Geneva, not looking at him, jerks her head toward the row of bottles, so he gets up and pours himself a shot, a very regulation shot. Settling back onto his stool, he fixes his eye on the spot on the wall, but something passes over it, pausing for a minute, a girl. Without even looking at her straight on, he knows that he recognizes her, but not from where.

She is tall, young. Her hair is blond, but not like Harry's own silvery yellow—more red, more gold. She is with a friend, like they all are. She turns her head and he remembers the curve of her neck seen at close range, an earring falling against the white of her skin. He has danced with her.

He remembers the feel of her dancing, polite, her bones all angled and arranged, the give of her flesh under his hand, her bent head, her hair stiff and fragrant from some of that stuff women use, each strand separate and gleaming. She sits at the bar with her girlfriend. He looks at the spot on the wall. He looks back at the girl.

"Geneva," he says. She is right in front of him, getting a beer for old Penfield, but she does not even look at him while she plunges her hand into the ice, flicks the top from the bottle, sets it square between the old man's hands where they are poised on the polished wood of the bar, fingers bent, slightly trembling. She takes the money from Penfield's pile of bills and change, rings it up, wipes her hands on the towel at her waist, and then, finally, looks at Harry.

"Send a drink over to the blond." He indicates her with his eyes.

Geneva turns her head to look. She looks back at Harry, her eyes narrow. "Al talk to you?"

Harry nods. "He did."

"If you screw the customers in your own bar, you'll find yourself flat on your ass with your dick in your hand someday."

"You can sew me a sampler with that on it, Geneva," Harry says.

"What do I care?" She goes over to the two girls and takes their order. When she brings their drinks, Harry watches out of the corner of his eye, sees her say something and indicate him with a jerk of her head. The girl has her head down so that he can see the part in her hair, blond to the scalp. Her friend looks at him, though, smiling, poking the blond with her elbow. She will not look up.

The glass with the drink in it sits in front of her on the bar, a light transparent color, slightly cloudy. Something with vodka in it. She moves her hand to the glass so that her fingertips just touch it, but she doesn't pick it up. Harry shrugs. He feels a pang, though. He feels the possibility of that hand, which has long thin fingers, a little bony at the knuckles, flattening to stroke, curling to cup or clasp.

He holds up his glass at Geneva, half rising from his stool to get his own drink, but she comes over and pours him a shot, a just-less-than-regulation shot which she pushes toward him along with her face.

"But if you screw Al over—do you hear me?—if you screw Al over, it'll be the end of you, Harry." She says this quietly. Not even Penfield, sitting next to Harry, could have heard her, if he was listening. *"It'll be the end of you, Harry."*

She draws back, taking the bottle with her. Harry puts his hand over hers on the bottle. "Leave it," he says. She snatches her hand out from under his. Harry watches her stride away. She moves fast and hard in the confined space behind the bar. She pulls a rag from the sink of soapy water and begins to do the stainless.

Charlie calls for another beer. "You can wait a minute," she says. "What are you, an alcoholic?"

When Harry looks back at the blond, her head is up. She is staring at the bottles on the top shelf, or at the mirror behind the bottles. Her friend is not there anymore. Harry settles back to drink slowly from his glass. He keeps his eyes at the end of the bar, on the television, on the two couples flirting with each other by the door. He does not watch her, but he can see her fool with a cigarette, shift on the stool, look in her purse for something. She drinks from her glass, taps her cigarette, shies away when the guy sitting next to her sways on his stool. She picks up her purse again, more decisively. She is going to go to the john, he thinks. He pours a little more into his glass from the bottle. She looks back to where the restrooms are—the door by the pinball game and the cigarette machine. She gets up fast, knocking her cigarettes on the floor, bends to get them, her head disappearing below the bar. She walks quickly past Harry, but he does not turn his head. He waits a minute. He stands up, feeling in his pockets.

"Hey Geneva," he calls. "You got change for a dollar?"

She springs the cash drawer open and slides the coins out without looking at them or at him.

"Need some cigarettes," he says, grinning at her.

He walks back, jingling the money. He inserts the coins into the machine one by one. He pauses and inspects the brand selection, waits for the sound of a door opening, of footsteps. He reaches into the machine and takes his cigarettes. He looks at them, then at the girl, who is just coming through the door. "Damn machine," he says. "They'll screw you every chance they get. Maybe this is your brand?" He knows that it is.

She puts her hand out and he drops the pack of cigarettes into it.

"Spit," Cynthia says, holding her hand cupped under her son's chin.

Joey spits his gum into her hand and lies back on his pillow. "I'm not tired," he says.

She wraps the gum in a Kleenex and puts it on the bookcase by his bed. "You've got to be tired. It's late. It's very late." Cynthia smooths her hand over the surface of the blanket, fingers searching for wrinkles. "I'll tell you a story, though."

"How about when the boys tried to ride the pig?"

"Not that one. This is about your Grandma Virginia and your Great-Aunt Louisa."

"Aunt Louisa in the nursing home?"

"Yes, but back then she was young. She and Grandma Virginia were young together, they were the youngest in the family, the babies."

"I don't want to hear a story about babies."

"Quiet. They were just the babies of the family, is what I mean. They were young, though. Grandma Virginia had long hair then, long and red like fire. It took her an hour to brush it and put it up in the morning."

"Why didn't she cut it?"

"Quiet now. Louisa's hair was red too, but it was dark, a kind of black red. They were the only ones who got their father's red hair in all the family. They slept together then, in the same room, here in this very house. They had the room in the front corner where my sewing room is now. The boys, their brothers, slept in the long back room with the sleeping porch where Harry stays. Their parents slept in Daddy's and my room, and here in your room is where the grandchildren slept when they stayed over. Virginia and Louisa used to sneak in and give them candy and talk and keep them up late. They weren't hardly more than kids themselves."

"Didn't they want to have their own rooms?"

"Families were big then. You couldn't expect to have your own room when there were ten or twelve in the house. But Virginia and Louisa liked sharing a room. They shared everything, and they felt it was them against the world, because they were born so close together, hardly a year apart, and so long after the rest of their brothers and sisters. Why, their oldest brother Stephen was born twenty-two years before them. He could have been their father. There was Stephen, then Gerald was two years younger, then the three girls—Vera, Mary Theresa, Anna, then young John, named after his father, and then a ten-year gap and then Virginia and finally Louisa."

"How come they didn't use birth control?"

"What kind of a question is that? Where did you hear about that?"

"Come on, Mom. From TV and stuff."

Cynthia stares at her son in bafflement. Why doesn't he watch cartoons? "Well, people didn't do that kind of thing then. They liked to have big families. Everyone did." She gathers herself together again and summons the mood of her story. "So then this house was full of people the whole day, the whole night. And they had parties, so that more people came over. Virginia and Louisa had so many friends they couldn't count them probably. They had a Halloween party once with one hundred people. There were one hundred caramel-dipped apples lined up in rows on the shelves in the pantry. All the girls made their special pies. The boys made a bonfire in the back—they got a permit for it. That was Gerald, he had friends in the police. Louisa dressed up as Mata Hari and your

Grandma Virginia was Mary Pickford, with her hair done in long curls. Her mother, your great-grandmother, did them up in rags the night before."

"Did kids go trick-or-treating then?" Joey yawns, sinking deeper into his pillows.

"It was more tricks than treats." Cynthia bends over the bed, rounding her shoulders protectively. It was too late for Joey to be up. Tomorrow night she would have to put her foot down and make him go to bed at a reasonable time. "To make a long story short," she says, "everyone came, all the hundred guests, and more, because they called up and asked if they could bring their friends and cousins and so on, so there were maybe a hundred and twenty, inside and outside the house, on the porch, in the basement, in the alley out back, in the attic maybe, who knows? But it wasn't like today, that you had to worry that they would trash your house. No, these were all nice kids, young people. And one of them, he was a friend of young John's, met your Grandma Virginia on the stairs. She was sitting on the stairs and he stopped and told her how the moon shining through the stained glass made a pattern on her hair and she looked up at him when he said it and they saw something in each other right away, in an instant."

Cynthia pauses and looks down at her son to see if he is listening. He is barely awake, his eyes slits, his breath already coming slower, one hand flung above his head.

"He sat down there on the stairs right next to her and they talked about their lives. He told her how he was planning to go in with his father in his store, and she told him how she was in high school and she was good at music and she wanted to be a music teacher someday, teaching piano and voice."

Cynthia sighs and smooths the turned-over edge of the sheet. "It was like a fairy tale," she whispers. "Both of them so fair—his hair was blond—sitting on the stairs under the stained-glass window. But then . . ."

She looks down at Joey asleep. "He walked down the stairs to get a glass of punch. He went into the kitchen and there was Gerald and John and Louisa, and Louisa poured him some punch and John introduced them." She lowers herself so that she is half-lying beside Joey, her head beside his on the pillow. She imagines them, a young Louisa with her dark cold eyes and that young man, William Walker, his hair like her cousin Harry's, and his hands and shoulders. The cup of punch joins their hands, a luminous poisonous pink.

The cold wind shakes the windows of the bedroom in the trailer behind the Maple Leaf. It is Al's trailer, but he never uses it. When he takes the trailer's keys out of the drawer under the cash register, it is to flip them to Harry, who sleeps there when he does not want to go back to Cynthia's. When he is too drunk. When he can't be with people. When he has a woman.

Lucette, lying in the bed beside Harry, knows nothing about this—about whose trailer it is, or when Harry might be found there. She knows that she is not the only woman who has been here with him, but she is not thinking about other women. She is lying so as not to touch Harry, asleep beside her, as still as a stone. She is turning over her feelings. Distaste, at being so close to another person, at having touched someone, having been touched, almost against her will. Triumph, that she made him see her, made him act. A sort of happiness that there is someone here in this rattling room who is older than she is, bigger, stronger. Fear, that she will be found out by her mother or the sharp-faced woman at the bar, or someone who might be at the window right now. She turns her head to look. There is no curtain, just a blind. The streetlight is shining in around its edges. When the wind blows harder outside, the blind rattles and whispers against the sill.

She is setting this act and this man against the others on her list. He is heavier, bigger. More silent. He is blond, the others were dark. He doesn't dress as well—his work boots are old, his leather jacket cracked and rubbed thin. Bev would laugh at his clothes.

Lucette moves her legs restlessly, and then stops when Harry moves toward her. He is still asleep, and she withdraws a little farther, until he is not quite touching her, although she can feel the heat of his body. It's a double bed, but there is only one pillow. She brings her wrist up to look at the numerals on her watch. It is four o'clock.

For just one minute, just one second, she thinks, and moves a fraction closer to the body next to hers, and then a little closer, until she can feel his skin all along the whole length of her side, her upcurved arm against his, her breast pressed against the wall of his ribs, her hipbone jutting into the soft side of his belly, her leg measuring its length against his. Under the old quilt they are warm, their moist skin bonds at the surface. When she pulls away, she feels the adhesion hold, then break.

Harry does not wake while she is putting on her clothes, but when she is ready, she bends over him and shakes his shoulder carefully. His eyes open with a jerk, but he lies there without moving, staring up at her.

"I've got to go," Lucette says. She waits but he says nothing.

"My mother, she'll be worried—" She wants to lie down again with her shoes and jacket on, her purse still slung over her shoulder. "I've got to go," she repeats.

Harry stares at her unblinking. "Okay," he says, finally. "I could drive you." He looks around the bedroom as if his car is likely to be in it somewhere, hidden under the pile of clothes in the corner.

"No, that's all right," Lucette says. "Thank you."

When she is walking home in the moonlight she counts things. Her steps from one end of the block to the other, the streetlights, the beats of her heart. She squares her shoulders and walks faster, in fear and exhilaration. Single cars slide past, ignoring the hanging red eyes of the traffic lights. There is no sound except the crunching of her boots on the snow, the click of her heels on the cleared sidewalk. She is afraid that she will meet someone, that someone will step out of one of the darkened doorways or from the empty porches. She walks faster and faster, slipping on stretches of shining ice.

· · ·

A hand on her shoulder wakes Cynthia. "What?" she says.

"Come on, Cyn, get out of the kid's bed."

She gets up, pushing into her stiff back with her knuckles, searching for the knot of pain. She pulls the door to Joey's room closed behind her, adjusting it so there is an inch-wide crack left for the hall light to come through. Her husband is ahead of her, the belt of his robe trailing behind him on the floor.

Instead of following him, she stands on the landing by the stained-glass window, spreading her fingers on the cold red pane and squinting to see through the colors. She wishes for snow, but nothing is falling through the empty air.

She stops to open Joey's door a little more, goes into the bath-room to check if the cold-water tap is dripping. She stops just outside the door to the empty room where Harry sleeps when he is there and listens to a tiny *skritch-skritch*. Mice? The branches of the sycamore rattling in the gutter?

She stands stock-still in the hall. What will she do tomorrow? What will she do? The stairs. She will take up the carpet just as her grandmother would have done, and then lay it down again and fix it under the gleam of the brass stair rods. She will send Louisa a card. She will buy Joey a new white shirt and dress pants. She will make a pie for dinner—will Harry be there?—yes, surely, because it is Sunday. She goes into the bedroom.

Lucette looks out the front window of the drugstore, and between the cards and posters announcing low prices and seasonal sales she sees that it is snowing, a snowy Monday in February. There are fat red hearts everywhere in the store—heart boxes of candy as big as wide-brimmed hats, crepe paper fold-out hearts that hang from the ceiling, tiny pastel hearts with messages on them. BE MINE. TOO CUTE. HEARTBREAKER.

Mr. Abruzzi is moving up and down the aisles, humming. He stops in front of Lucette and leans across the counter. "Let it snow, let it snow, let it snow," he sings to her. She folds her arms and leans against the register.

"Did you change the number on the 'Days to V-Day' sign?" he asks, then answers himself: "No, you didn't. But you know what, Lucette?"

"What, Mr. Abruzzi?" she says.

"I'm going to forgive you. You know why?"

"No."

"I'm going to forgive you because of the wonderful time we're going to have when you finally go out with me."

Lucette says nothing. She takes the tubes of protective lip gloss out of their display box next to the register and rearranges them, not looking at him.

"All I have to do is mention the dating ritual and you start to work harder." He takes the display box away from her. "Seriously, Luce. Why not?"

Lucette shrugs.

"I'm not a bad guy." He is fiddling with his tie, watching the slow progress of the store's only customer, a woman who is inching her way toward the register, distracted every few steps by another display. She is studying an arrangement of candy bars that are marked 3 FOR A $1—MIX 'N' MATCH. "So what is it?"

Lucette sighs deeply. She looks up at him. "Have you been smoking dope in back again?"

"That has nothing to do with my capacity for love. I can still be a total man for you."

"Cut it out, Mr. Abruzzi."

He looks back toward the woman. She has three candy bars in one hand and two in the other. She is frowning. "All right, this is serious now. I am asking you out for a date on Friday, four days away. To a movie. Very respectable. Tie for me. Heels for you. You pick the flick."

Lucette sighs again. "I can't."

"Oh. I understand." He whistles, smoothing the sides of his hair back. "Have to visit a sick friend? Have to wash your hair?"

"I've got someone." She punches the button that opens the

drawer and breaks open a roll of quarters, rapping it like an egg on the edge of the coin section.

"Got someone?" He leans farther across the counter. "Got someone? This sounds like a disease, Luce. What are we saying, here? Is this love? You've got this someone bad, is that what you're saying?" He shakes his head. "How come I'm always the last to know?"

"Excuse me, if you don't mind." The woman has come up behind him. He moves out of her way, stands back a bit and watches Lucette begin to ring up the woman's purchases. The two Dawns, thin Dawn Fried and fat Dawn Blake, come up the aisle carrying a box of cigarette cartons between them and let it drop on the other end of the counter.

"Dawn, have you heard?" Mr. Abruzzi says. They both look up. "Lucette here has got someone." He nods his head toward Lucette. "I'm depending on you, Dawn, to get all the facts. Take notes, children. There will be a quiz at the break." He turns and leaves them.

"What's he mean?" Dawn Fried asks Lucette.

"Don't be such a total dope, will you?" Dawn Blake says.

"I just asked a question, all right?"

"Fried, will you please get a life?" Dawn Blake says. "So Luce," she says as the woman gathers her plastic bags and goes out into the blowing snow, "who is it?"

Lucette stands with her hands on the register. She looks at the clock. It is a few minutes until her break. "Just a guy."

"Is he cute?"

"He's all right."

"What kind of a car has he got?"

"Fried, Fried, Fried," Dawn Blake says, shaking her hair, the curls of which are stiff and springy as wire. "These superficial questions. I'm ashamed for our sex. Better to ask the color and substance of his soul. Has he got charisma? What's his sign? Has he got it where it counts? These are the questions."

"Everybody hasn't got your kind of mind. Here, I'm not doing all these myself." She pushes the box toward Dawn Blake.

Lucette reaches under the counter for her cigarettes and lighter. "I'm going on break."

"I'll go now, too," Dawn Blake says, and follows her through the half-door that lets them out from behind the counter.

"Oh, you guys, you're not going to leave me up here all by myself," Dawn Fried says. "Come on, that's not fair."

"Tell it to your armpit, Fried," Dawn Blake says. In the elevator, she sings along with the oldies rock music on the loudspeaker. "Glad all over," she sings. "God, what crap. I bet Mr. Abruzzi used to fuck to this song."

"I don't think he's old enough," Lucette says.

"You ought to go out with him. Maybe he'll give you a raise."

"No thanks."

The elevator doors open and they step out into the dirty, neon-lit basement. There is no one else in the break room. Lucette sits down at one of the long metal tables and lights a cigarette. Dawn stands in front of the candy machine and pulls all the knobs, one after the other. When no candy drops down, she fishes in her purse for change. "You want a Snickers?" she asks.

"No," Lucette says. She slides down so that her head is resting on the back of the chair. "Why don't *you* go out with him?"

"That greaseball. But seriously. He's too nice. You know? Too soft. Too easy to push. Too drugged up. So what about this guy? More of Abruzzi's bullshit?"

Lucette shakes her head. "There's this guy I met when I was out with Bev."

"Cool." She looks at Lucette. "It is cool, I presume?"

"More or less." Lucette drops her cigarette on the floor and steps on it. "Did you ever go out with an older guy?"

"This guy's old?"

Lucette shrugs. "Sort of."

"Older guys." Dawn rips the paper off the candy bar. "What a trip. I like it with older guys. They're always on the spot with drinks and dinners and so on. And they're not always looking over your shoulder for something better. They're so happy that you're young, you know? It's like you don't have to do anything at all to please them but be there and be young."

"You've gone out with a lot of them?" Lucette asks.

"Only two," Dawn says, through the candy she's eating. "That's enough."

Lucette wonders what Dawn Blake is thinking, if she is thinking about the two older men, and how much older they were, if they were as old as Harry. She doesn't know how old Harry is, exactly.

Probably she could figure it out from things he has said, and from things she has found out about him. She knows that Harry's mother belonged to the Altar and Rosary Society when Lucette's grandmother did. Harry's cousin Cynthia was in a grade ahead of one of Lucette's second cousins. Harry went to the same high school as one of Bev's brothers, much earlier.

Dawn Blake sighs, stretches, balls up her candy wrapper. "Guess we'd better go."

Upstairs they sidle past the display of chocolate hearts wrapped in red foil that blocks the "Employees Only" door. "You'll probably get something nice for Valentine's Day," Dawn says. "Older guys are good for that kind of stuff."

Lucette thinks about this. She doesn't believe Harry is that kind of older guy. Should she give him something? But she twitches when she sees herself handing him a present, something red or pink. There are so many ways it could turn out wrong—his surprise, embarrassment, disapproval. What she would like is if he would pick her up from work, even in his truck, which the Dawns would find laughable. She would like it if at five he would be out there, double parked on Euclid in the falling snow, not caring if buses piled up behind him, backing up traffic. He would reach across to open the door for her and she would push his metal thermos and the tools off the seat before she got in, would find a place to put her feet among the stuff on the floor. He wouldn't look at her until he had started the truck and moved out into traffic, and then he would turn, one hand on the wheel, and say—what?

"Maybe he'll give you underwear. Older men are really into underwear," Dawn Blake says, reaching over the half door to unfasten it.

"Underwear? What are you guys talking about?" Dawn Fried says.

"No," Lucette answers Dawn Blake. "I don't think so."

Cynthia is folding the laundry in the kitchen. Derek's, Joey's, Derek's, Derek's, Joey's—she checks them off mentally, the socks, the T-shirts, the jockey shorts. Joey's underwear used to stand out, with Superman or the Ghostbusters on it, but now he wants to wear what his father wears.

"I got a letter from my brother," Derek says to her. He is drinking a last cup of coffee at the kitchen table before he leaves for work. "Paul's thinking about expanding his place."

Cynthia nods, and begins on Derek's ironed work shirts. Holding them up against her chest, pinned by the point of her chin, she buttons every other button and flips them over to fold in first one side, then the other, then three folds the other way. When they are turned over, they make a neat package, the collars standing up, the shoulders squared.

"Loretta sends her love."

Cynthia snorts.

"I don't know why you're like that about her," Derek says, swirling his coffee around.

"She doesn't have any use for me either," Cynthia says. "Aren't you going to be late?"

"I've got a few minutes," Derek says, looking at the clock. "Paul's doing pretty well, anyway, it seems. They sound happy."

"I could almost feel sorry for her, stuck in that piddling town in the Poconos. Clearmount—what a name, it sounds like some kind of airplane glue."

"It's nice scenery around there. You have to say that."

"Maybe for honeymoon couples that's enough, nothing to do but feel each other up and look at the trees." Cynthia laughs. "I don't know how they can stand it, Paul and Loretta, seeing all those kids mooning at each other, and all that tacky honeymoon trash all over. I couldn't take it."

"It's a business, isn't it?" Derek puts down his cup. "There's nothing wrong with making people happy. Nothing wrong with love and a certain amount of happiness to start off a life."

Cynthia puts the last shirt on top of the stack and leans against the table. "I like looking at things straight, not with all that pink wallpaper and heart-shaped this and that."

"I suppose you'd like it better if Paul took to running a funeral home. I suppose that'd be more honest."

"In a way. In a way, it would." Cynthia deposits the laundry in the basket and walks out of the kitchen.

Derek sets his coffee cup down with a thump. "Speaking of love," he calls after her, "I hear Harry's got a new woman." He goes to the sink to rinse the cup. "A new girl, I should say."

Cynthia pauses on the stairs. "I can't hear you, wait until I get back."

When she comes downstairs, she opens the refrigerator and gets out a lunch bag. "Now, what did you say?" She hands the bag to Derek.

"I said, Harry's got a new girl, a young one."

"Young? What does that mean?"

"Young. Just out of high school."

"Well," Cynthia says. "I suppose she can take care of herself."

"Pretty, too, I hear. Someone from the neighborhood. Name's Lucette Harmon, a little blond."

Cynthia repeats these words in her mind: a little blond. They seem particularly repellent. She sits down at the table and fiddles with the salt and pepper shakers, the napkin holder.

Derek pulls his coat from the back of the chair and picks up his lunch bag. "What else Paul said is that he'd like us to come down."

"I haven't got time to visit," Cynthia says.

"He'd like us to come down permanent. He could use me, with the hotel expanding. I'd like us to think about it." Derek puts his coat on. "All right?"

"And this house, what would we do with that?"

"It's just a house, Cynthia."

"It's part Harry's."

"Harry'd probably be glad to have the money we'd get selling it. Al wants him to go into business with him."

"Harry in business?" Cynthia presses her hand to her chest. "Harry? That's a laugh. He'd never manage it, never. And he'd never be glad to see this house go, have it lived in by strangers, how can you even say it? That shows what you know about family."

"Family is what we'd be going to. I'd think you'd be happy for Harry. He's not going to get another opportunity like this." Derek pauses by the door, his hand on the knob. "I've got to go."

"Go then. Go, now you've upset me." Cynthia turns away from him and looks out the window at the snow falling.

"Cynthia," Derek says, but she will not look at him. He sighs. "I'll see you tonight."

"I'll probably be asleep," she says. "I'm tired already."

The snow is falling. Harry lies on the bed in the trailer, looking out into the white afternoon.

The room is dim, gray. The no-color of the sheet over him is the same as the no-color of the wall and the floor and the old-style venetian blinds pulled halfway up. There won't be any work at the site today because of the snow. But he is going to get up in a minute, go across the parking lot to help Al set up. His body feels tired, lightened and strung thin as wire from the drinking last night, and the sex. Sex on Sunday. This sounds good to him. Maybe it's a song title. Maybe if there is no song, he should write one. Sex is different on Sunday than on other days, more deliberate, less careless. You must decide. Sex or church. Sex and church. Sex only. Church, thinking about sex. Sex, thinking about not being in church, thinking about the people in church, hands folded, eyes all looking in the same direction.

Harry does not go to church any more. Until his mother's move to the nursing home, he would drive her to Mass and pick her up. He used to go with her on Christmas and Easter, standing and sitting awkwardly, half remembering the hymns, holding her purse while she genuflected, the slow lowering of her heavy old body, the painful rising. He was not allowed to help her. He stopped going to church regularly when he was in high school. He and Louisa fought about it every week until he left home. When he came back from the army, the first Sunday he was back, he got up and drove her there, got out and opened the door for her, got back in and drove home. She watched him drive away before she turned and went through the heavy doors. She didn't say anything when she got in the car after Mass except that the sermon had been too long. Now she hears Mass from her wheelchair, if she is having a good day, in the home's cafeteria, the priest holding up the host from behind a folding table, no music but the sounds of metal on metal and the muffled voices of the staff in the kitchen making Sunday dinner. Harry still comes for Christmas and Easter and sits beside her in a folding chair. He doesn't stand or kneel. No one does. They all sit immobile, watching the quick antics of the priest as he skips back and forth behind the table, they suffer him to come among them with his gift of bread. When he gets to Harry, Harry holds up his hand, warning him off, and the priest passes by.

Harry moves into Monday. He walks through the snow falling to the back door of the bar. The beer delivery trucks come in a rush, and he and Al move back and forth pushing dollies loaded with cases of beer in clinking bottles. He shifts all the tables and chairs from the big room to the bar room so that Geneva can do the floor with a rented polisher. He checks the drain in the ladies'-room sink. At three he is beginning to think about how he wants a beer, but he holds off. All this time it snows, and when he opens the door to put trash out in the yard or passes the window in the corridor that leads to Al's office he sees it falling, slow and white, covering the tracks of the cars and filling up the footsteps of old ladies with shopping carts and children coming home from school.

At three-thirty he gets his truck and he and Al go to the Wholesale Club for supplies.

"Let's see, I need toilet paper, maraschino cherries, window cleaner. What else?" Al taps his pencil on the dashboard. "You think of anything, Harry?"

"New slush mat for by the back door."

Al writes this down. "I want to see if they got anything for Geneva's birthday, too.

The truck hums along in the fast lane on I-480. Harry is doing sixty-five, passing the cautious slower cars, flying over the snow that has not yet been plowed or salted.

"Slow down, Harry, for Christ's sake," Al says, tapping the pencil in a frenzy.

"It's a truck, Al," He slows down to sixty.

"Her birthday's the sixteenth. Barbara's having a little party. You know, just cake and ice cream. Think you might stop by?"

"Maybe. I never pass up a chance to see Barbara," Harry says. He hasn't seen Barbara in a long time.

"You haven't seen her youngest yet, except in my wallet," Al says, slapping his hip. "You could bring someone if you want, no problem."

Harry turns to look at Al. "Why would I want to do that?"

Al rubs his signet ring against his chin, pushing it through the bristles. "I thought maybe that Lucette."

"You want me to bring Lucette?"

"I didn't say I wanted you to. I said you could. If you wanted to."

Harry makes the turn to the airport road and swings onto 237. He switches on the radio.

"Up to you, of course," Al says, gripping the doorhandle as the truck bounces over the old train tracks. He looks over at Harry. "You been seeing a lot of her."

"So that means I should bring her over to Barbara's?"

Al taps his pencil some more. "Seems like a nice little thing," he says finally.

"She's old enough to vote, Al," Harry says, turning into the long curving driveway.

"Sure she is, sure she is." Al puts the pencil between his teeth and pulls out his wallet, shuffling through it for his membership card.

Inside, they push the cart between the thirty-foot-high metal scaffolds that hold truck tires, electric curling irons, marked-down artificial Christmas trees, giant boxes of detergent. Al likes to go up and down every aisle to see what's there and to remind himself of things he's forgotten. Harry manages the cart, following behind, watching Al as he walks slowly, eyes raised to sweep the contents of every shelf. Al picks up bottles to read the contents, stops to talk to the women who sit at their metal folding tables, offering minia-ture sausages, cut-up bits of microwaved French toast, taco chips with small paper cups of salsa. Al doesn't eat any of these things because his digestion is bad, but he is interested in the pros and cons of them. He leans against the nearest metal strut and asks the women about cooking times and cholesterol count. Some of them offer Harry their bits of food, looking at him with interest. "Who's your friend?" one of them asks Al.

"Oh, that's just Harry," Al says. "Say hello, Harry. This is Mary Elizabeth."

"Hello," Harry says. He moves on to the next aisle, Mary Elizabeth's eyes following him. He can feel them on his back, checking out his shoulders, his butt, and this feeling is not unpleas-ant, but he moves no slower, doesn't turn his head to catch her eye.

When they are loading the boxes into the back of the truck, Al clears his throat and says, "How's Cynthia?"

Harry looks at him, surprised. "She's all right." He slams the tailgate, thumping it with the heel of his hand to check that it's closed.

"I guess you'll be going over there tonight for dinner with her and Joey," Al says.

The seats of the truck feel cold through their pants and they both shiver. Harry reaches over to turn on the heater as he swings into the driveway, sliding just a little on a sheet of ice before the big tires grip.

"So?" he says to Al.

"Well, it's Monday," Al says. "You always go over to the house on Monday."

This is true. Harry starts to whistle a song from the jukebox. He stays in the fast lane for the comfort of the divider from which he can measure his distance—the lane markers are invisible under the snow. "I don't go every Monday."

"You're going today, though?"

"I suppose I am." He waits for what Al will say next.

Al fusses, first with his wallet, putting his membership card away, and then with his gloves, putting them on, taking them off, and putting them in his pocket. "I hear Derek wants to move," Al says.

Through his bare hands on the wheel and his foot just hanging on the lip of the clutch, Harry can feel the road, the bumps, the puddles of soft slushy snow, the slick patches.

"Where'd you hear that?"

"Derek told me. He wants to go in with his brother—you know, the one that lives in PA and has the honeymoon hotel."

"So, you had a talk with Derek." Harry thumps the wheel with his hand. "That's nice. That's very nice."

Al turns sideways in the seat. "It just came up. We were just talking, the two of us, he came in for a beer on his way home, he'd just got this letter—" He stops, watching Harry. "Anyway—"

"Anyway what?" Harry asks, his voice low and soft.

Al doesn't answer.

"Anyway what?" Harry says, louder.

Al watches the speedometer creep up, but he doesn't say anything. Harry turns the radio on and the strong singing voice of

Randy Travis streams through the truck, *hand, ring, marriage, love, forever,* swirling past them like the snow past the windows. Going fast like this, it seems darker outside, maybe *is* darker. The fast whipping angles that Harry makes around the slower drivers, the quick glances at dim shapes in other cars, the gleam of neon from the signs at the edge of the freeway—these are all like some lesson, some conversation. Harry looks at Al and sees that his lips are moving. He is sitting perfectly still, hands folded on his lap, legs crossed as if he were home watching TV, but his lips are moving, and Harry laughs.

A car pulls in front of him, going slow, and he taps the brakes, in sheer exhilaration bringing his hand down on the horn in a long blast, sliding sideways, still under control, then farther, across two lanes, still steering, still steering, feeling nothing at all where the road should be, just the smooth liquid glide that a skater feels, then the chunking bite of the tires against pavement. "Christ," he says, "Christ," when the car is in a lane and riding straight.

"Fucking asshole," he yells, and then rolls down the window and yells it into the snow. "Fucking asshole."

"Roll it up, Harry. It's freezing out there."

Harry looks at Al, and Al is smiling, Al is laughing. "You son of a bitch, you asshole."

"Same back at you," Harry says. He switches on the turn signal and proceeds up the exit ramp steady at forty-five.

Later, when Cynthia goes out to the backyard with the garbage, it is still snowing, falling straight and thick around her. When she has slid the bag into the can, she retreats to the back steps and looks out from under the shelter of the wooden canopy over the door. She hugs herself, but the cold feels good after the heat of the kitchen, the oven up to 450 degrees for biscuits. There are a few things that Cynthia makes very well—biscuits, baked beans, a lemon sponge cake from her mother's recipe, fried cornmeal mush. Otherwise, she tends to over- or undercook. She makes meals with no vegetable. She spends all her time on a fancy dessert, which does nothing to compensate for the strangeness and toughness of the meat dish. It doesn't matter. Derek doesn't mind what he eats, Joey doesn't like anything very much.

The snow looks like the flour shaken from her sifter fifteen minutes ago. When she scoops a handful of it from the railing where it has stacked itself up, she is surprised that it is not silky and dusty like the flour. Compacted in her hand it is hard and wet, halfway to ice.

There are no footprints, no markings of any kind in the back-yard except her own, a single line down the path in the middle of the lawn leading to the garbage can, which is invisible behind the rose trellis. When she was little, brought here by her mother to play with her cousins, Cynthia liked to sit on this stoop with her arms around her knees and think dreaming thoughts that had to do with the enclosedness of the yard, held in by the strong perimeter of the fence and the wiry line of rosebushes, tented over by the sycamore tree. And she liked the promised wildness of the back alley, the secret place behind the backyards, between houses, barely big enough for two cars to scrape past one another, the place where bad boys fought and set off firecrackers, where cats yowled.

It is five-thirty, another half hour until Harry comes. She wishes he would come now while she was watching, through the gate from the alley as he used to when he came over from his parents' house on the next street. When he was around, there would be an extra energy in the cousins' games, all those cousins she never sees now except at weddings and christenings and funerals. Cynthia was the oldest of a certain set of cousins, Harry younger by six months. Between them they kept the younger ones hopping, Cynthia thinks now. How did I ever come up with all those things? she wonders, shivering. The play they put on, the garage clubhouse, the doll and pet sale, the mystery club. How they had all begged to come and play here, in their grandmother's backyard. How happy their mothers must have been to have this place to bring them in that time before day-care, so that they—Virginia and Louisa—could visit with their mother and their brother and sisters who still lived there with her, could argue and laugh and talk at the tops of their voices. Cynthia has a number of sentimental thoughts about that time. One is that she and Harry were like Wendy and Peter Pan, rulers of that world of children, the backyard Never-Never Land, and Petey, June, Donny, Chuck, all of them, their own family of Lost Boys.

Inside, Cynthia lifts the lid to stir the stew, and then stands listening, trying to locate Joey. She can hear the thump of something against his bedroom wall—his heels? the basketball? She hears his voice—he likes to talk to himself when he runs his trucks over the rug, pretending to be now an announcer, now the driver, now an audience. Some day he'll be talking to girls on the phone, she supposes, but not yet. She opens the refrigerator to check that she has made the salad. There it is, red and green in the white bowl, covered by shiny plastic wrap.

Just out of high school would mean what—eighteen, nineteen? Twenty at the most. Derek is a fool, she thinks. Al Zaitchek a blabbermouth, an old woman, a gossip. Lives his fantasy life in Harry. Of course she knows that Harry has women. Lucette Harmon, she thinks, that would be Anna Harmon's daughter.

When she was young, Cynthia had lived in this same ten blocks between Denison and Trowbridge avenues, bounded on the west by Fulton and the east by West Twenty-fifth, as if that space was the kingdom of the blessed. All the relatives anyone was interested in lived within these limits, and most of her friends. When she walked up West Thirty-fifth to school, she walked up the center of the universe, counting off the streets one by one, lovely names—Riverside, Dover, Poe, Library, Daisy, Marvin, Woodbridge. She had felt sorry for the boys and girls in her class who lived outside the lines of the square.

Living now on Daisy Avenue, in her grandmother's house, she is in the center of this world. She knows it as she could never know any other place, no place in Pennsylvania, for sure. Derek didn't realize—how could he?—what strength she could draw from driving past her old house on Mapledale Avenue, even though it is painted a foreign salmon pink color, even though the new people have chopped down the willow tree in the backyard.

She sits down at the table and looks out at the snow falling, her hand spreading and smoothing the wrinkled dish towel over and over as she examines the map in her mind. The map that comes alive when she thinks about family, about the neighborhood, about her past, marked with glowing spots of old friendships, black rings of hate and old grudges, the stains of gossip that cling to certain families.

Poor Anna Harmon, Cynthia thinks, left by her awful first husband, then widowed by Frank Harmon after three years of happiness. This was what Anna's life had added up to—three years of happiness between miseries. A weak woman, Cynthia thinks now, giving in, lying down under it. She sits up straighter at the table, pushing her shoulders back.

But this Lucette could not be Frank's daughter, Frank had died only four years ago, maybe five. Must be the child from the first one, then. Could Anna Johnson Harmon have a daughter so old as to be out of high school?

The phone rings and she stands up to answer it, anxious—is it Harry, saying he will be late, will not come?

"Hello, Cynthia? This is Vicky. Joe can't find the time cards from last week."

"They're on the shelf over the coffee machine, in an old napkin box," Cynthia says, pressing her hand to her chest.

"Over the coffee machine!" Vicky shouts. "Wait a minute, Cyn, don't hang up. Did you find them?" She pauses. "He found them. So what're you doing?"

"Just doing dinner. Biscuits." Cynthia sits down again.

"Harry coming over?"

"Yeah. How's business?"

"Slow. But it'll pick up pretty soon when the party-'til-you-puke crowd gets rolling."

"I'd like to tell them a thing or two. Not a thought in their heads beyond getting drunk and fooling around."

"Oh, Cyn, they're just kids, they're young."

"Not so young that they can't think about something besides their own pleasure." Cynthia twists the telephone cord around her hand once, twice. "Having kids before they're old enough to know what to do with them."

"They usually manage to figure it out." Vicky laughs.

"But really. Look at people we went to school with, pregnant and married at seventeen or eighteen. And then what happens to your life? Look at Anna Harmon."

"Oh, that wasn't the trouble with Anna, and you know it. She got married late if anything. The trouble was who she married."

"Well." Cynthia untwists the phone cord. Lucette fills her mind, but she can't think of how to expel her, how to speak her name.

"I've got to go, Cyn. You'll be in the usual days this week?"

"Yeah." The sounds of the letters are wrong, she thinks. Lucette is a hard name, sharp, ungiving.

"Say hi to Harry for me. Tell him I still have the hots for him. Just kidding."

Cynthia hooks the phone into its wall cradle, and glances at the clock—Harry will be here any minute. She looks around quickly, but everything is ready, the food in its bowls or in the oven, Joey upstairs, she in her green sweater that is not dressed up, is in fact faded a little, but that fits her so that she seems softer than she is. She looks down at her torso and thinks it is a shell, a façade, too cool, hard—she presses her hand against her ribs and feels how she is warm, even hot inside, soft—a body that is still going on, not yet dead or resigned.

Well, everything's done anyway, she thinks, salad, stew, biscuits cut out, oven hot. She sits down in the rocking chair, ready.

By now the roads are salted, slushed up from rush-hour traffic, and the wheels of the truck make a slurping sound. Harry has driven this way hundreds of times, from the Maple Leaf to Cynthia's house. He sees the road winding down to the zoo, the long bridge over the valley, the new McDonald's where a little string of stores used to be on West Twenty-fifth, the big yellow block of the Jones Home where the orphans live. He looks up at its windows as always to see if there are any kids visible. He has never seen anyone, child or adult, on the grounds behind the iron fence.

As it goes up the alley, the truck makes the first tracks in the snow. He parks it snug against the garage so there is room for a car to squeeze by. It is too big to put inside. He swings through the gate and looks into the window of the garage. Floor swept bare, rakes hung up, a bag of salt by the door, it looks as it did when he used to sneak in there with girls, his body hot on the cool floor.

He walks up the path. It's wild back here, a mess. Cynthia likes it that way, though. In the summer he will come over and find her on her knees, hands in the dirt. For hours she'll be pulling things up, clipping, fingers and arms bleeding from long scratches. She'll come into the dimness of the house with her hair wild, full of leaves and petals, and lie on the floor of the kitchen to rest her back while Harry drinks iced tea made with real tea, real lemons, Grandma's recipe, steeped on the stove. Summer seems a long time ago, a long time away.

He puts his key in the lock, knocking on the door at the same time. Cynthia is there before he turns the knob. He takes off one glove and she takes his bare hand, pulling him inside. She pours him a cup of coffee while he takes off his jacket and hangs it on the hook in the old office behind the dining room.

"Sit down at the table and talk to me," Cynthia says. "I'll start the biscuits now you're here."

"Where's Joey?" Harry asks.

"Upstairs with his cars. I'll call him in a minute."

Harry holds the cup with both hands, warming them. "I was thinking about iced tea just now," he says.

Cynthia turns from the stove, her face pink from its heat. "I wish it was summer right this minute," she says. "I miss the heat and the sun."

"Maybe you'd like to live in Florida."

"Florida? Oh no," Cynthia says. "This is home, right here." She looks at him. "You wouldn't care for Florida, would you?"

"Me? No, I don't guess so. California was nice, though."

"Oh, California," Cynthia says. "Who can take California seriously?" She laughs and goes to the cupboard for the dishes. "But you're a man, you can go anywhere you want."

"You wanting to go any place, Cindy?"

"Where would I go?" She turns to look at him, a stack of plates in her hands.

"I don't know. You used to want to go places when we were kids."

"Oh, then. I was young, what did I know?" She puts the plates on the table and goes back to the stove. "I wouldn't want it back for a minute, not even to get rid of the gray hair or the wrinkles." She raises her hands to her face, lets them fall against her body. "I wouldn't. Would you, Harry?"

"You haven't got wrinkles," he says to her, watching her shoulder blades move under her shirt.

"No?" she says, without turning. "Oh, well. There are other things. I guess men don't notice like a woman would."

"I wouldn't say that. I've always been a noticer myself." Harry is aware as he says this of all the ages and bodies of Cynthia, the length of her arms and legs growing, the smell of her when they wrestled each other, her hair, silvery brown now, a darker shade of his own.

He gets up and stands behind her, takes the spoon from her hand. "Let me stir this. You sit down a minute."

"I should call Joey."

"It'll wait."

He stands at the stove, stirring, stirring the shallow lake of the gravy, waiting for the bubbles to spread and signal it's ready. He turns his head so that he can look at her, he holds her eyes with his. She plays with the strands of her hair. The yellow of the kitchen, the whiteness of the stove and the sink are bright as a halo at the edges of his vision. Nothing will change, he says to himself.

"I have a few wrinkles," she says to him.

"Not as many as most."

Cynthia puts her legs up on another chair. "You know, Harry, I can't remember, really, what my body looked like then, when I was young. Before Joey, when it was pretty okay. Why do you suppose that is? A kind of self-protective thing? So old women don't go into a deep depression or commit suicide? I mean, you have these pictures from then, of the prom and graduation, of your wedding. But those are all of the clothes you're wearing, and of your face, and that face looks pretty much like a different person. So who cares? But no one takes pictures of your body, thank God."

Harry stirs and stirs, still looking at her. "I remember what your body looked like," he says.

"You do, do you?" She swings her legs down from the chair and gets up. She takes two quick steps across the kitchen and grabs his shirt front. "Well, just forget it, see?"

He laughs.

She shakes him back and forth, smiling. "Wipe it from your mind."

"Got it."

Satisfied, she releases him and goes up the stairs. He listens to her footsteps going to Joey's room, hears them talking.

After dinner, they sit in the front room with Joey, the TV on to one of Joey's shows. Joey lies on his stomach, his chin propped on his hands, kicking the floor with the toe of his hightops. Harry and Cynthia sit on the couch, one at either end, in between them a stack of magazines Harry is looking through and a basket of odds and ends Cynthia is sorting. She holds the coupons up, close to her eyes, to see the expiration dates. She unsnarls thread from rubber bands and twist-ties, makes a pile of buttons on the couch cushion between them, denting the cushion with her hand so that they will stay.

"Do you remember watching *Captain Penny* when we came here to Grandma's for lunch?" she asks him.

"Pooch Parade," he says. *"The Little Rascals, The Three Stooges."*

"Who's the Funny Man?" she says. "I used to be afraid of Grandma when I was little."

"How come?" Harry riffles through the pages of his magazine, puts it down, picks up another.

"I don't know. She was so big, and she hardly said anything in English. She seemed so far away, like we lived on different planets. I was afraid of her, but I wanted to make her happy. I remember once she gave me a steak sandwich—did I ever tell you this? I came for lunch on a day when I wasn't supposed to, I forgot where I was supposed to be, and Mom wasn't here, just Grandma, no one else in the house. All the aunts must have been at work. The house was dark, no lights anywhere. She was probably almost blind then, it didn't make any difference to her."

"So what happened?" Harry says.

"Nothing, really. I could see that she didn't know what to do with me. Like it had been so long since her children were little that she couldn't remember how to talk to me or what to give me to eat. She didn't remember about *Captain Penny* and so I didn't get to eat on a TV tray in the front room like we always did. She set a place for me at the kitchen table, and she stood at the stove, all that big bulk of her moving around the kitchen in her slippers, remember her slippers? And she fried me up a steak sandwich like she would have for Uncle John."

"How was it?"

"Oh, it was terrible. So tough I could hardly chew it. But I ate it all, I sort of tore at it with my teeth, looking out at the neighbor's backyard while she watched me eat. She was smiling and saying things, half in Slovak, half in English. I felt so sad for her, that she had made me this horrible steak sandwich, but that it was her gift to me, like she was reaching across all those years, seventy of them, or eighty. How old was she when she died?"

"Eighty-eight? Eighty-nine?"

"Eighty-eight, I think." Cynthia rubber-bands the coupons, sighing, looking around the room. "She used to keep her TV over there, by the big bookcase, do you remember? Turn that down a little, Joey," she says. "Weren't you afraid of her?"

Harry says, "Not until I started bringing girls back to the garage."

"Harry!" Cynthia purses her lips and nods her head toward Joey. "Don't be a bad example."

"He's not listening." Harry puts his magazine down and watches as Cynthia paws through the stuff left in the basket, bits of thready lint, dirty old erasers, dead batteries, grimy scraps of paper.

"What's the matter, Cyn? I was just joking."

"That's always the way with me, saying it was just a joke." Cynthia holds up her hand when Harry starts to speak. "I know all about your girls, Harry. I'm not a prude."

"No one said you were—"

"I've got no interest in what you do with women, Harry, I want you to know that. Not that I'm saying you shouldn't, you can do what you like, sex is fine with me, as you ought to know, ought to know what I'm like by now, I mean—" she stops, holding the basket in both hands. "Oh, the hell with it."

Harry looks toward Joey, and she jerks her head impatiently.

"What's the problem here? What's going on?" Harry thinks of what Al told him about Derek and Pennsylvania, trying to guess if this has anything to do with Cynthia's mood. "What are you upset about?" he asks, and wonders if he should ask her about the house now, get it out into the open. "Maybe all this is too much for you—" he waves his hands around at the room, the house. "The cleaning. It's a big place."

Cynthia stands, her hands shaking. "What about the house? What about it?"

"Nothing about it. Sit down."

She stands, her fingers rubbing the weave of the basket, not looking at him.

"You might have thought of getting a newer house, a ranch

maybe. Derek always wanted more land. And you were talking about going someplace else before. Florida—"

"Never." She steps backward, bumping Joey with her heel, so that he looks up to see what she is doing. "I never think of it." She looks around her, at the ceiling, the stairs. "This is our family place. How could I think of someplace else?"

"Mom?" Joey says. "You're stepping on my pants."

Harry picks up the pile of buttons from the hollow in the cushion and slides them, cool and smooth like shells, between his fingers. He holds them out to her.

"Time for bed, Joey." She takes the buttons from Harry and puts them in her pocket. "What are you thinking of?" she asks.

Monday nights Harry usually stays at Cynthia's, often Tuesday and Wednesday, too. Sometimes Thursday. Friday, Saturday, Sunday, he sleeps in the trailer, or at a woman's place. On Monday nights, after Joey is in bed, they sit on the couch watching television and reading. Harry drinks, usually beer, Cynthia has coffee. They talk a little. At twelve or twelve-thirty they go upstairs to bed. Harry uses the bathroom, then Cynthia. They say goodnight, Harry still dressed, Cynthia in her nightgown and robe. She sits up in bed, he knows, after she closes her door, reading, he supposes. He goes into sleep like a diver, the deepest sleep he gets is at Cynthia's, in the bedroom across the hall from where she lies with her book. The hours of the evenings at Cynthia's are like even, clear-edged squares, pleasantly blank, filled up with the light from the lamps, the flicking pages of Cynthia's book, the comfort of slow drinking, the feel of the worn rugs under his feet, the sound of water running into the bathroom sink with the same splutter he has heard since he was old enough to wash his own hands.

Tonight, though, he doesn't want to sit next to Cynthia, or stay here at all. But he doesn't want to tell her this, or to leave without saying anything. So he sits, his eyes on the television where the end of a show for teenagers is playing itself out, tapping his fingers against the cover of the magazine he was reading.

Cynthia, already in her nightgown, stands halfway down the stairs, her hand on the banister. He can see the marks of the comb in her hair, the shine of her washed face. The nightgown is an old one, once red, now a faded pink. His fingers know the texture of it, for one night, when she drank whiskey with him instead of coffee, they had danced to 1940s records, jitterbugging with the shades pulled down, one last slow dance when he dipped her, both of them laughing, staying up so late that just as Harry closed the door of his room he heard Derek's car in the driveway, his key in the lock, and what he almost never heard, the soft sounds of Derek and Cynthia talking in their bedroom.

"I guess I'm tireder than I thought," she says to him now. "I think I'll go on up and read a little and go to sleep."

"All right," he says. "Maybe I'll take a little walk and turn in early myself."

"Oh, stay up, stay up. I don't know, maybe I'm coming down with something."

When he hears the door of her room close, he puts the magazine back on the stack and gets up, walks around the room, touching the television, the old piano. He hums. He thinks again of dancing with Cynthia, feels his hands on her back, the thinness of the cloth between their skins. One flesh, he thinks, a remnant of church teaching. When they were very young, he thought she was his sister. It had escaped his notice that other kids' sisters lived in the same house with them. What a girl she was, he thinks, the toughness of her arms, her wiry strength, how she would grit her teeth, would strain to best him at something. Her sweat had been as familiar to him as his own. The feel of her hair, her breath, her spit. He grins, happier now that she is upstairs, her sadness and upset contained. What a girl, he thinks, going into the kitchen.

He opens the bottom cupboard to get out the bottle of Old Crow that Cynthia keeps for him, and pours himself a quarter of a glass and a full glass of water.

· · ·

Lucette's mother, Anna, sits across from her while Lucette eats her dinner this Monday evening. She has no plate in front of her, although she has eaten most of a slice of bread and several pieces of cooked carrot. She watches the food on Lucette's plate and its progress into her mouth.

Lucette can ignore this now. The blinds are pulled all the way down to the sill, the curtains drawn across them. The watery green of the walls, the whiteness of the stove and refrigerator, the thirty-year-old radio on the shelf over the sink, the rattling of the furnace—they all make Lucette wish to leave, but this dinner is one of the things that she owes her mother, who cooks so seldom. She eats her carrots one by one and spoons up the pile of rice. She cuts the hamburger patty with her fork and dips it into the spreading circle of catsup her mother has poured in the center of her plate. She, too, has a slice of bread, which she breaks into smaller and smaller pieces. The carrots are all right, the rice goes down without chewing. The meat, though, is salty, sticky, done more on one side than the other. She chews.

"Maybe I put in too much marjoram," her mother says to her.

"It's just right," Lucette says. She knows, although her mother thinks it is a secret, that she is using the spices, when she cooks, in alphabetical order. It is not something they talk about.

Anna sighs and picks a round of carrot out of the pan. She holds it in her fingers, turning it one way and then another, but doesn't eat it. "Are you going to do your homework after dinner?"

"No," Lucette says. "I haven't got any." She takes a sip of water and another bite of hamburger.

"Of course, of course you haven't," her mother says. "How silly of me, how silly. I was back in the past, wasn't I? Let me get you a napkin, honey." She goes out of the kitchen and comes back with a pink cloth napkin. "Here's the pepper, too, for that rice. You like pepper on rice, don't you?"

Lucette takes the pepper and the napkin, putting them on either side of her plate.

"I remember how you used to do your homework right here at this very table," Anna says. "You remember?"

"Uh-huh," Lucette says, chewing faster. She swallows and starts to say something, but her mother is staring at the door to the hall, behind Lucette, as if she expects someone to come in. Lucette's shoulder blades itch, she wants to turn around and look, too. She knows who her mother is seeing there.

She feels the time her mother is remembering closing in around her, the old warmth of this room, the expectation of the gleaming dishes, the open windows, blinds flapping, curtains rising and falling with a wind from outside, the fountain of food and happiness rising from the stove, the refrigerator, her mother bringing out platters like a conjurer, every surface reflecting light, smooth to the touch. She makes herself look down at the floor, at the scurf of hardened dirt that has gathered along the wall, at the fingerprints next to the light switch, the rip in the blind. The tingling in her shoulder blades increases. She puts her fork down. "I can't eat this," she says to her mother.

Anna's eyes jerk back to her. "Aren't you hungry, honey? You don't eat enough."

"It's too tough. There's too much marjoram." She pushes her chair from the table, and bats Anna's hand away when she reaches toward her. She goes to the bathroom and, gulping, sits on the lid of the toilet. She counts to twenty-five and flushes. Screened by the noise, she throws up her dinner. She flushes again, washes her face. She can hear her mother moving around in the kitchen, talking. Lucette turns the faucet on to make the water run faster and more noisily so that she will not hear the voice, but she still does.

"Forget it, just forget it," Anna is saying, "I can't get up early enough to cook is the trouble, can't raise my head from the pillow, doctor's no help, no point in the doctor, not enough sleep, there is not enough sleep in the world." There is the sound of a dish breaking. Anna raises her voice. "You don't eat enough." Her footsteps come along the hall, shuffling. "You hear me, Lucette? Don't sleep enough, coming in late, never any breakfast, candy bars for lunch, won't touch a good dinner."

Lucette stands facing the door, puts her palms against it. She imagines her mother on the other side in the same position.

"Turn off the water, Lucy," Anna whispers into the crack between the door and the wall, just below the hinge. "It's a waste to let it run, it's a shame. I'll get up earlier tomorrow, I'll start cooking earlier. Nice to see a woman in an apron, he said. Bring me an apron home, Lucy."

"I have to go out, Ma," Lucette says in her normal voice.

"Go by Silverman's, they've got what I want. White with maybe a blue design, like a check or flowers. Take some money."

"I will."

"Are you done in there?" her mother whispers.

"I've got to wash my face," Lucette says. The water is still thundering into the bowl of the sink, the hole of a whirlpool has formed to suck it into the drain.

"I'm feeling a little tired, honey."

"Why don't you go upstairs, Ma?"

"I think I'll do that. Don't be out late."

Lucette doesn't answer. She takes one hand away from the door and turns off the water.

"I'm still your mother," Anna says, and then Lucette hears her slow steps down the hall, through the kitchen, the crunch of her slippers on broken china, one foot after another on the back steps, the low mumble of the TV.

Lucette comes out and cleans up the broken plate, the food on the floor. Picking up the hamburger with a paper towel, she feels sick, wishes she had eaten it even as it makes her gag to look at it. She throws away the contents of the pots and pans and washes them. She wipes her hands and dials the phone, and says into it, keeping her voice low, "Bev? What're you doing?" She waits, tapping her fingers against the wall. "Sure, I could come over," she says. Before she leaves, she turns off the kitchen lights and listens at the foot of the back steps. The light at the top of them is on and she turns that off, too, and goes out the side door.

In the cold air she breathes deeply, clearing out the queasiness, and the picture of her mother propped up in bed with her hand on the remote control, the only light in the room from the TV and the wavering underwater glow from the aquarium. It is three blocks to Bev's house, six minutes walking slow, three and a half minutes walking fast. Lucette knows every crack, every tree, every yard, the rusted barbecue grills that sit out all winter at one corner, the chained barking dog at the next.

She can hear the noise of Bev's family life two houses away, can hear through the double-paned windows the stereo playing and Bev's mother shouting over it. The kitchen light spills onto the walk along the side of the house, and when she knocks on the back door it opens at her touch, letting out more light and noise.

Bev's brother Ray is standing with his back to her, snapping his fingers, doing dance steps.

"Take my word for it, even you could do this, Mom," he says.

"Get out of here with those hips," his mother says. "Your father and I know how to do the dances we like." She is looking in the refrigerator.

"Waltzes. Cha-chas." Ray clutches his stomach. "Polkas, I bet." He groans and falls, rolling, on the floor. From there, he sees Lucette and springs to his feet. "Lucette, am I right or am I right?"

"Hello, Mrs. Archacki," she says. "Right about what?"

"Mom and Dad should learn some new dances. Life is passing them by. How can they really know their children if they don't appreciate their music?" He grabs Lucette by the hand. "Boogie with me, Luce. A demonstration."

"Don't pay any attention to him, Lucette," Mrs. Archacki says. "It's just hormones."

"Where's Bev?" Lucette says.

"Upstairs," Ray says, but he doesn't let go of her hand, he pulls

her out of the room and toward the stairs. "Listen," he says to her
on the landing.

"What?" She turns to face him.

"How about if I go out with you guys sometime?" He swings
her hand back and forth, and then pulls it flat against his chest.
"You'd have somebody to dance with all night."

"Come off it, Ray."

They look up at Bev, who has appeared at the top of the second
flight.

"I've got an ID," Ray says, dropping Lucette's hand.

"It's no good having an ID when you've still got that baby
face," Bev says.

Ray points an imaginary gun at Bev and pulls the trigger.

"Do you mind?" she says to him.

Lucette starts up the last few steps, but Ray drops and grabs her
by the legs, one hand on each ankle, and howls like a dog. She tries
to bat him away with her purse, but this unbalances her and she half
falls onto the steps. The youngest, Stevie, runs out of his room to
see what is going on, and Mrs. Archacki comes to the foot of the
stairs. She throws the dish towel at Ray, and laughs.

"Mom, will you make him stop?" Bev says.

"Come on, Ray. Stop bothering the girls."

Ray moans and pretends to bite Lucette's leg through her jeans.
Stevie pushes past Bev to join in, and Bev jumps down to put her
mouth next to her brother's ear. "I'll tell Mom what you were
asking Lucette," she whispers.

Instantly, Ray jumps up. "All right, all right," he says.

Disappointed, Stevie goes downstairs and turns the television
on, Mrs. Archacki picks up her dish towel and goes back to the
kitchen. Lucette and Bev go into Bev's room. Ray follows them
to the doorway and stands there a minute, looking at Lucette as she
sits down on Bev's bed.

"You're such a little pervert, Ray," Bev says. "Will you get out
of here?"

"I could tell Mom a few things, too."

Bev throws one of her stuffed animals at him, and he goes, laughing the hyena laugh he's been practicing.

"What a dolt, what a dweeb," Bev says.

"Oh, he's all right." Lucette runs her fingers through her hair.

"You're just saying that because he has the seventeen-year-old hots for you."

Lucette doesn't say anything. She knows how Ray feels about her, and she likes him, likes wrestling with him, likes him kidding her, likes his dopey grinning face pushed up at hers when she comes over to Bev's.

"So what do you want to do tonight?" Bev leans across the dresser to look at her face in the mirror. She blinks at her reflection, reaches for a tiny comb and combs her lashes with it. "You want to go to a movie?"

"I don't know," Lucette says. She turns around on the bed, takes the stuffed animals that are piled up there, and sits them up in a row against the wall.

"Are you going to see Harry tonight?" Bev asks. She lifts up bits of her black-brown hair and sprays them. When she is finished, they stand out from her head like the petals of a flower.

"He's at Cynthia's tonight."

"So you're not allowed to call him at Cynthia's, or what?"

"I'd feel funny."

"I suppose I'm not supposed to say anything about how weird all that is."

Lucette doesn't answer, she gets up and joins Bev by the mirror. She chooses a reddish-purple blusher and begins to brush it onto her cheeks in a strong upward diagonal. With a black-tipped wand, she draws a thin, shiny line just above her lashes. She bends over from the waist and brushes her hair down, away from her head.

"I mean, he doesn't even live in a regular place, half the time at his cousin's and the other half in that stupid trailer. Why does he hang out with her anyway? She looks like a witch to me. Does he even have a real job?" She pulls a bit of Lucette's hair and Lucette twitches away from her hand. "No, he doesn't," Bev answers herself.

"He works construction," Lucette says, still bent over. She stands up and flips her hair over. Fine as silk, it falls back into place, lying, as it always does, flat against her cheeks and ears, separating at her shoulders, falling like a cape over her back.

"Here," Bev says. "You should use this Dusty Rose shadow with that blush." She watches as Lucette smooths the powder onto her eyelids. "You know what I mean—it's not a paycheck job. He only works when they call him in, or when he feels like it."

Lucette takes the pocket mirror Bev offers her and studies the back of her head.

"Your hair looks fine," Bev says. "How do my eyes look? Do I need more blue?"

"No."

"Did you ever meet this Cynthia?"

"I've seen her around." Lucette takes a cigarette from a pack on Bev's dresser and lights it. "He's not going to introduce me to his family, for God's sake."

"Well, why not?" Bev says. She puts her hands on her hips the way her mother does. "Why ever not?"

Lucette shrugs.

"You'd think you were a prostitute or something." Bev checks her teeth for lipstick. "I dare you to call him."

"Cut it out." Lucette hooks her hair behind her ears and smiles, feeling her stomach contract.

"I mean it. I dare you to. Call and say to Cynthia that you want to talk to Harry, and then tell him to meet you, that you need him, that you want him. Give him a hard-on while Cynthia's right there stirring up some potion on the stove or whatever she does."

"Cut it out, Bev," Lucette says and grabs for Bev's hair. But Bev is too quick, dancing out of her reach, so Lucette catches her around the waist and wrestles her to the floor and pins her arms down.

"Crucify me, why don't you?" Bev yells, laughing.

Lucette rolls off her and they lie on the floor looking up at the ceiling, breathing hard. "I'm hungry," she says finally.

"You can have some spaghetti. Cookies, too, if you say you'll call him."

"Nope."

"Starve then," Bev says, and she sits up and pulls her blouse down.

"Your mother will give me some anyway."

They pick up their jackets and go downstairs. At the table, Bev watches Lucette eat a plate of spaghetti. "Mom?" Bev says.

"Hm?" Mrs. Archacki, still in her apron, is sitting on the chair with her feet up on another, flicking through the pages of *Bird Fancier*.

"If you and a guy were going out, you wouldn't be afraid to call him at home, would you?"

Lucette narrows her eyes at Bev. Bev sticks out her tongue.

"Well, we didn't do that when I was a girl, calling boys."

"Not even if you were going together?"

She puts the magazine down on her lap to consider. "It would depend on the circumstances." She looks over at Lucette, who looks down at her plate. "Now, though, I don't see why a girl shouldn't be the one to call. I used to hate waiting, myself."

Bev gives Lucette a look.

"Are we going to a movie or what?" Lucette says.

Later, after the movie, when Ray is in the men's room, Lucette huddles into the small protection of the hood around a public phone on Fulton Avenue and listens to the phone ring in Cynthia's house. She has practiced what she will say to Cynthia, the tone of her words, cold and precise. She holds her body tight against the thready sound of Cynthia's imagined voice, feeling Bev just behind her, clicking her lighter. When Harry answers, she has nothing ready to say.

"Harry?"

"Yeah?" he says.

"It's Lucette."

"Lucette, honey," he says, surprised. He sounds as if he is warm, happy. "What are you doing? What's going on?"

"Nothing," she says. "I wondered what you were doing."

"Not a thing."

"So, you want to do something?"

"I guess I might. I guess I do."

"Well, okay." Bev pokes her and raises her eyebrows.

"Where are you?"

"On Fulton, by the library."

"As close as that? I'll be there in three minutes." Lucette hears the click as he hangs up the phone.

When his truck pulls up, she is standing alone, waiting for him, hugging herself against the cold.

Cynthia thinks how she left Harry with that question on her lips—"What are you thinking of?" She can feel the words in her mouth even though that was not the last thing she said to him. She feels the unsaid hum of them in her throat.

Now, though, they are separated by the ceiling, by the floor of her bedroom. She can hear him roaming. She hears the brief running of the water from the kitchen faucet, imagines him settling down with a drink.

As she lies in bed, she thinks of how he said she has no wrinkles. He remembers how her body used to look. How he looked at her in the kitchen, took the spoon away from her. She holds these things in her mind, her body and his, fifteen years old, shadowy in the dim, cool air of the garage behind this house, cold even in summer, their clothes around them on the floor. There was nothing wrong in it, just curiosity, a rehearsal for what would come later, with others, that was how she'd thought of it then. They had barely touched, had only taken note of what was different, what was pleasant, what was strange about the other. All the times they had touched before, casual and unthinking—hitting, pinching, pushing, arms around each other's shoulders in victory or defeat or conspiracy—those times were less physical, less like a touch than that silent looking.

She had been happy then with his look and the purity of the space between them. They should have gone on, she thinks now, and behind her closed eyes, hovering ten feet over Harry's head, separated by lathe and plaster, she makes her remembered fifteen-year-old hand reach out to touch what was different about him, and what was the same. Something might so easily have happened to make them start, a noise, the sound of a car in the alley. They would have been afraid, half reaching for their clothes—and then, relieved, they would laugh, relaxing, their slackening hands drop-ping their T-shirts again, and continue to look at each other, but nearer now, having moved closer together in their panic.

When she falls asleep, Cynthia moves her hand restlessly over the blanket. She is dreaming about Louisa, her aunt, Harry's mother.

Louisa is dead in this dream, and Cynthia likes her better that way. Louisa tells Cynthia she has a new job teaching children. They sit, hands clasped, on the porch of a house across the street, the Biltner's house. The air is pleasant. It is summer, green and hot. Louisa smiles, Cynthia smiles.

They're late, Louisa says, but Cynthia is distracted because she can see Harry by the corner of the house. It is almost time for them to go away together. Who is late? she asks Louisa, urging the dream toward its ending. They still do it all the time, Louisa says. She is sitting up straight, just as she could before her strokes, and her speech is fine, but her eye, her dreadful eye, is staring, just as it does in real life, from the flat whiteness of her bed in the nursing home. Who does? Cynthia asks. She tries to make Harry notice her, to sway the curtains of dream, to influence events. Who is late? she asks, but Louisa is looking down the street toward the traffic on Fulton Avenue and does not answer her.

When Cynthia opens her eyes, her bedroom seems insubstantial, the yellow lamplight meager and cheerless. She looks at the face of the clock: eleven-thirty. She presses her eyes shut, willing herself to sink, to dissolve, searching for that corner of the porch, for Harry's hand, the street under their feet as they run from Louisa's eye.

But she can only half-dream, shapes and colors moving against the screen of her eyelids, the long arms of the rosebushes scratching at the windows and doors, Vicky-from-Convenient's voice on the phone saying words too low to hear, the hard tired feeling in her arms that comes from carrying a baby or loads of laundry.

So I'll be awake, Cynthia says to herself, and pulls herself up in bed. She leans against the pillow and feels the luxury and boredom of having nothing to do. Harry must be sleeping now, since the house is silent. He does this sometimes, she knows, drinks a few shots and stumbles up the stairs to bed. A wonder she didn't hear him and wake, she thinks, but maybe that was what woke her, the noise of Harry going to bed, where he must be now, quiet, he never snores. She listens for any sound, any rustling, and hears none, holds her breath and wills her ears to open. There is maybe a tick, a tickle of sound, a sliding? Something. Harry is in bed, not quite still, his breath moving the covers. It seems natural that she can feel him sleeping, breathing, turning in his bed, and she smiles, slipping back into sleep in the center of her house.

"You have to be home?" Harry says to Lucette as he reaches for the glass they've been sharing. Lucette has been drinking a lot of it, he sees, so he keeps hold of it. He has drunk more, but looking at their bodies next to each other on the bed, this seems natural, his being larger, darker.

"No," she says. "Not really." She reaches for the glass, but he holds on to it a little longer.

"Your folks okay about it?"

Lucette takes the glass and drinks from it. "There's only my mother."

Harry thinks of his dead father, the smiling picture that used to hang in Louisa's front room. "That's right," he says. "He ran off, your old man."

"He's dead," Lucette says in such a loud voice that Harry takes his hand away from her breast and sits up. She takes a long drink from the glass and looks at him. "My real father is dead."

"Sorry," Harry says. He stills his body, stares at the angle of ceiling and wall, breathing shallowly.

"A semi overturned in front of him and he ran into it," Lucette says. Her voice is even now.

"That's right," Harry says. Frank Harmon, he thinks. "Tough on your mother."

"Oh, she's all right," Lucette says. She looks down at his hand, picks it up and moves it back to her breast. She liked the feeling of it being there, how after a while she couldn't feel it as separate from her body. "So why don't you tell me something." She turns to him, looking him carefully in the eye. "Tell me how it was in the war."

"That's old history," Harry says, and leans his head back against the pillow. He moves his hand on her breast to distract her. "You gaining weight?" he asks.

"What?" She sits up and looks down at herself. "What do you mean?"

"Feels heavier," he says, cupping her breast.

"Would you like it if they were bigger?"

"No," he says. "Just fine the way they are." He leans down to put his mouth to her.

Her body feels slower to him, like fucking in a dream, he can't seem to hold her to the present. He imagines that she is still thinking about the war and her questions, and he moves impatiently against her to shape her attention so that it will fill the space their bodies make on the bed, in the room, in the trailer. The light on her hair is sharp and yellow so that the strands look metallic, though they are soft on his fingers. He feels the people and scenes that her question conjured up on the edge of his mind, but he ignores them and holds her hard against him, one arm around her neck and the other at the back of her thigh to urge her on. Just before the end, he looks at her through his nearly closed eyelids and sees that her eyes are glassy, turned up a little so that the whites show under the rim of the iris. He knows this is a sign that she is almost there, and he pushes harder into her, emptying his mind, waiting to go under.

Cynthia has to work today—Tuesday, four to twelve. She works twenty hours a week at the Convenient Food Mart, Tuesday and Thursday, four to twelve, and a four-hour shift on Friday nights, eight to twelve.

Since she was sixteen, Cynthia has always had a job, and never one she really liked. She was working in a bank when she started dating Derek, whom she had met at a wedding shower for a neighborhood girl, Loretta Gitlin. Derek was Loretta's fiancé's brother, and had only come to the shower to rescue him from the shrieking, paper-tearing, ribbon-pulling to come.

He had been waiting in the kitchen, drinking bright pink punch out of a cup that Loretta's mother had given him, the handle so small that he couldn't get his finger through it. Cynthia was cutting sheet cake, and Loretta's mother kept coming over to check that the pieces were equal in size. Cynthia was getting more and more irritated with Loretta's mother and with Loretta. She had come with her mother, because her mother had wanted to gossip with the neighborhood ladies—Virginia loved a chance to dress up and eat something sweet.

Cynthia had been irritated with Derek, too, hanging around watching her cut cake. She kept getting crumbs on the tablecloth, which upset Loretta's mother. The icing stuck to the knife, collecting more crumbs, so that she had to stop often to wipe them off with a paper towel. Her squares got less even and Loretta's mother kept taking her hand to show her with the knife how big they should be. She heard her own mother's high laugh in the other room and gritted her teeth. She cut viciously down into the cake. She wiped the knife hard, feeling the disgusting ooze and bulge of the icing under the paper towel.

"You're bleeding," Derek had said to her.

"Don't be stupid," she said.

He put his cup down on the counter and came over to the table, the dishrag in his hand. She looked down and saw that she had a long cut on the side of her index finger. Blood was running across her palm and along the length of her arm, dripping red into the snowy white cake. She laughed, and the kitchen dissolved around her, layers and layers of it melting away while she rose up like the levitating woman in a magic show, borne aloft, hair and dress trailing.

When she opened her eyes she was lying on Mrs. Gitlin's sacred pastel couch from which the plastic cover had been removed for the shower. The shower ladies were hanging over her. Her mother was holding Cynthia's arm straight up in the air, under Derek's direction. The sharp smell of sulfur was in her nostrils—Mrs. Gitlin was waving an extinguished match under her nose. Loretta was standing back, among her unopened presents, arms folded. Each and every element of this scene made Cynthia happy, the paleness of the couch under her shoes, the thin thread of smoke from the match, the feel of stretching in the arm her mother was holding up, the throb—not yet pain—in her cut finger, Loretta's cranky face, and Derek's serious one.

After she and Derek were married, she worked for a while as a bookkeeper at a small plating company, and then as the night manager of a restaurant. She quit that job when she was six months pregnant with Joey. When he was three she'd started doing some work at home for the accountant's office Derek worked in, but she got sick of that. For three years now she has been a cashier at the Convenient Food Mart near her house.

Cynthia thinks how to fill the hours before she has to go to work. The day drags at her. She could shop, she could clean.

Early this morning she looked out the kitchen window and saw that Harry's truck was no longer parked behind the garage. After Joey left for school she went up to Harry's bedroom and opened the door. The bed was smooth, unrumpled, exactly as she had made it up the day before. She could see the marks where, with the flat of her hand, she had smoothed the spread up and under the edge of the pillow. There were no butts in the ashtray on the table by the lamp, no dirty glass. She felt ashamed standing by the empty bed, remembering how happy she had been the night before when she thought she had Harry here asleep.

Now she sits in the kitchen rocking chair, ankles crossed, hands on the armrests. She feels a bad energy in her body, but it is not an energy that she can harness to cleaning the junk room or making a complicated recipe or shopping for new pants for Joey. She wants to drive, she decides. She could drive straight south or west, as she sometimes does, until she sees nothing familiar—the white fields, the dark solitary houses, the yards full of wrecked cars, the round empty faces of strangers. But there is not enough time, not as much time as she likes to have for that, only three hours.

When the idea of visiting her Aunt Louisa in the nursing home comes to her, Cynthia gets up from the chair immediately. She runs up the stairs to comb her hair and change her shirt. She puts on a sweater and brushes her teeth again.

She ought to take something with her. She looks around. No flowers. No books or magazines, Louisa does not read.

She is presented with this same problem every time she goes to the nursing home, and usually she ends up buying a box of turtle candy, which she once heard Louisa say she liked. But she does not want to do that, her energy is like an arrow that will not bend or waver. She goes to the dining room and opens one of the china cabinets. On the second shelf there are miniature shoes, mostly made of china, different sizes, styles, colors. She selects one from the back, a small one, green with a frill of china lace along its edges, wraps it in a tissue, and stuffs it into her purse.

The light outside hurts her eyes. The house is a dim house, green and shadowed in the summer, winter-dark now. She revs the car up to thirty-five, forty on the side streets, slowing down to fifteen for stop signs. On the West Twenty-fifth Street bridge, she guns it to fifty. The road is dry, no problem, she thinks. The sense of her own movement and Louisa's stillness makes her feel up to

Louisa, as if she can take this energy into Louisa's room and drive it into her like a nail.

The nurse at the front desk looks up at Cynthia. "Can I help you?"

"I'm here to see my aunt, Mrs. Walker," Cynthia says.

The nurse looks at the clock. "She's eating her lunch now," she says.

Cynthia takes her hand off the Formica counter separating her from the nurse, thinking what she will do while she waits. There is a coffee shop down the block, and she imagines walking into its green-and-pink interior, sitting at a little table, watching the other customers, picking up her coffee cup with an elegant turn of her wrist. There is a row of shops down there, maybe a library. She can't remember.

"But you could go in anyway," the nurse says. "It's nice for them if they have company for lunch."

"I don't want to be in the way," Cynthia says.

"It's quite all right, Mrs. Lynch," the nurse says, getting up. "I'll take you down there myself, I've got to hit the john."

Cynthia follows her down the hall, all the surfaces gleaming around her. "Does she have to be fed?" Cynthia asks.

"I don't think Mrs. Walker does," the nurse says, turning her head and slowing down a little. Her face is round, her chin pointed. She looks to Cynthia like an elf in the illustrations of certain children's books, sly, a trickster. "We encourage them to eat by themselves if they can. It's good for them, and the staff can use that time for something more vital." She laughs. "Sometimes it gets messy, though."

Cynthia remembers a photograph of Joey when he was learning to feed himself, mouth wide; he was splotched with what looked like green slime—strained peas.

"I'm sure it does," she says, and braces herself for a Louisa spotted with food.

But when the nurse opens the door, she sees that Louisa's bed jacket is as clean as her own sweater. She has been eating, but the tray on its swing-out table has been pushed aside and Louisa is lying back against her pillows. She has a roll still in her hand, but she is not eating it. Her head is turned toward the other half of the room, where the other bed is, and the window. She looks flattened, immobile, the hand with the roll is lax on the bed, barely holding on to it.

Cynthia counts back to see how long it is since she has been here. Almost two months, she thinks, just before Christmas. It's not that she has been remiss, it's not that Louisa is ever glad to see her. But has Louisa changed in those two months, become quieter, older, less alert? She stands by the side of the bed, and then takes Louisa's hand to slip the roll from her fingers.

Louisa turns her head, fast. Lifting her upper lip she makes a noise—"Uuurrr"—and Cynthia pulls her hand back. The feel of Louisa's skin disturbs her, it is so hot and soft. She can't remember the last time she heard Louisa make any noise at all.

Louisa stares at her with her good eye. The other, the bad one, is unpleasant to look at, the lid hanging halfway down, the way the pupil wanders, the cloudiness of it. But her good eye is worse. It is dark, shining, black, there is almost no difference between iris and pupil. She turns it on her visitors like a laser.

"Hello, Aunt Louisa," Cynthia says.

Louisa sets her lips together, thinning them. It seems to Cynthia that Louisa regrets having been surprised into making a noise, and she takes this as a good sign, that she has made Louisa ill at ease.

"I hope you're feeling okay," she says. She glances over at Louisa's roommate, who is looking at her with interest. "Hello," she says to her. She can't remember her name.

"I just thought I'd stop by on my way to work," she says to both of them. This lie comforts her, and puts her back into her role as mover, visitor, a productive force.

"It's cold out," she says, sitting down. "No snow, though."

Louisa looks toward the window and then back.

"Of course you can see what it's like outside, can't you?" Cynthia says. She turns her purse around and then puts it on the floor beside her.

"Harry asked me to stop by," she says. "He said you could use the company."

Louisa snorts. This sound is surprising, coming from her. It is so expressive, it is hard to remember that she doesn't speak.

"You can't tell her nothing about Harry," the roommate observes. "She knows it all, don't you, honey?"

Louisa continues to look at Cynthia. She has pulled herself up on her pillows so that she is half sitting. Because of the weakness in her left arm, her position is skewed to the side. Cynthia wants to even her out, to make her straight. But the idea that Louisa might make that noise again holds her back.

"Harry was over for dinner last night," she says. "We had quite a talk about the old days."

Louisa stares at her.

"About the neighborhood and so on. He and I and Joey ate together and watched TV."

"How is your Joey?" the roommate asks. She is crocheting something long and yellow that is draped over her bed, trailing on the floor.

"He's fine," Cynthia says.

"And your husband? It's Derek, right?"

"He's fine," she says. "He was at work."

Louisa drops her eyes. She seems bored, or disgusted.

Cynthia looks around the room for something to comment on, but there is nothing much there—two small bureaus, a metal cupboard for medical and hygienic necessities, the half-open door to the bathroom. The roommate's bureau is crowded with pictures, cards, small stuffed animals, a plant in a ceramic wheelbarrow, a partly eaten candy bar. Louisa's bureau is bare, and the white flatness of it reminds Cynthia of what she has brought. She reaches for her purse and feels in it for the shoe.

"I've brought you something," she says.

Louisa does not raise her eyes, but the roommate leans over to see what it is.

Cynthia brings out the shoe and removes its wrapping. She holds it out to Louisa on the palm of her hand. "It was Mother's," she says. "I thought you might want to have something of hers."

Louisa looks at Cynthia, and then at the shoe.

"I'll put it on your bureau," Cynthia says, but she hesitates. "Wouldn't you like to look at it first?"

She leans forwared with the shoe outstretched, and then, when Louisa doesn't take it, she puts it down beside her.

"That was Virginia's, eh?" the roommate says, and she sits up in her bed to get a look at it.

Louisa picks up the shoe with her right hand, and slowly brings her left hand over to meet it, almost dragging it through the air. The left hand unfolds clumsily and she drops the shoe into it. Her left arm waves uncertainly in front of her, some of the fingers uncurl rustily.

"Oh, be careful," Cynthia says, getting up, reaching for the shoe, but the hand continues to wave, to waver, and the shoe falls from Louisa's stiffened fingers. She sinks back on her pillows as it hits the bed and slides off, breaking on the shiny linoleum floor.

The shoe is shattered into iridescent green fragments. Cynthia picks up an unbroken bit of lace frill. "You smashed it," she says. "You did that on purpose."

Louisa moves her shoulders unevenly—a shrug?

Cynthia thinks of her mother, of her mother's hands, of the green china shoe in her mother's hand, of her mother standing in front of the china cabinet—and she is so angry she can hardly breathe. The stupidity of it, of her mother's death, and nothing left except things that can be broken.

"Well, she don't hold with knickknacks," Louisa's roommate says.

Louisa has began to turn her head from side to side, slowly at first, and then faster. Cynthia is filled with anger. She grabs one of Louisa's arms and shakes it, but Louisa continues to toss her head, her eyes glassy.

"No use to talk to her now," the roommate says.

Cynthia drops Louisa's hand and grabs her purse.

"That's right, you come back later," the roommate says. "And honey," she calls after Cynthia, "get that boy in here to clean up. Sure was a pretty thing."

"Old bitch," Cynthia says aloud in the car, backing out of the parking lot. She can still feel Louisa's skin against her fingertips, hot, moist, alive.

She presses her hand to her forehead as if to feel for a fever, but her forehead is cold. She forces the car to stay in its lane, her hands hard on the steering wheel, but it jerks left, then right, back to the left as she overcorrects. The clock on the bank rises before her when she stops for a light. It is only two o'clock, more than two hours before work.

She longs for a place to go, a curtained place, dim but filled with a cool, even light, empty space, long corridors. She would walk through it, looking out at a garden full of flowers and birds. She sees herself pacing the corridors, with no need ever to check a clock or be someplace for somebody, no one's dinner to fix, no one's laundry, no one's voice on the phone.

It feels as if everything is slipping away from her, sliding out from under her feet. Eyes still closed, she puts her palm against the window glass, and it is cold, almost painful to the touch.

A week later, Harry is at the Maple Leaf, waiting for Lucette. He feels a ghost of that date nervousness from high school, the pressure of a ghost tie on his Adam's apple, the sting of aftershave on his scraped cheeks. He sits at the end of the bar next to Tase Penfield, their brown bottles of beer in front of them, soldiers at attention.

"It's not like it was, Harry," Penfield says, the first thing he's said in five minutes.

"No," says Harry.

"The noise, the-the-the disrespect."

The Stones are playing on the jukebox. "You like the old music better?" Harry asks. He drains his beer and considers whether he wants another. At Cynthia's there is always enough whiskey, but with Derek there it might be different. Derek is not a drinker.

"I like the rock and roll, don't get me wrong. Those little girls in miniskirts, they're cute as hell. I like that Cher, a sexy woman, nothing wrong with that, is there?"

"Not a thing," Harry says. He decides on another beer, reaches over the bar to get his own, holding it up to show Geneva.

"It's not that." Penfield lifts his bottle and looks seriously at the wet ring it has left on the bar. "It's the general attitude."

"What do you mean?" Harry asks, his eye on the door. He wants to be on time at Cynthia's if he has to go, on time to get there, and then to leave in good time as well.

"It's the speed. People don't take no time. And that way of making everything out to be fun. I hate that. You see it on the news. They're smiling all the time. Earthquakes. Fires. Children burning. Floods. Armies marching. They smile at everything. You noticed?"

"I guess I have," Harry says. This was the time of the evening that Tase Penfield liked to talk, and was still able to.

Harry is itchy, restless, but he sits quietly, his elbow on the bar alongside Penfield's, his eyes steady on Geneva. She doesn't look at him, will not acknowledge him. He knows it annoys her to be watched, and sometimes he likes to annoy her. His eyes follow her as she puts a beer down in front of a boy with a spiked crewcut and a leather vest buttoned over a white T-shirt—the bottle makes a precise contemptuous tap on the wood of the bar. She stands in front of the boy without speaking until he gives her some money. Harry shakes his head. It's a wonder to him that Geneva doesn't drive away all the customers, but she doesn't. They give her tips, in fact, which she accepts with no thanks.

She is nice to Tase, though. Respectful. And her kids, she must have been all right with them—they're over all the time although they're grown, always stopping by the bar to say hi or bring something, a plant maybe, Geneva has a collection of plants with multicolored leaves. They're always inviting her and Al over for dinner. Harry is aware that Al once hoped he might be interested in their youngest, Barbara, but she seemed as untouchable to him as a nun, not to mention the problem of Geneva as potential mother-in-law.

What've you got against marriage, Al had asked him then.

"It's no fun," Harry had said, laughing, and Al had shaken his head and pretended he was going to sucker punch Harry. But that was it, partly. Marriage was serious, both in its good and its bad ways. Marriage would tip the scales, you would always be scrabbling to regain something. When Harry met someone, man or woman, and liked them, and then found out they were married, he felt sorry for them, sorry that they were held down so in their own life. Al was a mystery to him, how he could be so happy when he had to deal with Geneva every hour of the day.

Geneva is yelling now at a pair of women who had complained about how she made their Alabama Slammers.

"Guess they haven't been in before," Harry says to old Penfield.

"Al's a saint."

"Here he comes," Harry says. Al is running up from the back. "Hey, Saint Al." Harry and Penfield watch as Al inserts himself between the more aggressive of the two women and Geneva, who are shouting in each other's faces.

The boy Charlie has come in from the other room, attracted by the voices. He leans against the arch in the wall to watch, but it is almost over now, the noise level is falling. The women are repeating their main points, but without as much heat. Al brings two fresh drinks and this sets Geneva off again, but she is too disgusted to keep it up. She takes her apron off and throws it down, and in a moment she is out the door. None of the regulars is much surprised, she has done this before.

"Jeez, I thought it was going to be a catfight," Charlie says.

"Not with Geneva," Harry says. "She's a tiger."

"More like a catamount," Penfield says. "Lean, always waiting for a fight. Same color hair. I remember back in the mountains, this would be in nineteen and thirty something, we used to go on a hunt after them every once in a while, catamounts, when they'd been after the stock. Wily, they were."

"So did you ever get one?" Charlie asks.

"I got a few." Penfield drinks the rest of his beer and sits, his eyes on the bar.

Charlie waits for details, and Harry turns, too, to listen, but Penfield doesn't look up.

"It's not like it was," he says. He holds his bottle up, although Geneva has gone, and Al is still trying to calm the two women.

Harry leans over and gets a beer, uncaps it for him, sets it between the old man's hands. "Well, Charlie," he says, and just then Lucette comes in.

"Hey, it's Lucette," Charlie says. "Hey, Lucette, over here."

Lucette has already seen Harry, although she does not smile or wave. This is her way. Harry nods to her and watches as she takes off her coat and hangs it on the coatrack by the front door. She smooths down her sleeves and he sees that she is wearing a dress. He has never seen her in a dress before and he looks at her with interest as she walks toward him. She looks older, taller, her hair is arranged differently, more stiffly. He doesn't think he likes how she looks in the dress, though she is so pretty in it, soft, covered but revealed.

"Hot damn," Charlie says under his breath. "If she doesn't look hot, Harry, you lucky shit."

"Can it," Harry says. He doesn't like the sound of *lucky* in Charlie's mouth. Why should he be lucky? It is his bad luck that he has to go to dinner at Cynthia's, to eat with Derek, to bring Lucette. A bad evening, as likely as not. What's the point of Lucette looking good in that scene?

Al sees Lucette and comes over to take her hands. "A dress, Lucette," he says. "What's the occasion?"

She looks at Harry, but he says nothing. "Mrs. Lynch invited us to dinner."

"Cynthia?" Al says. He stops stripping the paper from a roll of Tums, his whole face registering surprise. "The two of you going to Cynthia's?"

"A family dinner," Harry says. He moves his teeth back and forth over one another. How had Cynthia made him say he would come? When she called him up to ask him over, to come over with his girlfriend, he had been silent for a minute. Then he had said, "Which one, Cyn?"

Cynthia had laughed. "You could hold a lottery, maybe," she said.

"So who comes, the winner or the loser?"

"That's up to you," she said. She hesitated. "So there's no one you'd like to bring over to dinner at my house?"

"I never think about having dinner at your house with other people."

Cynthia laughed again. "I heard you've been around with the Harmon girl."

"Lucette," Harry said.

Cynthia was waiting, it seemed to him, for something more. He held the phone loosely, tapping his index finger against the receiver.

"Well, you could bring her over," she said, finally.

"I don't know," Harry had said, and then, "I'll let you know."

Why hadn't he called and said he had to work or that Lucette was sick? He had thought that Lucette would refuse to go, she was so unsociable, never wanting to hang out at the bar, always ready to go as soon as he wanted. But she had said yes when he brought it up, and readily, he thought.

Lucette doesn't say anything now, but the way she is standing conveys to Harry that she thinks they should leave and he is annoyed by it. "How about another beer?" he says to Al. "And one for Charlie?"

"Thanks, Harry. I owe you," Charlie says.

"What about you?" Harry says to Lucette.

"Could I have a glass of water?" she says to Al.

Al brings the beers and fills a glass with ice and water for Lucette, and a glass of ginger ale for himself which he uses to wash down two Tums.

"So Cynthia asked you two to dinner," he says. "Isn't that nice."

"I never met Cynthia," Charlie says. "I seen her at the supermarket though. A kind of a skinny woman, isn't she, with long old hair, kind of brown?"

"It's just the family," Harry says.

"Derek going to be there?" Al asks.

"I guess he will be," Harry says. "It's not one of the nights he works."

"Cynthia's got a nice little boy," Al tells Lucette. "Joey. What is he now, Harry, seven or eight?"

"Eight."

"She works at the Convenient over by my ma's," Charlie says. "I seen her there, too."

"Cynthia lives in the old house," Al says, again to Lucette. "Harry's and Cynthia's mothers' old house. Many's the story I've heard about the parties they'd have, all the brothers and sisters. My parents used to go over there all the time, they were part of that whole crowd." He pauses, spits on the red stone of his ring, polishes it with his handkerchief. "That was a different time— music, dancing, a lot of conversation, some poker. The old people, they still talk about those two sisters, Virginia and Louisa Starnes, that was. Cynthia's mother and Harry's mother. Virginia's dead these eight years now and Louisa in the home." Al shakes his head.

Harry and Lucette look at each other. Harry wishes he hadn't gotten another beer. More than anything he wants to leave and drive for a couple of hours, no less, until the dark and noise of the car is all that he has in his mind. Lucette is inscrutable to him right now, but he doesn't want to know what she is thinking. He feels a pull from her, from her wearing a dress, her hand curved around her glass of water, but he doesn't want it, doesn't want to feel it.

"She has like a blue Chevy Nova, right?" Charlie says.

"It's the general attitude," Old Penfield says. "It's not like it was."

Cynthia is ticking off items on a list in her head. Set table, check roast beef, take pie out of oven. She wants Lucette to see— something—something about their family, Cynthia's and Harry's. She wants to convey, by the way the tablecloth drapes over the table, by the pattern of the plates and utensils on the cloth, by the very smell of the food, the whole structure of their life, hers and Harry's. She wants Lucette to see that she is outside of it.

This is just a family dinner, a friendly invitation for Harry to bring Lucette, this is how she presented it to Derek. Even so he was surprised.

"You want me there?" he had asked.

"Why wouldn't I?" she said. "You live here, too. We'll just get to know her. We're Harry's family after all."

"Why should we get to know this one?" Derek said.

"I just thought it would be nice," Cynthia said. She was washing dishes as they talked, her back to him. She looked out at the winter sun on the snow in the backyard. It was bright but not bracing, thin and cold.

"This one's more serious?"

"Oh, I don't think so," Cynthia said, moving her hands through the dishes in the sink. "I just felt like having people over for dinner."

Derek didn't say anything, and she wondered what he was thinking, if he was thinking how she never wanted to have people for dinner, how she never wanted to go over to other people's houses for dinner or anything else.

"So is Thursday okay for you?"

"It's okay," he said. He got up and put his hands on Cynthia's shoulders. "You look tired, honey."

"Of course I'm tired. I work all day, don't I?" She had moved her shoulders out from under his hands, washing, rinsing, stacking.

No candles, she thinks. They would never use candles for a regular dinner. Cloth napkins? No, she decides, and she puts out the paper ones she bought that are more expensive, buffed somehow to make them smooth, a fleur-de-lis pattern embossed on the surface. She folds them in triangles and lays them on the plates, their points facing right like a series of arrows. This is what is needed, a direction to the evening, a path that will move Lucette through here like a conveyor belt, in and out of their lives. She imagines traffic signs, or better, painted lines on the floor as in the hospital, different colors for different destinations. Lucette's line would be red, it would come in the front door, lead to the couch where she could sit before dinner, to the table, and then out the door forever.

Cynthia yawns, a jaw-wrenching yawn. She has been having trouble sleeping just lately. She sits down in the big wing chair by the fireplace. She puts her right hand over her left, smoothing the skin, starting at her wrist and sweeping down over the knuckles, down the length of her fingers, counting each time she starts over at the knobby bone of her wrist. When she gets to twelve, she lets the muscles in her neck go slack and leans her head against the back of the chair. Her eyes are open, unfocused, and eventually they go dark, the fuzzy blackness like a blanket. Eighteen, nineteen, twenty. She tries to feel her body—lump of tissue, bone, warm fluid—in the middle of this cold room, thirty-one, thirty-two. She uses her mind like a probing finger—to find where it is, the trouble she can sense all through her, but she can feel nothing, can hardly distinguish the stroke of her fingers on the back of her hand.

"Mom!"

She jerks up, her head snapping forward, hands abandoning each other, one clutching the arm of the chair. "Joey—" her voice is raspy and she starts again—"Is your room clean yet? What do you want?" She gets up, pulls her blouse down, straightens her skirt.

"I'm done with my room," Joey says. He sits down on the footstool. "Can I go outside?"

"It's almost time for Harry to come," Cynthia says. She looks down at herself, checking how she looks, puts her hand to her face.

"Just for a little while," Joey says, kicking his feet at the rug, pushing up a little ridge.

"It's snowing," Cynthia says, turning toward the window, although it is too dark outside to see anything.

"It stopped. Come on, Mom."

"Oh, go. Go, I don't care." She peers out the front door, cupping her hands on either side of her face. The air is clear and dark, the street empty. "Where's your father?"

"He's in the basement," Joey says, his mouth muffled as he pulls down his ski mask.

"Wear your boots," Cynthia says, but she doesn't look to see if he puts them on. She goes to the top of the basement steps and looks down. The light is on, but she can't hear anything. "Derek?"

She hears deep in the house the clink of metal on metal, outside, the scraping sound of metal on ice, Joey's sled. "Are you down there? Derek?"

The truck is a safe place, dim in the clear snowlit air all around, but Lucette wishes it on faster. She kicks at the stuff on the floor with the pointed toes of the shoes she is wearing, Bev's shoes.

"I got some tools down there," Harry says to her.

"Oh, *tools,*" she says, and watches him as he takes in her tone, his look unreadable. She twitches her legs, her thighs cold against the seat cover, lifts her body to pull the dress down farther underneath, so that her open coat falls back. She glances at Harry, he is looking straight ahead. The dress is borrowed from Bev. She had gone over to Bev's to change, to hide the dress and its unusualness from her mother. She hadn't told her mother where she was going, she never does. She smooths her hands down over the front of her dress under the coat, Bev's coat. "Is this the street?" she asks Harry, although she knows it is.

He grunts, down shifting. The street is like a river, the thick, scarred ice flowing between the banked-up snow on the lawns, the light of the streetlights gleaming on the shiny places, picking out the frozen hard ridges of old car tracks. Harry pilots the car down the middle of the street, letting the truck skid a little. Lucette shivers and starts when it slides. She looks out the side window, so as not to have to watch things coming toward them.

And then "Goddamn! Goddamn!" Harry shouts, the truck skewing sideways.

Lucette looks, she has to, afraid to see anything, a dark shape going one way while the truck slides on its own line.

Harry fights the wheel. The truck is sliding toward one of the parked cars. Lucette braces herself against the dashboard, one hand held against her stomach in a fist. The truck misses the dark hulk of the car, buries itself in the hard-packed snow just beyond.

"Goddamn," Harry says again, and jumps out of the truck, leaving the door open.

The cold air hits Lucette. She holds her palm against her stomach for a minute, her breathing hard and visible in the dark air. She looks out the door. The outside handle is jammed into the hard white snow bank. She wraps her coat around her and slides across the seat and out the driver-side door. Harry is in the street ahead, running—she can hear his heavy boots on the ice. The night is so bright from the moon that the streetlights could be turned off. Lucette stands on the street, chipping at the ice with the heels of her shoes. She looks at the houses. There is one with a porch light on, its door opens and the figure of a woman comes out, stands dark against it. The woman looks at where Harry is running and then turns toward Lucette. Lucette can feel her eyes, she thinks. She doesn't know what to do. She reaches inside the truck and turns off its lights, closes the door. Carefully, she walks over the ice to a shoveled driveway and starts toward the lighted house.

Her heels click on the sidewalk, sharp but comforting, she likes hearing this sound. She averts her eyes from the woman ahead of her, a form of politeness, watching the shoveled edges of the snow piles, the dusting of icy crystals on the sidewalk. As she gets close to the lit porch she turns her head toward the street. Harry is not in sight. She stands at the edge of the porch light's reach, not wanting to go up without him.

The woman, still dark against the light, is looking up the street, too. She turns to Lucette, taking on color and shape. "What's he doing?" she asks. She looks quickly at Lucette and says before she can answer, "You never know what Harry is going to do."

"I don't know," Lucette says.

They stand there a moment more in the cold silent air. Lucette knows this is Cynthia, but she doesn't want to say her name until Harry is there.

The woman shivers. "We might as well go in."

She holds the door for Lucette, and then stands for a minute longer on the porch. "Joey," she calls. "Joey, it's time for dinner." She waits, and then comes in, slamming the door behind her. "Derek," she yells.

Lucette stands on the rug in the hall, her coat unbuttoned.

"Men," the woman says to her, grimacing. She laughs. "Who knows?"

Lucette smiles. She thinks how this might be the wrong house after all, and the real Cynthia is in one of the houses on either side, waiting for her and Harry, maybe even that Harry is there in the right house, wondering where she is. She looks at the woman, who is smiling, reaching for Lucette's coat, and imagines that this is someone with whom she will be friends, that she will come over here and this woman will have cookies or banana bread set out on the table for her and they will talk in the kitchen, in the spring, in the summer, in the fall. Big sugar cookies, yellow, with raisins, glasses of amber iced tea, steaming cups of coffee or hot chocolate, she can see them, talking about women's things, two women with their heads together over a table, the tick of the oven timer, the sighing of the furnace.

"You're Lucette," the woman says.

"Yes."

Cynthia looks like Harry, and Lucette is surprised by this. Her hair is light like his, with maybe more gray in it. There is something in her face that is like his, although it is thinner, with hollows in her cheeks where Harry has solid flesh. The long arms, long fingers. The color of her skin is the color of Harry's where his is not weathered darker.

"I need to stir the gravy," Cynthia says.

She goes into the kitchen and Lucette follows her. It is old-fashioned, with yellowing linoleum, a wooden table and chairs, big scarred refrigerator. Lucette stands by the table. There is a window over the sink and she can see her reflection in it, sunk in the glassy darkness.

"Sit down, sit down." Cynthia is stirring in a pan with a long spoon. "Derek," she calls.

A door at the end of the room opens and a man comes in. "Dinner ready?" he says.

"Not quite," Cynthia says. "Is Joey down there with you?"

"No," he says. "Didn't he go outside with his sled?"

They both look at Lucette where she still stands by the table.

"Where's Harry?" he says.

"There was an accident," Lucette says.

"What?"

"We skidded into a pile of snow. There was something in the road."

Cynthia and Derek look at each other.

"My God—" Derek says, and he runs toward the front of the house.

Cynthia drops her spoon on the stove and follows him.

Alone, Lucette looks around. She goes over to the sink and looks at the dirty dishes, the ragged, squeezed-out cloth. Opening the refrigerator, she peers into the freezer compartment at the anonymous plastic-wrapped bundles, and below at the three eggs in the egg-shaped depressions on the door. She lets her fingers brush the spices in the spice cupboard, takes the broom out of its corner and sweeps it across the floor. There is a shelf with cookbooks stacked on it and a collection of oddments. She picks up, one by one, a pinecone, a marble rolling around in a baby-food jar, a ceramic owl, a pencil with a bat-shaped eraser, a khaki-green arm from an action figure.

She takes a cookbook off the stack and opens it. On the flyleaf, written in old ink, pale blue and scratchy, it says "Virginia Starnes, 1947." Underneath that, in different ink, it says, "eggs, vanilla, cream of tartar."

She puts it back and goes to the door that leads into the dining room, where the table is set for dinner. She walks through it, touching the backs of the chairs one after another, and into the front room, neat, pillows plumped up on the couch. She can see where a stack of newspapers has been shoved into one of the glass-fronted bookcases on either side of the fireplace. She goes into the hall and stands looking up the stairs. She can see a stained-glass window at the landing, and the light from it, a quivering red shape on the wall.

She puts one hand on the banister and begins to climb the stairs. They rise to a landing which she can just see over to where another set of stairs goes down, to the kitchen, she supposes. To the left she can see the first step of another flight leading up, no light up there, an angle of darkness falls across the landing. She knows that Harry sleeps here sometimes. It would be a room that showed only one person, the room with no kid things in it, easy to find. She is one step from the landing when the front door opens and they all— Harry, Cynthia, Derek, a little boy—rush in at once.

Harry has a grip on the boy's coat collar. Derek holds his hand by the wrist. Cynthia is white with cold, her lips almost purple, her hair standing out from her head as if it has frozen solid.

"What the hell were you doing?" Harry says, in a way that suggests that he has said it before and not gotten a good answer.

"Who were those boys?" Derek says. He taps Harry's arm, and

when Harry let's go of Joey's collar, he unzips Joey's coat and takes it off.

"Oh, Joey, Joey, what were you doing, why didn't you come home?" Cynthia is crying.

"Shut up, Cynthia," Derek says, and the two of them look at each other over Joey's head. "Calm down," he says.

Lucette had been ready to explain that she was going up to look for the bathroom, but no one is paying any attention to her. She comes back down and stands at the foot of the stairs.

"So what happened, Joey?" Derek says. He squats, balancing on his heels in front of the boy.

Joey is not crying, but his face is wet, his hair flattened on one side from his red wool hat.

"We were sliding," he says.

"You were sliding on the street, weren't you? Weren't you? Why would you do that, I told you not to—"

"Cynthia," Derek says. He looks into Joey's face and waits.

Lucette feels very warm, watching Derek's hands on Joey's arms. She feels faint. Derek has his back to her and his back is very broad and strong. Beside him Cynthia is like a wraith, a thin sick woman wringing her hands, her body bending like a vine. Cynthia moves back when Derek speaks, one step, then another. She drops to the couch, leaning on Harry where he sits on the arm.

"Tell me, Joey," Derek says.

"We were sliding," Joey says. "I didn't think there'd be any cars on the street."

"You knew Harry was coming, you knew that," Cynthia says.

Joey shrugs. "He always comes around back, by the alley. You always do," he says, turning to Harry.

Lucette looks at Harry to see what he will say, and is astonished that Cynthia is reddening, her cheeks hot as if with a fever. No one else notices this, as far as she can tell, Derek and Harry still focused on Joey.

"It could have been really bad, Joey," Derek says. "You know that?"

"I guess," Joey says. He looks into his father's eyes, it seems to Lucette. He blinks, and yawns.

"You could have been hurt, or one of your friends. Your Uncle Harry could have been hurt, or this girl." Derek turns to look at Lucette. "You weren't hurt?" he asks.

"No," Lucette says. She sinks down, back against the newel post, and sits on the bottom step.

"Harry's truck might have been damaged."

He runs both his hands down Joey's arms. Lucette shivers.

"I guess you're sorry," Derek says. "Aren't you?"

"Yes," Joey says, his voice a thread.

"We'll think about a punishment," Derek says. "We'll talk about it later. Maybe we can have dinner now?" He releases Joey and nudges him toward his mother.

Cynthia rises from the couch and catches Joey up in her arms. "Oh, Joey," she says, "Oh, Joey," and they both start to cry.

Harry gets up from the couch, and he and Derek move away.

"The truck okay?" Derek says.

"It's fine," Harry says.

"It's still sticking out into the street," Lucette says, and they turn to look at her.

"I turned off the lights."

"Better move it," Derek says. "I'll give you a hand."

Lucette would like to go with them, but they don't ask her to come. There has been a clear division—men outside, women and children inside. But she doesn't want to be here with Cynthia and Joey. They have stopped crying, but Cynthia has her arms wrapped around Joey, rocking him back and forth, talking to him in a low voice. For a minute, Lucette stays where she is, sitting on the step, her feet side by side in front of her on the gold carpet. But the hardness of the step and the weird energy she feels are too much for her. She gets up, walks from the hall to the front room, and stands next to the couch.

"I need to use the john," she says to Cynthia.

Cynthia looks up at her, and it is a different look, different from how she looked at Joey, or at Derek or Harry.

"It's upstairs," she says.

Lucette goes up quickly, almost running. In the second-floor hall, she pauses. She can see which is the bathroom, even in the dark the gleam of the tiled floor is visible. She goes inside and turns on the light. It is old-looking up here, too, white and green, dim even with the light on, an old, claw-footed tub.

She is nervous, reluctant to explore. She touches the sink and then turns slowly to look at everything—toothbrushes, towels, bathmat. She opens the medicine cabinet and then closes it. She takes off her high heels, turns on the water, and goes out into the hall, walking soft-footed. Four doors: which? She opens the one on the left and knows right away that it is the wrong one. It is the parents' room, stretching across the front of the house. She steps inside. She can't turn on the light, but it is lit from outside by the moon or the streetlight on the white-reflecting snow. The curtains are open and the shades are up. Drifting across the room, her stockinged feet brushing the carpet, she touches the bed, catches sight of her shadowy figure in Cynthia's mirror. She goes to the closet, the size of a small room with a small square window of its own, a huge pile of clothes on the floor.

She goes to the window and looks out at Harry and Derek working with the truck. They have moved the truck to the space in front of the house. The hood is open and Harry is bent over the engine, reaching in among the coils and wires. She admires how his pale hair shines under the streetlight.

Back in the hall, she listens. She can hear Cynthia in the kitchen, the noise of pots and plates, running water, and Joey's voice. She opens the door at the end of the hall—shelves, towels stacked up—the linen closet. The next door sticks, and she works the knob carefully until it pushes open. There is a light on in here, at the baseboard, a nightlight shaped like a turtle. Joey's room—bed half-made, shoes on the floor, a picture of an airplane on one wall.

One more door, the one past the bathroom. But when she starts toward it, she hears that the water in the bathroom is making a different sound. Although she didn't put the stopper in, the water is flowing silently over the lip of the sink, just beginning to puddle on the tiles.

When she has wiped the floor with toilet paper, not wanting to leave the evidence of a soaked towel, she feels sick. She has to go down now, has to be downstairs, but her stomach has convulsed, tight muscles around an empty hole, and she stands still. The side door below her opens and slams, she hears boots shuffling. She waits another minute until her stomach quiets, slides her shoes on, and goes down the front stairs, pretending that she hasn't seen the stairs to the kitchen.

Joey is sitting on the couch. "Are you sick?" he says.

"No." Lucette looks toward the kitchen, where Harry and Derek are talking to Cynthia.

"You were up there a long time," he says. "And the water was running. This girl at school that throws up a lot says that's what she does when she throws up. She turns the water on so no one will hear the noise."

"What are you watching?" Lucette says.

"Cartoons."

They both watch as running figures move in front of static backgrounds, all angles, charging with souped-up rifles in the crooks of their arms.

"This one is pretty dumb." Joey turns the sound up and down with the remote control. Every time he presses the button a line of green grows or shrinks across the bottom of the TV screen. "My favorite is this one where these kids all get sucked into a video game."

"Is that where they all have different powers?" Lucette has seen it on Saturday mornings, lying in bed at the trailer, waiting for Harry to wake up.

"Yeah. I like the guy who does magic, only he does it wrong."

Lucette sits on the couch next to Joey. She wishes they could sit there for a long time, just as they are, the TV harmlessly on in front of them, the smell of dinner in the air, the sounds of voices from the kitchen—Harry's and Derek's a low rumbling, Cynthia's higher, lighter, the voice of a woman interrupted in the middle of getting dinner. The idea she had about Harry's room recedes from her. She had imagined standing in the middle of it and learning something, but it seems silly now. She slides down a little on the couch and puts her feet up next to Joey's on the coffee table.

"Dinner's ready," Cynthia calls from the other room. "Joey, put on the record player."

Joey jumps up. "Can I pick?" he yells.

"You can pick, but it has to be from the stack on the little table."

Lucette turns around to watch, folding her arms on the back of the couch, her chin pressing into the bend of one elbow. Harry comes into the dining room and flicks the switch so that the chandelier over the table lights up, a hundred slivers of glass shining. Joey puts on a record and turns the volume up, the music flooding out as Derek comes in carrying roast beef sliced on a platter, fanning out around a center of parsley.

Cynthia is behind him, with a bowl of mashed potatoes like a white mountain, and vegetables, yellow-orange carrots, red tomatoes, green beans. "Dinner," she says again. She waves them to their seats, Derek at one end, Harry at the other. Cynthia sits on one side by herself, near the kitchen door. Lucette and Joey are on the other. Joey rushes to sit next to Harry.

"Let Lucette and Harry sit together," Derek says.

But Lucette doesn't want to disappoint Joey. "It's all right," she says.

"Well, if Lucette doesn't mind," Cynthia says, smiling at her.

Passing the bowls and platters Lucette keeps her head down. She can see the food moving around the table in a pattern—the carrots from Cynthia's hands to Harry's, the tomatoes flecked with small cubes of bread from Harry to Joey, the brown gravy from Derek to Cynthia—and the flashing of the silverware, the gleam of light on the white plates, the small colorful mounds of food sliding from the spoons. It is dizzying. She takes one slice of roast beef, one spoonful of carrots, one dollop of mashed potatoes, one stewed tomato, one thing in each quadrant of her plate, like four slices of a pie, north, south, east, west.

"Have a biscuit," Cynthia says, pushing the napkin-covered basket toward her.

"No thank you," Lucette says.

"You have to have one of Cynthia's biscuits," Harry says. "They're the only thing she can bake that's good."

"Oh, stop it," Cynthia says to him, slapping his hand with her napkin. "I know I'm not the cook my mother was. Try one, though," she says. "Lucette."

Lucette takes a biscuit and puts it on her plate between the carrots and the potatoes.

"It was my grandmother, mine and Harry's, though, who was the real cook. Remember, Harry?"

Harry grunts affirmatively, his mouth full.

"She used to have the whole family over for Christmas Eve, for Easter breakfast, right here in this dining room. And that was nothing to what it was like when all the aunts and uncles still lived here. The parties they used to have! My mother used to tell me about how wonderful it was, all their friends there, and how no one would leave, they were having such a good time, and finally Grandma would make them all breakfast to send them on their way."

"It's hard to imagine your Uncle John at a party," Derek says, reaching for the gravy.

"You only knew him when he was old," Cynthia says.

"He was pretty hard to take."

"He was unsociable, if that's what you mean," Harry says. He picks up his glass of water and then sets it down again.

"Uncle John used to keep his teeth in the refrigerator," Joey says.

"Why?" Lucette asks.

"That's your *Great*-Uncle John," Cynthia says.

"He said it killed the germs," Joey says.

"Don't talk with your mouth full."

"He had an extra set he kept in the freezer," Joey says. "He showed them to me once."

Derek laughs. "Well, why not? A lot of perfectly good storage space in there if you're a single person."

"Well, we shouldn't be talking about people Lucette didn't even know," Cynthia says. "Another biscuit? Anyone?"

The biscuits make the round of the table.

"Hear anything from Al?" Derek asks Harry.

"What about?" Harry says.

"I heard Al was trying to finance a new bar."

"Who told you that?"

"I heard something about it from the lawyer who's handling the estate, a client of mine. He said Al made an offer."

"None of my business."

"Cynthia and I've got a bit of news as well," Derek says.

"Did you tell Harry about the camping weekend?" Cynthia says to Joey.

"We're going on a camping weekend," Joey says. "It's a retreat."

"Retreat from what?" Harry says.

"You know, a retreat, like in church." Joey shovels up his carrots and starts breaching the wall of his mashed-potato dam, so that a trickle of gravy oozes out.

"Joey, don't play with your food," Cynthia says.

"So what are you going to do on this weekend?" Harry says.

"Nature walks and stuff. Reexamine our faith, Sister says. We're going to have a big bonfire. I'm going to collect pinecones. Eric says if you throw them in the fire they make a great noise."

"Eric?" Cynthia says. "Eric Kistner? I thought you didn't like him."

"He's okay."

"Was that Eric I saw out in the street with you?" Harry asks.

Joey looks at his mother. "I don't know."

"Eric." Cynthia puts down her fork. "I should have known."

Joey widens the excavation in his potatoes with his fork.

"That Eric is no good, don't you see that, Joey?"

"We can talk about this later," Derek says, but Cynthia pays no attention.

"It was Eric's idea to slide in the street, wasn't it? Who else was out there?"

Joey doesn't answer, keeping his head down.

"If he was any decent kind of friend, he wouldn't have run away, would he? Would he, Joey?" Cynthia leans across the table, and Lucette pulls her spine flat against the back of her chair.

"Cynthia, I can talk to Joey about this later," Derek says.

"It was just boys having a little fun," Harry says at the same time.

"Oh, fine. Fine for you." Cynthia throws her napkin down on the table. "I should thank you for not running over my son, I suppose, and thank my son for being such a regular boy, and thank Derek for being so fucking understanding."

No one says anything.

Lucette puts her fork down on her plate carefully, the slightest chink of sound. She rests her fingers on the tablecloth, rubbing the nap of the cloth very lightly. She keeps her eyes on the glass bowl of flowers in the middle of the table, but she can see without looking that Cynthia's head is bowed, her hands clenched on the edges of the table. Lucette's spine cracks with its straightness, her thighs twitch. She can still taste the carrots she has eaten, feel the track of them down her throat.

Derek half rises from his chair, but Cynthia forestalls him, pushing herself away from the table, knocking her plate against the bowl of flowers. It does not spill, but the water in it rocks from side to side, washing back and forth over the thin green stems.

"Just never mind," Cynthia says. "All right? Just forget it." She stands up and goes out, through the front room into the hall.

Joey is crying. Lucette feels her throat clench in sympathy, but she is cold, distant, as if she is floating away from the table, the

white table with its colors of food and its shine of plates frighten-
ingly small and distinct.

Harry gets up and goes out.

Lucette turns to look at Derek. He still stands half-crouched by
his chair. "I should go," Lucette says. In the larger silence, there
is the small sound of Joey's crying, the soft sound of Harry's and
Cynthia's voices.

Derek nods, not really listening.

She gets up, hesitates by Joey's chair. She picks up her coat and
puts it on. Cynthia is sitting on the stairs, Harry leaning on the
banister below her. Without moving, Lucette says, "I have to be
getting home."

Harry looks up. "I'll take you back in a minute."

"That's all right," Lucette says.

"Oh, go with her." Cynthia doesn't raise her head. "Why don't
you go?"

Harry straightens up.

Lucette turns to the dining room where Derek and Joey are still
sitting. "Good-bye," she says.

Derek catches up to her by the side door. "I can drive you
home," he says.

"No thank you," Lucette says, almost crying.

She opens the door and slides through the slice of cold that
pushes in, pulling away from Derek's warm hand. She stops to get
her bearings. Down the street the cleared sidewalks stretch black
under the streetlights, but the alley is shorter, and she crosses the
street and starts along it. With every step she takes, her shoes slide
on the thick, unsalted ice. She tries to stay in the tire ruts where
the ice offers a rougher surface, something for her heels to catch
on to, but it is difficult—the ruts run into each other, crossing,
recrossing, disappearing. The sky is full of ugly orange light, the
dead orange streetlights, the dull orange glare of the city. By the
time she turns onto Bev's street, her feet are solid and numb.
Sluggish, they drag from her ankles as she makes them step, step,

step. She leans her forehead against the front storm door, too cold to go around to the side, and hits her forearm against the glass.

Ray opens the door and she stumbles and falls against him. He puts his arms around her, one reaching up under her coat that has fallen open. "Mom?" he calls. "Mom?"

"Sorry," Lucette says. "I can't feel my feet. I can't feel anything, just a prickling."

"Any time, for you, baby." He hesitates, and then reaches down and catches her behind the knees. He grins as he carries her over to the couch.

In the clear white light of next morning the sleeping Harry turns over and over on the bed. The trouble is that the blind is up, and the cold from the cracks in the sash are twisting with the wafts of heat rising from the radiator, a braid of air. There is turbulence, the blind is flapping, something large is reaching from beside the bed, and he ought to get outside the window onto the small flat back porch roof. He turns over once more and wakes up.

The whiteness of this room, his room at the old house, is blank, featureless, and he shakes his morning head. He is lying on his back. Everything is the same, the one straight-back chair with his clothes thrown over it, the box of a dresser—dark wood hard against the white. The bed rings under him, white metal, a hammock of metal springs. White sheets, white pillow. Despite the radiator, the air is chilly, and a smoky wisp of his breath rises.

Harry shakes his head but it will not clear. Last night, driving through the grid of streets between Fulton and West Twenty-fifth Street, the truck pulling a little to the left—was it from hitting the snowbank, or was it like that before?—he had not found Lucette. Stupid kid. Stupid games. He had driven doggedly for an hour before he came back to the house.

And nothing was happening there, the kitchen light left on and one in the front room, one lit spot on the stairs. It was only ten-thirty. He found the bottle where Cynthia kept it, under the sink in the dim yellow kitchen, and took it back with him to the couch, where he sat in the circle of light—one drink, he thought, would do it. But it was so quiet, the air so empty. Were they sleeping up there in their beds? Were they awake, staring at the ceiling, crouched by the door to hear what he would do? Were they murdered, throats slit, the useless old lock on the side door hanging broken? He couldn't sit, couldn't pace because of the noise. He had gone upstairs with the bottle.

It stands now on the small metal table by the bed, brown liquid, like the wood of the chair and the dresser, not much left. He stretches his hand out to it, can't quite reach it. He's thirsty, a beer would be nice, but he eases his body up against the metal bars and reaches for the bottle. One quick one. He smells it, the pruney smell of sour mash, and his nostrils flare. When it is sliding down his throat, he begins to feel better, he begins to expect to feel better.

The cold air hits his legs as he swings out of bed, his balls tighten up. His clothes look limp and dead, are cold against his skin when he pulls them on. No time to hang them on the radiator. When he has his underwear on, and his pants, he knocks back another shot and it plunges through him, a hot shaft all the way to his belly, holding him up.

Dressed, he looks around. There is something in this room he needs. What? He opens the drawer in the metal table: a paperback book pushed to the back, a man and a woman curved and hooked around each other on the cover. Cynthia's, he thinks, and laughs. He sits on the edge of the bed and reads where it falls open: *one long curl of coal-black hair snaked down the whiteness of her back as she bent down over the bundle of her clothes on the bank of the river—*
Cynthia reading this? he thinks, and smiles. Does Derek know he's not hot enough for her? He takes another hit from the bottle.
drops of water like crystal beads hung from her lashes, the ends of her hair, the tips of her breasts
women, he thinks, all the parts of them, too much to hold,
moving in her, the long river grass soft as a cloud under them, her breath caught

He shifts on the bed to ease his erection, his hand loose on the cool neck of the bottle. She can't keep it in the other room, he supposes, where Derek could find it. But here. Cynthia lying on the white flatness of this bed, his bed, her breath coming fast *feels the blood pulsing in her throat, her life force pushing against his hand* Harry clears his own throat, turns the book over to look at the back. Tiny gold letters superimposed on a tangled greenness, a jungle, a woman seen through vines and flowers, her shoulders and back bare, the almost visible curve of her breast. "She came expecting to be safe and invisible," he reads, "but the jungle promised much more, of danger, deceit, and a passion that would overwhelm Lucette, a passion as powerful as the ruins and the gods they honored." Lucette! Damn, he thinks. But when he looks again, he sees that he has misread it. ". . . a passion that would overwhelm Jeanette . . ."

He puts the book back in the drawer and closes it. He puts the bottle down and caps it, tapping the top with his finger—no, no more.

The banister under his hands, smooth and thick. The bounce of the stair treads. He pauses to check the weather at the front door. The beautiful white light outside. Gray inside. Oh, Cynthia, he thinks, and he turns around as he hears her step behind him, puts his hand on the newel post to stop the swing of his body.

"Cyn," he says. "Got to be going."

"What about breakfast?"

She is holding another damn dish towel. Her light hair is smooth and flat, hooked behind her ears. *Her coal black hair.* Cynthia's back is bony. He takes the dish towel from her hands. "No breakfast."

"Let me make you some coffee, then," she says. "Did you find her last night, that girl?"

He reaches behind her and runs the flat of his hand down her back, feeling the jut of the vertebrae. "As bony as ever," he says.

Cynthia is perfectly still under his hand where he has let it come to rest at the base of her spine. He watches her breath come faster.

She squares her shoulders, he can see the knobs of her collarbone move under the white cloth of her shirt. "Got a lot to do," he says.

"Do you?"

"Forgot to make the bed, Cyn."

"That's okay."

"Nothing like family, right?"

She looks at him, a matter of raising her eyes, almost on a level with his. They used to measure, he remembers, their faces touching. Sometimes her nose, her mouth would be higher, sometimes his. One year for a while they were exactly the same, so that they could match their profiles like reflections, nose to nose, lip to lip. The center of her forehead is flushed red, her birthmark identical to his and to their grandfather's, a broad stripe almost invisible except when she cries or is angry or upset. He wants to set his own mark against hers.

The phone rings, but still they stand there while it rings, how many times? When it stops, Cynthia stoops to pick up the dish towel. She goes into the kitchen and hangs it on a nail by the sink. Harry follows her. With one hand, he searches for his jacket on the hooks by the side door. He'd like another shot, but not here. "Going to the Maple Leaf," he says.

"Fine," Cynthia says.

"You could come, too," he says. "Al'd love to see you." He likes the idea of having a drink with Cynthia in the strange dim daylight of the bar.

"I don't think so."

"Come," he catches her hand. "We could have a couple of beers, talk. What've you got to do that's so important?"

"I've got to go to work, if you don't."

"All right, then." He drops her hand. "I left the bottle on the table," he says. "I was looking for a Kleenex or something in the drawer, but there wasn't a goddamn one." He puts his jacket on and goes out the door, bursting out on to the sidewalk, fast through the yard, to the gate, to the alley.

. . .

"How long is it since you've seen him? That's all I want to know," Geneva says.

Cynthia sits down at the kitchen table in her coat and looks out the window at gray dripping March. "It hasn't been that long," she lies. "He was over here to dinner a while ago." She pulls on her hair, thinking.

"How long ago?" Geneva's voice in the receiver is like a thin and twisty wire.

It was three weeks ago, Cynthia knows, that disastrous dinner. "What is this, anyway? Why are you asking?"

"Has he even been over to see his mother?"

"I don't keep track of when he visits Louisa."

"All I know is that Al is breaking his back doing what Harry ought to be helping out with. He hasn't been here except to sleep in the trailer every once in a while, and he's made damn sure *I* don't see him, which means that he's got some brain left."

Cynthia looks at the clock. It's after nine. She unbuttons her coat and sets her purse down on the floor beside her.

"I heard him come in last night," Geneva says. "Banging around in the trailer. I thought I'd catch him this morning, but he must not have even stayed the night. And here it is another Saturday he's leaving Al to do everything. Has he even been working? What's going on?"

"Harry's a grown man." Cynthia says. "I'm sure he can take care of himself."

"I don't give a damn whether he can take care of himself or not, although it's plain to me that he can't. He's a drunk and a fuck-up and a loser, and if you can't see that you're letting family feeling or something worse get in the way of it."

"What do you mean?" Cynthia grips the phone harder. Her body feels too big for its skin.

"You know what I mean, Cynthia Starnes."

The sound of her maiden name silences Cynthia, and she bows her head over the table.

"But that's your business, I don't care about that. This is my problem—Al is working too hard. Get your cousin's ass over here, that's what I'm interested in. Tell him he's got a responsibility to Al. You got me?"

Cynthia sits a minute after Geneva hangs up. She is supposed to get her hair cut in half an hour, Vicky from the store is supposed to do it. She buttons up two buttons of her coat and then stops. She picks up the telephone, dials, and waits.

"Hello? This is Mrs. Lynch. I was just calling to inquire about my aunt, Mrs. Louisa Walker."

"She's doing as well as usual." The voice of the nurse sounds small and far away.

Cynthia taps the table with her finger. "Oh, that's good. I was thinking of visiting her and I didn't want to come if she wasn't up to it." She hesitates. "Her son thought he might not be able to get by for a while, so I thought I'd fill in a little. Not that I could take his place."

"He's been coming by pretty regular." Cynthia hears the rustling of papers.

"Well, I guess it was going to be a little later on that he'd be gone. He might have to go out of town, something about a job. Well—" She straightens up, her finger over the cut-off button.

"He's been the worse for wear, I hear. Not that he isn't always polite."

Cynthia pretends not to hear this. She says good-bye, takes her coat off, shrugging it onto the back of the chair. She pushes the phone away from her. What now? Harry on a binge again, and she the last to find out.

She taps her fingers, restless, puts her hand on the phone, but she can't think of anyone to call. If she calls the construction company, she will have to talk to Harry's boss, whom she can't stand, or the stupid bookkeeper with her sexy lisp. And what could they tell her? No use to talk to Al, he must not have seen Harry either, or Geneva would know. No drinking buddies to call, for when Harry drinks like this, he does it alone.

She hears the noise of Derek and Joey coming down the stairs.

Joey throws himself at her, a tackling hug. "I thought you had to leave," he says.

"Who was that on the phone?" Derek asks.

"Geneva Zaitchek."

"Al's wife?"

"She's worried about Al," Cynthia says. "She thinks he's working too hard."

Derek zips up his jacket. "Why's she talking to you about it?"

"Oh, I don't know." Cynthia gets up and goes to the sink. She turns on the water and fills a glass.

"What about Harry?" Derek says.

Cynthia drinks from the glass, looking out the window over the sink.

Derek comes up behind her. "What *about* Harry?"

"Nothing about Harry."

"How come Harry hasn't been over?" Joey asks.

"He's your Uncle Harry," Derek says. "I don't know why your mother lets you call him Harry."

Cynthia puts the glass back in the dish drainer.

"What about it, Cynthia?" Derek says.

"He hasn't been around at the Maple Leaf, Geneva says."

"Well, you know what that means."

"What?" Joey asks.

"We don't know that," Cynthia says.

"Did you call at work?"

"They wouldn't know anything. Last time, they didn't."

"Maybe he left town," Joey says.

"Cut it out, Joey. Go on, go outside." Cynthia takes him by the shoulders and marches him out the back door.

"I'll be out in a minute," Derek says. "There's not much you can do," he says to Cynthia.

"I know," she says.

"Just wait until he rides it out." He pulls his hat from his pocket.

"Well. See you later." He pauses at the back door, his hand on the knob, and looks back.

Cynthia pounds her fist on the sink. "It makes me so mad," she says.

Derek pauses. "You could call that girl. Lucette."

"Why would I do that?"

"He might be with her." He puts his hat on and leaves.

When he has gone, Cynthia calls Vicky and tells her she has to come a little later. She makes a pot of coffee, strides around while she waits for it to perk. What can she do?

She imagines getting in the car and driving through the city to look for him, through the dark, rough, hidden parts he disappears into when he does this. She goes upstairs to his room, goes in and sits on the bed, runs her hand over the blanket, her fingers looking for clues. The room is so empty that she despairs. There is nothing in the closet, she knows, except a garment bag with her own summer clothes in it. Nothing under the bed. Nothing on the little shelf over the bed. Nothing on the metal table. She swings her feet up and lies back on the bed, flushed hot, the skin of her bare arms, the back of her neck burning against the cold sheets. You bastard, Harry, she thinks. You jerk. She doesn't look over at the metal table. The drawer is still pulled out a little, his message. She thinks that if he's dead, she won't care.

She pushes the drawer shut with a clank. He must think of her as pathetic now. She thinks of the last time she saw him, of what she felt. When he put his hand on her spine—but this is too much, it makes her feelings rise in her throat, choking her. She knows exactly what he was thinking then—that they were the same, their same-colored skin, their light hair, the knobs and the length of their bones.

He wanted comfort, and she had frozen under his hand. He withdrew, he said that about the drawer so she would know he had seen the book. He had wanted her to hurt, too.

In the silence of the house, she hears the coffee boiling over the top of the the pot. She runs downstairs and pulls it off the burner as the whiskey-brown liquid cascades over the sides, splashing her hand, and then she goes to the sink to run the cold water. Holding her hand under it, she watches the way the same runnels form over and over. She can see her skin flushing redder through the clear water.

"You know this song, 'Love the One You're With?' " Mr. Abruzzi waves his hand, conducting the Muzak. "Lucette? Vera?"

"I asked you to call me Mrs. Simonski, asked you time and again."

"You'd think you were sixty. What if I call you Ms.?"

"I *am* sixty, as you very well know." Mrs. Simonski picks up a tray of nail polish and moves toward the back of the drugstore.

"Well, Lucette? 'Love the One You're With?' "

Lucette, standing by the register, shakes her head.

"It's Stephen Stills," the woman stocking cigarettes says.

Mr. Abruzzi swivels his head. "This is not Trivial Pursuit, Eileen, or should I say Ms. Dalziel?"

"It's all the same to me," Eileen says.

"Very profound." He turns back to Lucette. "But the thing is, the significant thing is the sentiment of the song. You get me, Lucette, or should I say Ms. Harmon?"

Lucette taps the tips of her fingers on the register.

"Love. The one. You're with." He gestures great flourishes with his hands, a circle for "love," pointing to her and himself. "With" he does by bringing his two hands together as if in prayer.

"I'm not into that sixties stuff," Lucette says.

"Now I was," Eileen says. "I definitely was. I did it all, everything you see on *Woodstock*. It was just what you did then. I don't think I wore a dress from 1969 until 1981. I had to get something for my mother-in-law's funeral in eighty-one and I got a dress. My husband almost fell over when I walked into the funeral home. I was late from work, you know? and had to come by myself, that was when I was doing bookkeeping at the factory. I walked in and he let out this snort."

"Very sociological, Eileen," Mr. Abruzzi says. "Very anthropological."

"Oh, we all know you've been to college," she says.

"But my point, Lucette, my point is the practical. Love. The one. You're with." He dances a little war dance in the aisle.

"The customers are going to be scared right out of the store," Mrs. Simonski says, coming up behind him. She takes out the file box where the developed film envelopes are kept.

Lucette rings up a candy bar for a teenage boy, and then reverts to her position, her hands resting on the register. The light in the store is bright, flickering on one side where the fluorescent bulbs are waning. Outside, the streets gleam with rain, car lights are on. When customers enter, they bring in a slap of wet and damp, the hissing of tires on pavement.

"I might need some time off," she says.

Mr. Abruzzi bows. "If that's what it takes."

Mrs. Simonski pulls a clipboard from under the counter. "You've got vacation coming, of course," she says. "Or is this sick time?"

"I guess vacation," Lucette says. She coughs and takes her hands off the register.

"Oh, angel choirs." Mr. Abruzzi imitates a prize fighter, clasping his hands over his head. "I shall array myself as a bridegroom."

"That's blaspheming," Mrs. Simonski says.

"Try Mexico," says Eileen. "That's what they said on TV last night. Mexico in March. Acapulco."

Mrs. Simonski snorts again, puts down the clipboard, and starts going through the film envelopes.

A horn blows long and loud in the street, brakes squeal, and they all look toward the window. Lucette watches them watching. Mrs. Simonski looks as soft as a pillow, her shoulders and chest covered in a flowered fabric, and Lucette thinks of putting her head there.

They could be a family: Mrs. Simonski the nagging, loving mother, Eileen the knowing older sister. Mr. Abruzzi, though, is too silly to be the father. Maybe the capering teenage brother.

There is no one in the store except one old woman in the back, muttering and hesitating by the shelves of vitamins. Lucette can see her in the surveillance mirror; she is putting a small box into her purse. From the size and color, it is the generic one-a-day multi-vitamin. This moral stealing—taking the cheapest available—stops Lucette's mouth, and she turns her eyes away so that the others will not see where she is looking.

"It's bound to be dirty," Mrs. Simonski is saying. "And expensive."

"Still, it'd be different," Eileen says. "Different food, different weather, different men."

"I don't fancy Mexican food myself." Mrs. Simonski says. "Nachos, for instance. All that gooey cheese."

Lucette's throat closes up, and she swallows twice to calm her stomach.

"Well, I'd go in a minute," Eileen says. "I'm tired of being here."

"Why, my dear Eileen, tired of all this?" Mr. Abruzzi waves his hand at the long aisles, the flickering lights, the revolving watch display. "I can't understand your thought on this. I really can't."

"Time for my lunch break," Mrs. Simonski says. "How many days do you want, Lucette, and when? So I can mark it down." She unlocks a drawer and takes out her purse.

"I'm not sure yet," Lucette says. "I'll let you know."

"Very wise," Mr. Abruzzi says. "We need time, time to lay our plans. Time to buy matching underwear. Black, with maybe a touch of red, a bit of lace—traditional, I know, but I'm that way."

"I might not even need it at all," Lucette says to Mrs. Simonski.

"White, then, bridal white, with bows, blue for me, pink for you." Mr. Abruzzi leans across the counter, lips pursed, reaching for Lucette's hand to pull her face toward his.

Lucette shakes the hand free. She shoves him with her open

palm, hard. "Leave me alone." She takes her purse from the drawer Mrs. Simonski has left open and pushes her way through the half door at the end of the counter.

"Take the afternoon off," Mr. Abruzzi shouts after her. "I'm easy to please."

"Act your age. She could have you up for sexual harassment," Eileen says to him.

In the elevator on the way down to the break room, Lucette sets herself to imagine being married to Mr. Abruzzi. She can see them in some fluorescent-lit kitchen, the table between them taking the place of the drugstore counter, listening to his sad jokes all day long. When the elevator stops, she goes to the coat rack and gets her jacket. She holds the alarm switch down with one hand while she opens the emergency door and slides out into the back alley.

She buttons her jacket and turns to the left, by the Dumpsters, to where the alley widens out to take delivery trucks, and edges past the piles of spilled garbage, averting her eyes and holding her breath. She emerges from between the buildings onto Superior Avenue, and walks quickly to the street at the other end of the Mall. At the marble railing, across a short space filled with ugly jumbled parking spaces, electric lines, trucks unloading, is the lake. Although the sky is heavy with clouds, the air is clear, and she can see the hard gray line of the horizon, dark clouds, darker lake.

She presses against the railing, feeling the sharp edge of it cutting into her. She lifts her face into the freshening wind, blowing harder here, so close to the flat plain of the water. The small white roughness of the waves moves toward her, she smells the lake smell—of fish and dampness—and sees the gulls pushing forward on the air. When she turns back to the city, the wind buffets her, she is carried on it, and walks faster to keep up as she crosses the street, the Mall, back to Superior.

She pauses at a phone booth by the Arcade and thinks about calling Bev. This might as well be her lunch break. But she is not hungry. She steps inside the hood over the phone and looks at it. Without putting any money in, she punches a number, slowly, her cold finger pausing on the hard little squares. She takes the receiver off its hook. Her throat is tight.

She takes a quarter out of her pocket and punches in a different number, which she reads from a scrap of paper. A receptionist's voice answers almost immediately, but just as quickly, Lucette pulls the phone rest down to cut off the call.

She punches the first number again, and hears the little tune of the beeps, singing even though she has put no money in. She holds the receiver against her cheek. There is no sound from the dead phone, not even a crackling of static. "Hello, Dad," she says. "Hello, Frank. It's Lucette."

The wind is blowing harder, pushing the clouds, tearing them so that slices of sky show through. The cold air swirls around Lucette's legs, pushing up under her skirt. People hurrying past, flat gleam of shop windows, the stone bulk of the library, the red eye of the traffic light—it is all moving around her where she stands, dizzy, lightheaded. She holds onto the edge of the phone hood, thinking hard to get things in line. If she tries, she can make it all right. She can count to five and turn her head to the left and there in the oncoming traffic will be Harry's truck. There is no reason that this should not be so, it is not so impossible. But she does not count to five. She did those tricks when Frank, her stepfather, died. Deals with God, promises, threats, the magic of numbers, of sacrifice. There are certain events that happen and then stand like great unmoving blocks in the world while everything flows around them.

Lucette feels tired. She has to go to the bathroom. She leaves the phone and goes around the corner, back to Euclid, back to the front door of the drugstore. She walks in like a customer, and stands in front of the counter.

Mr. Abruzzi blinks at her, not recognizing her for a minute in her coat, her wind-reddened skin. "May I help you?" he says, and she wants to say, yes, yes you may, help me, please, but instead, she reaches across the counter and flips his tie out of the V of his sweater. "Not in this life," she says.

· · ·

"You did what?" Cynthia says, two days later.

"I called her. Lucette." Derek is sitting at his desk in the basement, looking up at her as she stands halfway down the stairs.

"Well," Cynthia says. She comes down a step further, bending to get a better look at Derek's face. "What did she say?"

"She said she's seen him twice, when I pressed her for details. Really tight-lipped, she was. I had to drag every word out of her."

"Twice," Cynthia says. She sits down on the steps, thinking.

Derek taps his pencil on the desktop, and then pushes away the file he's brought home to work on. "I got the idea he was drunk when she saw him."

"She said that?"

"No. But I got the feeling something was wrong, and that's the thing that's likely to be wrong with Harry."

"Serves her right," Cynthia says.

"Why are you so set against her?" Derek asks.

They are silent. The furnace ticks, the tap in the sink drips, slow and regular.

"Does she know where he is?"

"That's all she said. I told you I had to drag it out of her."

"How did she sound?"

"She sounded unhappy. What difference does it make? There's nothing you can do."

"I suppose not," Cynthia says, and she gets up and goes upstairs. She closes the door to the basement, then stands there with her hand on the knob for a minute.

She looks at the clock. It is two-thirty, two hours until work. Dinner is ready, foil-wrapped in the refrigerator. She opens the door again and calls down the stairs, "I'm going to run over to the store. Do you need anything?"

"How about some duct tape?"

"Okay."

She puts on her coat and goes to the telephone table by the front door. She finds the White Pages and turns to H, runs her finger down the column of Harmons. Frank Harmon on Mapledale, still using his name. Living in the past, she thinks. She goes out to her car.

Maybe Lucette's mother won't be home, Cynthia thinks. But at least Lucette will not be there, it is too early for her to be back from work. She crosses the bridge over the freeway and turns onto Mapledale. Big shabby houses, set back a little. She peers out, looking for the address.

When she finds it, she parks in front, sits there. The house is painted white, old paint, gray with cracks, and grimy. Green trim. Leafless bushes. The front door, an old one, inset with an oval of glass. The blank, curtained picture window. The driveway two wavering lines of gravel and mud, invaded by grass. Cynthia sets her mouth, clicking her teeth together. She thinks about what she will say. Concerned, she's concerned about Harry? Wonders if Lucette has said anything? She wants to know about Lucette, too, but this will be something she picks up, subtle clues, things the mother will let drop unaware. She leans forward to get a LifeSaver from the roll on the dashboard. Butter rum. She sucks on it, eyeing the line of the curtains. Are they twitching, is someone pulling them open a crack? She's not sure.

She picks up her purse and opens the car door. Avoiding the slushy pools in the gutter, she goes quickly up the front walk. The wooden steps sag and creak a little, and the floorboards of the porch are springy, pulling away from the main frame of the house. Cynthia puts her finger on the doorbell button and pushes, but it is so aged looking, the paint cracked and peeling, that after a minute she knocks as well. She settles in to wait, the house looks so quiet, so dead.

But almost immediately she hears the muffled fumbling noises of someone approaching. Cynthia steps back a pace, hooks her hair behind her ear. A face is staring at her from the other side of the glass oval, a woman. She makes no move to open the door.

Cynthia clears her throat, waits. Then she tries to open the storm door, to talk to the woman through the glass, but it's locked. She raps on the outer door. "Mrs. Harmon?" she says.

The woman looks at her, unmoving. Her face is round and pale, and she is wearing something white.

"Mrs. Harmon," Cynthia says. "I just stopped by to talk to you."

The woman is turning away, fading back into the dimness behind her, so slowly she barely seems to move.

Cynthia grasps the handle of the storm door and rattles it up and down. "Mrs. Harmon!" she says. She presses her forehead against the glass.

The woman is opening an inner door.

"Mrs. Harmon, it's about Lucette!"

She sees the woman turn. She opens the heavy wooden door with its panel of glass, and the storm door. When Cynthia steps in, she pulls the inner door back and goes through it.

Cynthia follows her, taking off her gloves. She pulls each finger off separately, and folds them before she puts them into her pocket. She follows through the front room, so dark that she trips over a footstool, and through a dining room, the table shrouded in a sheet, into the kitchen.

The woman, Anna Harmon, sits down at the table, and after a moment Cynthia sits down opposite her. It is not as dark here as in the other rooms, but it is gray and cloudy outside, and the room is filled with that gray light, wavering and distorting.

"I'm Cynthia Lynch," she says.

"Do I know you?"

"I'm from the neighborhood. We've probably seen each other around."

"I don't know where the time goes. I hate to get up late. I tell her, I tell Lucette, get me up when you leave. It spoils the day if you get up so late, I tell her. Or maybe I forget to tell her."

"Yes, well," Cynthia says. "I know how that is."

"Sometimes I can't think now if I really said something or if I meant to."

"That happens, I guess."

"Or sometimes I dream I said things. If it's Lucy I dream about saying things to, it's hard to tell if I did or not. I might have, right? But if it's someone else, one of the neighbors or those that are dead, then I know when I think about it that it was a dream. Not when I first wake up, things are fuzzy then. But if I think. Or if I remember it later in the day, you know how a bit of a dream will come to you like a memory, then for a minute, maybe? . . . But if I put my mind on it I will know it was nothing but what happened in my head, sleeping.

"I wanted to talk to you about Lucette, Mrs. Harmon."

"You know my Lucette?"

"She was over to my house for dinner a few weeks ago with my cousin Harry—"

"That's one thing I worry about, she doesn't eat enough." Anna gets up, supporting herself with one hand on the table. "I'll get us some tea, how'll that be?"

"Oh, that's all right," Cynthia says. "Really—"

Anna reaches to the second shelf for two cups. The cups have tea bags in them already. She sets them on the table and turns on the gas burner under a dented tea kettle. "Are you from the church?"

"No," Cynthia says. She watches Anna where she stands by the stove, waiting, almost crouched over it. They do not speak while the water begins to rattle in the kettle. Cynthia unbuttons her coat. The blue flickering of the gas is the focus of the kitchen, a spot of color in the gray light. She looks out the window. There is an apple tree in the backyard next door, a big old one. Its branches are moving in the wind, shedding leaves dead since the fall. As she watches, an old man comes out of the garage carrying some-thing—a rake? a broom? Cynthia leans forward, squinting to see better.

"But I know you, don't I?" Anna says. The kettle is shrieking. "I've seen you before."

"Around the neighborhood?"

"You're a Starnes, aren't you, from over on Daisy Avenue?" Anna puts the cups, only half-filled, down on the table and leans forward, bringing her round face closer to Cynthia's. "Louisa's daughter?"

"Virginia's. Did you know my mother?" Cynthia takes her tea bag by the string and drags it around the cup. Anna's face is younger than she expected, spots of pink on the cheeks, high up, smooth white skin. Her hair, though, is gray, a hard iron gray.

"Not to say know," Anna says. "Only at church, saying hello after Mass. I miss that, sometimes, the church." She sits down again.

"Lucette's at work?" Cynthia swirls her tea in her cup.

"I'm always looking out for things to talk about with Lucette. Have a conversation, you know? I look out the window for the weather. I see if there's anything new outside—a strange car, someone painting or shoveling snow, whatever. I try to listen to part of the news, but it's hard—traffic accidents, people shouting at each other, about what? It's hard. If she doesn't come home."

Cynthia hooks the string of the tea bag on the other side of the cup and sips from it, trying to think.

"Nice to have someone here. Lucy doesn't like it when I talk to myself. But you know how it is."

"Oh, yes," Cynthia says.

"Not out loud, I don't. But I think things, sure—words, sentences. I say them to myself, you know, at the bad places in the day. When television is bad. When I go out on the porch to get the mail. When I am waiting to be tired. That's private, though, smooth"—Anna hesitates—"the words are smooth, like when we used to say Latin at the church. I miss the priests. I appreciated everything they did for me, the priests, and I believe they know it, though I don't come around now. You can tell them for me."

"I don't go to church," Cynthia says. She takes another sip of her tea.

"It's a shame, but what can you do? I miss how it looked for Christmas, the flowers, the candles."

"I was wondering about Lucette," Cynthia says. "If she said anything about how Harry is?"

"Harry?" Anna has been holding her cup in both hands, looking out the window in a dreamy way, and now she sets the cup down and looks at Cynthia.

"My cousin."

"Your cousin." She continues to look at Cynthia.

"They've been—" Cynthia stops, not knowing how to say it, "seeing each other," she says with distaste.

"Lucy's a good girl, I'm sure. Smart. She knows how to take care of herself," Anna says. She begins to twist her hands. "She didn't want to go to college, she said. I don't know, I don't know. If Frank were here to ask—no use to ask her father—wouldn't he say she should go? They have the community college, cheap with night classes. I say this to her, Frank, the community college, night classes, but he is not here, she says to me. He is not here, for Christ's sake, she says it to me in a loud voice. But even without college she's smart, that should count for something."

"Mrs. Harmon—"

"Anna, you might as well call me Anna. Sometimes I say his name to myself, not out loud. Frank Harmon. Anna Harmon. Lucette Harmon, though by law that's not her name." Her hands begin to pluck at her apron, then to twist it into a rope. "She would have it that way, that Frank was her real father, her chosen father. Lucy's a hard girl, some say, but I know how she really is. So like her father, and still I love her, how is that? But forget about it. Forget about all that. I'll forget about it now, forget it."

Anna's face, too, is twisting, the pink of her cheeks hotter, the white paler. Cynthia feels around for her purse. "I guess I'd better go," she says. "Thank you for the tea."

"It's not true I can't face things like she says, Lucette says. I know what happened in my life."

"That's right," Cynthia says stupidly, getting up.

Anna gets up with her, hands still twisting, still wringing her apron, and part of her dress now, too.

Cynthia goes through the dining room, Anna following, still talking, in a voice that is lower and lower, light and dry as a leaf, scratchy in her throat.

"What I like is to walk around the house, through each room, by the walls, I like to touch the walls with my hands."

Cynthia stumbles over a box on the floor and catches her balance by grabbing the back of one of the chairs pulled up to the table. She can feel the layer of dust sliding under her fingers.

"I stop at the windows and look at what is out there, rain now and white heavy clouds, and then go on. It isn't that I do this all the time, only once a day, once a day in the early afternoon when I feel strong. When I get to the front door I look through the small glass panes at the top, still tall enough, I haven't shrunk yet like my mother did when she got old."

Cynthia opens the inner door and goes out into the hall, fumbles with the heavy front door. Anna follows her right to the threshold, where she stops as if she's come up against a wall.

"What I like is to start with one thing, one clear thing that I have to know or do, sometimes I'll start the day with that one clear thing," she says. "You have to push that button before it will open." She points with her finger. "But then I start to see it in a different way, it gets mixed up with other things until it's as black as dirty as ruined as everything else. I blame myself, I tell Lucette. Yes, Ma, she says. Yes. No, of course she doesn't say that, she says No, Ma. No. But I do. I don't cry about it, I don't make a big fuss. This is something I pride myself on, that I know how to hold myself in the world. And Lucy, too, she keeps herself to herself." She watches as Cynthia opens the door and then the storm door.

When Cynthia is on the porch, she turns to look back, to say good-bye. Anna has not moved. "Come again," she calls. Her voice is thin and light. "It was nice having you."

As soon as she comes up the front walk, Lucette knows that something is wrong. The front door is open a few inches. She hears the sound of running water overhead, and waits to see if it will stop. But it goes on and on, and as she runs up the stairs, she thinks of other times, of water gliding silently over the edge of the tub, standing in great pools on the bathroom floor, water dripping from the ceiling of the room below.

Upstairs, she checks the hall carpet. There is no widening water mark, not yet anyway. She knocks, two small raps, and listens. There is a splash, the noise of a body moving in water.

"Hey," she says. She hears the sound of the water hitting the porcelain of the tub, hitting the wall and sliding down, a long continuous stream from the shower. Lucette looks at the bottom of the door. She knows that in the bathroom the air is thick, gray with warm fog, but the door fits tight against the carpet, nothing escapes.

She clears her throat, leans forward, putting her mouth to the crack. "Hey, are you in there?" she calls into it. She turns her head, puts her ear where her mouth was, and listens.

There is a wisp of sound, thin, watery. "Lucette."

"Come on out of there, why don't you?" she says, loud, in a cheerful voice.

"I like it in here," her mother answers. "I'm fine." She pauses. "I'll be out in a minute."

Lucette waits, thinking. "I'm hungry, aren't you hungry?" She listens, but there is no answer. "I'm going to fix myself something to eat."

"Is it time for dinner?" Her mother's voice is a little stronger.

"It's late, I think," Lucette says. "I don't know what time it is, I don't have my watch."

"Well, wait for me, wait."

She can hear her mother moving in the water, the squeal of her flesh against the white slickness of the tub, and she swallows to loosen the tightness in her throat, her stomach rising against it. She waits a minute and then says, a goad to her mother, "Well, I'll go and start things, okay?"

Lucette goes down to the kitchen and turns on the overhead light. There are two cups on the table, tea bags trailing down their sides. She stares at them. Both of them are more than half full. Nothing else is out of place. She goes through the house, turning on the lights, looking. Everything is the same. With a sick feeling, she imagines her mother sitting at the table, pouring boiling water into the cups, talking, sipping, maybe moving to the other side of the table, sipping from that cup, talking, in the dead gray air of the kitchen.

I am so tired, she thinks, so tired.

She goes into the downstairs bathroom, pulls her skirt up, her underpants and hose down, almost crying at the resistance of the material, the elastic cutting into her fingers, grabbing at her flesh. She sits on the toilet, leaning sideways so that she can rest her head against the tiled wall. She sits there until she hears her mother open the door of the upstairs bathroom. She makes a small pad of toilet paper and wipes herself, pushing the tips of her fingers into her body a little. She looks at the mark on the paper: a faint wet stain, hardly even yellow, nothing. She throws it into the toilet, pulls her clothes back into place quickly, covering up her lower body. The waistband of her pantyhose snaps against the skin of her stomach, fitting itself into the groove it has made.

In the kitchen her mother is banging the pots and pans around. Water is coming to a boil on the stove. She turns when Lucette comes in, a small square can of paprika in her hand. "We could have macaroni and cheese," she says. "It's filling."

Lucette sits down at the table. She watches as her mother gets out milk, butter, flour, cheese, the macaroni. Anna's eyes flick over the cups on the table, but she says nothing.

"I'll rinse these," Lucette says. She gets up and hooks her fingers through the cup handles.

"What?" Anna stirs the white sauce, her eyes on the wooden spoon cutting through the whiteness of the milk.

"These cups." Lucette picks out the tea bags and drops them in the garbage.

"That's good," Anna says.

Lucette holds the cups under water from the faucet and scrubs them with her fingers, puts them in the drainer. She tears off two squares of paper towel for napkins, takes two plates, two forks, the salt and pepper shakers.

"You can play the radio if you want," Anna says. "I don't mind."

"That's all right." Lucette watches her mother's hand, stirring, stirring.

"I don't mind noise," Anna says, stirring harder. "Not a little noise."

"Was someone here today?"

Anna holds up the spoon and lets the sauce run off it, a milky white ribbon. "Someone?"

"There were two cups out."

Anna looks over at the sink, at the two cups in the drainer. "Yes."

"So someone was here."

Anna turns off the two burners, lifts the macaroni pot and carries it over to the sink. "The colander, Lucette, quick!"

Lucette jumps up and gets it, slides it into the sink, and watches the stream of water and macaroni, tumbling like fish. They stand there together for a minute, watching the steam rise from the sink, warm on both their faces, then Anna takes the colander from her hand and pours the macaroni into the pot of sauce. She begins to grate cheese over it.

"Mother?" Lucette says.

"It was someone from the church."

"What did they want?"

"Just to talk, you know how they do. She seemed like a nice woman. She said very nice things about you."

"About me? She knows me?"

"She knows some friends of yours." Anna stirs the cheese into the macaroni.

"What was her name?" Lucette asks.

"I don't remember."

"You must remember, Ma."

"I don't remember." Anna's white, wrinkled hand is trembling as she shakes paprika into the pan. "She knew a friend of yours, that's all I know. Harry."

"Harry." Lucette gets up from her chair.

"You could bring your friends over, Lucy. I don't mind that." Anna looks over at her, eyes squinted small. "I can take a little noise. You know?" She brings the pan to the table and sets it down. She spoons macaroni onto Lucette's plate, a great sliding pile. She stands holding her own plate, looking at Lucette, and then sets it down again. "I don't think I'll eat right now."

"You've got to eat," Lucette says.

"Not right now." She sits down. "I'll sit with you, though."

Lucette feels her mother's eyes on her, watching her chew. She is starving, but when she has eaten half of what is on her plate, she can't go on.

"Are you sure you don't remember what her name was?"

Anna is looking out the window. "You know what, Lucy? Did I ever tell you this?"

"Tell me what?"

"Let me tell you a story. I wasn't beautiful like you are—"

"Oh, Ma—"

"No, you are, so light and fine, not mean though, like as you are to him in other ways."

Lucette screws up her eyes and pushes away from the table. She doesn't want to hear about her father.

Anna leans forward. "I was like I am now, but young. Stronger, faster. I was walking down the street fast and he caught up to me, me walking home alone and fast so as not to be among the couples. I saw you at the meeting, he said, Young Catholic Adults the meeting was. He said, I liked you right away. And me, not beautiful, young but not even very young any more, far enough along to have seen everyone marrying off before me, coming to church with babies in their arms and mine empty. Heavy is how I felt, though I was no fatter then than now. Heavy in my spirit.''

Anna reaches across the table and takes Lucette's hand. Lucette feels her mother's white, water-wrinkled fingers on hers with a terrible disgust that she tries to keep out of her face. She can feel her breath getting short.

"But here is the funny thing," Anna says. "He was beautiful. Shorter than me, slighter, more beautiful. What could he have seen at that meeting where I didn't even notice him? Me fanning myself with a paper, it was hot. My hair falling out of its curl. My dress filled out with big bony shoulders, slack across the chest. I don't know." She shakes her head. "When we stood in front of the altar I didn't have any questions, there was a shine that was on everything. And when we were married and I felt myself going farther and farther down I still didn't have questions. I didn't know the questions. When things were flying across the room and falling on me, I prayed for dark, for quiet, for space, for empty rooms with no noise. You know? Lucy honey?''

"Why are you telling me this?" Lucette is crying. "I hate you to talk about him, I hate it.''

"He's your father, though." Anna looks out the window again. "Not Frank. You can't forget that. I don't think about his face, how it looked when he was drunk, yelling, crazy. That's not healthy, some things it's better to forget. Forget about it, the good and the bad. Listen, it's no way to live, all that stuff falling on you. Just forget about it all. Forget it.''

"What about Frank, though?" Lucette flings her hand free of Anna's, and her mother's knuckles crack against the table. "What about him?''

Anna looks at her coldly. "He always had a care for what I could stand. You'd like to see me crying, I suppose. I know what happened in my life. I remember it all, Frank's hand on the wheel of his car or holding a wrench or reaching up to turn out the light, your little baby face folded up in a blanket, your father walking me home from the church—"

"Stop it, stop it," Lucette screams.

"Always, he said, the only woman, he knew me right away, he said, the woman he would marry, him drunk but not passing out, standing, standing like a tree, holding up my new dress my dish towel pulling at my curled hair filthy he said filthy can't clean can't cook, and him still in this world, not dead, not dead like Frank." Anna stops, out of breath. "I remember those things always. They are always falling on me."

Lucette stands up, she walks away from her mother's voice, she goes up the steps.

"Lucette?" her mother calls after her. "You haven't finished dinner."

Upstairs, Lucette sits down on the bed in her room, clasping her hands together on her knees. She is shaking, her body will not let her be still. She walks out into the hall, past the white and silent bathroom, past the extra room that was once her mother's sewing room, to the door of her mother's bedroom. The door is open, a crack of dark showing along its edge. She shuts her eyes and remembers one of the first things, that she is in that bedroom, in the golden dark of afternoon, she is standing, but not on the floor, holding on to something that stretches in front of her, barring her from the rest of the room. She looks at the great flat expanse of her mother's bed, where she sleeps with him, her father. She knows that she is standing in her crib, the light coming in from around the edges of the blinds has wakened her from her nap so that she can look across at the bed and hear the noise from the next room that is her mother, the sound of crying, her mother, she knows, crying on and on. Lucette grips one hand with the other, holding on to herself.

All evening, doing the dishes, folding clothes, taking out the garbage, seeing Joey to bed, Cynthia has held herself tight. She can feel the pressure of tears she will not cry, she can taste them. She imagines for one minute, her hand pausing among the dish towels, the happiness, the comfort of putting her head down on something, on someone, and letting them out, sobbing great gulping sobs, the wetness on her cheeks, cooling her burning eyes. She is so hot, so dry, so used up.

She bends over Joey now, kissing him goodnight with her dry lips, how soft the skin of his cheek feels against them. "Go right to sleep," she tells him.

"I'm not tired." He sits up in bed.

"It's late," she says, pushing him down, patting his pillow, pulling up the blanket and folded-over sheet.

"Tell me a story, okay?"

"I thought you were getting too old for stories."

Joey butted her with his head. "Come on, Mom."

"Well, lie down." Cynthia pulls the covers up again, smoothing them over his chest and shoulders. She puts her hand on his forehead, his cheeks, as if testing for a fever. His face is bright against the pillow patterned with faded action figures. She can hear the tick of the furnace and the small rattling noise of the window panes loose in their frames. The wind is rising, and it moans around the northwest corner of the house just as it always has.

"What shall I tell you?" she asks him.

"Tell me about how you went around the block," he says.

"That's not much of a story."

"Tell it," he commands her, wriggling down further in the bed.

"Well," she says, "I was little, only maybe four. I hadn't started school yet. And I was out playing in the front yard at our house on Dover Avenue and Harry came along from down the street. You remember he used to live down the street from us then, from the house where I lived with your grandma and grandpa?"

"Yeah," Joey says, twisting under the covers.

"He wanted to use my wagon to carry some stuff over to this friend he had on the next street. Lefty Price, that was."

"What kind of stuff?"

"Oh, I don't remember. Some comic books, I think, and some junk he found in their garage that he thought they could use to build something."

"So, then what?"

"So, I wanted to go. And he said I was too little and that my mother wouldn't let me go. I knew that was true, that she wouldn't if I asked her. So I told him that it was all right, that I had gone around the block all by myself the week before when he wasn't around."

"But he didn't believe you."

"No, he didn't. But I made him take me anyway."

"And then Grandma came out and looked around and you weren't there—"

"She was crying and screaming, yelling my name. I could hear her when we rounded the corner coming back. It was a very long block, and we were little, and then Harry had hung around talking with Lefty for a while. It must have been forty minutes or more that we were gone."

"So what did Grandma do when she saw you?"

"She ran toward us holding out her arms," Cynthia stops, choking on her words, grimly fighting the stone in her throat. "Holding out her arms—"

"And her skirt was flying behind her," Joey says.

"She picked me up and kissed me and spanked me at the same time, yelling at Harry all the while." Cynthia pats Joey's hand and gets up. She goes to the window to pull the blind down a fraction more. "Time for sleep."

"But what about the next day?"

"You remember all that."

"Come on, Mom."

"I had to stay in the next day while the other kids played. I sat in front of the picture window and watched them all day long." As Cynthia says this, her throat tightens again and she is afraid that she will cry after all. Not in front of Joey, she thinks. She pulls the curtains across, lining them up in the middle of the window, pulling the folds straight.

When she has turned off the light and closed Joey's door except for a crack, she stands, one hand on the wall. What could I have done? she thinks. Her actions stretch back into the past, a long line of them, wrong, misguided. Particular events rise up before her and she turns her head aside, looks at the floor. How she'd disappointed her mother. Failed as a mother herself, a wife. She remembers, she remembers. Her faithless hand pouring Jack Daniels for Harry. Her refusal to ever go all the way, ever go beyond a certain safe point. She sees Louisa's face when she last went to visit her, Louisa shrugging, sneering. And Harry, slamming the door. Why hadn't she gone with him? What would it have hurt?

She moans, goes into her bedroom and lies down on the bed. She thinks how it would have been to go with Harry for a drink in the afternoon, the cool echoing dark of the bar, the light slanting through the small high windows, the dusty amber beer bottles, Harry laughing and talking with Al. She would be leaning over the bar with him, their elbows touching as they drank, their knees pressed against the solid wood of the bar, the jukebox maybe playing, loud in the empty afternoon.

Composing herself, she turns over to lie on her stomach, her cheek pressed into the weave of the spread. This is how it happened, she tells herself, and she pulls reality into a new shape.

We went out to get a beer. We drove in the truck. The Maple Leaf was empty except for Al. We had a beer.

She makes herself see Al holding up a pitcher with draft, golden liquid filled with light, a magic drink.

It was warm in the bar. I took off my coat, shrugging it off my shoulders. It fell onto the floor.

She waits for the feel of the cloth sliding, the friction of cloth against skin, she feels it, she shivers.

Harry was smiling. Al had to leave, the phone? Geneva calling? A beer delivery? He won't be back. We were alone in the warm afternoon dark of the bar, the jukebox playing. We might dance, might do anything. There might be an earthquake, a snowstorm. A nuclear war, so that the door opens to a dead empty world.

But Joey? her mind interrupts.

Back in the bar, Harry was smiling. His arm on the bar touching hers. She makes her dream self turn to Harry and say Lucette's name, lightly, laughing.

He said—

What does he say? Cynthia presses herself against the bed as if it is a lover, she rubs her face against it, dragging her mouth across the clothy ridges, moves her body against its pressure, grabs the spread in great bunches and pulls it toward her. She bites down on a mouthful of cloth, and feels, finally, tears coming, spasms in her throat, wetness, the tight place in her opening up.

I hate this, she thinks. I hate it.

Leaning across the bar, Harry almost loses his balance. He rocks back, keeping his hand on his drink, congratulates himself on his recovery. Smart about some things, too damn smart. "Hey, honey," he says to the barmaid.

"Last call," she is yelling. She comes over to Harry and plants her elbows on the bar between them, cups her hands to hold her chin. "Last call," she says to him, smiling.

"Not possible," says Harry. "Not fucking possible."

"It is, though." She waves her hand around, taking in the people clutching each other for the last slow dance, the ugly yellow of the lights coming up like doubtful daylight.

"Hey, Hallie," someone yells. "What about my seven and seven?"

"I'm coming, I'm coming," she yells back. "So? Last call, Harry?"

He leans forward to focus on her face.

"Is this one of our nights, Harry?"

"Wait," he says. "Wait."

"I got other things to do, if you don't," she says, lifting her hand, pretending elaborately to examine her nails, each one glinting violet in the light from overhead.

Harry reaches over the great distance of the bar's smooth shining surface and grasps her arm just above the wrist and holds on. "Last call?" he says.

"Yes," she says.

"Okay," he says.

"Well, all right then." She tops up his glass and whips away to do her side of the bar, flicking change that flashes with light, pouring liquid in silvery streams, making the glasses ring as she picks up empties, tossing the cans and bottles in the trash like a basketball star.

Harry would like to put his head down, not to sleep, just to rest his eyes from the lights that are jumping and circling in front of him. It is necessary to sit up straight, Geneva will be watching him like a hawk. But no, he remembers, this is the Empire. No Al, no Geneva, a different set of people. He is in exile.

He has not seen Al for how long?—he tries to think—a week? two weeks maybe. He lifts his glass and drinks, bourbon and ice cubes smooth from melting slide down his throat. He has not seen Cynthia, either. This seems to him a good thing, but he wishes that the music was loud and pounding, fast and cheerful the way it was before. Now it is slow, the notes sad, drawn out, sweet and mournful. He turns his head to look at the couples on the dance floor. They are moving with the music, swaying back and forth, their arms wrapped around each other, faces buried in each others' necks, hands stroking, curved on the others' curves. They move as if they are underwater, as if they are drowning. When their faces turn to the light, their eyes are closed, or only half-open, blank, blind.

He remembers dancing earlier, with a small dark woman, bouncing across the dance floor with her. But maybe that was someplace else, some other night? He looks up to scan the opposite side of the bar, a long oval of wood, filled with faces, late-night smiles, the Empire, he is at the Empire. Hallie.

When the band stops playing, he drinks the last of his bourbon and crooks his finger to Hallie.

She comes and pours a short one in his glass. "Drink it up quick, Harry."

He remembers that he is going home with her. He thinks about how it will be, he sees them on her bed, in her room. She has a waterbed, the room is like a jungle, filled with plants, fifty of them maybe. And fish tanks, the room is never dark, suffused with the eerie purple glow that lights up the cubes of water. Hallie feeds the fish at night, leaning over the tanks, naked, her dark silhouette against the lighted, quivering water. He sees Hallie leaning over him, connected to him, they are pushing for it, that's nice, he thinks, and a tendril of some plant curving overhead, reaching for his mouth and his eyes like a snake— He knocks back the shot and shivers. That has happened already. That has already gone down.

He stands up, pushing himself away from the bar. Around him people are getting their coats on, women emerging from the john, their hair combed and fluffed one more time, men checking their pockets for Trojans, the barmaids sweeping up the night's litter. He'd like to see Joey, he thinks. He starts for the door.

"Harry!"

He turns. Hallie is waving to him. "Parking lot," he calls to her. He pushes his way through the crowd, squeezes past a man and woman writing each other's phone numbers on matchbooks, staggers slightly, catches himself.

"Evening, Harry." Roger, the owner, seventy-two, ex-cop, nods to him.

"See you," he says, stepping carefully around the the corner, through the door, outside. The night is cold, bitingly dry. He looks for Hallie's car—a Chevy, he thinks, blue, a bent right-front fender—but all the cars look alike. He makes his way down the line of cars slowly. The sky is full of stars, high and sharp. He puts his hand on the trunk of one of the cars to steady himself and is surprised by the cold smoothness of it. He stops and leans against the car. There is no wind. The cold air fits against him like a skin.

He has a sense of how far he has gone. Not too far. Not far enough yet. He measures the days behind him, a unitless stretch that he feels with his mind for the space they have taken up. Not too far. Cynthia, Al, Louisa are at the other end of that stretch, their small faces, their hands. Lucette. Not far enough. He measures what space he has left, how far he can go.

"Harry?"

"Lucette?" he says, turning toward the voice.

"What?"

He assembles the face, close enough to kiss. Hallie.

"Are we on?"

He lifts his hand, how heavy it seems, and skims it down over the shape of her head, just touching the halo of her hair. "Hallie," he says.

"You're drunk, Harry," she says. "We can just go home and sleep. Come on."

"Hallie," he says. "You ever meet my nephew? Joey?"

"I've seen him," she says, leading him toward her car. "I saw you with him in the supermarket once."

"I've got some things I've got to do."

"Tomorrow, Harry."

"Hallie. I ever tell you about Vietnam?"

"What about it, Harry?" She holds his elbow while she unlocks her car. The door opens and he falls into the black hole it makes.

"I didn't go, Hallie, did I ever tell you that?"

"You told me."

She shuts the door and he leans back. There is the suck of the air from the driver-side door, and she is sitting beside him, close. He reaches for her, feeling for the warm curve of her breast under the slippery stuff of her blouse.

"Home first, Harry," she says, reaching for the ignition.

But he pulls her over and kisses her, pushing her mouth open with his tongue.

"Jesus, Harry," she says. "You might as well cut it out." She pulls her coat closed. "You know you won't be worth a damn by the time we get anywhere near a bed."

Harry falls back into his seat as the car moves forward.

As they walk to the trailer behind the bar, Lucette presses Harry's hand several times, more for luck or comfort than to get his attention. He is drunk, but not staggering. He has been drinking beer all night, and whiskey only once every hour or so, when someone wanted to do shots. He is drunk enough to be hazy if you ask him complicated questions, drunk enough to forget where his car is, not drunk enough to pass out. Lucette steers him through the parking lot, past the caved-in asphalt patch like a black pit in the darkness, around the hulking cars of the bar patrons who are still inside waiting for Al or Geneva to say last call. He is just drunk enough, she thinks.

"Hey Harry, old Harry," she says, shaking his arm a little.

"Old enough to be your father," he says. He steadies himself on the rusty yellow Camaro that belongs to Charlie, looking across the street at the house with the shutters, dark except for a window high up on one side. "Old enough to know better," he says.

Lucette wants to lean against him, or push him back on the cold metal and kiss, she is so happy to have found him. She has been looking for him for days, going to the places she thought he might be, sitting at bars, pretending to drink her beer, waiting for him to find her. She wants to put her hand on the back of his neck where his hair is short like fur. She can do what she likes with him when he is as drunk as this. She can be as loving and silly as she wants and he will smile. She could put his arms around her waist and hold him around the neck and tell him she loves him. But she stands beside him touching just the sleeve of his shirt, feeling his flesh hot through it, although it is cold enough to snow.

"Aren't you cold?" Lucette asks, just for something to say. She knows he isn't. He wears his jacket open in the dead of winter. He owns no hat or gloves or scarf.

Harry doesn't answer. He takes out a cigarette pack, offers her one, and when she shakes her head, lights one himself. The match burns on the hood of the Camaro where he drops it.

"I'm trying to quit," she says.

Harry runs his hand down her back, slowly, from her shoulder to her thigh. She twitches it off, and takes a step, still holding his arm, to draw him away from the Camaro.

"How about we go to the Empire, honey?"

"It's too late," she says, pulling on his arm. "It would be closing time when we got there." She tugs a little at Harry's arm and he sways upright. She wants to be inside, out of the glittering shining night, with the lamp lit and the electric stove burner glowing red under the tea kettle.

"Haven't got the key," he says, patting at his pockets.

"I got it from Al." Lucette had waited until Geneva was in the back room and made herself go and ask Al for the key to the trailer so there would be no hitch later on. She couldn't bear to ask for it in front of Geneva. Al had winked at her. "You take care of Harry," he'd said, like he says practically every time he sees her. "Tell him anytime he wants he can move in there permanent."

"Al's a good guy," Harry says. Committed now to going into the trailer, he makes a rush up the steps, and goes right to the bathroom. Lucette fills the kettle and turns on the stove. She sits down on the only chair, the last one of a vanished kitchen set, then gets up, repositions it so that it faces the couch squarely, and sits down again. Harry hangs uncertainly in the doorway. She gets up to make the tea so he won't notice she's been waiting for him, but the water isn't ready yet. She gets out cups.

"Do you want some tea, Harry?"

"No tea."

She puts tea bags in the cups. She gets out the coffee can with sugar in it and sets it beside the cups. The water still isn't ready. She licks her finger and sticks it in the sugar and licks it again. Harry sits on the couch. From outside someone would see only the small yellow squares of the lamplit windows and maybe her shadow moving back and forth.

When the kettle sings, Lucette pours, and spoons in sugar. Carefully she carries the cups into the living area. She puts Harry's on the arm of the couch by his hand and holds her own, balancing it on her knee when she sits down.

"Harry," she says, "I have to talk to you."

"What?"

Here she sticks. Harry looks at her, as if waiting patiently for her to go on, but really, she knows, it is all the same to him just now if she speaks or not. Perhaps he is the wrong kind of drunk, she thinks. She likes it when he is drunk and forgetful of everything but his body, driven, when he takes sex like a drug. But when he is like that he will not listen to her at all. He listens when he is drunk desperate and hollow, when liquor makes him remember everything that he usually holds under. She doesn't like him like that. She is afraid for him, and of what his clear-seeing eye will see and make come alive in his life, and in hers, because she is with him.

He looks at her now as if she is a flower, a picture on the wall. If they went to bed he would hold her and move in her as if she were water or earth, and he would fall asleep holding her for safety.

"Harry," she says, leaning forward so that he will see her. "I'm late, my period's late."

"It's all right," he says.

"I'm probably pregnant, I'm going to have a baby." Lucette puts her tea cup on the floor and clasps her hands together tightly, digging her nails in to keep a hold on the moment.

"I know, I know," he says. He sighs and puts his head back and closes his eyes.

"What do you mean, you know?" Lucette looks down at her stomach. Did she look different already?

"It'll be all right. What'd the doctor say?"

"I haven't seen any doctor." Lucette looks hard at Harry. His eyes are still closed.

"It'll be all right, they won't find out."

"Who won't?" Does he mean Cynthia? Lucette feels cold, the vinyl of the chair is cold against her thighs. "Who won't, Harry?"

She gets up, kneels down in front of Harry and closes her cold fingers around his arms.

"Harry, it's me, Lucette. Listen to me."

He opens his eyes, blue, hazy with drink. "Lucette?" he says. And then something about his face changes so that he looks less drunk. What was it? she tried to think later. Was it that his eyes cleared or got sharper? Or that his face shifted into its watchful daytime mode? The small expanse of skin between his eyebrows draws together, he takes a short, sharp breath, his lips stretched as if to smile or frown. "Lucette," he says again.

She lets go of him and gets up. She trips on her cup, spilling the tea on the thin rug. She looks around her, at the old lamp with its torn shade, reluctantly given by Cynthia, the single chair, the scarred end table littered with beer cans and ashtrays, the miniature sink and stove, the almost empty cupboards, the dark door that leads to the bedroom. Her purse is lying on its side next to the sink, and she goes over and picks it up. She hears Harry getting up behind her.

"Lucette," he says. It warms her, hearing him say her name again—he does not say it often, he is not a name-sayer—but she doesn't turn around. "What's wrong, honey? What's wrong?"

There is a temptation to tell him everything all over again, what she said, what he said, what she has guessed. Or not to tell him but to scream it at him, and to say all the true hurtful things she knew or had heard about him—drunk liar fucker screwed-up bastard. The other temptation is to say nothing, to give him no satisfaction, to keep her face plain and smooth, not to cry, not to raise her voice. To leave and say nothing.

"Go on over to the Empire, Harry. You can probably make it there by last call," is what she says. "You go on." She looks around at him at last, as he stands by her. He is leaning against the wall by the counter, watching her in the way she loves that takes her in all at once, eyes, mouth, body, breath. His hair is silvery in the lamplight. He raises his hand to massage the back of his neck as he often does when he is puzzled or concerned. She moves back so that he will not touch her.

"Whatever it is, Lucette, whatever it is . . ."

She turns and slings her purse over her shoulder and goes out, stepping carefully down the tilted metal steps.

The next morning the snow is melting, the wind is blowing. Lucette knocks at the back door of the Maple Leaf. No one comes to answer for a long time. She knocks, and then waits in an attitude of exaggerated patience, knocks again. She looks over her shoulder several times as if she thinks someone across the street or in the next-door house might be watching. She has never been here before in the daytime.

She is giving Harry a chance. Either he will be here and she will tell him in person, or he won't be here and she'll leave him a message. She doesn't know what she'll do if no one is here, except that she will still be going away.

Thinking about it makes her head hurt, but she can't stop. How she is pregnant, how she and Harry are going to have a baby. How she told him last night but he still doesn't know. She thinks it over and over, with different parts of it in closeup each time: her clasped hands, Harry's closed eyes, his sharpening gaze, the teacup lying on its side, Harry's breathing as he stood behind her, the feel of the steps under her feet, the headlights of cars sweeping over her as she walked home.

It is worse that even now, Harry doesn't, she is pretty sure, know what is wrong. He has forgotten, has left what she said behind in the place he goes when he drinks. And worse because now she can't discuss it with him anymore.

The knowing sticks in her throat: Harry has slept with someone else. She knows he must have because the news of the baby was old to him, but not Lucette's old news. Someone else had said the same words to him—Lucette can almost hear this other voice, low and throaty—because he was drunk, he thought that Lucette was that woman, just for a minute. Lucette tries not to think who it might be. The secretary at the construction company. One of the women who hang out at the Maple Leaf, who say his name in a knowing way. The barmaid at the Empire, who always has her eye on Harry, who must have taken him by the hand one night when he was there without Lucette.

She knocks again, and Geneva opens the door. Lucette hoped it would be Al, but she asks in a cold voice for Harry.

"He's not here," Geneva says.

"Oh," Lucette says. "Can I leave him a message?"

"I don't take messages."

"Is Al here?" Lucette asks her.

"Al's asleep."

Lucette thinks about breaking down, telling Geneva everything. Geneva might soften, wake up Al, make some coffee, talk about what bastards men are. But Lucette doesn't want Geneva to know. It is bad enough that Geneva probably knows that she loves Harry. She probably thinks that she is just a kid, that Harry doesn't take her seriously, that she is just a piece of tail.

After Geneva closes the door, Lucette stands a minute thinking. What she wants is to tell Harry, sober, about the baby so he would know who it is that was talking last night. She would tell him and wait to see what he said. Then she would ask him for some money. Then she would tell him she is going away. This plan is built to be dismantled at any point that Harry says the right thing. What the right thing would be is not certain. It would be what makes her forget the images of Harry with the barmaid from the Empire, what makes her love Harry in the old way, what takes away this coldness from her heart and body.

She goes and sits on the steps of the trailer. Harry is not inside, she knows, because his car is not here. There are a lot of places Lucette cannot go: She can't go to Cynthia's house; she can't go to the Empire. She can't go home, because she left her mother a note saying she is never coming back. She sits looking at Charlie's yellow Camaro, still here with a flat tire. It is warm enough to be summer today. A bird is drinking from the puddle by the end of the trailer. The back door of the bar opens and Al comes out, dressed but wearing slippers.

"Geneva said you were at the door, and then I looked out the bathroom window and there you were. Did you need anything?" he says, watching her. He looks over his shoulder at the back of the bar.

"Al," Lucette says, "tell Harry I'm pregnant and I'm going away." She stands up. "Okay? Will you tell him that?"

"Going away where?"

"I don't want to say where. Will you tell him?"

"I'll tell him, but maybe you ought to do it. You could call him, Geneva won't mind if you use the phone. You could call him at Cynthia's right now, or at work, he might be at work."

"Will you tell him, Al?"

"Yes, okay. But wait a minute. Come with me a minute." Al leads her across the parking lot and through the back door. Inside, the bar is lit by the sun, but it is cold and dim in comparison to its nighttime self, when neon glows in the corners and cigarette smoke wraps around the barstools and the racks of upside-down glasses. Al opens the cash register, holding his hand over the bell and sliding the drawer out very slowly. He reaches behind the slots and gives her a stack of bills without counting them.

"Here," he says. "This is to take care of yourself. Harry can pay me back later."

"I'm still going away."

"Take care of yourself and go away for a while. But don't forget about Harry. I know, I know how he can be." He shakes his head. "I've known him a long time, Lucette." He takes her hand and pumps it solemnly.

They hear Geneva's voice raised from upstairs. "How long are you going to take with that brat?" she yells.

Al grins. "Remember now," he says. "Remember what I said."

Outside in the sun again, she looks at the bills in her hand. They are all fifties.

"Did you ever touch someone who was dead?"

"No, I didn't." Lucette leans her head back against the arm of the couch. She brings her hand up to look at it, this hand that has never touched a dead person. "They're cold, I know."

"It's more than that." James Gandy pauses to sip from his mug of tea. "It was like, oh, you know when you touch someone, but you do it real slow. Maybe you're sneaking up on them and you move your hand up toward their arm, say, real slow, and just before it gets there you feel something between your hand and their arm. Something comes out from their self to meet you." He demonstrates with his hand, sneaking it toward Lucette, drawing it back.

"Static electricity?"

"Not just that." He pauses again.

Lucette stretches her legs. Her ankles rest on the other arm of the couch.

"Well," he continues, "when you touch the hand of someone

who is dead, there is nothing. The thing that pulls your flesh to their flesh at the last moment, that's gone. It's flat. Only skin."

"Just shut up about it."

"All right. But I've known a fair number of dead people. My father, my grandmother, my mother. Aunts and uncles. My high school math teacher. My cousin James, we had the same name. He died in Korea."

"And you touched them all, I suppose."

"Don't be smart. About my cousin James. It does a strange thing to you to see your own name in an obituary and on a slab of marble. 'James Gandy, Korea' it said, and then the dates. I think it was a milestone for me, to see that. That may have been the beginning of it, now that I think of it." He sits up in his chair, the tea slopping over the rim of his cup. "This is really interesting, Lucette."

"What is?"

"It's a new connection." James Gandy gets up, grunting a little. "I'm going to write it down before I forget it. And then I'll come back and you can tell me about your day."

"Okay," Lucette says. She too has a cup of tea, which she is balancing on her stomach. If the baby was out, free in the world, she couldn't do this, she thinks, couldn't balance a cup on its head or shoulder. Now it is only a barely visible filling out of the flatness of her stomach.

She sighs, and rubs her shoulder against the back of the couch, old, heavy, covered in dark-red velvet. The couch is like a boat, a velvet boat, dark wood curved around her. She rocks in it, in the stillness of the room. At the windows the curtains whisper and stir in the breath of heat rising from the registers. Through her half-closed eyes she can see the thin yellow sunlight seeping in, a doubtful April sun. James Gandy's cat, Lex, is lying on the window seat. He likes to fight with the white, semitransparent folds of the curtains, but now he is sleeping, stretched out in a rectangle of sun among the flats of little plants straining toward the light.

"Here, Lucette, this is most interesting." James Gandy comes back and sits down in the wicker armchair, which creaks and squeals under his weight. He opens an old black ledger. "You see, I cut it out at the time, I'd forgotten that. Here it is."

Lucette moves her cup to the arm of the couch and sits up. She takes the ledger and looks at the picture, the young blank face, the army hat, the half column of print, the list of relatives stubbornly still alive. "He doesn't look like you," she says.

"Who could tell, in that getup? But he didn't. I was twenty-eight, he was twenty-one, just a kid to me." He takes the ledger back and stares at the picture, smoothing the stiff yellow tape that holds it down. "But you see, even at the time it impressed me, that's interesting, don't you think?" He closes the book and leans back in the chair, which squeaks some more. He looks at the ceiling. "If he was to come back right now, what would we have to say to each other, I wonder?"

"If he came back now, you might not recognize each other," Lucette says. "He'd look old, maybe."

"Look old?" James raises his eyebrows, small semicircles in his round face. "You mean he'd show signs of aging? I've forgotten signs of aging, you know, from the balloon."

Lucette looks at him, waiting for him to go on, as she has before when this has come up. He looks back at her, his face cheerful and bland, waiting. If she asks, he will tell her.

"I'm hungry," she says, "are you?"

"I've hardly eaten anything all day," he says. He closes the ledger with a clap that brings Lex's head up.

In the kitchen, James Gandy sits at the table watching as Lucette heats the can of soup that they will eat with crackers and cheese. When it is his turn to cook, they eat stews and soups and casseroles with dozens of ingredients, homemade bread, spicy spreads and compotes, weird combinations of vegetables. But he seems to like what Lucette cooks—Campbell's tomato, grilled-cheese sandwiches, tuna macaroni, omelets—just as well.

"So how was it at work?"

"It was okay."

"And the brothers Wittgenstein?"

"Witkowski."

"Witkowski, of course. Are they the same?"

"They weren't speaking to each other today. They kept giving me notes to pass back and forth." Lucette takes a cigarette out of her pack and leans forward to light it on the stove.

"They're crazy, you know." James plucks the cigarette from her lips and throws it, lit, into the garbage. "You're supposed to stop."

Lucette does not resist. The cigarettes don't taste the same, they are stale and rough, like the crumbled bark of trees.

"What were the notes about?" He offers her a substitute, a stick of candy, lemon-yellow striped with white, from a glass jar on the window sill.

"The coffee machine." Lucette sucks and lets the flavored saliva collect in her mouth.

"Oh, wonderful! The coffee machine?"

"Phil wants decaf and Jay doesn't." Lucette pours the soup, thick and pink, into the bowls, white china bowls with small purple flowers painted on them, a thin line of what James has told her is real gold around their edges. She sets the bowls on the bare wood of the table.

"You'd think they were still eight years old." James picks up his spoon and begins to eat. "What about the old man?"

Lucette takes a handful of crackers and crumbles them into the soup until it is sludgy. "He didn't come in today. He's still mad at Phil about the expense-account thing."

"It is his company, after all," James says, considering. "If he wants to put his teeth-cleaning on the account, why not?"

"Phil says it has to do with taxes."

"Oh, Phil is too stodgy. He always was. But I told you what they were like, you were warned."

"I don't mind them," Lucette says. She stirs her soup with her spoon. She lifts it to her mouth, sips, swallows, and is suddenly tired, as if the soup is a sleeping potion.

James is watching her. "You should get to know the girls in the factory. Some of them are your age, surely?"

"I guess." Lucette yawns. She sets her spoon down.

"You ought to have a nap," he says. "You ought to get them to bring in a couch for you. The old man could use it, too."

Lucette makes a face. "He'd want to share it."

"Go, go to bed, go." James makes shooing motions with his hands.

Lucette's bedroom window looks out on trees, bushes, sky. Standing there, it is hard for her to remember that she is still in the city. She can't even see the greenhouses, they are hidden by a line of fir trees. She leans her head against the glass, looking north, back toward the places she has left, so close, just the other side of the West Twenty-fifth Street bridge. She is tired, so tired she can hardly lift her head from the pane, cannot undress or turn back the covers. She falls on the bed, her head against the cold, smooth pillow, and sleeps, her hand by her mouth.

Lucette is dreaming: In another universe, Lucette has told Harry about the baby when he was sober. This other-universe Harry too has slept with the barmaid from the Empire, but he keeps it to himself. They are going to be married, they are being married, Lucette is walking down the aisle in a mist of white lace with Frank, her stepfather. Father Lawrence ahead is smiling, forgiving her for all those years of no church, smiling ruefully, ironically, as if to say, "What was it all for? So unnecessary, for here we all are." Lucette holds her stepfather's arm carefully and with joy—he is her support, but he is fragile. He will have to be very cautious, to rest a lot, to eat nourishing foods, but he is here, has just gotten back this very day to walk with his arm through Lucette's. Her mother will have to clear the stuff out of his workroom, Lucette thinks. Lucette and she will have a long talk, for there are things they both have to apologize for, and it will be difficult. They reach the altar and Lucette is suspended between the two men, Harry and her stepfather.

"Who gives this woman?" Father Lawrence asks, smiling.

Lucette's hand trembles on her stepfather's sleeve. Harry turns his head slightly in anticipation of her presence at his side.

"Who gives this woman?" Father asks again.

Lucette turns to her stepfather. "Sorry, honey," he says. Blood is crawling down one side of his head. His right hand is dripping with blood, and he holds it carefully away from her white dress. He presses her fingers and withdraws his other hand. His eyes are turning up in their sockets. He is falling down, he is dead. Lucette falls, too, her face is pressed against the cold marble of the church floor.

But she is awake, and the cold against her cheek is her own cold hand, and the cold air rattling the glass of the window, in which, when she sits up, she can see her darkened unfamiliar face against the night outside.

Now would be the time to think about her stepfather, to hold him in her mind like a friend, like someone living. Well forget it, she thinks. Just forget it.

Lying on the bed, she is adrift, she is an island. No one knows where she is. James Gandy, of course, knows, and at the electronics factory her current address is in the files that she herself now presides over. But no one else. She has told Bev where she is, made her promise to tell no one, but even Bev hasn't been here, hasn't seen this room, this house. This pleases Lucette. No one will know anything about her unless she tells them, she can pick and choose what she says.

She has told James Gandy that her stepfather is dead (though she called him her father), that her mother is crazy. He knows she is pregnant, but nothing about Harry.

On the other side of leaving, it is hard to remember her panic and fear, the trembling in her fingers as she stuffed the money Al gave her into her purse and walked away. It seems that it was all planned or ordained, now that she has done each thing to bring her here to this hour, this room. The newspaper she bought, the ads she circled, the bus she took, the miles of hard sidewalk she walked.

Now, in James Gandy's house, Lucette gets up from the bed and goes over to the table pushed up to the window. James Gandy helped her drag it in here from the unfinished part of the attic. It would serve her as a desk, he said. It is an old wooden kitchen table, painted green, and it just fits into the window gable. When she sits down and looks out all she can see is the sky, it is like being at the controls of a space ship.

She pulls a calendar toward her and counts the months again. She opens the drawer in the side of the table, a silverware drawer, James Gandy told her, and takes out the envelope with her money in it. With the money that Al gave her and what she got when she closed out her bank account, there is nearly fifteen hundred dollars. She does not want to have to spend this money. It is for after, she thinks, this and what she can save. She needs money for the hospital, but she has no idea how much that will be. She has not even been to the doctor yet, having an idea that if she puts it off, it will cost less. It is hard to get her mind around these details, or to have a clear picture of the baby, though she believes this is something that will come. She knows that she will go away when the baby is born, but not where. There is a stack of books on the table, books about other places. Oregon. New Mexico. She pulls them toward her and opens one, but does not read. She sits looking out the dark window.

Lucette gets up from her table-desk to go to the bathroom. This is a symptom, she knows from the books she got from the library and now from Dr. Spock, a paperback presented to her by James Gandy. Between her room at the back of the house and her bathroom there is a stretch of unfinished attic, bare wood floors, echoing, dusty. There is a naked light bulb with a chain hanging from it, but she doesn't turn it on. She can hear squirrels chittering on the roof sometimes, and pigeons fluttering and moaning. This bathroom is exciting to her, its cool porcelain surfaces, the cold white light that comes in through the high window. One wall is the diagonal of the roof, which slices the space over the bathtub. Everything is green, leaf-green sink and tub, jade-green tiles, pale creamy green paint on the ceiling and upper walls. There is a mirror that folds out into three panels installed on one wall, and an old wooden, marble-topped vanity table that, like her table-desk, came from the dark recesses of the attic. Her bedroom is nice, but she wishes that she could live in the bathroom. The bathroom is what made her want to stay in this house when she was still unsure of James Gandy, aware that she probably had to, since the price was cheap, not knowing if she could bear to live with someone who talked so much and was so friendly.

She flushes the toilet and turns on the faucet in the sink and holds her hands under the water. She would like to take a bath. She loves to see the water rushing into the green tub, to pull the silvery green shower curtain and enclose herself like a secret under the slanting ceiling. But she is still tired. Her hands and arms feel heavy. She stands in front of the small mirror over the sink and pushes back the flat shining strands of her hair. She likes the look of herself, white face, blond hair, against the green.

"This bathroom is the *pièce de résistance*," James Gandy had said that first day. "I put my soul into it."

Lucette had followed him in through the door and blinked at the green and silvery light, an underwater room.

"It's a little dingy," James Gandy said, running a finger along the edge of the sink. "It hasn't been used since my aunt lived here, that was when Mother was still alive. This was her apartment, so to speak. I built the whole thing, this and the bedroom." He looks around gloomily. "She hated it, though."

"Hated it?"

"She didn't like the green. She said it washed her out. And she found the unfinished part of the attic disturbing. Heard noises, and so on."

The minute she'd seen it, Lucette had longed to run the water in the sink and the tub, to submerge herself like a dry and dusty plant, to feel herself expanding in the water, and now, although she is tired, she turns the water on and watches the tub fill. James Gandy has given her candles for when she doesn't want to use the fluorescent light over the sink, and she lights them now, one fat and white, another thin and green, and sets them on the wide edge of the tub. Sighing, she steps into the water, sliding down until it is up to her neck. She watches the flickering of the candles and the shadows on the silvery shower curtain. The attic is full of drafts and eddies of wind, she can hear the noise of it in the tall pine trees outside, a sighing.

She thinks of how she came to James Gandy's house. Leaving her suitcase in the locker at the bus station. Looking at places in Lakewood and Parma, too expensive, trying to keep away from her own neighborhood, afraid to stray too far. She was at the Pick'n'Pay on State and Brookpark, having bought a doughnut and a banana for lunch, when she saw a notice on a yellow index card on the store bulletin board: "Furnished room for rent, private bath, must be plant/cat lover sympathetic to spirit expansion, rent negotiable." It was an address on Schaaf Road, a street familiar to her, but out of the way of her usual haunts.

When she first saw James Gandy standing in the frame of his front door, she had found his size intimidating. He was several inches more than six feet, but so large, so rounded that he hardly seemed tall unless you stood next to him. His face was smooth-skinned, with a high flush on his cheeks and large forehead. She took a step back from him, her hand on the railing of the wheel-chair ramp. There were no steps at the front of the house, just the ramp.

He had been holding the cat, great golden Lex, and he pushed him out toward Lucette like an offering, trying to make him hold his paw out. "He's disappointing today," James Gandy had said to her. "He only wants to sleep. I've threatened him with a kitten, though, maybe that will liven him up. What do you think?"

"I don't know," Lucette said. She looked back at the street, thinking of how far she had walked, maybe for nothing.

James Gandy stooped and opened his hands to let Lex pour himself onto the ramp. James had leaned against the door frame, yawning, staring at the sky, streaky white clouds chasing across the pale spring blue. "I don't know," he said, echoing Lucette. "Would I really do it? It would be nice to have a kitten again."

"I've never had a cat," Lucette said. She repositioned the strap of her purse on her shoulder, ready to go back down the ramp.

"But you look so potentially sympathetic, a potential cat person." He held his hand out to her, a big hand, broad palm, long fingers. "Do you think you could live with Lex? And this"—he waved his hand at the big old house, its peeling paint, the bushes, the wheelchair ramp, the screen of pine trees, a long row of greenhouses behind them—"can you live with all this? Tell me, I've forgotten, what is your name?

"Lucette."

"The whole of it, please."

"Lucette Harmon."

"Lucette," he repeated after her, breathing it, "Harmon. That's very nice, much more euphonious than my own. Which is James Gandy. Not elegant, but it has energy." He held his hand out more insistently, waggling it at her almost, and when she took it, he tucked her hand into the crook of his elbow and turned her around to walk back down the ramp. "We'll just take a look at the grounds," he said. "A tour of the manor, the master inspecting the fields. Do you feel like the new governess?"

Lucette walked beside him stiffly. They turned at the bottom of the ramp and made for the back of the house. Here she could see that the land sloped away gradually, a long sweep of what had once been lawn, now grown over, and beyond that the jumbled, glinting streets, houses, mills, smokestacks of the city. Several rows of greenhouses lined one side of the old lawn, their glass panes reflecting the ragged clouds.

"What is all this?" she asked him.

"The family business, my dear. I feel more and more like the rakish old lord, though I am neither dark nor sardonic. Built up by my grandfather, one of the first settlers in these here parts, and carried on by my father, not to mention the females of the family. This long stretch of high ground all along Schaaf Road once was the shore of Lake Erie in some primordial time, and there is this wonderful well-drained soil, because of the sand, you see. I hang on by my fingernails, becalmed on this high sandy ridge. Gandy Farms." He waved his hand. "Grandiloquent, no? Though there was a farm, singular, at first. Now we are hemmed in by the city."

"Your family?" Lucette looked back at the house behind them, a collection of towers and gables and porches.

"All dead now. It's only Lex and me that have to approve of you." He spun her around. "But you have to see the room before you decide. Come." And he led her up toward the back door through a maze of little brick paths between beds of dark soil, with lonely scattered groups of drooping white flowers. "It's a pity there's nothing to look at but the snowdrops, but it's a north-facing slope, it can't be helped."

And Lucette let him draw her on, up the hill, through the banging screen door, into the warm interior of the house.

At first she thought he was crazy, but she took the room anyway, because it was cheap and because of the bathroom, because she didn't want to look at any more places. He had driven her downtown to get her suitcase out of the locker at the bus terminal and she had moved in that day, had been sleeping between the white sheets of the bed under the uncurtained window only six hours after she had walked up the wheelchair ramp.

The first week she had resisted his overtures as best she could. She stayed in her room, eating granola bars and apples that she bought at the store on the corner where the bus let her off when she came back from looking for a job downtown. But he was too much for her. He talked around her silences, tempted her with savory-smelling food, dropped Lex in her lap, dragged her out for tours of the greenhouses, where he told her the Latin names of the plants. He is not a twisted recluse, she has found. His neighbors like him. He runs his business in an efficient, lackadaisical way. He knows everyone around here, and they know him. It was James Gandy who got her the job at the factory, for he has known the old man, old Mr. Witkowski, for a long time.

When Lucette finishes her bath, she blows out the candles, first the white, then the green, and walks in her bare feet across the dusty attic floor, placing each foot carefully so as not to pick up splinters. She is tired, she has to work the next day. She calls down the stairs to James Gandy that she is going to sleep and he calls something back to her up through the floors of the house that are between them.

Sighing, she gets into bed in the dark and lies on her back, her hands folded on her stomach, the sheet folded over the blanket and pulled up to her neck. He is walking around downstairs and she follows his progress from the front to the back of the house. She hears the door to the attic groan open and then his heavy steps coming up from the second floor.

James Gandy stands outside her door, breathing quickly from his climb. He is leaning against the wall, she knows, from the slight thud of his palm against the plaster. "Did you say you were going to bed?" he says through the door.

Lucette sits up. "Yes," she says. "I'm sorry I didn't yell louder."

"I was coming up anyway," he says. "I need that box with my father's papers in it. I'll see you at breakfast?"

Lucette lies down and listens to his steps descending. It is amazing, she thinks, how quickly she has gotten used to him.

At the West Side Market on Saturday, Lucette stands considering, apples or pears? James Gandy is ahead of her, strolling past the cabbages, his hands in his pockets. She can hear him humming. The man behind the stand weighs her fruit and adds up the prices on a piece torn from a grocery bag. Lucette looks to where she can see James Gandy's fine thin brown hair and broad pink neck over the heads of the crowd. "Wait," she says to the man, and runs down the wide aisle between the stalls.

"Hey," she says when she comes up to him.

He turns abstractedly from the mound of pale-green space-alien vegetables, small and cabbagelike with tiny vegetable arms growing from their sides and tops. "Would you like some of these for dinner?"

"I don't know," she says. "The fruit," she gestures back to where the man is waiting with the bags in his hands.

"Yes." He turns and walks back with her, stopping once to shake hands with the woman selling baby carrots. She wipes her hand on her wide white apron and giggles. "My protégée," he introduces Lucette.

The woman smiles at Lucette. "You got a good man here," she says, her eyes going to Lucette's waist.

Lucette flushes and opens her mouth to speak, but James Gandy takes her by the elbow, waving good-bye to the woman. "Don't mind," he says. "These people are good Catholics, they love the idea of a baby."

"How did she know I was pregnant?"

"I believe they claim they can see it in the eyes, these old women. Don't mind."

Back at the fruit stall, James Gandy counts money out for the man, who smiles as he twirls the bags and twists a plastic tie to close them. He says something in Spanish, smiling.

"He says a beautiful day, a beautiful woman," James translates for Lucette. He begins to hum again as he packs their purchases into the wire shopping cart he has brought. "We might have a cup of coffee, hmmm? Before we trek back."

He sends Lucette to buy two cups, six creams, two sugars, and a carton of milk, and they cross West Twenty-fifth Street to sit in the little concrete park on the corner of Lorain Avenue.

Lucette drinks her coffee in tiny sips, looking at the people—the mothers with children pushing up against them, the old women with wire carts like James Gandy's stuffed with wrapped parcels, old men with their faces turned up to the hot spring sun.

"I can remember when there was a snack bar here. Alexander's it was called, I think." James waves his hand at the edge of the park. "They had the most wonderful greasy French fries. I used to go there for my lunch when I worked at the bank that was here,

Cleveland Trust. I'd sit at the counter and talk to the kids from the Catholic high schools further down Lorain who used to cut school and go there for Cokes and those French fries. I thought I was very sophisticated, very suave, I can tell you. I thought I was better than God to them. That's how you think when you're twenty-three or so." He sighs pleasurably, and sips his sweet white coffee.

"What have you told people about me?" Lucette asks.

He turns to look at her. "Only the facts," he says.

"You told people I was pregnant, had left home, about my parents?"

"Are you upset, Lucette?" He raises his hand to shade his eyes.

"I just want to know."

"Well." He sets down his cup and puts his hands on his broad knees. "I've told people that you are a young woman on her own in the world, pregnant, renting the room in my attic. No dissembling. No extrapolating. You wouldn't have had me lie?"

Lucette takes another sip of coffee. "No," she says, but, she thinks, why say anything at all?

"You're not happy," James Gandy states.

Lucette shakes her head.

"No it's okay or no you're not happy?" he asks.

"I'm happy," she says, "but—"

"I've been stupid, I see." He drinks the rest of his coffee in a gulp. He hands her the cup, stuffed with empty cream containers, to throw away, and starts off with the cart. "But it's a way I have, I have to tell the truth," he says without turning his head. "I learned it in the balloon."

In the car, Lucette waits for James to say something, but he drives straight down West Twenty-fifth without speaking. When they pass Mapledale, Lucette feels the pull of her mother's house, her mother inside it wrapped in her thoughts, but she refuses to look that way, keeping her eyes focused on the place ahead where the buildings stop at the bridge. There where the sky is larger, a great arch over the zoo in its tree-filled valley, she feels safe, she is out of the neighborhood.

She looks at him every once in a while, but he does not turn to her. His large pale face is blank, eyes flickering to follow the traffic. Lucette leans her head back against the headrest. She feels cradled in the softness of the seat. It is a huge car, an old Cadillac, that moves like an ocean liner down the street. James has his strange ways, she thinks, but they are not so bad.

She is tired today, another symptom, "the fatigue of early pregnancy," one of the books called it. These small things—going to the bathroom more often, tiredness, the tickle of nausea when she brushes her teeth—it is hard to believe that they mean anything. If it were not for the fact that her periods have so definitely stopped, she might never have noticed these faint stirrings of her body. But even so, she never wakes without remembering—I am pregnant. Somehow her body must know.

James Gandy has never brought up abortion to her, although he must have wondered if she had considered and rejected it. He has been delicate with her, tactful. She sighs, thinking about his courtesy, his willingness to talk if she wishes, to keep silent if not, to cushion her, feed her, entertain her. She feels herself sinking away from consciousness, rocked with the motion of the car on its excellent suspension, and the scenes and objects of her life with James Gandy rise and circle her in a slow tornado—the bathroom's green grotto, the spaceship window, the solid white candle burning with a steady flame, Lex's fur-circled eyes—the white-painted wooden kitchen table grows until it is a mile-high plateau, the aisles of the greenhouse twist and bend away ahead of her, she is walking, dragging her numb left foot, when will it open up ahead? Plants brushing her arms and face . . .

The car stops, and Lucette opens her eyes. They have pulled into an unfamiliar driveway next to a boxy little bungalow, painted pink with bright-green trim.

"Wake up," James Gandy is saying to her, as he roots among the packages in the back seat. "We're here with a purpose, smooth your hair down a bit. Here," he thrusts a wax-paper-wrapped bunch of tulips at her, pink streaked with green. "You take these."

He leaves her to follow him up the swept concrete sidewalk that leads to the front door. "No flowers," he says, after ringing the bell. "They won't have them. Not a bush, not a tree."

She sees that the lawn grows right up to a concrete border that edges the foundation of the house. "Who won't?" she asks him, but the door is opening.

"Why, James!" A tall, pale old woman opens the door. "Here you are, when we least expected you. May was just going to play on the organ."

"Who didn't expect him?" A second woman, a little shorter, her white hair loose and wild, pushes from behind the first. They are both wearing the same shade of pink. "I was thinking, God strike me dead if I wasn't, that it's just the sort of day that James turns up."

"Let me introduce you to my new roomer," James says as they crowd into the small front hall. "Lucette, these are my old friends Helen and May Skrovan."

"James, you thing you, you know May's a Skrovan only by birth. She's been married," the tall woman says to Lucette. "But she won't give up the name."

"I'll call myself Skrovan if I like," the shorter woman says, pushing her hair out of her eyes. "Why not?"

"Oh, well," Helen says, giving in. "Tulips, James? Not yours, I suppose."

"They are, though."

"Oh my," May says. Taking them from Lucette, she brushes her face with them.

"I don't know why you're doing that, they have no smell," Helen says.

"It's just *you* can't smell them anymore." May thrusts them at Lucette. "They do, don't they?"

They have a smell, Lucette finds, a thin, wild, nectar smell, but she doesn't want to take sides. She looks at James Gandy, who immediately reclaims the tulips and marches with them into the house, calling for a vase.

"And May must play for us. What will it be, May, to go with the tulips? Brahms? Stravinsky?"

May laughs. "No classical, James, not today." She sits down at the organ in the tiny living room. "I have a new songbook." She holds her hands high above the keys and shakes her wavy white hair.

"Oh, stop," Helen says to her. "She thinks she's Liberace."

May lowers her hands and begins to play a song to which James hums along. " 'Downtown,' " he whispers to Lucette. "Petula Clark."

Almost immediately, Helen begins to talk to James Gandy in an undertone that does not carry to where Lucette is sitting. She lets her head rest against the back of the chair, a plumply cushioned rocker. It is a small room, very full, not only of the usual sort of old-people furniture and knickknacks, but also with filled boxes and paper and plastic bags, stacks of magazines neatly tied with twine, unidentified objects wrapped in newspaper or tissue. There is a card table in the corner with some of these objects on it, half unwrapped, along with rolls of tape and sticky labels, a collection of Magic Markers, and a small metal box.

"I'm holding my own," she hears Helen say to James Gandy, and she turns her head to pay more attention to the conversation, but the two of them have moved closer together on the couch, and dropped their voices even further. May, her back to them, plays on, singing aloud occasionally to accompany herself. "I fought the law," she sings, "and the law won."

When May has finished, ending with some extra-loud chords, they go into the dining room, also tiny, also crowded with bags and boxes. Helen hands James a plate for the jelly doughnuts he has brought. "Very nice," he says, turning it over to look at the bottom.

"I expect to get as much as ten dollars for it," Helen says as she passes napkins. "There isn't a lot of yellow depression glass around."

James Gandy offers a doughnut to Lucette. "Helen and May do

the flea-market circuit," he tells her. "And they have a table at the International Bazaar on Sundays."

"That's over on Brookpark and Hundred-and-fiftieth," May tells her. "You should bring her, James. I'm sure she'd love it. You'd like to come, wouldn't you?" May takes a big bite of her doughnut, and powdered sugar flies, falling down the front of her dress. "Oh, blast."

"Watch your language," Helen says. "You don't have to come," she tells Lucette.

"There are a lot of young people there," May argues. "And it's very educational. There are people from other lands. That Indian gentlemen who sells cassette tapes." She looks at Lucette to see what she thinks.

Lucette smiles. She doesn't know what she ought to say.

"We'll be sure to come sometime," James says, "before I have to open on Sundays to sell annuals."

"We could have gotten Saturdays as well," May says, "but we like to be flexible."

"And we have our aerobics class on Saturdays," Helen says.

"Helen is the more fit of the two of us," May says. "You should see her do those routines."

"Well, May has bad arches. Twenty-four years ago she stepped off a curb and her arches fused."

"I can do the stretches better, though." May twists her arms behind her, one elbow pointing toward the ceiling and one toward the floor, and turns around so Lucette can see that her fingertips meet between her shoulderblades.

"Well," James says, wiping powdered sugar from his hands. "I have to be off, girls."

"You have to call us 'women,' you thing you," Helen says.

Lucette gets up.

"Oh, you can stay with us," Helen says to her, motioning her to sit down.

"Yes," May says. "James will be back before we have to go to our aerobics. Although if you did come along it would be all right.

Our instructor, she's the sweetest thing, as thin as a little stick, a blond like you, she wouldn't mind at all if we brought a guest. It's three dollars for one time, although you don't have a leotard. You look very limber though, maybe it wouldn't matter."

"Don't be silly, May. She's not going to go to aerobics with us."

"Where are you going?" Lucette says to James Gandy.

"Just a little side trip," he says, putting a hand on her shoulder. "You wouldn't be interested. But really," he leans down to whisper in her ear, "I'm leaving you here for the conversation. It will be educational." He straightens up and then mouths to her with exaggerated movements of his lips, "Be nice to them."

"But when will you be back?"

"Really very shortly," he says, and he whisks out the door and is gone.

"Well, now," Helen says. She comes back into the dining room, where Lucette is still standing by the table. "Maybe you wouldn't mind sorting buttons with us while we talk?"

"Must we do buttons?" May says. "I'm sure Lucette would rather do jewelry, wouldn't you? Wouldn't you like to do earrings? Or necklaces?"

Lucette sits down, puts her hands in her lap. If she had any aunts, she would know how to behave with these old women, and she is angry with her mother, no sisters, no brothers, no use. "Earrings would be fine," she says.

"You see?" May says to Helen, who purses her lips.

"But I don't mind buttons," Lucette adds.

"I'll do buttons," Helen decides, "and so will Lucette, if she doesn't mind, and you do jewelry, May." She brings some shoeboxes to the table, and May drags over a large plastic bag filled with packages and small bags.

Helen gives one of the boxes to Lucette, an incredibly old shoebox with the picture of a smiling, faded woman in a fifties haircut and small pointed white collar. It is half full of buttons, all sizes, all colors. "Sort them by color," Helen says, "and put them in these plastic trays."

"They sell better that way," May says. She is tumbling out the contents of the bags, winking, chiming piles of costume jewelry.

Lucette bends her head over the button box and puts her hand in. They are smooth and cool, and she dabbles her fingers in them, sliding them over her palm. She takes a handful and spills them out onto the table, sorting the red from the blue from the black from the white. They click pleasantly against each other.

May reaches for one of the doughnuts, but Helen taps her hand with one of her long fingers. "Don't," she says, "you'll get the merchandise sticky."

"Oh, all right," May says. She looks sideways at Lucette, smiling a small three-cornered smile. "Start, why don't you?" she says to Helen.

"Yes." Helen sits up very straight. "About James." She appears to look out the dining-room window, although her hands continue to sort buttons, dealing them out like poker chips.

Lucette stops sliding and clicking the buttons, her hand stilled, touching and then drawing in one large button, from a coat maybe, gray shot with dark red streaks. He's sick, has cancer probably; she thinks of his face, pink not with health as she thought, but with an unhealthy, unnatural flush; sees him, his house, her room, the green bathroom, receding from her, collapsing in on themselves. No wonder, she thinks, no wonder, feeling the skin of her forehead draw together, her mouth pulling apart into an O.

"It's just that James doesn't like to have to explain himself," May says, still smiling.

"He thought, from one who has known him a long time," Helen begins, pursing her lips.

"What do you mean, from one?" May stops trying to fasten a chain of purple beads around her neck. "Don't take it all on yourself."

"It's merely a manner of speaking."

"He's sick?" Lucette asks.

"Sick?" They both look at her. "I wouldn't like to call it sick," Helen says. "Some might."

"But not us," May says, leaning forward over her piles of jewelry. "He's been the dearest, sweetest, why, what he's done for us—"

"Well," Helen says sharply, "we needn't talk about that, I don't think." The two sisters look at each other for a moment, Helen's eyes glittering, May's face unsmiling, going blanker.

Lucette looks from one to the other, wanting to get up and go through the boxes and bags to the front door and out, to wait for James Gandy on the sidewalk. But suppose he doesn't mean to come back? She thinks of how all her stuff is at his house, maybe right now he is there packing it. Bundling her out. She grips the table.

May reaches out and pats her hand. "You're upsetting her, Helen."

"Oh dear." Helen shakes her head. "Listen. It's just that James has a different outlook on life than most people, he's got some different thoughts—"

"Good thoughts," May interjects.

"Yes. He believes in the good of things, he sees the good side. In fact, there's not a thing wrong with the way he lives, better than many a Christian—"

"Better than most!"

"Don't go too far, May. It's just that what makes him think the way he does is a little different, that is, he believes, he thinks he saw—"

"I don't think you ought to say it that way, you're making him sound crazy."

"You tell her, then, if you can't be quiet," Helen says, subsiding in her chair.

May reaches over and takes Lucette's hand. "It's really simple," she says. "James saw what he calls a balloon, and went up in it, and talked to them that was driving it, and it changed his life. That's all." She sits back and takes up a pair of earrings and holds them up to the necklace lying on her chest. "He doesn't like it if you call it a UFO or a spaceship. Sensationalizing, he calls it."

"A balloon?" Lucette says.

"That's it." She puts the earrings down and picks up another pair.

Helen has picked up a handful of buttons, but she doesn't start sorting them. "I feel sure that James wanted us to give some kind of, I don't know, background, for his philosophy, to relate it, you know, to Christian thought—"

"Oh, ppfff. I don't know what Helen likes to make a big fuss about," May says to Lucette. "James likes to talk about the philosophy. He just can't take the first part, having to tell about the balloon. Now, if it was me, that'd be the fun thing, what it looked like, what they looked like. He never told us as much as I'd have liked to hear."

"Now that's over, you can talk to James about it," Helen says, starting to sort buttons again. May, too, starts to separate the piles of jewelry in earnest.

Lucette sits back, waiting to feel something, nervous, afraid, angry, but instead she begins to laugh, and when the two old women look up at her, puzzled expressions on their faces that make them resemble each other more, she laughs harder, the sound going up higher in her throat. They watch with concern while she laughs and then starts to cough and hiccup. Helen brings her water in a small squat glass with cherries painted on it. May gets up and pats her back softly until she stops.

"You want to watch out for overexcitement," Helen says.

"Oh, I don't think that matters," May says.

"I'm fine," Lucette says, "really." She drinks some water.

"Well, of course you are," May says. "You're pregnant, though, aren't you?"

"Oh, May," Helen says. "Can't you ever keep a thought to yourself?"

"James told you?" Lucette asks.

Helen clears her throat. "James said particularly that we were to say that he didn't tell us anything about you at all, and he didn't."

"That was it, you see. What else would there be to hide about such a pretty, nice young girl, except a baby?" May says sadly.

"No need to blush," Helen says, although Lucette is not blushing, she is too dumbfounded to do anything. "We haven't led completely sheltered lives, you know."

That night, after dinner, when James Gandy is out in the greenhouse, Lucette goes into the front hall and sits down in the armchair by the telephone and calls Bev. "Can you get out?" she asks her.

"Sure," Bev says. "I'll come and pick you up. Give me directions."

Lucette hesitates. When she first moved into James Gandy's house, she had called Bev right away to tell her where she was. But Bev hasn't been here yet, they've only talked on the phone. Somehow she doesn't like the idea of Bev being here, even only at the front door. "I'll meet you at the corner of Schaaf and Broadview, by the gas station."

But Bev insists that she will come and get her, and when Lucette goes out to wait for her, she's glad, because it's raining lightly, tiny slivers of cold rain. When she gets into Bev's car, she feels her throat aching, her eyes wet, it is all so familiar—the overflowing ashtray, Bev's purse gaping open on the floor, the gear shift covered with duct tape, the small stuffed dog hanging from the rearview mirror. She tries to keep her face turned away so that Bev will not see her wet cheeks, but Bev is all over her, crying herself, hugging, hitting Lucette with her balled-up scarf.

"You creep Lucette, God, how I missed you." She pulls back and looks at Lucette. "Wait, am I squeezing anything? Are you crying?"

"No," Lucette says, "it's just a symptom, really."

"A symptom?"

"It's hormones, you know—going crazy."

Bev starts the car. "Where do you want to go?"

"I don't care. Anyplace."

Driving toward McDonald's, Lucette feels tension rising higher and higher in her, and she tries to bring it down, rubbing her fingers lightly back and forth over the armrest, noting each time they pass over a roughened, cracked place. The cars in the other lane seem to leap at them, each one a potential accident. "How is everyone?"

"Mom's fine, Dad's fine, Ray and Stevie are fine," Bev grins at her. "Ray heard me talking to you on the phone. He tried to make me tell him where you were and what you were doing, but I got rid of him. He still has one major crush on you."

"Maybe you should tell him I'm going to have a baby." Lucette realizes that this is the first time she has said "I'm going to have a baby," not "my period is late," not "I'm pregnant" and she starts to sweat.

"And break the kid's heart?" Bev pulls into the McDonald's parking lot. "Do you know what you're going to do with it? I mean," she says, when Lucette doesn't answer, "are you going to come back with it and like, live with your mother, or are you going to get a place, or are you going to give it up to somebody else, or what?"

"I don't know," Lucette says. She thinks of "after" as a different country. She has to go there, but she doesn't know how she will act or what she will do or say.

Bev looks at her, tapping her fingers on the steering wheel. "Oh, Luce, it would be so nice if—"

"If what?"

Bev shakes her head. "I don't know. I guess, if we could be happy about it."

"You mean, if I was married," Lucette says.

"It isn't the being married so much, there are people who have babies and aren't married. But this going away, no baby showers—"

"No pink and blue bunnies?"

"You know what I mean."

"You're thinking of you, Bev, of what it would be like if it happened to you." Lucette bites at the skin on her finger. "I guess you think I should be home with my mother, *my mother,* and that she should be buying booties."

"Oh, Luce."

"She's not like your mother."

"All right, Luce. Don't." Bev looks down at her hands on the steering wheel.

McDonald's is nearly empty, only an old man hunched over a cup of coffee, and two preteen girls with Happy Meals.

"So, how is everyone else?" Lucette says again.

"Your mother's okay." Bev drips her French fries in a mixture of catsup and mustard. "I mean, I haven't heard anything that she's not."

"Are you still going with Jimmy?"

"No." Bev laughs. "I got mad at him last week. He was singing one of the songs he does with the band, and he was staring at this girl in the back all the way through. Maybe he thought I wouldn't notice. Anyway, we had a fight and that was it. It's okay though, I was getting a little tired of his attitude." She pops her straw through the hole in the top of her soda. "Don't you want to know about Harry?"

"I guess," Lucette says. She has gotten a milkshake with the idea that it would be healthier than Coke, but it tastes flat and strange to her, too thick in her throat.

"Well, he's moved in with his cousin Cynthia totally now."

"What?" Lucette looks up.

"Yeah. I think probably because his friend, that guy Al, died. The one that owned the Maple Leaf."

"Al *died?*" Lucette has imagined that things would be going on in their usual way, people moving along their accustomed lines.

"He had a heart attack, I think, about a week after you left. I was going to tell you when we talked before, but I forgot. I think he left Harry some money or something. I got this from Jimmy, when they were still playing their gig there. He heard about it in the bar, how Al left Harry something and Geneva was mad on account of it. Oh yeah, and I think Cynthia's husband left, too. I don't know why."

"I can't believe all this," Lucette says.

"Why not? Cynthia sounded like a bitch to me." Bev swirls the ice around in her cup.

"I mean about Al." Lucette sees her hand taking the money from Al, his hand closing the cash register drawer, the stone of his ring winking. She hears Geneva calling from upstairs.

"Well, he was old, I guess."

"He wasn't that old, it's just that he was bald. He was only a little older than Harry."

"I told you Harry was too old."

"Oh, shut up."

"Sorry," Bev says, not looking very sorry. "Well, that Al was a nice old guy, I guess. Lucette, have you been to the doctor yet?"

"The doctor?"

"Yeah, the doctor. I was talking to my mother—"

"You told her about me?"

"We were talking about one of my cousins, don't have a cow. But you're supposed to have prenatal care. My mother says it's important."

"I was going to go pretty soon."

"Look, Luce, if you're going to have this baby, you better get serious. Do you even know how far along you are?"

"About three months, I think."

"How about if you make the appointment and I'll go with you?"

"I don't know where to go."

"You go to Metro, my mother says. They've got an obstetrics clinic and you go in and fill out these papers and then they charge you how much you can afford. You call, and I'll take you."

Lucette hesitates, stirring her straw around and around in her milkshake, thick and pink like paint in the cup. "James Gandy would probably take me, if I asked him to."

"Who the hell is James Gandy?"

"You know, the guy whose house I'm living in."

"Oh, him. Don't be dumb, you don't want to go with some guy, everybody'll think he's the father."

They both laugh. "Okay," Lucette says. "I'll call you."

"So what's he like, this guy, what's his name?"

"James Gandy."

"What a dumb name. Is he a geek or what?"

"He's all right. You should see my bathroom—it's all green, the sink, the tub, everything. I've got a little table with a mirror—"

"A vanity table," Bev says. "God, I've always wanted one of those. Show me when I take you back."

"I don't know," Lucette says.

"What, is this guy weird, he doesn't want you to have visitors?"

"He's really nice. He's got a cat named Lex, and these green-houses, that's his job, the greenhouses. We share cooking, every other day."

"And he's not married? How old is he?"

"I don't know," Lucette says. She pushes her milkshake away.

"I get it, another one of your old guys. Older than Harry?"

"Cut it out, it's not like that."

"But is he older than Harry?"

Lucette admitted that he was.

"That old and not married. Makes you wonder."

"He's got these women he's friends with." Lucette says. "These two sisters."

"Lots of them do. What's the house like?"

"Big. Lots of plants everywhere. I don't know."

"You've got to invite me in sometime when he's not there, if he's fussy. But I bet we'd get along great. I've always wanted to meet someone who's gay."

"I don't think he's gay," Lucette says. Really, she has no idea if he is or not, but the picture that Bev has drawn—James, unmarried, having lived with his mother, his cat, his plants—doesn't seem to be a true one, or maybe just not complete. The things that she might add to round it out—his preoccupation with death, his curious unadultness, the things that Helen and May told her about him—she can't explain these to Bev.

A pair of headlights from out in the parking lot sweeps over them, and they look around. The old man is still sitting in his booth, but he has fallen asleep and is snoring, a little buzz of sound. The two young girls have their heads together, whispering, one of them scratching her grubby ankle with careful long fingernails, each painted half blue, half pink. The employees are fighting in low voices behind the counter, as they always do when there aren't enough customers to keep them busy. Lucette watches the girl who is supposed to be doing takeout toss her ponytail, which is threaded through the hole in the back of her McDonald's cap.

"God," Bev says. "I'm so bored."

"Thanks."

"I don't mean now. Well, now—but not because of you. It's a drag not having anyone to go out with. Couldn't we go out sometimes?"

"When I'm pregnant?"

"You don't show yet. And anyway what difference would it make? You don't have to drink."

"I have to be careful of money. I don't want to see anyone I know."

"We could go to different bars, out in the suburbs or some-place." Bev bounces a little in her seat. "That would be fun—new places, new guys."

"Fun for you."

"Your life's not over yet." Bev pokes Lucette. "Think about it, okay? Wait, though, I know what we can do tonight. You want to go to one of those home parties?"

"You mean like Tupperware?"

"Yeah, but it's not Tupperware, it's something else, I can't remember what. This girl from work is giving it, so there won't be anybody there you know."

Lucette starts to shake her head, but Bev catches it in both her hands before she completes the first swing, and makes it nod up and down. "Yes? Come on, it'll be fun, it'll be weird. Let's do it."

"All right, all right," Lucette says, smiling, and they get up and go out to the car, Bev dancing a little in the parking lot.

"It'll be great, you'll love it. It'd be better if we were stoned, but you ought not to do that, and anyway I don't have any, too bad. This girl that's giving it, Joan, is nice but sort of uptight, you know? Look in the glove compartment, I have the invitation in there. Baltic Avenue, right? That's in Lakewood, I think."

"You don't know where it is?"

"I can find it, don't worry. What time does it say?"

Lucette leans forward to take advantage of the streetlight. "It says seven-thirty."

"That's perfect, it's only a little after that now. We'll just miss the hanging around at the beginning when everybody's trying to get a good chair. Hold on," Bev says, and she puts her foot down on the accelerator as they hit 117th Street.

They bounce over the pavement, nipping through stoplights. Bev stubs out her cigarette. "I can't believe you quit smoking," she says. "That's so scary, that your body can just tell you not to smoke anymore." She looks over at Lucette, her face pale in the dark car. "So do you feel anything?"

"Like what?"

"You know, like something moving inside?"

"No." Lucette looks out the side window to avoid the onrush of the world in front of them. "It's too early, I think."

"I don't know if I could put up with that. It just seems too weird, you know, like having a fish swim around inside you. My one uncle told me about how they used to swallow goldfish— college kids. That's what I imagine it would be like. I still don't like fish because of that."

"The books say it's different from anything else." Lucette rubs her fingers on the cool glass of the window. "I'm afraid I won't be able to tell when it happens though. You know?"

"Listen, are you going to have natural childbirth? Who's going to the hospital with you?"

"I don't know," Lucette says, and trembles on the edge of feeling bad, but before she can, Bev grabs her arm.

"Well, can I? You'd like me to, wouldn't you?"

"Do you want to?"

"Yeah, sort of. I really do. I want to see what it's like before I do it myself."

"Well, okay."

"This'll be great. I'll be really good, Luce."

"Maybe you can pick up a doctor while you're at it."

"Hey, maybe two, if I have the time."

They laugh, zipping up West Boulevard, under the sweeping branches of trees edged with miniature leaves. Lucette leans her head back and with her eyes half closed lets the lights—headlights, streetlights, traffic lights, neon signs—slide over her face, streaks of white green red orange pink blue. She is happy just now, to be with Bev, to be out sliding through the lights, skimming along the road. She feels potent—she can handle all of this, no problem. It's just a matter of stretching out her hand. She imagines how she will move among the people and events of her life and order them all, majestic, loving, happy.

After they drive up and down Baltic a while, Bev decides that a certain double house, white with dark-red trim, is the place where Joan lives, and they park and get out. They are giggling, holding on to each other. Bev takes Lucette's arm and pretends to hoist her up the steps. "In your condition, my dear," she says. Every time she says "In your condition," they laugh.

Fifteen minutes later they are seated, Lucette on an upholstered footstool, Bev on the floor beside her, listening to Joan introduce the party organizer, Maureen Rivera. "Call me Mo," she says, but she is old enough so that Lucette can't imagine calling her anything but Mrs. Rivera.

It has turned out to be a home astrology party. Joan and Maureen Rivera are both in costume. Joan's is just a maroon silk kimono, the kind that goes with a matching nightgown, with cut-out stars and sickle moons pinned onto it, and a cardboard witch's hat with a scarf pinned to the tip. Maureen Rivera is wearing a very glamorous gypsy costume, lots of jewelry winking and clanking, ruffly blouse cut low to show off her large, firm, freckled breasts, a swirling, many-colored skirt, a black wide-brimmed hat over a kerchief. Joan keeps picking at her kimono, pulling it away from her legs, readjusting the front to keep it closed over her chest as if she isn't wearing anything underneath, although when she stands in the kitchen doorway, Lucette can see the shadow of a blouse and skirt showing through.

"Everybody was supposed to wear an appropriate costume," Joan says again. "It said on the invitation."

"Oh, I lost the card," Bev says. "It's lucky I remembered it was tonight."

"Now the first thing we're going to do is play a game," Maureen Rivera says. Everyone groans, and she smiles good-naturedly. "You're each going to tell us your name and then one of us will tell you something about yourself. You go first, Joan."

"Um, you all know me, my name is Joan Helwig."

"I'll be the first predictor," Maureen Rivera says, and she closes her eyes. "Joan Helwig is a very—" she pauses, "GENEROUS person." She opens her eyes and smiles her big smile. "Now how do I know that?"

They all shift in their seats and look at each other, but before they get really uncomfortable, she answers herself. "All I have to do is look behind me." She gestures at the buffet table, each bowl and platter covered with plastic until after the presentation. "Joan has set out all this food for us, not just a few carrot sticks, or some measly crackers and a piece of cheese, but—what?"—she turns to look—"stuffed things, miniature cakes, these little things with the cherries on them. What is it? It's a banquet, for God's sake! And that's how I know, without knowing another single thing about Joan—she's GENEROUS!"

Joan bows her head, smiling and blushing. "I didn't do absolutely all of it," she says. "Eleanor brought the cheesecake tarts, and I had the prune roll leftover frozen from Easter, that was my mother's . . ."

"So, you next," Maureen Rivera says, pointing her purple fingernail at the woman sitting on the couch behind Lucette. "What's your name? Stand up, honey."

"I'm Shirley Powell."

"Okay," Maureen Rivera says. "What about Shirley? What can we say about Shirley?"

They all look at her, and she stands stolidly under their gaze. Lucette feels Bev twitching at her side and knows that she is suppressing laughter. We can say she likes to eat, Lucette thinks, for Shirley is fat, solid and square under her dress that's printed all over with tiny flowers.

"Come on, ladies, what do you know about Shirley?"

"I know she's the terror of the stockboys at Higbee's," a woman in back says, and they all laugh, even Shirley.

"Now, now, that's not what we're looking for. How about someone who doesn't work with Shirley."

"Um, we know she likes flowers?" a thin girl contributes, biting her finger. "From her dress?"

Lucette feel Bev's shoulder start to shake, but Maureen Rivera is pleased. "That's it, that's it, all we have to do is look at Shirley and we think of flowers, a garden of flowers, isn't that right?"

"A field of flowers," Bev breathes into Lucette's ear.

"Now what about you, sweetie," Maureen Rivera says to Bev, who jumps up with alacrity.

"My name is Beverly Archacki," she says, "don't wear it out."

"What do we know about Beverly?"

Bev poses, hands on thrust-forward hips.

The woman in the back speaks up again. "We know she is very popular with the men."

Everyone laughs, and Bev does a little shimmy-shake inside her short skirt.

"Well, all right, I guess that'll be enough," Maureen Rivera says when the laughter dies down. "So what was the point of all this?"

"That Bev dresses like a slut?" the woman in the back asks in a good-student voice, and Bev pretends to throw a cushion at her.

"That we all know things, that we have capacities we're largely unaware of, that if we know these things about the present, about people unknown to us, why couldn't we know other things?" Maureen Rivera lowers her voice. "Things about the future?"

The point of the party, it develops, is to sell things associated with fortune telling and astrology—tarot cards, small crystal balls, horoscope charts, and also what Maureen Rivera calls "related merchandise"—crystals to wear as jewelry, candles and incense to burn during seances, T-shirts that announce the wearer's astrological sign, or that say "Have We Got Karma Together?" or "I'm Clairvoyant—Just Think Your Phone Number At Me."

After the presentation, Joan removes the plastic from the bowls and platters, and they fill little paper plates with food and wander around looking at what is for sale.

"I don't know," Joan asks Lucette. "Do you think I'll make any money if I have my own party? All I get for this one is a dream-interpretation book and my personal horoscope. I had to tell her my birth hour and minute for that, though, and you know, I have this feeling that I got it wrong, so it probably won't work for me at all. What do you think?"

"I don't know," Lucette says. "Maybe most of it applies, if you're pretty close." Her plate is filled with food from the buffet table, but now she isn't hungry, at least not for these small cut-out circles and squares and triangles of food.

"And I don't know if I can do the presentation," says Joan.

"It didn't seem too hard," Lucette says.

"That was just the first part, there's more in a minute."

Maureen Rivera is explaining to Shirley that this can be a year-round business, how the parties are more popular in the fall, of course, because of Halloween, but that they address concerns and questions that are legitimate any time of the year. Shirley nods, a look of deep discomfort on her face.

Bev is sifting through the merchandise laid out on a card table. "Look at this," she keeps saying, holding up things for the others to see—a book called *How to Hold a Seance;* a cloth panel of dream symbols to embroider in different-colored threads; dream-interpretation books and dream journals; charts to coordinate your horoscope to your biorhythms. "Here, Luce, this is definitely for you." She holds up a needlework kit for Scorpio and wags it in Lucette's face.

"Are you Scorpio?" Joan asks.

"No," Lucette says. Her face is hot.

"A new boyfriend?" one of the other women asks, and they all turn to look at her, she feels the pressure of their gazes—those she knows slightly, those she knows only as they figure in Bev's stories about work. She looks at Bev, who is pantomiming that she's sorry. "I'm pregnant," she says, "I'm going to have a baby in October, I guess."

"A baby?" they say, "how wonderful," and they pull in closer to ask about her weight gain, her morning sickness, her sleep habits, if she wants a boy or a girl, if she has names picked out. Lucette smiles. She keeps her left hand out in plain sight, spread on the cushion of the couch to show that she has no ring, and miraculously no one asks about the father. She leans against the back of the couch answering questions. Bev is writing down the names and phone numbers of doctors with good recommendations.

"But this is very good," Maureen Rivera says, cutting through the voices of the other women. "We have a future event to project our thoughts at, how nice. Do you perhaps have the conceptual date?"

"The *what?*" Shirley asks.

"The date that the child was—you know, begun."

"No," Lucette says, but she thinks of that first night at the trailer, wondering, could it have been then? And although she tries to push it away, the trailer, its flapping blind, the twisted sheets, and Harry's big warm body up against the length of hers are there in the room with her, as if Maureen Rivera can see them, has called them here.

"It's no matter," Maureen Rivera says. "When is your birth date?"

"June fifteenth," Lucette says.

"That's very interesting, very good, a Gemini. And we can do a general chart for a newborn. That will give you an idea of what's in store." She stares at Lucette, measuring her, finding her out with the instruments of her eyes. "And your due date, when is that?"

Lucette hesitates, and Joan says, "Tell her, Lucette," and some of the other women echo her. "Come on, Lucette, when will it be?"

It seems to Lucette that everyone in the room has drawn closer, that they are all listening, and although a minute ago she felt warmed, enclosed by their questions, now she feels separated, offered up to Maureen Rivera's eager black eyes and her curving purple nails. She looks at Bev, but Bev only shrugs again, as if to say, get it over with so we can go.

"October thirty-first," she says. She is sure that this cannot be right.

One of the women laughs, a thin sound. "Ah," Maureen Rivera says, drawing it out. "An auspicious date. Let me see." She picks out a book and opens it on her lap, keeping it open with her palm, but she doesn't look at it. "I can tell you some things, I think." She looks at Lucette, into her eyes. "You want to know will this baby be a significant person, you want to know if this baby will have health, happiness, fame. Maybe if this baby will be a boy or a girl, it is possible I might tell you that."

She leans toward Lucette and takes one of her hands, Lucette feels the tips of the long, exquisitely manicured nails lightly scratching her skin.

"Or other things you might want to know, I can maybe tell you those, if you let me."

Lucette wants to pull her hand away, but everyone is looking at them, and she can't find the right moment to do it. Maureen Rivera has begun to look through her book, keeping hold of Lucette. Lucette is acutely aware of the coldness of Maureen Rivera's fingers, the heavy weight of the broad palm. To her horror, she feels her throat begin to ache, to close up, her face is hot, flushing, there is a pressure behind her eyes, and she is afraid she can feel the push of tears, any minute they will be running down her face.

"Isn't it bad luck to do an unborn baby's horoscope?" Bev says.

"What nonsense," Maureen Rivera says, not looking up from her book.

"No, I'm sure I heard that." Bev has pushed her way forward, to a place by the couch where Lucette is pinned by that hand. "Haven't you guys heard that?"

"Um, I don't know," Joan begins.

"It's up to you, Luce," Bev says. "But if it were me, I'd say, why take a chance?"

Maureen Rivera looks up at Bev, her black eyes small and opaque. "It's not you, though."

"Oh, come on," the mouthy woman in the back says. "I don't think she wants to do it anyway, do you, honey? Do mine instead."

"We will do yours next," Maureen Rivera says. She takes a firmer grip on Lucette's hand.

"What is all this bull? I came to have a good time. Do mine, or let's just forget it."

"Oh dear," Joan says, "oh dear, now what?" She picks up a brownie and puts the whole thing into her mouth.

Maureen Rivera digs her nails into Lucette's palm, then drops it onto the couch. "I'm a professional," she says, "I don't need this shit," and she begins to gather up her stuff. Joan flutters around her. The other women pretend not to watch these preparations for departure, quickly beginning half-a-dozen conversations.

Bev drops down onto the couch next to Lucette. "We'll go in a minute," she says into her ear.

As soon as Maureen Rivera goes out the door, they all begin to talk and laugh. "Wasn't she creepy?" Joan says. "Things went so bad, she'll never want me to give my own party, thank God."

"The T-shirts and all were nice," Shirley says, smoothing down her skirt, "but I don't hold with that other."

"You don't need to hear creepy stuff when you're pregnant, it's bad enough without that."

"I don't believe in it anyway."

"All this future business is not what you ought to be worrying about," Shirley says to Lucette. "You ought to be worrying about if you're drinking enough milk. You know, if you don't get enough calcium you can lose your teeth."

"Oh, that's an old wives' tale, Shirley," someone says, and they are all off again, with conflicting remedies, prescriptions, predictions. A girl if you're carrying high, low for a boy, the swinging-needle method, the glow you're supposed to have, swollen ankles and fingers too puffy to wear a ring, how you want to burn your maternity clothes, not being able to bend over, get out of a chair, lace your shoes, cut your toenails. The pain of labor you are supposed to forget, how you gather yourself up at the last, and then, having given your all, must give more. They sit back, exhausted, thinking about it.

"But it's worth it," Shirley says, and they all echo her, yes, it's worth it, when you hold that baby in your arms, you know what it was all for.

"Yeah, you'll love the brat, with that cute little baby face," the mouthy woman says. "At least until he's two and starts tearing the house apart. God save you from twins, honey."

In the car on the way home, Lucette feels as tired as if she has walked miles.

"Did they upset you, talking about eighteen-hour labor and all that?" Bev asks her.

"No," Lucette says, and the truth is that she is not upset, she has no feelings at all down where she is, the bottom of a hole, a deep well, black and airless, where she lies unmoving.

Step by step, Lucette advances down the central aisle of the greenhouse. She has a pair of scissors in her hand to snip dead leaves from the healthy plants. The air is moist and still, warm with yellow light, it smells of the geraniums she is trimming. It is nearly the end of May, and they are beginning to bloom, their small petals unfolding separately, the heavy heads drooping. She stops to watch a bee fly in one of the open panels in the roof, propped up earlier by James Gandy for ventilation. The bee flies in circles, confused by the profusion of flowers in endless crowded rows.

Lex has followed her, and looks up, interested in the bee for a minute. He yawns and Lucette yawns back, warm and drugged with hormones, with the light coming in, the moist gingery smell of the plants, the gold of the cat, the visible softness of his fur, his little witchy eyes. The hanging plants—purple verbena, thick green-leaved ivy, Chilean bridal veil—barely sway in the warm air; the tall stalks of lilies and the bouquet clusters of white, root-beer-scented viburnum quiver.

Lucette feels soft, her body like the modeling clay they used to play with in kindergarten that took the impressions of their fingers, even of the grain in the wood of their desktops. Every morning she goes to work, takes the mass of papers that appears overnight and channels them into their proper places: the filing cabinets, or the desks of her bosses, or large brown mailing envelopes. Every day she droops over her desk after lunch, not sleeping quite, but in a sort of waking trance from which she rouses herself to answer the phone or mediate between Witkowski the father and the Witkowski sons. Every afternoon she comes back to James Gandy's house and falls asleep on the couch in the long, empty dining room. Then she gets up and eats what James has cooked. He cooks all the dinners now, saying that she can do her share later, when she has gotten over the sleepy part of her pregnancy.

In the lengthening evenings she goes outside, sometimes to

work in the greenhouse, sometimes just to walk about the lawn or sit in one of the lawn chairs watching the sky. James will drift out to sit next to her, often with one of the baby books. When he finds something he thinks applies to her, he reads it out loud. It has barely gotten dark when she starts to feel sleepy again, her head, her eyes are heavy, and James closes his book with a clap and escorts her into the house and says good night as she goes up the steps. By ten she is in bed, sleeping deeply. Her very sleep seems to make her tired and heavy.

The only time she feels light is in the bathtub. She takes a long bath every night, no matter how tired she is, and then a quick one in the morning.

Lucette waves the bee away and it flies off down the rows of geraniums. She likes the humming quiet of the greenhouse, she likes to be there alone. James is always there with a book, a pillow, a glass of juice. He had sulked a little when she went to the doctor with Bev. He says now that he likes Bev, that she is "an antidote." When she comes over he leaves them alone, withdrawing after giving them plates of cookies and drinks, adjusting their chairs, their cushions, bringing Lucette a little Japanese parasol that used to be his mother's if the sun is in her eyes.

"Are you sure he's not gay?" Bev would say before she started in with whatever news there was. She always made sure she drove by Lucette's mother's house so she could tell Lucette that every-thing seemed to be all right.

"Did you leave the milk?" Lucette would ask. Bev bought half gallons of milk with the money Lucette gave her and left them in the old milk-delivery box by the side door. Lucette knew that her mother had enough of everything else for a long, long time, stacked up in rows in the cupboards in the side hall.

Bev would go on to talk about other news—a guy she'd met, someone from high school she'd seen in the supermarket, a bar they used to go to that was closing. She would never say anything about Harry, though, until Lucette asked her.

"Him," she'd say. *"He's* fine, I'm sure." And then maybe she would say that she had seen him at the Maple Leaf, or at a new bar. "I don't know what he's doing there," Bev would say, "besides drinking." She would concede that he appeared to be working behind the bar, to be in charge somehow. "Maybe he's managing it for Al's wife, that old witch." She would watch Lucette carefully while she talked about Harry, but she never asked if she still cared about him.

Sometimes Bev threatened to walk right up to Harry next time she saw him and tell him he was going to be a father—"drop it like a bomb in his lap." When she said this, Lucette felt a prickling on her arms and the back of her neck, a quickening of her breath. "Don't you dare," she would say, "don't you dare do that." After Bev was gone, she would sit in her chair, the images Bev had created dancing and jabbering in her mind, watching over and over how Bev confronts Harry and how he sobs or smiles or turns away, trying on how she might feel.

She walks further down the long aisle of the greenhouse, toward the door at the other end. At a certain point the geraniums give way to impatiens. James Gandy claims not to like impatiens. He only grows them for the trade, they are very popular right now. They have an essential triviality, he says, a mindless expansionism, perfect for the mindless gardener. But Lucette thinks the colors are nice. She likes the way the small plastic containers are illogically color-coded: a white slash of paint for white flowers, pink for pink; but green for coral flowers, blue for fuchsia. The color-coding is done by temporary workers James hires, high school boys who silently water and prune and pot, listening to their Walkmans.

It is so nice here, she thinks, like a house, with a roof, walls, a floor. But not like a house, for the walls and the roof are transparent, the floor is dirt. James has let vines grow up the south side, and when the wind blows, the leaves ruffle and slide over each other so that the wall seems to be moving. Tiny plants grow on the floor, refugee seeds that fell from the long potting tables and took root. There is a constant musical drip from the irrigation system. Birds and butterflies fly in through the door or one of the opened roof panels and flutter for a while above the long rows of flowers and green leaves before finding their way out. Long slow notes of classical music fall into the gold and green quiet from the sound system James installed to encourage the plants.

Lucette pauses to rub the velvety nap of a geranium, the scissors dangling from her other hand, feeling the trancelike state come over her, hardly aware of Lex prowling around her ankles. But as she stands there, starting to drift away, she hears the crunch of gravel by the door at the other side of the greenhouse. She turns, expecting James, but it's not James—with the sun shining through the door she can only see that it is a man, a tall man.

The scissors slide from her fingers. "Harry," she says, her voice barely getting past her lips. She knocks over the geranium she has been fingering, its opening bloom falling onto Lex, who yowls and shoots sideways. Lucette's eyes open wider to the dust-powdered sunlight, her lips part, her nostrils dilate, her fists unclench and she takes a step toward him.

"Lucette?" he says, his voice cracking and rising with the question. He steps forward, too, away from the glare, and in the cool green light that filters through the vines, she sees his young face red with razor burn, lanky arms and legs, his purple-and-green windbreaker.

"Ray." Lucette breathes out hard with the shock of it.

"You're not mad at me for coming, are you?"

Lucette shakes her head, unable to say anything.

"I know about everything," he says, coming farther in, "and it's cool. I know you're, you know, knocked up."

Lucette bends to pick up the scissors, and then holds them with the points to her other hand, testing their sharpness. "How do you know?"

"I heard Bev talking to Mom, asking her stuff."

Lucette nods, not surprised that Bev has told her mother.

Ray grins. "And I followed Bev a couple of weeks ago. I heard her talk to you on the phone and when she left I went after her. Just call me 007."

They both look at Lex, who is prowling between them, head cocked up at Ray as if waiting to be introduced. "But how—" Lucette begins.

"It was cool, Luce. I called up one of my buddies right away— don't worry, he doesn't know anything about you—and he came over and we waited in his car all slumped down and when Bev came out we just waited until she was up the street a little and we came along behind her. It was easy."

Lucette looks at him, unable to think of anything to say.

"Maybe I'll be a detective, what do you think?" He strikes a sinister pose. "Private Investigator Archacki. You can be my secretary, Luce, what do you think?" He picks up one of her hands and waggles the fingers. "Do your nails at your desk, like in the movies?"

She laughs, and pulls her hand away. "You're so weird."

He smiles, relieved, and takes her hand again. "You want to go somewhere?"

"Where?"

"Anywhere. I've got a car."

"Your buddy's?"

"No, it's Mom's. I'm supposed to be going grocery shopping. But I've got lots of time. That old guy's gone, isn't he?"

"How do you know?" she asks, letting him pull her down the aisle toward the door.

"The power of deduction, my dear." He taps his head and grins again. "I waited until I saw him leave and you alone in here. Are you excited to see me?"

Lucette shakes her head at him, but she is smiling.

"You're so excited you can't speak," he informs her. "I understand." He takes her hand and pulls it against his chest. "My heart, too, is like—full." He sticks his other hand inside his shirt and makes it hump up in the double thump of a heartbeat under her palm.

"Oh, shut up," Lucette says.

They agree to go for a ride first, and then Lucette will come along with Ray to the grocery store. "We'll go to the one on Ridge," Ray says, "and we won't see anyone we know." He points the car south on Big Creek Parkway and twitches in and out, changing lanes, nipping through yellow lights.

"You drive like Bev," Lucette says to him.

"I drive like Evel Knieval," Ray says. He sneaks a look over at her. "You don't look any different."

Lucette can feel the waistband of her jeans pushing into her stomach, and she sits up straighter.

"I thought you'd be fat." Ray reaches over and punches her arm. "But you look really fine, you look the same."

Lucette looks down at herself. It's true, she really is nearly the same. Ray stops at a traffic light. She looks at him until he senses her glance and turns.

"It shows with my clothes off," she says. She sees the corner of Ray's mouth turning up, one of his semi-lewd remarks coming, and she holds his eyes seriously until he looks away.

When they get to the end of the Parkway, where there is a lake with ducks in it, they get out of the car and go to stand by a wooden railing. Ray leans morosely on his elbows, making quacking noises to annoy the ducks. The small park is full of children chasing each other, throwing Frisbees, playing some game that involves tossing a football through the chains of the swings. There are a few couples walking with hands linked, their heads leaning toward each other. One of the women is pregnant. Lucette looks away when she notices her.

"Is school almost over?" she asks Ray.

"Yeah," he says, kicking the bottom rung of the fence.

"You going to the prom?"

"Nah. I figure I'll go next year when I'm a senior, but the junior prom is uncool."

"Couldn't get a date?"

"Hey," he protests, "I could have gone with Eddie Collins's girlfriend's best friend. He was going to fix me up."

"So what happened?"

"I just wasn't that interested. She was too big."

"What do you mean"—Lucette pokes him with her elbow—"too big?"

"I mean too big—she was a fucking Amazon." He holds a hand up to show how tall she was.

"Too much woman for you?"

"No way," Ray says, assuming a pose of dignity. "I just prefer my women more compact." He rubs his arm against Lucette's. "About five-six?"

"I'm too tall for you then, I guess," she says. "Five-seven."

"I can be flexible."

They watch the water dance in front of them. A fish leaps in a silver arc, almost too quick to see. "Did you catch that?" Ray yells. "Did you see that fish?" He grabs Lucette around her shoulders, as if with excitement, and shakes her. He takes his hand away slowly.

"We'd better go back if you're going to go shopping," she says.

At Finast, they push the oversized cart slowly up and down every aisle to jog Ray's memory, for he has lost his mother's list. They giggle over each selection. The things that they know are for Bev are particularly funny—her hair spray, her low-fat cottage cheese. They push the cart in turns, pointing out peculiarities in the shoppers surrounding them, all of whom seem terribly adult to them. Women weighted down with various sizes of children, old women with their permed hair carefully wrapped in chiffon scarves, old men leaning on the carts, their canes hooked over the handles, married couples deliberating over brands of tuna or frozen vegetables. They seem like citizens of another country.

In the checkout line, they bump up against each other and read the tabloid headlines in stifled whispers. "Listen," Ray says, "how about if you don't tell Bev."

"That you followed her?"

"Yeah." They watch his purchases roll down the conveyor belt to the waiting hands of the bagger. "I could come again. If you want."

They push their cart outside, and pause on the edge of the vast parking lot. "All right," Lucette says. "I guess."

When she lets herself in through the back door James is in the kitchen tearing lettuce for salad. "Where were you?" he says. "I went out to the greenhouse and found only the evil Lex prowling after birds."

"I just went for a ride," Lucette says. She picks up a peeled carrot and eats it in tiny bites, shaving off a half inch at a time with her teeth. "With Bev."

"You should have invited her in." He gives her a handful of raw green beans. "Here, that should hold you until dinner. I thought we'd eat outside. It's still so hot. And then, if you're not too tired, I have some interesting things to show you."

He looks at her secretively as he says this, and she knows he means something from the collection of clippings and statistics through which he documents and cross-references what he calls "synchronous happenings."

"Okay," she says. "I won't be too tired."

Lucette has found a knit top that, by accentuating her chest, makes her waist appear smaller, and she looks at herself in the three-way mirror, holding her arms up to get a good view. James is taking her out for dinner for her birthday, along with Bev and Helen and May. From the front the top looks fine, although her torso seems blocky, straight up and down. From the side, her stomach shows, protruding in a slight but unmistakable curve. She sucks it in. "How do I look?" she calls to Bev, who is sitting on Lucette's bed.

"Fine, I guess." Bev puts down a book on New Mexico and picks up one on breast-feeding. "Are you eating enough?"

Lucette turns to stare at her. "What do you mean?"

"You look sort of thin." Bev comes into the bathroom to get a better look.

"What do you mean, thin?" Lucette says, touching her stomach.

"Except for that. You're eating for two, you know."

"You sound like your mother."

"My mother never said anything like that in her life."

"Well, where'd you get it from?"

Bev doesn't answer. She sits down on the edge of the tub and fingers one of the candles, and then picks up the soap and sniffs it.

"Lily of the valley," Lucette says. "What's the matter with you?"

"Nothing."

Lucette returns to her reflection. "You don't have to go if you don't want to."

"You didn't ask about your mother."

"So how is she?"

"My mother went to see her. She's okay."

"What'd she do that for?"

Bev picks up the soap again and holds it to her nose. "She just thought she would."

"You told your mother about me, didn't you?" Lucette's face is stiff in the mirror.

"What if I did?" Bev leaps up off the edge of the bathtub. "Why shouldn't I? I felt like I needed some advice, okay?"

"What do you need to talk to somebody else for? What about me?" Lucette throws down her hairbrush. "It's my baby. It's me that's losing my hair. It's me that's sick."

"You look fine to me."

"What do you know?"

Bev sits down again, and Lucette picks up the brush and passes it over her hair a few more times. "So, do you still want to go out to dinner?"

"I guess." Bev fidgets, drawing one leg up to lie along the length of the tub edge, wiggling around on the hard porcelain. "You didn't ask if I bought milk for your mother."

"So, did you?"

"Yes, I did."

"Wonderful."

"Jeez!" Bev explodes, jumping up again.

Lucette turns to look at her, eyebrows raised.

"All right, here it is," Bev says. "I've put up with a lot from you, but now . . . I want to be there for you, but—I don't know."

"What do you mean, you've put up with a lot from me?"

"Only since we were in sophomore year, only since you went limp on me."

Lucette starts brushing her hair again, trying to calm herself, to breathe. The words "sophomore year" bring with them long halls, beige, echoing, herself walking through them in an envelope of silence. "There were reasons," she finally says.

"Everybody has reasons."

Lucette looks at herself in the mirror, watching her lips form the words. "My father *died.*"

"Nobody's life is perfect."

"What would you know about that?"

"My life is not perfect."

Lucette throws the brush down, it clatters on the tile floor. She is trembling, her love for Bev's life rushing over her—their house warm with yellow light, the fullness of it, mother, father, daughter, the extra padding of two brothers, Bev in her own room with the twin bed for guests, her closet full of clothes picked out by her mother, paid for by her father, the kitchen with dishes closed away in cupboards, the boots and shoes in a jumble on the newspaper put down in the back hall.

"How can you say that to me?" Lucette says. "How can you?"

Bev has started to cry. "And he was your *step*father, anyway. Your stepfather." She runs out and starts down the stairs, going so quickly she seems to fly.

"He was my *father,*" Lucette screams after her. She sits down on the top step, breathing hard. She hears the questioning tones of James Gandy's voice and Bev's voice, quick and light, answering. She waits for the slam of a door, but nothing comes. She gets up and goes back into the bathroom and looks at herself in the big mirror. She pulls the purple knit top down again, stretching it over her hip bones, and brushes her bangs once more. She doesn't hear the door opening and closing or Bev's car starting up and pulling out.

When she goes downstairs, Bev is standing in the front hall with James, looking at the floor. "I have very strong feelings about harsh words. Some people find me ridiculous, I know," James says. "But how damaging such words are. For everyone. Everyone in the immediate vicinity."

He takes Lucette's hand, and Bev's. "You're friends, aren't you?" He shakes his head. "What if Bev went out the door and drove into a car accident? What if Lucette had an aneurysm?—it happens. Even as young as you are. How would you feel? How would I feel if I let this pass and you were forever separated in this life?" He brings their hands together and waits for them to look at each other, which they do, finally.

"Now," he says, "can we be nice with each other? Can we go out? What about it?"

In the car, James tells them about the restaurant where they are going to celebrate Lucette's nineteenth birthday. "It's May and Helen's favorite restaurant, the Olde Country Buffet. Have you ever been there, Bev?"

"No." Bev is clicking and unclicking her seatbelt in the back seat.

"It's an experience, believe me. The food is good except for the vegetables. They're like one's grandmother's, the life cooked out of them. That's what the whole thing is, like going over to your grandmother's house for dinner, the smell of food cooking, a crowd of people. Except that there's classical music piped in. My grandmother hated any kind of music except polkas and 'Ave Maria.' " He looks over at Lucette, who is sitting straight-spined, her head turned toward the side window, and then back at Bev, who is slouching down in the back.

Lucette feels James's wish to make them smile and talk, to bring them together, feels it pushing against Bev's obstinacy and her own resentment. She feels such coldness toward Bev, she doesn't understand herself. She is tired of waiting, tired of living inside her head. She lets the front yards, traffic lights, high blue sky, sun winking in and out between the trees slide by and sets herself to think of something else, to take herself out of this car, away from James and Bev and their emotions. She thinks about the times she has seen Ray as if she is remembering a vacation.

The last time she saw him was yesterday. She closes her eyes and replays it against their dark screen, first shadows, angles, and lines, a kind of mental blueprint for the flesh and light of Ray's face when he turned it to her on the new roller coaster at Cedar Point, screeching with delight. And then, as she goes farther, the scene takes on color and depth. He had cheap tickets because it was the day his school was going to Cedar Point, and he had offered one to her hesitantly, in case she was worried about running into someone.

They were in the habit of riding in the car when they went out, sometimes stopping at out-of-the-way fast-food places for something to drink, sometimes going to movies in the crowded pastel malls of the far suburbs, the foreign parts of Cleveland where no one they knew ever went. But Cedar Point seemed safe, far away. "Who would we see?" she said. "Who cares?"

She had taken the day off from work, telling old man Witkowski that she had a doctor's appointment. The whole question of her condition embarrassed him, she knew he wouldn't ask further.

Ray picked her up at the bus stop on the corner of James's street. The sky was gray, high thin clouds with long jagged rents showing blue spaces stretched longer and thinner with the wind. The wind pushed the car around on the highway as well, even Mrs. Archacki's big old Buick. For a while Lucette sat stiffly within her seatbelt, holding herself against the shocks of the wind. But eventually she relaxed, and as they began to drive through country— cows grazing, long rows of tiny corn plants—she fell asleep, her head nodding against the headrest, and slept until they slid to a stop in the parking lot and Ray shook her, looking into her face intently to see if she was awake.

It hadn't been any different from other times she went to Cedar Point. There were the same rides, the same long waits in straggling switchback lines in the sun, the same strange intimacy with the person who stood in line with you, the two of you isolated in the chattering, jiggling crowd, a still spot where you were looking at each other, waiting your turn. And the rides themselves, even the new ones, the same swoosh and slide, the screams, the spinning sky overhead, the same helpless fall against each other's bodies. Ray had been afraid that she would be affected by the fiercer rides, that she would feel sick, but if she felt any twinges at all they were submerged in the flying, pounding, twisting, turning motions of her body as it conformed to the parabolas and high curves of the rides.

They had ridden the new roller coaster eleven times. The last few times she felt giddy and high, as if she might take flight at the top of the first, biggest hill, the restraining harness bursting away from her as she rode into the sky. They stayed later than they had meant to, so that she had to call James Gandy and tell him she was meeting Bev for dinner. They wandered around the park as the lights were coming on against the clear dark blue of the sky, red and green and pink neon lighting their faces and their hair. On the way home she had slept again, without the seatbelt on, half lying across the big front seat, the top of her head just touching the side of Ray's leg.

Now in James's car she touches her hair, thinking of all that, as they pull into May and Helen's driveway. May is waiting for them on the front steps, wearing a dress, white printed with bunches of violets scattered across it, each bunch tied with a curling pink ribbon. She says that Helen is coming with the mailman. Lucette gets into the back seat with Bev, letting May have the front seat next to James. "Thank you, sweetie," May says. "So what do you think about Helen and the mailman, James?"

"I wasn't surprised."

"Oh, you, you're never surprised." She turns to the girls in the back. "He won't allow himself to be, I believe."

"Put your seatbelt on, May."

"But, James," she says, "what about my karma? Maybe I'm supposed to die being thrown right out of this car." She laughs, but when James clicks the seatbelt button at her she takes it and puts it on. "Now, tell me, Lucette, how are you? And who is this?"

Lucette introduces Bev, not looking at her.

May bounces in her seat a little. "I'm very pleased to meet you. Isn't this wonderful? Going out with these beautiful children? I feel almost parental, if you will allow me, James?"

"Certainly I will allow you," James says, turning the car smoothly. They proceed east along Snow Road.

They meet Helen and the mailman at the entrance to the restaurant, and go in together, to wait in a line that seems long to Lucette, although May and Helen exclaim at its relative shortness, compared to other times they have been there. Helen picks up a bunch of tiny printed menus that show what will be served on all the days of the week and passes them out to the others. "Roast beef, ham, barbecued ribs, breaded fish, macaroni and cheese," Lucette reads. "Mashed potatoes, corn on the cob, beef-vegetable soup, cornbread, iced pecan rolls. Various desserts."

"This will be very good for you," May says to Lucette. "You'll be able to get all your food groups."

Helen has introduced her friend the mailman as Mr. Stephen Hamm, May trying to catch Lucette's eye and make her laugh. When they have moved down the line a bit, she leans over to Bev and whispers that she could never go out with a man named Hamm.

"Why?" Bev whispers.

"Oh, I just couldn't," May says aloud, and laughs.

Lucette looks over the half wall separating the line from the diners at the splendors of the Olde Country Buffet, its long steam tables of food, its skinny, perky servers, its pink-and-gold decor. There are two lines of people moving along either side of the heaped-up mounds of food, they bunch together and then slide apart like beads loose on a string. At the end of the steam tables there is a boy in a tall chef's hat standing over an enormous hunk of roast beef and another of ham, dexterously cutting steaming slices on request. When they reach the cash register, James pays, and they join the lines in front of them. Each of them takes a tray and silverware. Lucette takes a plate, but May nudges her. "Take two," she says. "One for salad, one for the rest. See?" And when Lucette looks, she sees that all those ahead of her have two plates on their trays.

"Look at that guy," Bev says to her, pointing to one of the employees who is keeping the mounds of food at their mountainous height. "Doesn't he look like Ray?"

He does, a little, the way his hair falls across his forehead, and Lucette is about to say so. But her antagonism toward Bev is still there, she is holding onto it. "I can't see it," she says.

"Who's Ray?" Helen asks from the other side of the steam tables.

"My dumb brother," Bev says. "A real goon."

Lucette takes some salad and some beets, and then, pressed by May, some Waldorf salad. There are two steaming wells filled with soup, but she passes these by. Then there is a series of long, deep trays over a reservoir of steaming water: green beans cut French-style, mashed potatoes swirled like icing, lima beans in tomato-red sauce, corn on extremely regular cobs. She takes a dollop of mashed potatoes and a small pile of beans. She slides one piece of baked fish onto her plate and lets May talk her into one scoop of macaroni and cheese. When she gets to the kid in the chef's hat, she asks for one slice of roast beef, although Helen urges her to try the ham as well.

"The ham!" May whispers. "She wants you to try the ham!"

James, ahead of them, is waving, he has commandeered one of the servers to put two tables together for them. "You can get dessert later," Helen says.

"And you can come back as many times as you want." May looks contemplatively at her own two plates, piled six inches high. "I never can make it past twice, though."

At the table they all exclaim over the smallness of Lucette's portions. She says she just likes to try out a bit of things first and then go back when she knows what she likes. She picks up a piece of salad with her fork and puts it into her mouth.

Bev, across the table, is staring at the family next to them, and catching Lucette's eye at last, she jerks her head, pointing them out so that Lucette will see, too. There are nine of them—a wife and husband, a grandmother, another adult who looks as if she is the wife's sister, and five children—everyone except two of these people is grossly overweight, eating as if in preparation for a famine. The two thin ones, one of the children and the wife's sister, have as much on their plates as the others, as if they hope to catch up. Bev rolls her eyes at Lucette, smiling, but Lucette can't smile back.

She sees the food on her plate as a duty, something that is outside her that must go in, fuel to keep going, propel her body over the roads, through the houses of the world. When she picks up a sliver of green bean it seems momentous, charged with responsibility. When she puts it in her mouth it is tasteless, no amount of spice could make her taste it.

"You know what I like about it here?" May asks, shoring up her mashed potatoes so that the gravy doesn't run into her salad.

They all look at her, waiting.

"The bread pudding," she says. "Wait till you taste it."

"May has always been a great dessert eater," Helen tells the mailman. "I've never cared for it myself, except maybe a piece of cherry pie now and again."

"That's her way of reminding you all that she's thin and I'm not." May pats her stomach. "I've stopped worrying about whether I'm a figure of fashion or not."

"You are beyond fashion, May," James says, holding his fork suspended, loaded with a chunk of roast beef swathed in mashed potatoes and gravy. "I have always found you most attractive."

"Oh, James, that is so nice of you to say when I know what store you set by telling the truth." May smooths her hands down the skirt of her dress.

"Every word is gospel."

"I like your dress," Bev says. "Those violets."

May whirls away toward the dessert table, her skirt fluttering.

"Still, she eats too much saturated fat. I wish you'd give her a copy of that diet you were telling me about," Helen says to the mailman. "I know what you think about diets"—she waves her hand at James—"don't even bother to say it."

He inclines his head, his mouth full.

"James believes that the body knows what it wants, and that you should listen to it," she says to the mailman and Bev.

"If your body wants beets, you must eat beets," James says. "If you crave chocolate cake, then, by all means, eat chocolate cake."

"I've heard that pregnant women sometimes eat dirt," the mailman says, smiling.

"Gross," Bev says.

"Oh, Stephen, surely not?" Helen says, holding her hand in front of her mouth like a fan.

"It's a fact," James says. "A phenomenon known as 'pica.' A craving that is a result of mineral deficiencies. Imagine, Lucette, going out into the garden and cutting yourself a nice slice of dirt."

Helen shudders delicately, and Lucette takes a tiny bite of macaroni and cheese. It has a comforting stodgy feel on her tongue and she takes a larger bite, filling her mouth. She sees Bev look up, her eyebrows rising, and at the same time, a hand falls on her shoulder.

"Is that Lucette Harmon?"

She turns around, her mouth full, and sees Mr. Abruzzi standing over her. She has never seen him anyplace except the drugstore, and for a minute she doesn't recognize him. He is dressed differently, too. Instead of the pastel short-sleeved shirt, the tie, and the dark pants he always wore in the store, he has on a red-and-green-striped rugby shirt and shorts, baggy around his thin legs that are

furred with dark hair. She touches her purse. Does she have everything? Can she leave right now?

"Lucette," he says, hopping nervously from one foot to the
other, "I'm overwhelmed."

Lucette swallows the rest of the macaroni, and breathes deeply.
Bev is looking quizzical, Helen inquiring, James inscrutable. The
mailman is smiling, pulling on his tie. Her terror subsides, there is
nothing he can do to her.

"Introduce me, Luce," he says, his hand still on her shoulder.
She shrugs it off. He is looking at James and the others with a slight
smile that she imagines is contemptuous.

"These are friends," she says, determined not to say their names,
feeling defiant and protective, sitting in the midst of this rag-tag
group of old people.

"I remember you," he says to Bev.

"I don't think I've had the pleasure," Bev says, giving him her
drop-dead-you-creep smile.

"You used to come into the store and go out to lunch with
Lucette," he insists.

"I guess I don't remember," Bev says.

"So," he says, giving up on her, "what's new, Luce?"

Lucette's hand moves to cover her stomach, she sits up
straighter. "Nothing."

"That's my Luce," Mr. Abruzzi says. "Tight as an oyster."

May comes back with two bowls of bread pudding, one with ice
cream on top and one without. She puts them down on the table,
notices the new arrival. "And who is this?" she asks, smiling
flirtatiously.

He rounds the table in a flash, takes her hand. "Vincent Abruzzi.
A former admirer of Lucette's," he says, sending Lucette a lan-
guishing, sidelong glance.

"May Skrovan, if you please." May holds her wrist at such an
angle, they seem as if they are about to dance. They all look at
Lucette.

Bev seems to be having trouble with her face, she holds her napkin over her mouth. Lucette realizes what they are thinking, James and Helen and May, and she is angry at Bev again, for finding it funny. She stands up abruptly. "It was nice to see you, Mr. Abruzzi."

"But Luce, after all this time." He drops May's hand. "Listen, can't we talk a minute?"

"Oh, all right."

Lucette drops her napkin on her chair, and as they move away from James and the others, he grips her arm above the elbow in the nervous, grabby way she remembers.

"You're so uptight, you must be straight," Lucette says. "Did you miss your fix?"

"High on life, Luce."

"Nice shorts."

He draws her over to the alcove where the coatrack is. "But Luce, what are you doing here with all those old people?"

"Friends, I told you." She looks at his clothes, their rather careful coordination, the color of the shorts a lighter shade of the green in the shirt—gift clothes, worn to please someone. "And who are you with?"

He blinks and blushes, dark red coming up under his olive skin, unexpectedly attractive. "My mother." He glances over at the window where a tiny woman sits perched in a booth, her dark eyes fixed on her son.

"What'd you say to her about me?" Lucette watches as he fumbles with his reply.

"I told her, a former employee—"

"Don't you want to introduce me?"

He looks at her uncertainly.

"Did you know I'm going to have a baby?" She pushes out her stomach a little and watches with satisfaction as he blushes again. "Aren't you glad we never went out? I might have said you were the father."

He shuffles his skinny legs, looking over at his mother. She is eating something with small, quick bites, her eyes still fixed on them. "I'm not like that, Luce."

"That's right." May and Bev are waving for her to come back. "All talk, no action. I've got to go."

"Is that why you left? Have you got a job?"

"I've got a job."

"Well . . . " He looks at her, his cheeks drooping.

Lucette feels a wave of longing, suddenly she wishes very much to go with him, back into the safe boredom of her old life. "Go on," she says. "If you're sure you don't want to introduce me to your mother." She smiles at him, a nice smile, full power. "Doesn't she want grandchildren? Or do they have to be Italian?" She gives him a push, her open palm on his chest, the first time she has ever touched him, she thinks, and sees from his face that he is thinking this too.

He grins back at her. "Yeah, they have to be Italian."

Back at the table, they have a surprise for her birthday. Not a cake, they don't have birthday cakes at the Olde Country Buffet. But May and Helen have produced from their purses candles and candle holders, pink and blue and yellow, and they have stuck them into a flock of cake squares from the dessert table. All the candles are lit. "Not nineteen pieces," Helen says, "that would be wasteful." There are nineteen candles, though, two or three of them to a piece. Lucette's piece has the most candles, five. They sing "Happy Birthday" to her, James in a resonant baritone, the rest in thin piping self-conscious voices, aware of the amused eyes of the other diners.

Eating her cake, which is bright pink with confetti flecks of chocolate, Lucette concentrates on Ray. She will be seeing him tomorrow, or maybe the next day. He will be the same as he always is, she thinks. She can depend on him.

· · ·

Bev has parked her car in a doctor's space, she goes toward it with total confidence, swinging her purse. "What did he say about your not gaining weight?"

"He didn't say anything. And I have gained weight."

"I can't see it."

"You told me yourself that your mother only gained fourteen pounds with you."

"That was because her doctor bullied her. Now they say you should gain twenty or more pounds. She asked me if you were wearing maternity clothes yet. I hate to think what she'd say if she saw you."

"You're getting boring, Bev."

Bev puts on her sunglasses and pulls out, her arm cocked out the window. "Where were you when I called you last night?"

"Last night?" Lucette studies one of the pamphlets that the nurse gave her on the way out.

"James said you were in the greenhouse, and then he came back and said you must be out for a walk."

"Don't go down Twenty-fifth."

"All right, all right." Bev goes straight on Trowbridge to make a wide circle around their old neighborhood. "You don't like to go for walks, Luce."

"I was sort of bored."

"You haven't seen Harry, have you?"

"Harry?" Lucette turns her whole body around in the seat to look at Bev. "I would have told you if I'd seen Harry." She feels her face getting hot, though, as if she is guilty.

Bev pulls into their old McDonald's. "I don't know if you would have. I feel like you're not telling me stuff."

Lucette doesn't know how to answer. Not telling Bev things, not telling her about Ray, that is not so bad. But actually lying to her? She imagines saying that she has only been with Ray, very casually: Well, I've been hanging out with Ray. It was no big deal.

What would Bev say? First she'd be mad because Lucette would

rather be with Ray than with her. And then she'd want to know
why. She would look at Lucette as if she is crazy—Ray? that goof?
Lucette wants to keep them separate.

She can't explain to Bev how she feels safe with Ray. She can't
explain why they have kept it secret. At first it was because Ray
had followed Bev, had spied on her when she was talking on the
telephone, things Bev hated. It seemed that this was all they were
agreeing to keep from her, these small betrayals. But after a while,
after Ray had come again, twice, three times, it became clear that
the whole thing was to be secret from Bev.

"Is it James? Is there something about James you're not saying?"
Bev says.

"God, no," Lucette says. "How do you mean?"

"I don't know what I mean." Bev opens her door and gets out.
"I just know something's going on." She looks at Lucette across
the top of the car.

Lucette shrugs. "I don't know what you're talking about."

"I guess I can't make you tell me."

When Bev drops her off at work after lunch, Lucette is listless.
The sun coming through the grimy office windows is irritating, the
hum of the air conditioner makes it hard to think.

Lucette pushes aside the pile of folders she has been cross-filing,
and puts her head on her arms. She wishes she could sleep, wishes
that she felt as she did earlier in her pregnancy when she walked
through the days in a sleepy haze. But that has passed, and she is
wide awake now. With her eyes closed, she tries to imagine herself
into happiness as she used to when she was in high school, falling
in love with boys who ignored her. It was very important then to
think up real situations where the miraculous meeting might take
place, every detail had to be right, no cheating. The motivations
had to be right, too. And she didn't allow herself to make physical
or personality changes, to give herself a better body, for instance,
or make herself wittier.

She remembered how she used to do it, sometimes lying in her
old bedroom in the dark, the sound of her mother's TV between

her and sleep, too low to hear what was being said, too loud to ignore. Or sitting at her desk in school, head propped up on one palm, pencil in hand but lax and unmoving. She would open that door in her head and walk in. It was a world as much like her own as she could make it, but darker, as if somewhere the blinds were drawn too far down. In there, she could work things out. Not easily—for there were problems to overcome, difficulties just as in life—but if she took her time, she would think of something. Sometimes she believed that she could influence the course of events if she concentrated hard enough, if she paid enough attention to detail—the exact shade of his hair, the precise placement of her hand.

But now, opening that door, she waits for the familiar rooms and streets to form around her, and as they do, waits to think of what will make her happy, so that she can arrange what will happen, what will draw it to her. What will it be, what does she need?

"Lucette." It's old Mr. Witkowski, and she is glad it's him instead of his son who has caught her drowsing over her desk.

"What?" she says, and then realizing that this doesn't sound enough like an employee answering her boss, "Anything I can do for you?"

"It's time to go home," he says. He glances down at her stomach as he always does. "I hope you're getting enough rest."

Lucette flushes and begins to make an excuse, but he waves his hand at her, and she sees that he wasn't criticizing, only expressing concern. "I'm fine," she says. "Really."

He stands there, the sun shining through his wispy white hair, visibly trying to think of something to say, his lips moving, making little clicks and chirps of sound. "Well," he says. "That's fine. Tell James I sent my regards."

"I will."

"He's a fine man." He hesitates. "In spite of . . ." he trails off, his lips working again. "We've always gotten along."

Lucette gets up and sidles past old Mr. Witkowski, who is still standing there as if he has more to say. But when she waits at the door, he only waves his hand, dismissing her.

Outside, the air is stunningly hot, the sun like a blow to the head. There is no breeze in the bus shelter, but out of its shade she feels dizzy, too tightly bound inside her clothes. On the bus it is even hotter. The air conditioning isn't working, and the driver has opened the square panel in the roof. Illegally, he leaves the door ajar between stops, but the air inside is undisturbed, a hot, damp, unmoving mass. Although this is a different bus than the one that took her home from her old job at the drugstore, the people could be the same, the same old men with empty hands, the same old women counting their numerous bags and paper-wrapped parcels, the same bored teenagers writing furtively on the seats and side panels. The bus driver is whistling, but he can't possibly be cheerful, driving this lumbering thing all day laden with these sick, unhappy people, just out of reach of cooler air. Lucette finds a seat at the back and sits there swaying with the movement of the bus like a limp underwater plant.

As she walks the long stretch of sidewalk from the bus stop to James Gandy's house she swallows her feelings, but each heavy footstep makes her more miserable.

"I prescribe limeade," James says to her. "Limeade out on the back porch where there is a small breeze."

He takes her purse, hands her a round paper fan, pushes her toward one of the Adirondack chairs. She lets her head fall back against the upright wooden slats and listens to the clinking sound of a spoon against glass as James mixes fresh-squeezed lime juice with water and sugar. The limeade is cloudy, swirling with bits of lime pulp that cling to the ice cubes like lint, but she drinks it anyway, almost in one gulp, and he pours her another.

"The greenhouse was like a sauna bath when I turned on the sprinklers. Lex would not accompany me, he's run off someplace."

"Smart cat," Lucette says, letting her arms and legs spread out, limp.

"It's not even summer, not until Friday. Not that the calendar has anything to do with the weather, necessarily." James pours himself a glass of limeade and sits down heavily on the old glider.

The back porch is screened in, and the light coming through the screens is darkened, broken up, so that there is the illusion of a cool dimness. The hulking old pine trees at the side of the house sift the small breeze through their branches and magnify the sound of it, a cool whirring. Lucette closes her eyes.

"So what did the doctor have to say?"

"Nothing."

"Nothing?"

"He never says anything much." Each time she goes to see him, the doctor looks at her chart—to see what, Lucette doesn't know—and asks her how she feels and she says she feels fine and he asks her if there are any problems and she says no and that's it.

"And you say he's Swedish?"

"Yes."

"Not, of course that I have any great recognition for differences of nationality."

"No." Lucette rolls her head back and forth slowly, feeling the alternate pressure of the wooden slats against the bones of her skull.

"But it's interesting that you have a foreign doctor who is yet not Indian or Filipino. Of sociological interest. And what about work?"

"Oh—" Lucette opens her eyes. "Mr. Witkowski said to give you his regards."

"How are they all getting along, the Witkowskis?"

"They argue all the time unless they're not speaking."

"A very nice illustration of the battle between the generations, the father and sons competing for that scarce resource, power." James shakes his big head, looking ruminatively at the ground. "I can't say that I was immune to it myself. Of course, that was some time ago, before everything else."

Lucette half closes her eyes, thinking that this sounds like the beginning of one of James's rambling speeches, and she waits to see what he will say, willing to let the rise and fall of his words put her into a restful trance. With her lids lowered, the greens of the lawn and trees run together a little, and the massed colors of the flowers chase each other across them. The sound of cars on Schaaf Road is very low, a buzz no louder than that of the bees weaving in and out of the blood-red spires of the hollyhocks at the corner of the porch. She is sleepy, her misery still present, but banked down under the soft color and sound of the afternoon.

But James doesn't say anything more, and eventually she opens her eyes and looks over at him. He is still sitting on the glider, hands clasped between his knees. Lucette wants to ask what he is thinking. "Bev said to say hello," she says instead.

"Did she? How nice." James lifts his head as if it is a great weight. "More limeade?"

"No," Lucette says. She watches James through her half-closed eyes.

"Did I ever tell you, Lucette," James begins, and then stops.

She opens her eyes and continues to watch him while he thinks, his pink face immobile, skeins of thought sliding across it.

"Did I ever tell you about this whole thing I have apprehended about the mechanics of sexual selection, et cetera?"

"No." Lucette stays limp, her legs splayed out, but each limb is suddenly rigid, maintained in position by a fine nervous tension.

"There is this network, this structure of perception I was given to see." He hesitates, then plunges on. "All of it, the unconscious strategies of youth, their affinity for the methods of sexual display, makeup, the arrangement of the hair, how it is necessary to sneer at old people from cars, that disgust—you can see it raw in Bev or boys in rock bands—a repulsion for all that is old and physically corrupt."

He stops, takes his handkerchief from his pocket, and wipes his forehead and upper lip. "I'm not saying it's absolutely a bad thing, you understand. How can anyone wish to repress the desires of teenagers for sex, and all that goes with it?—it's so pure, so fated. Anyway, what I'm saying is that I can see all this, it was a gift I couldn't reject. I tried, I could see that it would make me maybe crazy and socially unfit. Why should I have to know these things? To see the whole plan of the world unrolled before me like a map or a diagram of the soul, what they call programming, how certain things are meant to happen, biologically, evolutionarily, race survival, the destiny of the body. And then why this regret when that part is over? Outliving your usefulness, the body not meant to live past forty, the race still unprepared for its unexpected longevity."

He shakes his head, still not looking at Lucette. "The body hangs on like someone at the end of the party that you wish would go home—doesn't know what to do with itself—the mind, the emotions are looking ahead to dissolution, there are tears, yearning, a desperate scramble for power or love, anything to replace the disappearing physical imperative that gave shape and purpose to every waking, every sight and scent, every movement of blood, every breath.

"I couldn't refuse to know it. But it made it impossible for me to participate. I knew too much."

Lucette feels her face burning. She, too, has lowered her head, is looking at the wide gray boards of the porch floor. James has stopped talking, seems to be waiting for her response. "So?" she says.

"I thought that was the purpose of it, the knowing—to be a repository of knowledge. The point being that someone had to know and that that someone had to be on the outside. But now I think possibly that there is to be something else."

Inexplicably, Lucette vividly remembers sitting in a classroom when she was fifteen and listening to a priest who had come in to lecture her Christian Marriage and Family Living class on premarital sex. The regular teacher, Sister Jane Gabriel, sat to one side in a straight chair, hands clasped on her knees, and the priest lounged on her desk and outlined the case against sex before marriage, anticipating all objections, since questions were not encouraged.

"Some of you may be wondering if we are not supposed to engage in, ahmmm, sex before we take our nuptial vows, why we reach maturity somewhat earlier than the usual age for marriage."

He paused, to allow them to entertain this doubt. "God in his wisdom has allowed this lapse of time for a purpose, as always. This period is meant to be a period of waiting, of learning. You mature early, that is, become, ahmm, pubescent, so that you have this time in which you can contemplate the possibility of the celibate life, a life without, ahmm, sex. Which it would be so hard to do," he says, smiling and nodding at the nun, "if we were thrust immediately into the thick of it, into the necessity of the, ahhmm, marriage bed."

Lucette sits up, her head buzzing. She runs her tongue over her dry lips. "Did I ever tell you about this priest we had in my Christian Marriage and Family Living class?" she asks him, and then is horrified to have said "marriage," "family."

But James pays no attention. He gets up from the glider. "I admit I didn't realize it at first. When you came I only saw you as a friend, another traveler in the world. Maybe, selfishly, as a listening ear, someone young, without a hardened net of preconceived ideas. And I thought I could be a help to you as well." He looks back at her briefly. "Forgive me for spelling all this out, but I feel I need to. I thought I would be a father figure, a substitute for a lover, who would not demand or trouble. However, I was quite wrong." He sighs. "I've constructed this life at some cost, and I thought I was settled in it. You'd think I would have learned that one thing by now—the mutability of all things."

He turns around and looks at Lucette. "I'm explaining this all wrong."

"It's very interesting." Lucette is no longer hot, she has gone prickly cold all over. Her fingers seek something, a cigarette, she realizes, after all these weeks.

"Another man would have been thinking more pragmatically," James says in a musing tone. "That's one of my faults, to be caught in the theoretical realm." He cocks his head, terrifying Lucette with his smile. "Maybe I ought to explain what happened to me? Maybe I ought to start there?"

"Oh, no, really, it's okay," Lucette says. She cannot bear it if now he begins the story of how he was taken up in a space ship, although she has wished many times in the past that he would tell her.

"Too far back?" He taps his fingers against the screen that separates him from the hollyhocks. "Ancient history. I don't want to bore you with all that." He stands, head bent, silent.

Lucette thinks wildly what she can do to prevent him from going on. She could get up and leave, but somehow she can't make herself do this. Inconveniently, the baby begins to move in her, and she is amazed, under everything else, how comforting this wavery slippery motion can be. But she puts this away to think about later. Now she concentrates on James, willing him not to go on, thinking she can drop her glass, one of James's mother's cut-glass water goblets, and surely this will distract him, or she might begin to cry, or say that she feels a pain in her stomach. She sits up tensely in her chair, bracing herself on its wide flat arms.

"You're very young, Lucette," James says, as if this is a new fact to him. "I know, of course, that youth doesn't equal stupidity." He looks to her for agreement, and she nods stiffly. "But when one is young, one tends to treat events as adversaries, to fight and put up barriers against what is happening, to you and around you. This is one of the most useful things I've learned—although as you see, I am still learning it—that events occur and we must turn to them, move with them, greet them, so to speak. That what takes place is meant, not in the sense of fate so much, but in a larger philosoph-ical sense. An event happens, so it is a fact. Before it happens, that event is as improbable as anything else. But afterward, it is inevitable."

"Do you mean free will?"

"Not at all. This is about events, not about our actions. Al-though, of course, our actions become events after they take place." James resumes his tapping of the screen, disturbing the bees crawling into the open flowers of the hollyhock. He laughs. "This is ridiculous. I'm getting too abstract. I only mean to say that I can see now that your coming, your future baby, that this was brought to me for a reason, that I have to respond to it, that I am just the right person to respond to it. That's what I mean to say. That I am here, in this place, at this time, for this baby."

"I don't know what you mean," Lucette says.

"Just that. I'm here."

"You mean," Lucette pauses, swallows, wipes her damp forehead with the backs of her fingers, "that we should get married?"

"Marriage?" James laughs. "Oh, dear Lucette, no, not that. I'm not such a fool. I'm saying that you came here because there was a place for you and for this baby. That's all. This house, so large, so empty. Myself, so useless. Your need. The baby arriving like a comet. These things have come together."

Lucette says nothing. With one hand on her stomach, she waits to see if he will say more.

But it appears he is finished. He takes a deep breath, as if he has been running. "We don't have to talk about this any more. You'll want to be thinking about how we will arrange things." He turns and goes to the door that leads out to the terrace. His hand on the knob, he turns, "You must know, of course, that, in all this, I consider you to be totally free. You understand?"

"Yes," Lucette says.

"Good." He goes out the door and across the terrace to the lawn, to disappear into the nearest greenhouse.

When he has gone, Lucette goes limp again and begins to sweat, to feel the heat. She thinks with longing of her jade-green bathtub, of the cool, green-tinged air of her bathroom, but her legs are too weak to take her there.

"Mom thinks I've got a girlfriend," Ray says to her the next day.

"Who?" Lucette rubs her fingers over the old seat cover, feeling relief to have finished work, to be in the car with Ray, driving. Driving away from all of them, she thinks.

"You."

"What does that mean?"

"Don't get excited. I just mean because of borrowing the car all the time. She put two and two together and got E equals MC squared. She thinks it's cute."

"What does Bev think?" Lucette says.

"She doesn't think anything. You know she doesn't care what I do as long as I keep out of her way. We're made in the shade." Ray snaps his fingers. "So what do you want to do? I've got to pick up bread and bananas and some other stuff, that was the price for taking the car."

"Listen, Ray, how about if you let me take the car for a little while. I could drop you off to do the shopping and then pick you up and then we can go someplace else."

"I don't mind taking you. Where do you have to go?"

"It would save time, though, if I did it while you were at the store."

"We've got plenty of time. I don't have to go to work until ten tomorrow."

"Hey, you need your sleep," Lucette says, lightly punching him in the shoulder.

He mock-punches her back, pulling the punch elegantly, barely brushing the skin of her arm. "Come on, let's just go. There's only about five things on the list. What's the problem?"

Lucette sighs. "I guess it's more like I need to go someplace by myself."

"By yourself? Where do you need to go by yourself?" Ray tries to look into her eyes. "To see your mother?" he guesses.

Lucette looks down at her hands. She shakes her head. "Just someplace I have to go."

Ray looks at her, puzzled, and then his eyes widen, the corner of his mouth turns down. "I get it. It's him."

Lucette sneaks a glance at Ray. He is sitting with both hands on the wheel, his jaw sticking out. "It won't take long," she says.

"Far be it from me," Ray says, not looking at her.

"I can give you some money for gas."

"God, Lucette." They pull into the supermarket parking lot, and he gets out. "Do what you got to."

Lucette watches how he walks away, taking long strides, his shoulders squared, and then she slides over behind the wheel.

It has been a long time since she has driven a car. Mrs. Archacki's Buick is upholstered like a sofa. She glides down the street in it, trying to extend her consciousness out to its edges so as not to hit the cars parked on her right. For a while she feels light, excited. She has forgotten how different it is to be the driver instead of the passenger. Being driven makes her feel enclosed—someone's darling, princess, captive—and sometimes this is pleasant. But, driving, she splits the air ahead, the world parts for her.

She is nervous, but it is agreeable, a tightening of her skin, a sharpening of her sight and hearing. The sounds of traffic ping against her eardrums, the metallic click of her signal as she turns onto Broadview Road is very definite. She is conscious of the straight line that she will drive along to Al's Maple Leaf. Of course, it is not Al's bar anymore, and she wonders whose it is now. His wife's, Geneva's, probably.

Stopped at a traffic light, she looks around, and it is so much the same that she is shocked. The same storefront that promises alterations for five dollars, the corner store that never keeps its tenants for more than six months—someone is trying to sell ice cream there now. The carpet store where no one is ever seen buying carpet—it was Bev's idea that it was a front for the Mafia.

She drives on, a little more slowly than the people in back of her would like. But although they honk, she persists until they pass her. She feels better with no one behind her to observe, to urge her forward. She lets the car glide down the hill past the cemetery. Here is dangerous territory. She rehearses in her head an excuse, a reason why she might be here. She is going to the drugstore a little further down, as anyone might, to buy toothpaste. She visualizes the tube, can feel its bulky smoothness in her hand.

The next light turns green for her before she gets there, and she gulps in an intoxicating breath. She is in just the right place, doing just the right thing. Her scalp lifts and prickles, and she turns the radio on for the happiness of the noise, although she hardly hears what is being played. Her idea is that she will see Harry as she drives by the bar. Not at all impossible, it is the time when things are being set up, a slack time, a time of going back and forth, in and out. Or she might see him driving, coming back from some errand. Or standing out on the street, talking to one of the beer-truck drivers. The Bud guy always comes late.

As she gets closer, her breath is quicker. She has no plan. "Come on," she says, "come on."

When she sees the sign of the bar on her right, a little sooner than she expected, it is like a blow. She holds herself tight against the sight of Harry that she feels ahead of her, and notes each thing as she approaches, the triangular break in the sidewalk, the green letters on the sign, the old wooden door with its head-high square of glass. And as she turns the corner, the air-conditioner that hangs out over the sidewalk dripping a rusty stream, the stand of weeds that has grown up around the telephone pole, the dusty blue chicory flowers spearing out. Chicory root was ground up and used to make coffee when there was no coffee, she hears her stepfather's voice telling her, and shakes her head. The gravel of the parking lot spilling out onto the sidewalk, the old wooden fence that separates it from the yard next door, overgrown with a glorious rambling rose. The trailer. She pulls over and parks across the street, her fingers trembling on the wheel.

The trailer looks empty, deserted, the blinds drawn tight against the sill, the steps a little askew, but this is how it has always looked. Harry's truck is not among the cars in the lot. But he might have gotten a new one. She monitors the light, the air for his presence. It seems to her that there is movement in the trailer, some subterranean tremor. She thinks, he is in there, he really is. For all her thinking, imagining, she didn't expect to see him, this might have been a practice run for the real event. She isn't prepared, but even while she's thinking not now, not yet, she concentrates on pulling him with the force of her will, drawing him, so that he must come out, open the door, set foot on the steps, cross the gravel. She can't go there. But if he comes out, then anything will be possible.

But, she is thinking, I *could* go over there. She imagines herself opening the car door, crossing the smooth, red-brick street, feeling the hard pointiness of the gravel under her shoes, putting one foot on the first step, the door knob turning in her hand—all this can happen. She reaches out for her purse, stops, opens the car door with dry fingers, stops, swings her legs sideways and sets her feet on the smooth brick pavement, stops, all the while keeping her eyes on the trailer, on the screened rectangle of the door.

A car is coming down the street, and she pulls her legs in, watches the driver as the car passes, an old woman with bright silver hair in curlers. When she looks back at the trailer the door is opening, someone is backing out, bending over the lock. At once she sees that it isn't Harry, too slender, not tall enough, and her mind races ahead, Geneva has kicked Harry out, has rented the trailer to someone else, has installed a relative, or a lover, why not? Did she really love Al? But the person turns, and she sees that it is a woman, not Geneva though. A woman who hurries across the parking lot to her car. As she fumbles in her purse for the keys, her face is turned to Lucette, her long lank hair falling forward. She swipes at it with her hand. It is Cynthia.

Lucette's first thought is to leave, and her hand reaches out to the keys, still in the ignition. But Cynthia herself is going. Cynthia's car pulls out and Lucette ducks, half lying across the seat. She feels her pulse beat where her upper arm is pressed to her temple.

After a minute she sits up. Now that Cynthia is gone, things seem less intense. Maybe if she stays, she can find something out: why Cynthia was here (for she never used to come to the trailer), or where Harry is. She could get into the trailer and look around, she still has a key, but this doesn't appeal to her. She might be found there by Geneva or Cynthia. She could wait outside in the car to see when Harry comes back, with whom, how he looks. She could then decide whether to talk to him or not. Or he might see her here, sitting in the car like a private detective on television. This feels bad to her, she doesn't want to be caught that way, waiting for him, spying, yearning. She clasps her hands, thinking, nervously weaving her fingers. She could go into the bar. The chances of being seen are greater than if she went into the trailer, but still it is what she wants to do. Even if Geneva is there, she will not be trapped as she would be in the trailer.

She gets out of the car, the strap of her purse wound around her wrist like a weapon. She crosses the street, almost running, and starts toward the front door. But then, considering, she stops. The side door is probably open, it often is in the afternoon, and if she goes in that way, she can approach the main bar quietly, maybe without anyone noticing. She tests the knob of the side door; it is open, she slides inside.

And here it is, the Maple Leaf bar in the afternoon, so different that at first she thinks Geneva has made some major change since Al's death. But it is only the time, the soft gloom of daylight seeping in, and the fact that it is empty. There is no one behind the bar, no movement at all, and Lucette takes a few steps further in. She stands in the arch between the two rooms. The dance floor, the tables, the stage are in a more complete darkness, like a cave. She lets her fingers rest on the smooth gleaming wood of the bar, as if something might rise from its polished surface. Here is Harry's habitual bar stool. There, the seat where she sat the first time she came with Bev. Here was where Al used to stand, his hands spread out on the bar.

"Believe I know you."

Lucette turns quickly. In the dimness by the door she sees a man at the very end of the bar. "Who's that?" she says.

"Tase Penfield." He half stands up. "Left me in charge. Geneva."

"Oh, hi," Lucette says, retreating.

"Believe we've met."

"Where's Geneva?"

"Gone to get her son-in-law. Just left, though, you'll have a wait."

Lucette considers. "I guess I could wait for a while." She ap-

proaches the bar and walks down to sit two stools over from the
old man, who is regarding her with more attention than she
expects from him, from what she remembers.

"Little blond girl, came in with that manhunting dark girl, am
I right?"

"Yes," Lucette says, almost laughing to hear Bev described this
way. *And then he called you a manhunter,* she imagines herself
telling Bev.

"I could draw you a beer."

"That's all right."

"Geneva said I could go ahead if someone came in. You're
someone."

"No thanks, really."

"Al's gone, you know."

"I heard."

"It's not like it was."

Lucette nods. She wonders if he will bring Harry up, or if she
will have to ask something. She wonders how she might push the
conversation.

"Left the new bar to Harry." He turns to her, his eyes peering
out from his caved-in face. "You knew Harry, if I'm right."

Lucette assumes what she hopes is a bored, time-killing air.
"How *is* Harry?" She wishes she was still smoking, a cigarette
would help.

"Some might say he's doing well."

"But he's not?" Lucette hears too much interest in her voice,
but old Penfield doesn't seem to notice.

"Got the new bar. Got a regular place to live."

"Where's that?"

"On Daisy Avenue, over to Cynthia's. His cousin, you know."

She remembers what Bev told her a while back. She sees again
Cynthia bent over the trailer door, locking it, her shoulders
rounded, her dark, short-sleeved shirt, her thin, tanned arms. How
she picked her way across the gravel as if she was barefoot, her
dirty-blond hair falling forward, how she tucked her head down

getting into the car. It is extraordinary how much she remembers of that little time, it couldn't have been more than thirty seconds.

"I'm surprised he's living at Cynthia's," she says, listening to her voice. It sounds perfectly normal, rather far away.

"A woman'll do what she has to, I guess."

Lucette looks at him, wanting to ask what he means. She is thirsty, his beer looks good to her, but she knows that if she drank some it would taste wrong, its wonderful bitterness soured by her body's reaction. It's hopeless, she thinks, letting her cheek fall onto one palm.

"I knew his mother, of course."

Lucette lifts her head. "Harry's mother?"

"Louisa." He nods. "*And* her sister. Fine women." He shakes his head, as if it is the preamble to some further point. "Cynthia, now." But he says nothing more, his head keeps shaking though this seems to have nothing to do with what he has said.

"I guess I'd better go, I guess I can't wait any longer for Geneva," Lucette says. There are many more things she would like to ask, but she is getting nervous. Each shadow that flicks across the square glass panel in the front door makes her twitch and start.

"Geneva does take her time."

She picks up her purse from under the stool.

"You might wait a bit, now, and likely Harry would be coming by."

"Oh, no," she says, "no, it was Geneva I needed to see. About—" she waves her hand, trying to think why she might want to see Geneva, but nothing comes. "Geneva," she says firmly.

Old Penfield nods and raises his beer glass to her, salute and farewell.

She feels as if she has been in this watery darkness a long time, amid the smoothness and gleam of the wooden surfaces, the dim shine of the glasses and bottles, the dark reflections swimming in the mirror. Old Penfield is a ghost, white face, white hands, his soft gray shirt and pants, his hand dancing on the surface of the bar, almost steady as he raises his glass to his lips.

Lucette drives down Broadview Road as if she knows where she is going. She had almost forgotten, in the bar's dark bubble of time, that she has to pick up Ray, but now she has, at least, a place to go. She points the car toward the supermarket. She no longer worries about being seen, or thinks about seeing Harry, she is invisible, she is no longer a player in this world.

She lets her mind settle on Geneva, recasting her in her new role: a widow. She believes that Geneva would have been impassive at the funeral, even noble. She would not have removed her dark glasses, hiding her grief behind them. She is living her life now as if it is a process of receding from Al, as if a great wave carries her farther and farther away from the time they were together. Lucette can't imagine Geneva reacting like her mother, who folded in on herself when her stepfather died. Geneva would take no shit, even from death.

When she stops the car in front of Ray, he gets up from the sidewalk where he has been sitting barricaded by bags of groceries. "You took long enough," he says.

"You said you only had to buy about five things." Lucette fights the desire to lie down and put her cheek against the smooth upholstery. "So what now?"

"I don't know. Do you want to go to a movie?"

"God," she says, hitting the palm of her hand against the steering wheel, "not a movie."

"You want to get a hamburger?"

"I'm not hungry."

"We could just drive around."

"I want to go someplace. Someplace quiet."

"The park?"

"No." She feels a revulsion at the idea of peaceful greenness, trees, happy people playing Frisbee.

"Edgewater Beach?"

She shakes her head.

"The old folks home? The cemetery?"

Lucette has an image of where she wants to go. It is dark, silent except maybe for a sound like the wind, a rhythmic rushing. No windows, no doors, no walls. She would float there in the smooth blackness, her lips and eyes soothed by the warm dark. She shakes her head again, not looking at Ray.

"What's the matter, Lucette?"

"Nothing," she says, but she knows that she says it in such a way that he will not believe her—with a trace of sullenness, of hysteria.

Ray, his arms full of groceries, looks at her bent head. She can feel his gaze, his worry.

"Maybe you should just take me back," she says.

"What would make you feel better, Lucette? Just tell me, give me a clue."

Lucette turns, letting her lids sweep up to take in his whole face, his eyes. "I don't know," she says, with that same sullenness. She lets her head fall back, lets herself go slack against the seat.

"I know where we could go. I've got a buddy who just moved into his grandfather's house because his grandfather's in the hospital. He's supposed to be house-sitting, you know? We could go there. He wouldn't mind."

"I don't want to see anyone," Lucette says, her eyes still closed.

"I'll call first, okay? Do you want to go over there if Leonard won't be there? We could talk or whatever."

"I guess so," Lucette says. "I guess that would be all right."

She watches as he calls from a public phone in the parking lot. He stands braced against the glass wall of the booth, rapping his fingers against the door. He runs back to the car, grinning. "Leonard said no problem. He said take as long as we like. He was going to go and see this girl he knows out in Mentor."

"What did you tell him?" Lucette slides over and he gets in behind the wheel.

"I told him I wanted to bring a girl over."

"Oh, you did?"

"Yeah." Ray shrugs, apologetic. "I had to tell him something."

Later, when Lucette thinks about this evening, she knows she is remembering it as if she knew the outcome. But now, being carried through the golden light and the evening's stretching shadows, she is only conscious of being tired, very tired, of wanting to fall, to slide, to lie down, even while part of her scrabbles away in her head, determined to find a way not to give in.

But she persists in remembering it as if she and Ray were taking part in a game, a complicated one, but one that they knew so well that each step led naturally to the next. Each touch, each glance was part of this game. Their heads inclined toward each other across Leonard's grandfather's kitchen table while they drank the wine Ray found in the refrigerator—Ray topping up his glass each time the level sank below half, Lucette nursing an inch of pink liquid. Their arms and shoulders brushed with an electric touch when they got up—for more wine, or to go to the bathroom. Their voices sank lower and lower, or broke into laughter.

Lucette remembered that at one point, late, after ten, their hands were lying on the table, their arms only half an inch apart. She wasn't drunk, but there was a hard, gleaming edge to things that she remembered about being high, a clearness that yet denied all responsibility. They were talking about her body, the progress of her pregnancy, and he kept saying that he couldn't tell she was pregnant. Laughing, waving his hands, he claims that he doesn't believe that she is pregnant at all.

"I am, though." She too is laughing. "If only you could feel how tight my clothes are."

"I don't believe it. It's one of those—what do they call them?—hysterical pregnancies."

"How do you know about hysterical pregnancies?"

"Hey, I've watched soaps," he says, and they both laugh.

"You can tell if I have my clothes off," she says. "Then you can tell for sure."

They look at each other, their hands still close but not touching.

"Well, I want to know for sure," Ray says.

"What for?" Lucette looks down at her hand; it feels full of energy, she imagines she can see her pulse jumping.

"I've got a scientific mind."

"All right then," she says. He laughs, thinking maybe that she is kidding, but then as she unbuttons the buttons at the neck of her blouse, he starts to get up, as if he expects that she will move to another room, or pull down the blinds. But she continues to undo the buttons, not looking at him, turned slightly away. She unhooks her bra and then unzips her skirt. She pushes the skirt and her underpants down over her hips so that they only just hide her pubic hair, lets her bra and her blouse fall off her shoulders, and then turns back toward him. Her breasts are exposed, and the gentle, solid curve of her abdomen. His hands are still on the table, and his mouth is half open. His look is like a warmth, she turns in it as if it is the sun. She doesn't feel, as she has often felt, lumpy and awkward, stretched and swollen. She feels as if she is more beautiful than she really is, that something has been added to her, that she is the container of this new beauty.

"You see?" she says. "You see?" She feels very happy, and later, when they are lying on Leonard's grandfather's bed, both of them naked, she is still happy. Ray's face is hidden against her shoulder, his hand on her stomach, the fingers splayed out wide, his breath warm on her breast. She thinks that this could be their house, and this bed with the pale orange light of the streetlight falling across it, their bed. This is love, she tells herself, how had she been so stupid before?

Lex is prowling the long window seat in the dining room, stopping every once in a while to put his nose to the glass, streaked with rain driven against it by the wind. James sits in his big wicker chair, arranging papers in piles on the floor in front of them, grunting a little each time he bends over. Lucette has been reading *TV Guide*, but now she puts it down on the table, gets up to lean over the window seat, and peers out.

"It's not raining so hard."

James pauses to look out the window. "The rain comes hard and then subsides. That sounds so nice, is it a quote?"

"I don't know."

"There will be a lot of customers tomorrow."

"Because of the rain?"

"Because it's the last Sunday in June. It's a communal impulse apparently, just before the Fourth. People realize they haven't gotten those petunias or pickling cucumber plants."

"Whatever," Lucette says, tapping her fingers against the glass, irritating Lex so that he springs from the window seat and bounds away under the dining table.

James picks up *TV Guide,* and begins to page through it.

Lucette goes to the door between the dining room and the kitchen, to look out the windows at the other side of the house.

"Settle someplace, please. You're making it hard to think. And Lex is spooked."

Lucette bends down to coax Lex from under the table, but he withdraws further, a bright ball of gold in the shadows. She flops onto the old velvet sofa, and then, twisting her body awkwardly, turns and lies down, pillowing her head against the big overstuffed red-velvet arm.

"Have you ever noticed the prevalence of an idea or a theme over a night of television?" James runs his finger down a page of *TV Guide.* "For example, tonight it is the problem of trust. Here, at eight o'clock, one pretty girl has to decide whether or not to trust a stranger who says he needs fifty dollars. And at nine-thirty, another pretty girl, who is, we presume, just as brainless and conventional, gets involved with a stranger who claims to be a record promoter. What do you suppose it means?"

"I don't watch those kinds of shows."

"You don't watch as much television as most of your peers, I've noticed. Why is that, do you think?"

A picture of her mother, sitting limp and blank in front of the blue glare of her old Zenith, comes to Lucette's mind. "I don't know."

"My mother disapproved of television when it first came out, but she became very attached to it, especially to Westerns. They used to show a lot of Westerns, particularly on Saturday and

Sunday afternoons, in the late fifties and sixties. Roy Rogers and so on."

"What did your father think of television?" Lucette closes her eyes, breathes deeply, feeling the blood move through her body. Her fingers twitch, and she places them on her stomach, lightly, delicately, not letting down the full weight of her hand. She can feel her skin's contact with the velvet nap of the couch through her clothes.

"He thought it was a fine invention. But in moderation. That was his key word, moderation. Did I ever tell you about my father?"

"You said something about him and the greenhouses, the business."

"The fact is that he was a sort of saint, a bit unreal. You couldn't annoy him, couldn't anger him. If I had found out, as in the plots of soap operas, that he was not my father, I would not have been surprised."

"Why not?"

"I fear he was too good for me." James puts down *TV Guide* and sighs. "I wasn't fine enough to be his flesh."

"You make him sound like he was God."

"Not God. But he almost wasn't human. Maybe someone halfway down the evolutionary road to a new incarnation. He had no debt to pay, no quarrel. If he had been a talking man—he wasn't, he was silent more often than not—but if he had been, people would have followed him anywhere because of his goodness, it was possible to feel in the air around him how good he was."

"It sounds like he'd be hard to live with." Lucette gets up from the couch and wanders into the front room to look out at the street.

"Not at all. He was good company. A little hard to reach sometimes. My mother used to rap him with whatever she had in her hand—her knitting needles, her glasses—if he didn't pay attention to her." James begins to put his papers together in crosswise stacks. "Here, take this pile," he says to Lucette as she comes back into the dining room. He picks up two more stacks and rises awkwardly. "Come, I'll tell you where to put them."

There is the sound of a car in the driveway, and Lucette turns her head toward it.

"I wonder who that is?" James says, turning with her.

"It's a friend of mine," Lucette says. She hesitates. "I meant to tell you he was coming over."

"Someone you met at work?" James asks.

They stand, both holding the slipping piles of papers, facing each other.

"No. It's someone I knew before."

"Well?" he says, waiting to hear what else she will say.

Lucette breathes deeply. She hadn't found the right time to tell him.

She and Ray have been meeting every day, sometimes only for fifteen minutes, but twice for several hours. They went to Leonard's house most of those days. They had seen the neighbors looking at them speculatively. "Wouldn't they love to know what we're doing?" Ray said to her exultantly, stretching his long skinny arms over his head, all bone and muscle and tendon, as they lay on the bed in the late afternoon light. Lucette thought that probably the neighbors had guessed pretty accurately what they were doing. But she didn't care, she didn't know them, they didn't know her. They didn't know what her life was like, didn't know what she and Ray thought and felt.

Ray is a virgin, or he was, and this makes Lucette feel tender toward him, protective, as well as triumphant. His shuddering, shouting climaxes make her happier than her own would, for she hasn't had any yet. She feels curiously removed from her own body.

She loves it when Ray touches her, she loves holding him. She takes his hand and guides it to her neck, her breasts, her hips, the insides of her thighs, and his touch makes her skin buzz with feeling. But it never builds, it never carries her over. This is probably because of being pregnant, she tells Ray. They kiss long kisses that leave her tongue and lips sore. When they don't go to Leonard's grandfather's house, they find someplace where they can kiss and embrace, under a tree in the park, against the paneled wall in the back hall of the building where Ray works. When they press their clothed bodies together like this, rubbing and twisting, Lucette sometimes comes, but she hides it from Ray, it seems wrong to do it this way and not when they are doing it for real.

James is still waiting for her to say something. The bell rings, and she takes a step toward the front door.

"I know you've been meeting someone, Lucette."

"It's Ray," she says. "Bev's brother," as if this is a negation of what he has said.

"Ray."

"Ray Archacki."

The bell rings again. "Let's let him in, shall we?" James says, and he goes to the door and swings it open, Lex running out, past them.

Ray is standing in the front hall, grinning, his hands hanging at his sides. They all stand there, not moving into the front room, although the hall is crowded. Lucette and James are still holding the papers.

Lucette shifts her stack to one arm, and says, "James, this is Ray Archacki. Ray, this is my landlord, James Gandy."

Ray sticks his hand out, and James shuffles the armload of papers to put his own out to meet it. "The landlord greets you. Beverly is your sister?"

"Yeah," Ray says. "Yes." He looks at Lucette.

"Maybe we could go in and sit down," James says, and he leads the way. He dumps his papers on the dining-room table and comes back to the living room, turning on lights. They all sit down, James in a massive wooden rocker, Lucette and Ray on the couch, one at each end.

Lucette hasn't spent much time in this room, which has the air of a dust-sheeted museum, although there is no protective covering on the furniture. The drapes are rarely opened.

"Here, let me get rid of those," James says, taking the papers Lucette still holds.

While he is putting them away, Ray and Lucette look at each other, signaling—yes, I am here.

They watch as James lowers himself into his chair, and for a moment they all look at one another, James turning his massive head from Lucette to Ray and back, Lucette darting glances at the two men, Ray meeting James's eyes solemnly, without blinking.

"I feel as if we ought to be having tea," James says. "Revelations over the crumpets. There are revelations?"

Lucette sees Ray is blushing, and she is annoyed. She moves a little closer to him, stretching her hand out to touch his elbow, jogging him. "Ray and I are going to get married," she says.

James nods, and rocks the chair gently, his hands on its arms, pushing with his toes.

"Did you hear me?" Lucette asks.

"Yes, certainly."

"We mean it," Ray says, and Lucette taps his hand to make him be quiet.

"I'm sure you do," James says. His face, all of him, is immobile as he rocks very slightly back and forth.

"I just wanted to tell you," Lucette says, "I wanted to let you know first."

"And will you be moving out?"

Ray and Lucette look at each other. "In a while," she says. "If that's okay."

"Certainly, certainly."

James stops rocking. "Well, I do think a drink, don't you? There's some wine, I believe. Lucette, would you get it, and some glasses?"

"Now?"

"Why not? It's in the refrigerator in the vegetable bin. Wine experts frown on keeping it refrigerated," he says to Ray, "but what can you do? Not everyone has a cellar."

Lucette gets up and goes toward the kitchen, then turns back, reluctant to leave them alone together. "Which glasses should I get?"

"The best ones, the crystal, of course," James says, keeping his eyes on Ray.

In the kitchen, the glasses clink against each other, nervous little chimes, as she puts them on a tray with the bottle. "Where's the corkscrew?" she calls, but James doesn't answer, and she paws hurriedly through the silverware, and then scrabbles around in the junk drawer until she finds it.

When she gets back, Ray is clearing the coffee table under James's direction.

"Just put those magazines on the floor, and that bowl can go on this little table." James hitches his rocker closer to the coffee table and opens the bottle, drawing the impaled corkscrew out with a flourish. He pours the wine, which is a very pale yellow, filling two glasses three-quarters full. Into the other, which he hands to Lucette, he pours about a tablespoonful. He holds up his own glass. The glasses collect what light there is in the dim room, so that the wine glows as if each glass is a lamp. "To the future," he says, "may we embrace it."

Lucette takes a sip, barely wetting her lips. Ray, clutching his glass nervously by the stem, drinks half of his wine. She can hear the sound of his gulp loud in the silence.

The doorbell rings.

"Another visitor. And I thought it was going to be a quiet afternoon." James sets down his glass, from which he doesn't appear to have drunk anything, and goes to the door.

"What did he say to you while I was gone?" Lucette whispers to Ray.

"He asked me how old I was." Ray takes her hand and puts it between his.

"What did you say?"

"What do you mean, what did I say?"

"Never mind."

"Come in, come in," they hear James say. "We're having a celebration, you must join us."

Bev rushes into the room as if she has been ejected from the hall, and stops, one foot skidding on the throw rug. She clutches the door to keep her balance. Ray and Lucette let go of each other's hands.

"What are you doing here?" Bev says, struggling with the heel of her shoe, which is caught in the fringe of the rug.

"Did you follow me?" Ray jumps up.

"My God, Lucette, what are you doing? Are you crazy?" Bev goes to Lucette and kneels down by her, putting her hands on Lucette's knees.

Lucette draws back. "I don't know what you mean."

"Just wait until Mother finds out what you've been doing," Bev says to Ray, flinging down her purse.

"That's right, run to Mom. And anyway I'm not ashamed of what I've been doing."

"And you"—Bev turns to James—"you're supposed to be an adult."

James shakes his head and sits down.

"You don't even know what's going on," Ray says.

Bev sits in one of the armchairs and folds her arms. "All right. So tell me. What's going on?"

Lucette has a moment of deep, despairing doubt, but she makes herself look at Bev. "Ray and I are getting married." She picks up her glass and takes another small sip. "We're in love." She puts her hand out without looking at Ray, and he takes it.

Bev moans. "You can't, you can't. This is so stupid." She beats her fists on the padded arms of her chair. "Can't you do something?" she says to James, "since they're obviously out of their minds?"

She turns back to Lucette. "I knew you weren't telling me something. And you," she says to Ray, "no, I don't even want to talk to you. Why did you have to, Luce?"

"You don't know everything," Ray says. "It was me at least as much. I came and found her."

"You followed me?" Bev says, and Ray nods, grinning.

"You slimeball! He's just a teenage pervert, can't you see it, Luce?"

Lucette sets her wineglass down with a click, but doesn't answer.

"Another guy's baby, Ray? You're only seventeen, you asshole."

"Just stop it," Lucette says. "Just cut it out. This only has to do with me and Ray."

"And what about Harry? What was all that about?"

Lucette lowers her head. "We hope you can accept it, but if you can't, it's just too bad."

"I'll tell you what's too bad," Bev says, reaching for her purse. "What I came over to tell you. Your mother tried to kill herself."

Lucette feels the room falling away from her, the still center, and she puts out her hand to hold on, but nothing is there. The others recede, their faces growing smaller, the furniture, the walls vanish.

Then she is lying on the couch. She can see her feet propped up on the opposite arm, impossibly far away. Her blouse is unbuttoned almost to her bra, there is something cold and wet on her forehead.

"She's all right," she hears Bev saying crossly. "She used to faint in church all the time in grade school."

"Shut up," Ray says. He is fanning her with a magazine, its pages flopping and hitting her on the nose. She bats it away with her hand, her fingers feel languid and bloodless.

"Are you all right?" James asks.

She looks up at his face hovering over Ray's shoulder, round and pink. "Yes." Her body feels very heavy, and she drags it up, props herself on her elbows.

Bev is still angry. "My mother heard from someone at work that lives on your street. She's been in intensive care, but she's coming home in a couple of days."

"What happened?" James asks.

"She slit her wrists in the bathtub with the shower running full blast. That's how they found her before she was gone, because the shower was hitting the wall where the window is and water was running down the side of the house. Some old guy next door went over, and when he couldn't get in, he called nine one one."

Lucette pushes away a picture of her mother's white slippery body being dragged out by men in uniforms. "So what?" she says. "That doesn't have anything to do with me. I've got my own things to take care of. You think it's any joke having a baby? I don't have to go back there."

Ray puts his arm around Lucette.

"This is so disgusting." Bev swings her purse to her shoulder. "Get a life, Lucette. This is the real world. You know you haven't got a choice—you have to go back, no matter what other disgusting plans you think you've got."

On the evening of the Fourth of July Cynthia counts fourteen pairs of underpants, fourteen pairs of socks spread out on the bed in her bedroom. She has bought extra so that Derek will be able to go two weeks without doing Joey's laundry. Probably it will be Loretta who will deal with it, but it gives Cynthia pleasure to provide so generously for her son. She is letting him go away from her, but her hand and her eye are still on him, she has him in the circle of her care. And he will only be gone for a month.

She can hear the dog across the street whining, a low accompaniment to the occasional boom and flash across the still-light sky. It is only eight o'clock, no one will set off serious fireworks for a while. But every now and then some kid in some backyard is unable to resist the tempting bunch of bottle rockets, thrust loose in a bucket or an old coffee can, and then there will be a spate of them, one beginning, others answering, and the machine-gun rattle of a string of caps.

The dog, a young German shepherd named Precious, isn't a neurotic dog. Last year's Fourth hardly phased her. But a few weeks ago she was banished to the porch at night, and she is suffering. Cynthia and Joey have been much taken up with this, wondering why she wasn't allowed to sleep in the house as she had for more than a year. Cynthia doesn't know those people. She can't keep track of who lives there and who might just be visiting.

Joey wants to kidnap Precious and spirit her away to some place where she will be happy, a farm, he says, where she can run and catch squirrels. He has made friends with her, sneaking over to feed her bits of bologna and leftover meat from dinner. He is worried that she will miss him while he's gone to stay with his father in Pennsylvania.

Cynthia smooths everything after she has folded it, pressing it with the flat of her hand. It's hot, a sort of contained hotness. She can see the wind blowing the branches of the trees, but the windows shut it out, closed this morning to hold in the night's coolness. She can feel the house quiet around her, the still air of each room quivering. This is one of the things she has discovered since Derek has gone, the quiet in the house. When she comes in from work, that quiet is waiting for her, filling the square shapes made by floor, ceiling, walls. And now Joey is going, it will be even more quiet.

She has never lived alone. She pauses, her hand on one of Joey's

T-shirts, tracing the outline of Batman's cape that swirls across it. She tries to imagine it—living always with the emptiness of the house around her, using only one plate, one cup, one fork knife spoon, glass, the floors that knew the imprint of her foot only, the quiet that would be unbroken unless she chose to bring someone through the door. She thinks she would like it.

The closest she has come to living alone was when she was away at college for a year. She had a roommate, Rosemary something, an Air Force brat, very popular, who was out nearly every night, coming in just after curfew with carefully rearranged hair, lips shiny with reapplied lipstick. She would drop onto the bed and tell Cynthia the amusing things her dates had said. Cynthia, not popular, would have spent the long hours between dinner and curfew lying on her bed or sitting at her desk, bony knees pressed together as she struggled with calculus or papers on *The Catcher in the Rye*. She saw Rosemary only for that little time at night, before they shut off the light and turned over, each in her separate bed, pulling the coarse, laundry-marked sheets up over her shoulder. Rosemary was nice in her way, Cynthia thinks. She could be funny, she could do imitations, had taught Cynthia to sing "Up in the Air, Junior Birdman."

But that aloneness, although it had been so close and so stifling, settling down over her every evening like a blanket, was nevertheless a sort of populated state. Rosemary was still present, in her books scattered over the desk and bed, her clothes half-pulled from their hangers and falling from her dresser drawers, the smells of her perfume and bath salts floating in little pockets in the air that Cynthia would run into when she walked about the room, batting them away like insects. And there was the sense of waiting for her actual presence, which grew stronger and stronger as the evening went on, sometimes making it hard for Cynthia to read or do math problems, so that she had to get up and pace, or go down to the basement for pop from the machine. Sometimes she turned off the lights and lay on top of the thin brown bedspread with part of it scrunched up under her and masturbated, though she didn't know then it was called that.

Cynthia shivers, thinking about it. Even now that she knows this is something everybody does, it still keeps some of its private, unique, shameful quality. She puts the piles of clothes into Joey's suitcase, along with other things she has collected on the bed—his comb, a new toothbrush, handkerchiefs. He has packed a duffel bag himself with baseball cards, squirt guns, comic books, his sleepy-dog. She looks out the window—it's not dark yet, but the air is less bright—and then at her watch, almost eight-thirty. Harry and Joey have gone to set off bottle rockets at Loew Field, they'll be another hour at least.

And of course she won't be alone now either, because Harry will be here. She goes downstairs, stopping to admire the squares of candy-red light the stained-glass window makes on the floor of the landing. She looks at the kitchen clock, comparing the time with what her watch says—maybe thirty seconds difference. The blue of the sky is deeper, more purple.

She measures coffee into the pot, but stops before she turns it on. Does she really want any? She wants something, but not coffee. Besides, maybe Harry will want some when he comes back, before he has to go over to the bar. He is helping out at the Maple Leaf tonight, since Geneva expects a holiday crowd, drunk with patriotism.

Instead, she picks a peach out of the wooden bowl on the table and goes into the back yard, full of the golden evening light. She sits on one of the old wooden lawn chairs, angling it so she can look up into the depths of the sycamore tree. The leaves are shifting in a restless movement, shudders that pass from one branch to the next. It is like looking at water moving, but deeper, since she can see the layers of motion, each rank of leaves ruffling and subsiding in turn. She can feel the same wind that moves the leaves, little rushes of air that slide along her skin and lift her hair. Irritably, she pushes it back from her face and runs her eyes over the back of the house. It looks as big as a cliff from here, white and nearly unbroken on this, its north side, except for two windows, one in the kitchen, one just under the peak of the roof, and then the dark screens of Harry's sleeping porch.

She tries to decide if the chimney looks slanted. The gutter is pulling away a little at the corner. She frowns. She should have told Derek before he left, Derek should have noticed himself. It is typical of his lack of interest in this house.

"Harry can take care of all the details," he had said.

"This is not just Harry's house."

"I *want* it to be just Harry's house."

Cynthia combed her hair, looking at herself in the hall mirror. "You've never liked this house."

"The house is fine." Derek reached over and picked a bit of lint off her shoulder. "I just want something new."

"You're asking me to pick up and leave my life."

"I'll be going, Joey will be going. What have you got here that's so important? An old house, a bum job at Convenient. You can't leave that?"

"That's not all—"

"Friends? You never see anybody except those women at work, and you don't care about them."

"There's Louisa. I have an obligation."

"You hardly ever go there. She doesn't like you."

Cynthia put her comb into her purse, and snapped it shut. "I don't want to go. Doesn't that count for something?"

Neither of them had mentioned Harry, although he was in both their minds, Cynthia is sure. Derek has never understood how it is with the two of them. He has never wanted to acknowledge how important Cynthia is to Harry. And to leave now, when things are coming together for Harry, how could she do that?

Cynthia doesn't miss Derek, although she is pleased to get his letters. They are full of the details of setting up a new accounting system for the hotel, of the changes Derek is helping Paul implement, the new addition they are planning, the redecorating.

Cynthia reads them over, smiling, thinking about Derek, happy to be using a hammer or a screwdriver for a change instead of an adding machine. Derek is sparing in his mention of Loretta, but she is implicit in the background as part of the "we" who take a break over coffee and sandwiches, as the person who shows Derek how to use a staple gun to attach a fabric panel to the wall. This is one of the things Cynthia dislikes in Loretta, this efficiency with her hands—the sawing, sanding, nailing—that she has developed since her marriage to Paul. She used to be one of those useless women whom Cynthia despised, women who planned to work only until they caught a husband, and then to sit forever with their manicured hands folded in their laps.

Writing back is more difficult. It is hardly worth writing down what she is doing—Derek knows already—and she doesn't want to tell Derek what she is thinking about. She could write about the gutter and the chimney, although now that she looks at it with her head at another angle, it doesn't seem to be leaning.

The light is draining from the air. The smaller fireworks come more quickly, punctuated by the single rattling boom of an M-80. Cynthia cranes her neck to watch the long arching trajectory of a bottle rocket. It isn't yet dark enough to see the color of its sparkling trailers. She gets up and walks into the front yard. From here she can see, all down the street, small groups, darting figures that come together and then scatter, a sizzling stream of sound and color exploding from their center. She starts to walk down the street, enjoying the sound, the small trails of smoke, the sharp smell of cordite. The boys know her, but they ignore her, an adult, except when their eyes meet hers accidentally, and then they say what sounds like " 'Lo–Miz–Lynch" over their shoulders, moving away from her. She nods at them, letting them escape.

It is cooler walking under the line of old shade trees. Cynthia is wearing an ancient sundress, faded from coral to pink, and it flaps against her legs. She would like to take off her shoes and feel the flat smoothness of the big square pieces of slate under her feet, but she is constrained by the thought of the boys, and of her neighbors, many of whom are sitting out on their porches on gliders, their heads and shoulders swaying, rocking slowly in the shadows. She speeds up, feeling sweat break out on her upper lip, walks faster to the corner where Daisy meets West Thirty-fifth, then turns out of sight.

Here, she pauses. Which way? She considers, bending to slip the sandals from her feet, and then turns left, north, toward Trowbridge, the church, Blessed Sacrament, and Joey's school, which she and Harry once went to.

She puts each foot down lightly, watching for broken glass. This sidewalk is full of landmarks for her: Here is the lawn where she and Harry once found $6.87 in change frozen into the snow. A little farther on is the crosswalk to the other side of Trowbridge, where the guard, a seventh grader, had threatened to report Cynthia for crossing without waiting for his protection. Here, on the corner by the pink house with the white curlicues, she first saw the word "fuck" written on the sidewalk when she was in second grade. She had at once known it was a bad word. She had sounded it out, moving her lips voicelessly, feeling it against the back of her palate.

Approaching the school yard, which doubles as the church parking lot on Sundays, she stops to put on her sandals. There are two small boys hammering caps a little farther down, but suddenly they snatch up their stuff and run away, the hammer hanging down absurdly long against the short legs of the smaller one. Cynthia looks back and sees one of the priests coming across the school yard, black cassock swinging. Her reaction is the same as the boys'—she straightens up and turns to go, but it is too late for her.

"Mrs. Lynch?"

She turns. He is the older priest, the monsignor. "Hello, Father," she says, rubbing one foot nervously against the other. There is a stone in her shoe.

"It's Cynthia, right?" he says, smiling.

"Yes. How are you, Father?" He has been at the parish since Cynthia was in high school. She pulls at the straps of her sundress, wishing she had worn a bra, aware of her nipples rubbing against the cloth.

"Fine. I was about to step over to the church and make a visit."

"Oh, good." Cynthia hunches her shoulders a little, and then, seeing that this makes the front of her dress gap so that the tops of her breasts are just visible, she stands up very straight, and folds her arms across her chest. "I was taking a walk, getting some air."

"I see Joey isn't playing softball this summer. I hope he's all right?"

"He's fine. It's just that he's going to visit his father. Tomorrow. He'll be gone."

"Ah," the priest says. He fumbles with the skirt of his cassock and brings out a handkerchief. He refolds it and wipes his forehead and the back of his neck. "Visiting Mr. Lynch, is he?"

"Derek's in Pennsylvania," Cynthia says, nervously pinching her arms. "It's a business thing, with his brother, he's helping his brother out with some problems he has, and some building."

He refolds his handkerchief again and replaces it. "It's good to have a family, isn't it?"

"Derek and his brother are pretty close."

"What sort of business is Mr. Lynch's brother in?"

"Oh. He has a grocery store." Cynthia looks up at the sky. It is darker, the priest's eyes are receding into his shadowed face. "I ought to get going. I have to finish packing for Joey, he's out with my cousin."

"Harry Walker," the priest says, meditatively.

"Nice to see you," Cynthia says, backing away. She walks quickly to the corner of Trowbridge and Fulton, trying not to come down hard on the stone in her shoe. She crosses against the light, darting in front of a car full of teenage boys. A little farther down Fulton, she stops and takes off her shoe, shakes the stone from it. She can't believe that she lied to the priest—what is his name, anyhow? She didn't want to tell him that Derek's brother had a honeymoon hotel, how silly. But she laughs. He'll never find out.

She walks down Fulton, bouncing a little on the balls of her feet. Another car of boys goes past, whistling and yelling, and she puts her shoulders back, head up. She knows it is only because the light is going that they paid her any attention. If she had been under the streetlight they would have gone past silent. But even to project the illusion of attractiveness is nice. She is aware of her body, her arms swinging, her legs pacing strongly down the street, the long tail of her hair just touching her bare back between her shoulder-blades.

July fourth, she thinks. There is a lot of the summer left. She should make plans, do summer things. Harry is working hard, he would appreciate some relaxation. A picnic, maybe. She might take some time off from work. The month that Joey will be gone stretches ahead of her, filled with days on which things might be done, might happen.

When she gets to Thirty-fifth, she goes as far she can toward the freeway and then stands there, looking across, holding on to the chain-link fence. She tries to remember when she could walk from where she now stands to the other broken half of Thirty-fifth, a half mile away—imagines her fourteen-year-old self walking in the thick humid air, one careful foot, then the other, over the concrete and weeds and the moving metal backs of cars. She feels a separation from what is on the other side of the freeway, and a longing for it, for her parents' old house, Harry's parents' house, the extinct Dairy Dell.

With a sigh, Cynthia turns and walks back toward Daisy. A block ahead she sees a group of kids and a few older men gathered in the middle of the street. It is dusk now, the dark tangible and grainy in the air, and she walks more slowly, wanting to watch whatever it is they are setting off. It is something big, it takes extensive consultation. Some of the smaller kids shoot off caps and wave sparklers while they wait, and there is a double boom—two M-80s.

As she hangs back, dragging the toes of her sandals along the sidewalk, a police car pulls up just behind her and she watches as they go up to one of the houses. The door is answered by a woman whose little dogs immediately start yapping. Cynthia knows exactly why the police have come—the woman's dogs were neurotic and yapping constantly and she threatened to call the police if they didn't stop setting off M-80s and they didn't and so she did. Walking very slowly, Cynthia sees that all down the street they have passed the word and stilled the pops and sparklers until it is safe. Cynthia stops and leans against a tree and watches the cops talk to the woman for a minute and then go down the steps and back to their car, where they confer and then drive away.

The boys are coming back into the street one by one, and by the time she is close enough to see what they are doing, the crowd is as big as it was before.

"Now then," she hears one of the men say, and they all spring back. A car pulls up and stops in response to the held up hand of an old man, his belly straining against suspenders, his shirt sleeves rolled up.

Cynthia waits, the man in the car waits, the roving group of boys is stilled, and when the fountain of gold begins to roil and spark, there is a rustle among them, they all watch, heads thrown back as it jets and thrusts into the air, the stars of it flung higher than the trees. When it has sputtered out, the car starts up and passes through. "Thanks, buddy," they say to him. Such happiness, Cynthia thinks, such futility and sorrow. She has tears on her cheeks.

It has to do with this group feeling that comes out with the fireworks, these illegal, individual, on-the-stoop-on-the-block-in-the-vacant-lot fireworks. Not fireworks that the city would set off for you and you would go to a designated place to see, sitting passive and stupefied on a blanket, but fireworks you set off yourself, risking burned fingers, singed eyelashes, optical injury, fireworks that rose up in showers of stars high over the city where anyone who was looking could see them. And the noise to go with them, loud enough to knock you down. It is so touching, this simulated war, simulated gun and mortar fire, simulated stars and thunder. It kills Cynthia. It lays her out.

When she gets close to her own house, she walks faster, thinking that she will change, she feels sweaty. As she hurries around to the back, she hears the phone ringing, and runs up the back steps, bangs in through the screen door. She picks up the phone, pulling the strap of her sundress up over her shoulder. "Hello?" she says.

There is a roaring, and then an indeterminate rush of what sounds like whispering. She knows she should hang up at once, and she takes the phone away from her ear, but then waits one more second—and the voice comes, a louder whisper, smooth, deep, "I'm waiting for you, babe."

Cynthia moves the phone farther away from her ear, until it is almost at arm's length. There is no more sound. Very slowly, she replaces the receiver, trying not to let it click. A trickle of sweat runs down her back. She hears Harry's truck, the slam of the door, Joey's running feet. In a minute, they will be inside. She passes her hands over her face, and pinches the cloth of her sundress to hold it away from her body, but there isn't any cool air to flow in and soothe her.

When they come in, she is still standing with her hand on the phone. When she takes it away, she can see the wet marks from her fingers. "Did you have fun?" she asks Joey.

"I got to light some." He jumps around the room making zooming rocket noises. "You should've come."

"And who would do your packing?" Cynthia looks at Harry. He is standing by the kitchen window, rubbing the curtain between his fingers.

"You could have done it tomorrow morning."

"You have to leave early, remember?" She moves over to the table, putting herself into Harry's line of sight. "Go on upstairs now, Joey, and get ready for bed." She waits until he is gone, then touches Harry's arm. "Do you want something to drink?"

"I've got to get going."

"You've got a minute, surely?"

"Geneva's expecting a crowd."

"Let Geneva wait ten minutes. She doesn't own all your time."

"She misses Al."

"Misses ordering him around," Cynthia says. "I made iced tea. Like Grandma's."

"Well, now," Harry says, "I have time for a glass, I guess."

"Go sit outside and I'll bring it."

When Cynthia comes down the back steps, Harry is sitting at the picnic table, slumped over a little. He has lit the citronella candle. His hair looks white, almost silver, out here in the dark. Cynthia leans over him, resting a hand on his shoulder as she pours the tea. She sits across from him, watching as he takes a long drink from his glass. She sips from her own, and then holds it against her face for the coolness. "You remember these? The jelly glasses?"

"They were Grandma's," Harry says.

"We used to fight over them, who would get the one with apples and who would get peaches."

Harry shakes his head.

"We broke one, fighting over it," Cynthia says. "It was the grape one, that was the one we both liked best."

"I don't remember." He sighs and looks up into the dark heart of the tree, rubbing his neck and the back of his head.

"I had a piece of the glass stuck in my thumb. You must remember. Your mother took it out." Louisa's dark-red hair falling over her arm as she worked with the tweezers. Cynthia shivers. "And then she made us both go upstairs and stay there for an hour, in separate rooms. I was in Grandma's bedroom and you were in Uncle John's."

Harry shakes his head. "Now I remember the glasses, but not all the rest."

Cynthia remembers her rage at being imprisoned inside on a hot summer day, and by her aunt, not even by her mother. Her grandmother's bedroom had smelled of the cinnamon-and-rose-petal mixture that she made herself. There was a bowl of it on her dresser and another in each of the big closets. The windows were kept closed from early in the morning, to keep out the hot air of the day, and the cinnamon-rose smell was overpowering, less and less pleasant. Cynthia had walked around sniffing carefully, trying to find some part of the room where the smell was less noticeable. She opened the hall door to breathe, and to see if Harry was visible, but Louisa heard her and yelled up the stairs that she should shut the door and stop fooling around. She had held her breath, but try as she would to extend the breath-holding periods, at last she would have to breathe in great lungfuls of the hot air, so horribly spiced and perfumed.

"I tried to call to you through the crack under the door," she says to Harry. This is not true, but she likes the idea of it. "I put my face down on the carpet and called very softly. But then I got afraid that your mother would come up and open the door and smash my face in, so I got up." She can almost see this happening. "I was afraid of your mother."

"I've got to go," Harry says. He drains his glass. "Give me another to take with me?"

Cynthia pours it for him. "You weren't afraid of her, I suppose."

"Of my mother?" Harry laughs. "Of course I was. She was terrifying."

Cynthia considers this. She doesn't believe that they are thinking of the same sort of fear, or even of the same woman, when they think of Louisa.

Harry stretches his arms over his head and then gets up.

"Aren't you going to say good night to Joey?"

He cups his hands to his mouth. "Joey!"

Almost immediately, Joey's head appears against the screen on his window. "What?" he yells.

"Good night!"

"Good night!" Joey bellows. And then, "Are you going to be up in the morning when I leave?"

"You can wake me."

"Okay," Joey shouts.

After Harry has gone, after she has said good night to Joey, Cynthia comes outside again, for the coolness. There is still an occasional distant pop of fireworks, but the neighborhood is quiet. She drags one of the lawn chairs out into the middle of the yard and lies down on it. The moon is high in the sky and the world is full of its white light, almost as bright as day, a day with no colors. Cynthia raises her leg and looks at it in the light of the moon, silvery and slender; it is transformed. Her dress is shades of gray, not a sundress now, a moondress. The roses are shadowy cups of tender white petals, their branches and thorns as black and complicated as ironwork.

Tomorrow, Cynthia thinks. Everything will start to be different. She will think out a plan for freedom. She is thinking about separateness, separation, she doesn't imagine divorce, just that Derek will be away, and she will not have to bother about him. That Joey will come back after she and Harry are "happy together"—that is how she thinks about it, and Derek will work, will live, will write letters. This doesn't seem strange to her. It will to some, though, she will have to protect them all from the knowledge or comments of others.

But that is in the future. Now she will be alone in the house, and also with Harry, a fairy tale, the good sister reunited at last with her transformed brother. She looks up at the house brooding over her in the night, at the dark blankness of its windows, the hard, sharp peak of the roof. She closes her eyes and stretches her limbs, sure that she can feel on them the flow of light from the moon.

The next day, Cynthia stands behind the cash register, watching Vicky Sloper ring up a six-pack of beer. Vince, the boss, watches from where he is sitting on an overturned milk crate by the magazine rack. When an ID has been properly asked for and given, he lowers his eyes to his newspaper.

"He looked to be about sixteen," he says to Vicky after the kid has gone out.

"It was a good ID," Vicky says, unphased. She and Cynthia exchange a look.

Vince rattles his paper. He lays each section aside carefully as he finishes reading it. When he is done, he will fold them all back together, return the paper to the rack, and go into his office. When the door closes behind him, Cynthia and Vicky will settle into conversation. For now, Vicky pages through the new *Easy Rider,* Cynthia busies herself with the cigarette shelf and the miscellaneous collection of things under the counter, straightening and sorting. She is much neater at work than she is at home, it is a joke between Vicky and her. Vicky barely lifts a finger at the store, but her house is like a model home waiting to be shown, no evidence of the inhabitants.

"Do we need to do the cooler tonight?" Vicky asks, her eyes on a double-page spread of a big Harley over which a woman, all thighs and hair, is draped. She shakes the magazine at Cynthia suggestively.

"The boy'll do it." Vince always calls the current stockboy "the boy," no matter how old he is.

On Mondays and Wednesdays, Cynthia is the night manager, but the other nights she is just a cashier. This arrangement has been worked out partly to acknowledge her senior status (since there are hardly ever any raises) and to give Vince's son Dino a few nights off. As it has turned out, Dino has four nights off, since Vince has been unable to stay home on Fridays and Saturdays. He believes the weekend to be a signal for bums and troublemakers to come out of hiding and zero in on his store, where they will shoplift and spill things on the clean floors and try to molest the cashiers. He has the tenderest concern for the cashiers. When he hires one he sighs, shaking his head, at taking her away from her more proper, happier place, at home. He feels bad if they have to do any of the heavy work, and often ends up doing it himself, shooing them away. If male customers hang around and talk to the cashiers, he comes up to the front and makes himself obvious, restacking the newspapers, peering at them from between his heavy black eyebrows and his pushed-down glasses.

Cynthia and Vicky, and the other women that work there, Martha, Jody, Louann, agree that he is a nice old guy. Sometimes if he stays up front too long, they will start to talk about notorious customers who gave them a hard time: The guy who used to come in once a week and beg gray-haired Martha to meet him at the Dart Inn. The bald guy who wanted to marry Jody, the youngest of them, telling her he was part-owner of a restaurant and winery. The one who used to tell whoever was there that his wife had told him to go and get laid because she certainly wasn't going to do it again. The weird guy who would come in to buy *Playboy* every month and then would stand outside the glass front of the store, looking at the pictures and at the women inside, back and forth, back and forth. Vince hates these stories, they make him more and more uncomfortable, and after three or four of them, he will fold his paper, replace it in the rack, and disappear. They will hear him banging boxes around in the back, cursing and muttering in Italian.

Today, though, he gets through the paper in record time, and before Vicky has finished paging through her magazine, he is holed up in the back office, playing a Benny Goodman tape that Cynthia can hear faintly underneath the radio rock music from the store speakers. Cynthia has been wanting to talk to Vicky, but now she lounges against the cash register, tapping her fingers, unable to decide what she wants to say. "How was your week?" she says finally. They haven't worked together since Monday.

"It was like shit, that's how it was," Vicky says with a satisfied air. She scoots down and brings out a cigarette and lights it. Vince has a two-way mirror to monitor what goes on in the store, but everyone who works there knows where the blind spots are.

"What happened?"

The corners of Vicky's mouth turn down, a sort of smirking smile that is her response to almost everything. "Handsome started a gig out at this bar at a bowling alley on Brookpark." "Handsome" is how she refers to her husband, Ralph. "I had to go out, of course, and sit there for five fucking hours, even though the cat was sick and the only babysitter I could get was that boy from down the block who drools."

"You *had* to go?" Cynthia asks.

"If your husband is as goodlooking as mine, and you're as ugly as I am, you have to go out and establish territory. I sit there and glare." Vicky demonstrates this look, pulling the corners of her mouth down even further, narrowing her eyes.

"And that does it?" Cynthia laughs.

"I have to reinforce it every once in a while. God, I hate going out and listening to them play. The same fucking songs, the same old-beer smell, the same disgusting ladies' rooms. Listen, you should come out with me some time."

"You make it sound so attractive."

"It's better if there's someone to talk to. When was the last time you went out?"

"We went to a movie last week."

"We?" Vicky pulls on her cigarette.

"Joey and I."

"Bambi?" Vicky asks gloomily. *"A Hundred and One Dalmatians?"*

A customer comes up with bread, milk, and a two-liter of pop. She wants some salami from the deli, which Vicky slices for her, meanwhile asking about the rummage sale that the church they both belong to is running. Cynthia watches the dark-pink slices fly, falling into a rounded tower on the white paper. She puts the heel of her hand to her neck and massages the tight curve between head and shoulder. Her neck hurts, and her shoulder, her scalp, the bone of her face just in front of her ear and down the side of her jaw. This is one of the things she has been meaning to ask Vicky about. Vicky has a library of medical books including an encyclopedia cataloging every ailment known to modern science. Whenever a customer mentions a symptom or illness, Vicky looks it up and is ready to offer advice on the next visit.

"Don't you ever go over to that bar where Harry works?" Vicky asks when the woman has gone. Their conversations take place in the bits of time between customers, sometimes suspended for as much as an hour if they hit a busy period.

"The Maple Leaf? Not for a while."

"What about the new place?"

"It's not open yet."

"That was something, Harry getting left a whole bar. I pray to God no one ever leaves Handsome a bar. I'd never see him."

They stand there in silence for a minute, leaning against the counters that form a little enclosure around them. The glass front of the store, backed by darkness, is a mirror. She can see herself and Vicky embedded in the bright, crowded interior, and, deep in the blackness behind them, the moving lights of cars on West Twenty-fifth. A truck pulls in, and then two more cars and a van, the beginning of a rush. Vicky stubs out her cigarette, and they work for a while without speaking. Vince drifts up, checking for trouble, but this is not one of those nights. No one pulls a gun, no one tries to run out with a twelve-pack of beer, no one makes smart remarks. Vicky has a word for everyone. Cynthia envies this a little.

When the rush has subsided, Cynthia leaves Vicky at the counter where she is ringing up candy bars and Southern Comfort for an old woman from across the street, and goes to walk up and down the aisles, checking to see if anything needs to be replenished. She waves to Danny, the stockboy. He is putting up extra beer. She points to the milk, gesturing that he needs to get some more of the 2 percent.

After three years, she knows every inch of the store. She knows what is displayed in each of the aisles, how there is the bread, followed by crackers and cookies in one aisle; in another, soups and meal-in-a-can things like beef stew, and then canned vegetables. She knows the whine of the cooler fan, the rush of cold air and misting of the glass when its doors are opened. She knows the place on the floor where there is a damaged tile that the buffer will never clean properly. Since she is now sometimes night manager, she even knows the office built against the back of the cooler, so small that it can hold only a desk and chair and two filing cabinets.

Since she is back there, she knocks on the door of the office. There is a rustling inside, and then a pause. Vince opens the door, smoothing his hair back from his bald spot, as bashful and furtive as if he had been looking at pornography, but Cynthia knows that he has only been sleeping, tilted back in his chair, his legs on the desktop. "I need Monday off," she says.

Vince looks at the calendar, poking it with his thick, crooked finger. "Let's see. You're on with Martha."

"I think Jody can come in." In fact, she knows that she can. The cashiers arrange the exchange of days off among themselves. Talking to Vince is a formality; he likes to be consulted.

"Well. I'll put that in with a question mark." He erases Cynthia's name and writes Jody's in pencil. "Wait a minute, now, wait a minute, you're night manager that night."

"I talked to Dino already, and he says he'll look in."

Vince shakes his head. "Look in? What good is that?"

Cynthia doesn't answer, waiting for him to talk himself around to it.

"He wants me to retire and he talks about looking in? Is that serious?"

"Dino's all right," she says. "He'll come in eight to eleven, that's when it's crucial. And he always drives by later to see that things are okay."

"He drives by after the bars close."

Cynthia shrugs.

"You'll talk to Jody?"

"Don't worry," Cynthia says. "I'll take care of it." But Vince stays in the doorway looking at her.

"Anybody bothers you up there, give me a ring," he says.

She nods, poised, waiting.

"That's what I want Dino here for. You need to be seen. That way they know you take an interest, you're not some absentee owner." He retreats into the office, shaking his head. "Bring Joey by some time," he says, closing the door. "We'll give him a free ice cream."

When Cynthia gets back to the front, one of Vicky's neighbors is there, leaning over the counter looking at the *Easy Rider* centerfold.

"So what's the idea?" Vicky is saying. "That you want one of these babies"—she slides her finger over the Harley—"between your legs so much you're willing to put up with the big slob who owns it?"

"You're a scream," her neighbor says.

"It's no laughing matter." The corners of Vicky's mouth turn down. "What do you say?" she says to Cynthia.

"I don't know."

"She doesn't know."

Vicky's neighbor laughs. She picks up her bag of bread and milk and Hostess cupcakes, and then sets it down again. "Did you hear about Tina?"

Vicky shakes her head.

She lowers her voice, and Cynthia and Vicky draw a little closer, although no one is around to overhear. "She got a positive on her test, that smear, you know."

"You're kidding," Vicky says. "She's only, what, thirty-seven," she says to Cynthia. "You mean her on the corner with that snotty little girl?"

"Tina. Yeah. I couldn't believe it."

"It's supposed to be eighty-five percent curable if you get it early," Vicky says. She assumes her cigarette-smoking position in the corner by the bigger cash register, lights one, and takes a long drag. "Total hysterectomy, then chemo."

"It makes you think, though," her neighbor says. "Well, I've got to go. 'Bye, ladies."

"The scary thing about that kind of cancer is how you can have no symptoms," Vicky says. "Makes you treasure your every ache and pain."

Cynthia's hand goes up to rub her neck. "I've had this pain in my neck and shoulder," she says. "You ever have anything like that?"

"I get an ache in my back up high, by my shoulder blade," Vicky says.

"This is more by the back of my head. But on the side."

"I don't know about that. You want me to look it up for you?"

"It's probably nothing," Cynthia says.

"So what are you doing this weekend?"

"Nothing."

"Nothing? Your husband and kid are gone, you're a free woman and you stand there and say 'nothing?'" Vicky fluffs her hair out. "I'd have some plans, I can tell you."

"I'll find something to do."

"You're probably thinking how you're going to do some really crazy thing like clean the closets."

Cynthia laughs. "You know me better than that."

"You want me to come over and cut your hair? I'm off tomorrow."

Cynthia picks up a piece of her hair. "Does it need it?"

"I know you've got this idea that everybody should have their hair cut once a year whether it needs it or not, but, honey, live a little."

"I don't know if I'll have the time."

Vicky stubs out her cigarette and studies Cynthia with a professional eye. "We could layer it."

"The last time I had layers it took forever to grow it out."

"The idea is you get it trimmed every once in a while. But okay, no layers. Just a cut. What about some color?"

Cynthia puts her hair back behind her ears with a protective gesture. "Color?"

"Just to cover the gray. You can do it back to your own color." Vicky goes over to the magazine rack and while Cynthia rings up beer and chips for two kids in surfer shorts and motorcycle boots, she pages through one of the women's magazines. "Here," she says, holding the pages flat on the counter in front of Cynthia. "This is something like your natural color, right?"

Cynthia picks it up to see it better. The picture shows a young woman bending forward in such a way that the tops of her breasts seem about to fall out of a very demure gray suit. She is serious-faced, as if considering a new plan for world peace, her eyes far away on some invisible horizon, but her hair is blowing furiously, its dark-blond strands spinning around her small head. One strand has fallen across her mouth, pointing up her pale-pink lipstick. Cynthia is rather taken with this picture, although commonsensibly rejects its charm for herself. The girl's hair is the color of autumn grasses, a dark brown-gold. "It was a little lighter than that," she says.

"Easy enough."

"Well." Cynthia puts the magazine back on the counter between them. "I'll think about it."

"I'll bring the stuff over. Tomorrow, about three. And you can think about how you want your hair cut."

"I just want the split ends trimmed."

Vicky makes a face, an intensifying of her corners-of-mouth-down expression. "You ought to get rid of some of it. It makes you look old, that long hair does."

"Long hair is a woman's glory," someone says, and they turn, and then, seeing who it is, sigh together. "Hello, Mr. Bast," Cynthia says, helping him to pile his purchases on the counter, catching things that his arthritic fingers let slip. Vicky begins to ring them up.

"My wife's hair was so beautiful, so long," he says, carefully placing a package of bologna next to one of pepper cheese. "Long enough to sit on, even when she died."

"She wasn't sitting on it in her coffin, I suppose," Vicky says, too low for him to hear.

"No lock of her so glorious hair was ever touched by the scissor," he says, as Cynthia takes a lettuce and a package of tomatoes from his hands. He does all his shopping at Convenient, since he no longer drives.

"It must have been lovely," Cynthia says, loud, so that he can hear over the racket of the cash register.

"So lovely. Let me tell you this one thing, how in 1937, this was in our little village, she was seen by a man from Budapest, a famous poet, his name would mean nothing to you now," he says accusingly, "but he was a great man, a very great man—" He fumbles with the last of his groceries, some packs of Beeman's gum, and Vicky snorts, stabbing the keys with her fingers. "This man saw her sitting by the fountain in the square, and he made a poem for her, for her beauty, mentioning special her hair."

"Twenty-three sixty-seven," Vicky says.

"I will bring the poem when I come in next," Mr. Bast says to Cynthia. She helps him pack his purchases into the child's wooden-sided wagon he has left at the front of the store. He pauses with the door open, the wagon halfway through it. "Nowhere in the Bible does it say that a woman had her hair cut, is it not so?"

They watch him disappear into the darkness.

On Monday, her day off, Cynthia falls back onto the couch, her bags falling from her arms. She has been shopping, on a spree which started out harmlessly as a trip to the mall to get earplugs from the sporting-goods store for Joey. She planned to send them as a treat, it would make him happy to get a package in the mail. Then she meant to leave and get some things for the dinner she was going to make for Harry. But she had paused to look in the window of the store that sold wicker furniture. There was a sale, and she went in.

When she came out of the mall, dazed by the sun and heat, her skin still cool from the air-conditioning, she was loaded down with bags.

She is half-worried, half-elated at having spent all this money. How much did she spend? She could figure it out, but deliberately she puts the numbers out of her mind before they add up by themselves and reproach her.

She pulls the bedspread out of its bag and holds it up to see if it still looks as nice, and then she gets up and puts it on the dining-room table. It looks fine, much nicer than any of the tablecloths she saw. She gets the candles and puts them in the middle. They look a little lonely, and she thinks she will find her purple glass vase and pick some roses to put in it, imagining the light-pink petals of the flowers and the dark rose of the candles against the smooth broad stripes of color on the table. She puts the brass elephant by the candles, where it looks strange, but nice. Harry will find it odd, eating in the dining room, just the two of them, but he will not complain. She pulls the flowered pillows out of the bag and stands them up on the couch. They look wrong, too new and bright against the old, darkened green damask upholstery, but she leaves them there anyway.

The last bag has her bathing suit in it. She especially doesn't know why she bought the bathing suit. She takes it out and goes upstairs, where she tries it on again in the dim light of the big front bedroom. It is a shiny electric blue, with an inner construction that makes her breasts stand out, slightly pointed, something a rock star might wear. She likes the difference, she looks both slimmer and more voluptuous. She reaches up to her hair, which is also different, a little shorter, not much, she wouldn't let Vicky cut off more than an inch. But the top is shorter, shaped, and she has bangs, which Vicky says will round her face more youthfully. She holds them away from her face, and underneath she is still the same.

The phone rings, and Cynthia hesitates, unable to decide whether to put on a robe over her bathing suit, but the sound is urgent and she runs down as she is.

"Hello?" she says, picking up the phone.

No one answers. She strains to hear if there is the flat silence of a dead line, or the hollow ringing void that means someone is there, not speaking. She decides there is really no one. She reminds herself that it rang at least six times before she got to it, and whoever it was might well have thought no one was home. Still, she stands holding the receiver until she remembers she is in front of the dining-room window in her bathing suit. She doesn't see anyone outside, but her body curls inward, her shoulders coming down and forward, her arms protecting her chest, her legs pressing together. She draws back from the window, and then, half-crouching makes her way to the front hall and, breathing hard, runs upstairs. She strips off the bathing suit, kicking it away, and puts her underwear and shorts and T-shirt back on. But before she goes downstairs again, she puts the suit on the bed, smoothing it, adjusting the straps so that they angle away properly from the pointed cups that stand up all by themselves.

Then it's later, and Harry is here, they are eating dinner, steaks made on the grill, thick slices of tomato and onion and cucumber, crusty chunks of fried potato, sweating glasses of amber iced tea. Harry doesn't comment on the new tablecloth or the fact that they are eating in the dining room, but he picks up the brass elephant occasionally and cradles it in his hand while they talk and eat. They both drink—Harry whiskey, Cynthia wine. She tells him about shopping, a tumbling narrative, her words falling over themselves as the wine rises to her head. He sits listening to her, smiling, his thumbs stroking the smooth gold of the elephant, laughing when she tells him about buying it, buying the candles.

"It was like being drunk," she says, wiggling her fingers, plunging them into her hair. "I only meant to buy the earplugs for Joey. I don't know what happened." She shrugs her shoulders, pursing her lips. Her body feels soft, malleable.

"So you bought candles—"

"Yes, these," she picks one of them up and tilts it a little to see the wax run, hot and transparent against its pink solid body.

"And the elephant—"

"And the cushions, over there, on the couch."

"And the tablecloth—"

"Yes, but it's really a bedspread." She strokes it with her hand. "It's called polished cotton, that's why it's so shiny."

"And what else?" He leans back, still holding the elephant.

She gets up and runs into the kitchen. "These," she says, holding swizzle sticks topped with flamingos. "Let's have them in our drinks." She puts one in his whiskey, and one in her wine glass, but it looks silly there, too long, poking out of the top. "Wait," she says, and goes again into the kitchen, coming back with a tall glass filled with ice. "Pour me a shot, I'll keep you company."

Harry pours the whiskey, and it snakes over the sharp corners and flat surfaces of the ice cubes, smoothing them, warming them. Cynthia slides the swizzle stick in and stirs, making the ice chatter and ring in the glass.

"So you bought the candles and the tablecloth and the elephant and the cushions and the swizzle sticks. What would Derek say?"

"He'd say it was financially irresponsible." Cynthia raises her glass and drinks, heat sliding over her tongue, down her throat, hitting some central point in her chest and spreading, exploding. "And that's not all I bought."

"More?"

But she thinks Harry is beginning to look bored. His eyes are hidden by their lowered lids, he has put the elephant down, it lies on its side on one of the broad stripes of the tablecloth. "Let's go outside," she says. "It will be so nice and cool in the dark. We'll have the scent of the roses. Here—" she gives him the candles to carry out, she brings their glasses and the bottle. Outside, they relight the candles and set them on the picnic table, where they burn soft and yellow. Harry drags the two Adirondack chairs together and sits heavily in one of them, sighing and stretching out his legs.

Cynthia stands over him, sipping at her glass, tipping her head back to look at the night sky, taking great breaths. "Don't you want to know what else I bought?" she says.

"Sure," Harry says. "Sure. What else?"

"I'll show you," she says, and waving her hand at him, she goes back into the house. She is still carrying her glass, and she stops to sip from it at the bottom of the steps, and again in the doorway of her bedroom. She sets it carefully on the top of the wardrobe and undresses. Her clothes fall away from her body and she leaves them where they drop. Naked, she goes to the bed and takes the bathing suit by its straps. It seems to float up her legs, over her stomach, no sticking or pulling. Her breasts fall into the cups, the straps slide up her arms and lie flat and shining on her shoulders. She picks up her glass, turns out the light, goes down the steps, turns out the lights in the front room. She is hot and clammy, and she longs for the cool of outside. She picks up the elephant from the dining-room table and sets it on its feet, and then turns the light off, as well as the small shaded lamp on the desk by the window. In the kitchen, she turns off the overhead light, flicks off the light over the sink, and steps onto the back steps.

The house is dark behind her, all the light comes from the sky and from the two candles on the picnic table. Harry is a dark mass on the ghost-white frame of the chair, and she drifts toward its twin, next to his. When she is halfway across the yard, she stops, suddenly shy. She can't tell if he is looking at her. "What do you think?" she says, and drinks some more of her whiskey, posing, one hand on her hip, shoulders squared.

"What is it?" he says, leaning forward, the dark mass of him shifting.

"It's a bathing suit, what'd you think?"

"Come closer," he says, "I can't see it."

She comes the rest of the way across the lawn, holding out her glass. "Pour me another shot." She stands in front of him while he pours from a bottle she can barely see, a smoke of darkness into her glass. "It's got this panel in front to make me look thinner."

"You don't need that."

"Maybe not. I just liked it. But there's this panel, here," she takes his hand and puts it against her stomach under the ribs of satiny cloth. "It's a miracle of engineering, just to hold me to-gether."

Harry doesn't answer, and she drops his hand, and sits down suddenly in the other chair. "I'm so happy, it's so nice that you're here, under this sky, this tree . . . " she tries to think what she wants to say. The smooth slats of the chair are hard under her legs. Isn't this better than that trailer? she wants to ask him. The whole dark world is opening up around them, the two white chairs, the two candles, one for Harry, one for Cynthia, under the dark hanging cliff of the house. Cynthia's skin is alive in every molecule, feeling the touch of the air as well as the chair slats and the smooth cold of her glass against her fingers. The world is vibrating, singing.

"What's that?" Harry says, his voice very close in all the world.

"What?" Cynthia says. The world is ringing in rhythmic bursts.

"It's the phone," Harry begins to rise.

"It's the phone," Cynthia echoes, and grabs his arm, holding him back. "It's only the phone, who cares?"

They sit together, legs angled toward each other, each with a hand on a glass, listening to the phone ring in the dark house.

All right, Cynthia thinks. Okay.

"How was your day off?"

"It was okay," Cynthia says. She stands again by the cash regis-ter, across from where Jody stands, filing her nails.

"So what did you do?"

"Nothing much. I went shopping." Cynthia pauses. "Harry came over for dinner."

"Your cousin, right? He's not bad-looking for an old guy." Jody rolls her eyes in a way that she means to be knowing. "He's not married, right?"

"He's too old for you." Cynthia yawns. She can still feel the effects of last night's alcohol.

"I'm not interested or anything," Jody says. She ducks down by the front register in the spot that can't be seen from the office in the back, pulls a brush out from the drawer and begins to brush her hair, pouffing it out and curling it over her finger. "Kenny's enough trouble for me, who needs another one. You want to watch something?"

"I don't care," Cynthia says. "Put on what you like." She yawns again, and when Jody looks at her curiously, says, "I had trouble getting to sleep last night," although this isn't true—she passed out and slept like a stone.

Jody points the remote control at the television mounted on the wall over the magazine rack and flicks through the channels. The television is a new thing, Dino's idea. He says that people will stay longer and buy more while they're waiting to see the end of a scene in their favorite soap, or the score at the end of an inning. Vince objected at first, saying that it would distract the cashiers from their work. "That's us women," Vicky had said to Cynthia, "so weakminded, can't have more than one thing at a time in our brains."

"I saw this preacher show yesterday," Jody says. "The Reverend Plant, you ever watch him?"

Cynthia shakes her head, which is heavy and dull.

"He has this whole town down there, in Alabama or someplace, schools and apartment buildings, supermarket and a mall."

"He must be raking it in," Cynthia says.

"They've even got a hospital. He had his daughter on and they were saying how she had her baby right there in this hospital. She said the doctors were speaking in tongues in the delivery room."

"Who'd want that?"

"You wouldn't catch me having my baby there." Jody shakes her head again, and her straw-colored hair moves stiffly around her thin little face.

Cynthia's eyes fall to Jody's stomach, which is flat, almost concave between the knobby protrusions of her hipbones.

"When I have one, I mean. Kenny says why not start early."

"I can think of some reasons." But Cynthia imagines how it would be if she had had Joey when she was Jody's age, twenty-one. He'd be seventeen or eighteen now, nearly on his way in the world, going to college maybe. She'd be free to start some new thing.

"Don't worry, I'm not ready yet. I want to party for a while." Jody wiggles her hips when she says this. "A baby is the end to good times. I know that from my mom. You were smart to wait until you were older to have yours."

"I wasn't *that* old," Cynthia says. "Twenty-nine."

"Kenny says he doesn't want to wait until he's too old," Jody says. "But I tell him lots of guys get married late and it works out fine. You could be as old as your cousin and still have a kid, no problem."

"Harry?"

"You know, I saw that girl he used to go with, last week— where was I? At the discount drug? Or no, Kenny and I were out to eat and I saw her in the parking lot in a car with someone. Whatever happened with that?"

"I thought she moved away," Cynthia says. Her heart is pounding.

"I'm pretty sure it was her. A blond, right? Around my age?"

"I don't know."

"She was pregnant, I'm pretty sure. It wouldn't be Harry's though, I guess. Wasn't that over a while ago?"

"I don't know," Cynthia says. The blood knocking in her temples is filling her skull with a headache. "I really couldn't say."

Two teenage boys come in and Jody rings up their bottles of pop, their small bags of chips, their candy bars, flirting with them in a halfhearted way. Cynthia busies herself at the deli counter, needlessly wiping down the slicing area, rearranging the pieces of fried chicken in the display case.

She is thinking about the spring. Harry's last disastrous drunk, his reappearance weeks later, no mention of the dinner with Lucette, no mention of Lucette. She hadn't asked him, hadn't dared. She knew he wasn't happy, but she'd been sure that was because of Al, Al dying, all the upset with the will, the worry of the bar. Of course, he'd have been feeling bad about that.

Cynthia bags for Jody, a steady stream of customers passing them by. She is sure that they broke up. That's a fact. And she'd heard that Lucette was gone—good riddance, she'd thought, hanging on Harry, bringing him down, not the right age for him, always thinking about herself, no doubt, as a young girl would. No wonder he went on a spree. I would myself, Cynthia thinks, easing a box of detergent into a paper bag, sliding in a bag of Cheetos with a newspaper between to keep out the soap smell. She remembers the rising excitement she got from the whiskey last night. She slaps a "Sold" sticker on a twelve-pack of beer and wonders if she could ask Jody how far along the girl might have been, how many months, this girl who might have been Linda, Louise, Luella—she imagines herself fumbling for the name when she talks to Jody, but she remembers it all right—Lucette, Lu-cette, it whistles soundless in her teeth.

When the rush subsides, Jody drags out one of the upended milk cartons they sit on when it's slack and settles down, leaning her head back against the counter, way back so that the cartilage in her throat stands out. Cynthia swallows. Of course, she can't ask. Jody would know at once that she thought it was Harry's baby. Not that it possibly could be. "Do you want a pop?" she asks.

"Sure," Jody says.

Cynthia rings them up on their tabs.

"I'd rather have a Coke than a beer any day," Jody says.

"I don't drink much," Cynthia says.

"I like a peach schnapps when I go out. Or Amaretto. Or something like an Alabama Slammer. You ever have that? It's pink and it tastes like some kind of fruit juice. You drink it in shots."

"I don't think so."

"It's really good if you don't like the taste of alcohol."

"I'm supposed to go to the opening of my cousin's bar in a couple of weeks. Maybe I'll try it then."

"That's weird, but I guess it happens a lot."

"What?"

"Well, you know. A guy who drinks and he has a bar."

Cynthia stares at Jody, who is sticking her tongue into the neck of her pop bottle. "What do you mean?"

"It's, you know, ironic. I mean he's got a drinking problem, right?"

"He drinks a little too much sometimes," Cynthia says. She takes the empty bottle from Jody and puts it fussily into the recycle bin.

"Did you ever think about having an intervention for him?"

"A what?" Cynthia says, although she heard. She even knows what it is.

"When all these people who are close to the guy, or the woman it could be, I guess, they get together and talk to them so they'll get help."

"I don't think that's necessary," Cynthia says. Harry just needs to cut down, she thinks. Last night he was fine, mellow, smiling, lying with his head against the back of his chair, relaxed. He'd drunk only a little—a beer when he came, a half glass of whiskey, maybe a little more. She likes that smile he gets, lazy, deep.

"Whatever," Jody says. "How about we watch Oprah?"

She switches the channel again and they watch, Jody intently, Cynthia blankly. She is counting, figuring. Harry would have told her. Or she would have seen something, some difference in him, some deeper trouble. Surely there wasn't enough time, it would have to have happened almost right away, he didn't even know her before February, did he?

On Oprah, there is a group of psychics, mediums, prophets, astrologers, crystal readers. Most of them look quite normal, dressed in suits and dresses, legs neatly crossed. They look like anyone's aunts or uncles, interrupted on their way to the family reunion.

One of them, a woman about fifty in navy blue with matching pumps, is holding an object that belongs to someone in the audience, a wallet which she clasps tightly in her hands. She rocks back and forth, her eyes closed, her glasses on a chain swaying across her chest. The other professionals look on, bored but polite. Oprah stands holding her mike loosely, her hostess-intense look on her face.

"I love this stuff," Jody says.

Suddenly the woman's eyes open and she gets up from her seat so fast that it falls over behind her. Did she make it do that? Cynthia wonders. The woman holds the wallet out in front of her like a divining rod. Her knees are trembling, she seems only barely able to stand, and Oprah starts forward, maybe to catch her, or to stop her.

"I see a little girl running up the aisle," she says. Her mike has come unclipped, but her voice is loud, like a bell, booming.

"A little blond girl," she says.

There is a woman crying in the back, the camera zooms in on her. The woman whose wallet it is.

"A little blond girl, she looks so happy." Her voice goes up higher. "Can't you see her?"

"Oh, stop, stop," the woman in the audience is moaning, trying to get out of her seat.

"She has brown eyes. Such brown brown eyes." She drops to her knees and sways, her arms still stretched out. When she speaks her voice is lower, lighter, a resonating whisper. "They grow older on the other side, dear. They grow and change." The screen goes blank, cuts to a commercial.

All the hair on Cynthia's neck has risen.

"What a performance," Jody says. She turns to ring up a six-pack for a kid whose ID she asks for.

Cynthia gets up and goes down aisle one. She bows her head over the candy and gum racks. What is it, oh what is it? Confused thoughts twist through her head, her dead mother, Louisa lying in her white bed, Joey gone where she can't touch him. What will she do if Harry has a baby?

Slowly she goes down the next aisle, and the next. She has picked up the broom as camouflage and pushes it in front of her, gathering the bits of gray fluff, the gum wrappers, the cigarette butts. She can hear Joey talking with the kid buying beer, and him laughing, but less and less as she gets farther away. In the last aisle, they are indistinguishable from the noise of the television.

I can handle this, she thinks. He doesn't care that she's back, or he doesn't know. She is gone just as much as if she was in Alaska, gone from him.

Going home, Cynthia walks tough, squaring her shoulders, subduing the sway of her hips. She projects maleness, toughness, her loose jacket hiding her body, her hair stuffed inside the collar. This is a game she plays walking home after midnight when the street is dark between the streetlights. Her steps are almost soundless, her feet in tennis shoes gliding into contact with the sidewalk. No one will bother her, no cars will stop or even honk at her, she is invincible, invisible. She likes it, though, this quick breathing in of risk. She likes to be the only thing moving on the dark street, likes the cherry-red glow of the stoplights that change whether there are cars or not.

As she walks she thinks of what she will do. The summer that she longed for in January is almost over, but there is still time— time to have picnics, to find wonderful summer recipes, to go out and do things. For a minute, she imagines she might have a party, buy more cushions, more candles. It never seemed possible to have a party with Derek, but Derek is gone.

She walks past the police station and the rows of black-and-whites, waxed and shining under the halogen parking lot lights. The house lit up, people talking, laughing, music playing, all the lovely food of summer—tomatoes, yellow peppers, orange melons and peaches, purple plums, green grapes. People spilling out of the house onto the porch and the lawn. Who would they be, though? She needs to meet people who would come to such a party, people who would be beautiful and interesting, full of character, sympathetic, warm. Right now she can think of hardly anyone she might invite. Vicky, the other women from the store. Their husbands. Her next-door neighbors, pried from the maze of hedges in their backyard, might they be interesting? Some of her cousins, the ones she can stand to see. What a mismatched group.

The party will have to wait, but that's all right. She walks on, big-shouldered, smiling. She will find out about Lucette, just to know what's what, not that it matters. She will make Harry come on a picnic. She'll go to the opening of his bar, she'll get a new dress for it. She'll have a drink when she gets home.

It's darker in the house now, but every surface, every object is familiar to her. She walks through to the kitchen, drinks a glass of water.

When the phone rings, she moves quickly to get it. It's Harry, she thinks, he needs something at the bar, she imagines herself driving through the night to take it to him. Or Derek, calling when the rates are low. But when she gets to the phone, has her hand on it, she waits while it rings a fourth time, a fifth, six, seven, eight. When she picks it up, she does not say hello, she holds it to her ear like a sea shell and listens.

"I'm waiting," it says to her. "I'm waiting for you. I like your long hair."

"It's not that long," Cynthia says into the phone. "You don't know anything."

Stupid jerk, she thinks after she has hung up. Idiot. If I were a man, she thinks, I'd never do that, never call a woman and say stupid things. Doesn't he know they can trace those calls? She sits down in the front room and turns on the light. Her hands are trembling. She turns it off again and sits in the dark.

I can handle this, she thinks. I can handle everything. She has an image of herself with her arms held out, each finger a beacon, each hand an anchor, all the days ahead like beads on a string she will slide past her, numbering them, biting them to test their soundness. She gets up and turns on the television. She will watch Johnny Carson, and then whatever is next. It is only two and a half hours until Harry comes home.

Cynthia is straightening up before she goes to the opening of Harry's bar, picking up magazines. They are a magazine-reading family, even Joey. She picks up *Vogue* and turns over a few pages that already show fall clothes, serious-faced models cocooned in wool and cashmere. Not yet, Cynthia thinks. But her ear registers the whirring and chirping of the cicadas outside. It is the end of July already, summer is past its peak, the real summer of June, July, August.

She adds *Vogue* to the pile that she is keeping and picks up last week's *TV Guide*. She hasn't read any of the articles, and now they seem stale. She turns to the answer column at the back, her favorite, and reads:

I've been arguing with my husband and brother-in-law for at least a year, and now the kids are starting to agree with them. At the beginning of our favorite show, there is a crowd scene on the street with a mailman waiting for the traffic light. They all insist that it's John Astin, who used to be on *The Addams Family*. I am absolutely positive that it's not.

Mrs. J.C., Mundelein, IL

Doesn't this woman have anything better to do? But still, Cynthia finds herself sympathizing with this embattled sister, her family (all male?) turning against her, member by member, the elusive mailman taunting her weekly from the screen.

She puts *TV Guide* in the wastebasket and picks up an aviation magazine, where she reads about a virus that begins as a cold sore and ends as amnesia that may last for a week or longer, a possible hazard to pilots. Surely to everyone, Cynthia thinks. She tries to imagine what it would be like to have amnesia—not to remember your own life, your husband or child. Not to know whom you loved, whom you hated. She gives a shiver. To be so free in the world, with not even a name to tie you.

This day, the evening of it, stretches before her unbroken. The magazines were the last of what she had to do before she pays attention only to herself, to getting herself ready for tonight. She wants Harry to be proud of her, she wants to look good next to him.

What if no one comes, though? This has run through her mind a dozen times in the last week, and each time it makes her cold, and each time she soothes herself—they will come, everyone loves Harry, even if only his friends come it would be enough for the opening. Anyway, they love to drink. She feels about the opening as if it is a party she is giving, she is full of fear and responsibility.

Outside, the wind picks up a little and the heavy dark blooms of the red rambling rose nod on their trailing stems. Cynthia opens the garage door and reaches for the garden scissors that hang just inside. She grasps the stems firmly between the thorns as she cuts the roses, forming them into a loose bunch to carry into the house, her hand a cup. She picks out a vase, one of her great-grandmother's, a green glass sphere, and sits at the dining-room table, clipping and nudging the roses into a pleasing disorder. She stands and looks around to see if there is anything else she wants to take upstairs. The phone is lying on the table, off the hook, and she hesitates, thinking whether to call Vicky and see if she's coming tonight. Later, she decides.

She carries the roses upstairs, sets them on the little table by her bed, the first thing she will see in the morning, and goes to her closet. She takes out the dress she will wear tonight, a new one, full-skirted, dark red like the roses. She drapes it across a chair, lying ready for her to embody it. She sets her good shoes side by side in front of the chair. She takes off her clothes and throws them at the laundry basket. Naked, she walks to the bathroom and stands on the cool white tile floor, testing the warmth of the shower. The water in the pipes sounds for a minute like the phone ringing and she tenses, straining to hear, until she remembers that it is off the hook. She steps into the water, lets it stream over her, parting her hair, sheeting off her chest and arms.

At seven, she is downstairs again, wearing her underwear and a robe. She opens the refrigerator. It is almost empty—there is just a quart of milk, a carton of cottage cheese, two lemons in a bowl, two vanilla yogurts. In the vegetable drawer, a head of lettuce rolls around with a couple of tomatoes and a cucumber. The door shelves are crammed with condiments and bottles of half-used salad dressing, but the main part, how white it is, how empty, how the refrigerator light shines in the spaces between the shelves.

Cynthia spoons two scoops of cottage cheese into a bowl. She picks up one of the three plums in a bowl on the table and slices it on top of the cottage cheese, admiring the white and purple and translucent green against the blue of the bowl. She sits at the dining-room table next to the phone, the long rays of the late afternoon sun streaming across her hands as she eats. When she has scraped the last bit of white from the bowl, she pulls the phone over and dials.

"Yes, I'm coming," Vicky says. "You don't mind if I bring Handsome, do you? I've got the chance of a babysitter and he hasn't got a gig."

"Why not?" Cynthia says.

"Never leave a man alone with time on his hands, that's what I say. What are you wearing?"

"That new dress, I told you."

"Oh, right. Well, I'm not wearing a dress, too serious for me. I'll wear my good jeans."

They both laugh. Cynthia has never seen Vicky in anything but pants, although she has a vast wardrobe of them, from jeans to satin harem pants that bell and sway around her ankles.

They arrange that Vicky will meet Cynthia at the bar at around nine-thirty, and Cynthia puts the phone down. She will sit and drink her coffee for a while, maybe look at *Vogue* and the other magazines she hasn't had time for. She wants to use them, gobble them up, so that she can throw them away with a sense of accomplishment. She hooks her finger through the handle of the cup and lifts it, and the phone rings. She has forgotten and left it connected.

This time she lifts it immediately, ready to fight, strengthened by this afternoon of peace. "Hello." She allows no question in her voice, no wishy-washy rising lilt.

"What have you been doing on the phone so long?"

"What do you mean?" she says, taken off guard.

"I've been trying to call you all afternoon and it's been busy," Derek says.

"I think the receiver was tilted a little," she says, "you know, not right on the button. And then I had to call Vicky just now."

"I was starting to get worried," Derek sounds angry.

"It's a good thing you called," Cynthia says, "because I'm going out tonight."

"Out where?"

"The opening of Harry's bar." She brushes her hand down her robe-covered thigh.

"It's tonight?"

"I'm going with Vicky. And her husband."

"That's good. Listen, Joey wants to talk to you, but before he does, I want to know when you're coming down."

"I thought we agreed that I'd stay here and keep my job for a while, to save money."

"God knows we'd be better off if you sold the house and came down here, even without a job."

"You agreed that we didn't have to sell the house."

"Didn't have to sell it *yet*. But that's not what I meant anyway. I mean when are you coming down here for a visit? You've been saying you'd come all summer. I thought you'd come when Joey did, and then you said you'd come last weekend, but you didn't. So when can you?"

"It's been hard." Cynthia twists the phone cord around her long fingers, the bones of her knuckles standing out white between the black winding plastic. She feels the beginning of the pain in her head, her neck. "The other women are going on vacation and so on."

"Cynthia, I haven't seen you since May, except for that time in June when I came up to get the van. I miss you."

Cynthia knows she is supposed to say she misses him, too, and it is even true in a way. She misses his friendly bulk in the house, his cheerful acceptance of her moods, his way of smoothing over what goes wrong. But she thinks that saying any of this will undermine, even endanger, the pleasure, the rightness she feels in being alone, alone in the house, alone in her life. And then there is Harry. She has to be here for Harry. "I thought you were coming for a week in September when you bring Joey back for school."

"We have to talk about that."

"What's to talk about?"

"We'll talk when you come down. How about next weekend?"

"I'll have to check with Vince."

"Well, do it." Derek sounds tired. "Here's Joey."

Talking to Joey, Cynthia feels good. He sounds so happy, he hasn't had time to miss her yet. He is learning how to fish from one of his cousins, he has played with dogs, seen raccoons and deer. He asks about the dog across the street, and Cynthia feels guilty that she has forgotten about it. She half-lies, saying that she has waved to it, and that it wags its tail at her. When they are finished talking, she is smiling. "Say good-bye to your father for me," she tells Joey, absently rubbing her neck and shoulder. She forgets to leave the phone off the hook.

When she hears the truck in the alley, she is washing her bowl and spoon. She leans forward over the sink to see if it is Harry, and it is, he is walking up the path by the garage, tapping the wall lightly, absentmindedly. She meets him on the back steps, clutching her robe, closing it at the neck with one hand. "You're here," she says.

"You wanted me to pick you up, right?"

"But you're early." Cynthia relaxes her grip on her robe, and ties the belt more tightly.

"I have to take Geneva. You almost ready?"

"Almost ready!" Cynthia gestures with her hand, a bit of sign language that is supposed to indicate her robe, her uncombed hair, the absence of makeup. "Well, I can hurry, I guess."

"How long will you be?" Harry eyes her, as if noticing for the first time that she isn't dressed.

Cynthia calculates. "Twenty minutes. No, fifteen."

"I can't wait that long. There's a delivery coming."

"But Harry—"

"You can drive yourself, can't you?"

"I didn't want to drive the car," Cynthia says, but when he looks at her, questioning, she is unable to explain why.

"You could come with your friend, what's her name."

"She's coming with her husband." Even as she says this, Cynthia is aware of how stupid it sounds. "Why are you taking Geneva anyway?"

"She asked me if I would."

So did I, you idiot, Cynthia thinks. "Why couldn't one of her kids take her?"

Harry shrugs. "I have to go, Cyn. You come when you're ready." He grins at her, and pulls a lock of her hair.

Cynthia slams the screen door after him and stands there watching his back as he goes through the gate. She goes upstairs, putting her feet down hard on the steps, very precise, very neat, straight and centered on the tread.

She doesn't want to go with Vicky and her husband and have to sit in the back seat, third wheel to their tight coupleness. She doesn't want to drive herself, for she wants Harry to drive her home. She is holding the thought of this drive in her head, late at night, the truck gliding through the empty streets, both of them tired, a little high, flushed with success. She will have been a help to him, charming customers, available for advice or a quick confidence boost. It won't be the same if they come home separately. It is the drive together, enclosed by the cab of the truck, thinking the same thoughts, that holds the magic.

She sits on her bed, thinking. She could drive there and then something could be wrong with her car? But Harry could fix it or get one of his friends to do it. She could pretend she felt sick, too sick to drive? But he would just think she'd had to much to drink, it would create the wrong atmosphere. The car looms, a great metal encumbrance, dragging her down.

And then she realizes: She can walk. It isn't so far, not terribly far. She calculates. A ten-minute walk. In heels? But she can wear her old sandals and carry her good shoes in her purse. She smiles and tilts the clock toward her. Almost eight-fifteen. Twenty minutes to get ready, ten minutes to walk, say fifteen to be sure, she'll be there just before nine. Plenty of time to help with the finishing touches, at least Geneva won't be able to take the credit for that. She jumps up, lifting her dress from the chair, and swirls it over her head.

At ten-thirty, Cynthia is pretending to drink a seven-and-seven, her new dress hanging limp down the sides of a bar stool. Nearly everyone in the bar is up on the floor dancing to the band's rendition of "Pretty Woman." The only people sitting at the bar are Cynthia, a group of three young men, Arabs, and Tase Penfield, who has his back to the dance floor the better to ignore it.

The bar takes up one-half of the big room, it's nearly forty feet long. It curls back on itself, a horseshoe, so that you can sit on one side and have a look at who is drinking on the other. This half of the room is lined with mirrors, one of Al's ideas, it makes the bar look twice as populated and festive. The other half has a smooth springy wood floor for dancing, surrounded with tables, and the stage for the band like an altar at the end of it. Over the stage is a computer-generated board on which messages appear urging customers to consider the specials and not to forget to tip the barmaids. This too was Al's idea. "It's like a memorial," one of the regulars from the Maple Leaf, Charlie, had explained to Cynthia earlier. "A fucking memorial." His silent friend, improbably introduced by Harry as Beaner, had nodded.

Cynthia sees, looking out over the room, that these two, Charlie and Beaner, aren't dancing either. That makes seven of us, she thinks. But of course Harry won't be dancing. And Geneva is sitting at the best table at the head of the dance floor, flanked by her two daughters and their husbands, like the queen mother. That's twelve. But no, she sees that only one of the husbands is sitting with Geneva, nervously drumming his fingers on the table. Cynthia searches the dance floor and finds the two daughters, both dancing with one of the husbands, laughing and making exaggerated shimmying motions with their hips and arms. And there is Harry! Cynthia sits up straighter to see who he is dancing with, but whoever it is is short, lost in the crowd. He isn't moving much, just shuffling his feet back and forth, but he is smiling at some focus among the bodies in front of him. He ought to be keeping his mind on business, Cynthia thinks. She stretches her neck, waiting for a glimpse of his partner.

"Harry's feeling good."

Cynthia settles back in her seat and gives the old man a repressive look. "Yes."

Old Penfield turns back to the bar and drinks a minuscule amount of his beer, head down. When the song is over, Cynthia waits for the dancers to disperse, maybe for a chance to talk with Harry, but they stand jigging a bit on the dance floor, waiting to see what the band will play next. When it starts, it is a slow song, "Imagine," an old John Lennon song that Cynthia finds incongruous for a country-and-western band. But the dancers don't seem surprised, they turn to each other, fall into each other's arms, and sway with the music, barely moving, each pair of tightly clasped bodies held in the looser embrace of the crowd.

How these people dance, hardly resting, stopping only to down their drinks and order more. Cynthia thought that only the young people would dance, but the middle-aged and the old are on the floor as well. Cynthia feels sidelined. She has that high-school–mixer feeling of serial rejection, the eyes of men prowling for partners sliding over her again and again. Even the three Arabs seem ready to join the dance, they have drawn closer to the floor and are eyeing a group of women hovering by the door, just arrived.

Cynthia signals the barmaid for another drink. She is unused to being in a bar. The last time she went to bars at all was the year after she came back from college, when she used to go out with the women she worked with at the bank. But then it was in a group, there was someone to talk to. She had been invited to sit with

Geneva, but she had gotten out of that, edging away after saying hello and being introduced to the daughters, the husbands. Geneva had taken notice, though. Cynthia had felt her eye on her as she slid away to sit by the bar. And where was Vicky? She looks at the door for what seems like the fiftieth time, but Vicky, with or without her husband, is not framed in it. The group of women is still there, talking with Charlie and his friend, and with the Arabs. Then there is a split, the Arabs and the women move to a table together, and Charlie and Beaner are left standing alone with the rent-a-cop Harry has hired for the night.

Charlie sees Cynthia looking over and waves. She takes a sip of her drink, pretending not to see, but a minute later, he is perching on the stool next to her. "Hot band, huh?" he says.

"They're all right."

"The drummer is a friend of Harry's. Well, I guess you knew that."

Cynthia hadn't.

"You looked lonely is why I thought I'd come over." Charlie picks at his fingernails as he says this, his eyes down.

"I'm just waiting for Harry."

"Yeah, I hardly got to talk to him myself."

Neither of them says anything, the silence filled by the band. The dance floor is less full, since the song they're playing, "Tequila Sunrise," is neither fast nor slow—people aren't sure how to move to it. Cynthia sees old Penfield hold his beer bottle up, but these barmaids, not knowing him, don't recognize his signal, and continue chatting in a knot by the sink. The bottle sinks back to the surface of the bar as if it is too heavy for him to hold.

"You changed your hair," Charlie says.

"What?" She has almost forgotten he is there, she is watching for Harry, who isn't dancing now, he's moving from table to table, talking to people he knows, smiling at the women, flirting probably, exchanging more serious conversation with the men.

"You got your hair cut or something. Am I right?"

"Yes. A couple of weeks ago."

"I knew it. It used to be longer, right?"

"Right." Cynthia wonders if she should call one of the barmaids for the old man. He is sitting, head bowed, hands on the bar, so still he might be dead.

"I've seen you around. You drive a Chevy Nova."

"Yes, yes, I do."

"Jeez, that's a good car. Friend of mine had a Chevy Nova once. Drove it to death, though. He killed the car, you know what I mean?"

"He did?" Cynthia feels the high-school–mixer feeling even more strongly. This is the stuck-with-a-loser part.

"If it had been anything but a Chevy Nova, probably would have only taken half as long. To drive it into the ground, I mean. You know?"

"What happened to your friend?" Cynthia says, looking around for Beaner.

"He got creamed in a motorcycle accident."

"What?"

"That was after he got rid of the Nova though." Charlie takes a long pull at his beer.

"I meant your friend who you're here with."

"He's around. He's got his priorities."

"Oh." They sit in silence again, listening to the band play "Cocaine."

Suddenly, hands come from behind Cynthia and cover her eyes. "Guess who?"

"Vicky!" Thank God, Cynthia thinks. "Where have you been?"

"Handsome was in a sulk." Vicky tosses her head toward Ralph, who is talking to the cop at the door. "I had to hit him with some guilt. So, am I breaking anything up?"

"Just talking," Charlie says, sliding off the stool. "Just passing the time, is what I mean to say." He slips away without saying good-bye.

Vicky orders straight gin on ice with a twist of lemon, and a beer for her husband. She holds it up when it comes and waggles it in the air to attract his attention. He ignores her. "He thinks he's giving me a hard time," she says with gloomy satisfaction. "What the hell. You want to dance?"

"No," Cynthia says.

"You haven't had enough to drink, probably. I can never dance until I've had two of these." She taps the side of her glass with a fingernail. "Handsome, now, he'll dance at the drop of a hat. I can see him sometimes when he's playing, his feet jigging away up on stage, wanting to be out on the floor." They look over at Ralph. He has made his way over to the side and is standing in the midst of a group of little tables where he can watch the band, oblivious to the fact that he is blocking the view of several people sitting near him. "Christ," Vicky says. "He wants to get up and jam, I can tell. If we're lucky, they won't let him."

"He's not so bad, is he?" Cynthia asks, her eyes on Harry, who is standing by Geneva's table, talking to one of the daughters.

"He's fine on guitar." Vicky searches her bag for cigarettes, and then for matches. "But it's drums he'll want to play." She lights a cigarette. The corners of her mouth droop farther, and she shakes her head. " 'Wipeout.' "

"What?"

"The song. 'Wipeout.' It's got a drum solo." Vicky sighs.

"So, who was your friend?" she asks after a minute, waving her hand in Charlie's direction. He is standing near the door again, leaning awkwardly against the wall, a bunch of balloons hanging just over his head.

"He's just some kid Harry knows, someone from the Maple Leaf."

"I don't know, Cindy, he looked interested to me. He might be a hot one."

"Please." Cynthia makes a face. "I'm old enough to be his mother."

"The older woman–younger man. It's a done thing. Jody told me she saw it on Oprah."

"So?"

"So there you go."

Cynthia laughs, the idea of skinny Charlie filling in for the stereotype younger man, tireless, muscled, athletic—it's too silly. They both laugh, covering their mouths, snorting over their drinks. "Stop it, will you."

"When Derek's away, the mouse will play."

"Stop it," Cynthia says. "I'm serious now."

"What's so funny, girls?" Ralph comes up and reaches between them for his beer.

"Just talking about men, sweetie." Vicky pinches his cheek.

"Can't get in the middle of that, can I?" He removes her hand from his cheek and glides away. They turn to watch him.

Cynthia looks at Vicky.

"He's not mad anymore," Vicky says. "That's just for form."

"Is he always like this?"

"Oh, he's a tiring man." Vicky yawns widely. "I need ten hours of sleep to deal with him."

This sets them off again, and they are still laughing when Harry turns in their direction. Cynthia continues to laugh as he comes toward them, watching his walk, slow, rolling, no stagger. He hasn't been drinking.

She allows herself to catch sight of him, smiles and waves. She holds herself carefully—it seems so plain to her, her delight, the wave that rolls through her body, that Vicky must notice. She widens her peripheral vision to take in Vicky on her left, but Vicky, still laughing, is looking at Ralph as he makes his way along the other side of the bar, she hasn't even seen Harry.

"Ladies," he says, laying a hand on Cynthia's shoulder, on Vicky's.

"Things look good," Vicky says.

"They do," he says, but his eyes keep roving around as he talks to them, checking over and over, searching.

Cynthia sits quiet under the weight of his hand. She wants to dance with Harry. She telegraphs this to him, letting the feeling rise, it seems, from her skin to his, but when she says his name, the eyes he turns to her are preoccupied. "Harry," she says again.

He snaps into focus. "What can I do for you?"

A dance, she thinks, looking into his eyes. Dancing. Dance. "How about a drink?"

"That would be nice," Vicky says morosely. "Gin up for me."

Harry signals the barmaid who has been hovering near them. "One more for these two. On the house."

"And what about for you, Harry?" the barmaid says.

"Nothing for me."

"Nothing at all?" she says, drawling out the last word.

"Not at the moment," he says, smiling at her.

Jesus, Cynthia thinks.

"I saw you dancing," she says when he turns back to her.

"You did, did you?"

With who? Cynthia wants to ask. You bastard. "Got to keep the customers happy, I suppose."

"That's about it," Harry says.

"Men don't like to dance," Vicky says, shaking her head. "It's a proven fact."

"What about Ralph?" Cynthia asks, feeling she has scored a point.

"Oh, Handsome, he's unnatural. My husband," she explains to Harry, pointing to the corner table closest to the band where Ralph has insinuated himself, writing down notes on a joke cocktail napkin, ignoring the waitresses who want him to buy a drink. "He's not a man," Vicky explains. "He's a demon from hell sent here to torture women. It's my mission in life to save others at the expense of myself." She laughs, a long trilling giggle.

"We plan to get drunk," Cynthia says to Harry.

Vicky nods. "We plan to dance."

Harry bows. "Well, I'll leave you ladies to it." He hesitates. "Geneva wanted to know why you didn't sit at her table. She asked where you were."

She knows where I am, the old witch, Cynthia thinks. "Are you saying I ought to go and sit with her?"

"No. I'm just telling you what she said." He turns and goes to the back, toward the pool room.

"You are going to dance with me, aren't you?" Vicky asks, poking Cynthia with her elbow.

"I guess so." Cynthia downs the melted-ice remains of her last drink and takes a long gulp of the new one.

"It'll come back to you," Vicky says. "And besides, when the floor is this crowded, no one can see you if you stand in the middle."

At one o'clock, they are out there, dancing hard to the band's version of "Mony, Mony," laughing, so hemmed in by moving bodies that they can barely take a step, can only stand and shimmy, along with fifty other sets of hips and shoulders. Ralph and Vicky have made up, and he is dancing with the two of them, although having a partner is beside the point. A woman two feet from them is dancing as furiously as they are, all by herself, nodding and smiling to anyone who catches her eye. Cynthia has a pain in her side, but she keeps on shaking until the final chords, and then she and Vicky fall on each other, exclaiming and laughing.

"I've got a stitch," Cynthia says, holding her side. "I think I've got to visit the ladies' room."

"Come on, then, I'll go with you." Vicky taps Ralph on the shoulder. "You—behave yourself."

In the ladies', they have to wait, fifth and sixth in line. There are only two stalls, and one is occupied by someone who is not coming out. "Bad idea to come on the break," Vicky finds her lipstick and outlines her lips.

"I like that color," the woman behind them says.

"Coral Mist," Vicky says, holding it up for her inspection.

"I wouldn't be able to wear it, though," the woman says, shaking her head. "Coral makes me look flushed, what with my natural pinkness." She pats her stiff, upswept hair, a violent mahogany brown. "Now on you, with the nice pale skin and the hair. You got a little bit of red in your hair, you know that?"

"No kidding?" Vicky clicks her lipstick shut.

"Don't mind me."

When Vicky goes into one of the stalls, the woman turns to Cynthia. "Now you got that nice fine type of hair. Where'd you get it cut?"

"I did it," Vicky yells from inside the stall.

"You got a nice separation in the layers," the woman shouts back. She takes a lock of Cynthia's hair and rubs it between her fingers. "I'd think about a permanent, though, if I was you."

"A permanent?" Cynthia says. She is warm and giddy from dancing, the perspiration drying cool on her arms.

"A body wave is what I'd think about." She cocks her head to one side, studying Cynthia. "Don't mind me. I'm a beautician."

"Your turn," Vicky says, pushing Cynthia toward the stall.

"I think I know you," the woman continues, as Cynthia goes inside. "I think we have a mutual acquaintance."

"Who's that?" Cynthia says. She feels like laughing as she sits down on the toilet. She is so happy, the blood racing through her veins from the dancing, the flat pinkness of the paint on the wall next to her, the high trilling of the woman's voice from outside the door. She leans her head against the wall, feeling the paint's smooth skin against her forehead.

"That'd be Mrs. Jacqueline Gitlin," the woman says. "She's one of my ladies. I do her hair Fridays, every Friday at nine-thirty sharp."

"Mrs. Gitlin?" Cynthia says. It seems to her that her voice squeaks, and this is very funny.

"That's right. Her oldest girl Loretta is married to your husband's brother."

Cynthia pulls up her underpants and pantyhose and looks down at herself to see if anything is rumpled or hanging out.

"Isn't that right?" the woman says to her as she emerges.

"Mrs. Gitlin, yes, that's right." She looks at herself in the mirror, swaying toward her reflection. She looks tousled, but in a good way, she thinks, like the models in magazines who are supposed to look as if they have just gotten out of bed.

"Come on," Vicky says, "they're playing our song."

"Nice to meet you," Cynthia calls as they go out.

"Don't mind me," Vicky says in a high voice. "Don't mind me, I'm a beautician."

"Mrs. Gitlin's beautician," Cynthia says. "Don't forget that."

"All right I won't. I absolutely will not forget it."

"I'm afraid—" Cynthia says, laughing.

"What? What?"

"I'm afraid Mrs. Gitlin needs more than a beautician, the old hatchet face."

"Is she really some relation to you?"

"Her daughter is my sister-in-law. Loretta. We're as close as we can be."

"How close is that?" They plop onto bar stools.

"I'm in Ohio," Cynthia says, drinking the last drop of her drink. "And she's in Pennsylvania."

"You girls took your time," Ralph says.

They turn around and look at him. "Go away, baby," Vicky says. "We're about to have a deep conversation."

"You're as high as a kite."

"Go away, go away." Vicky flaps her hands at him, and he goes. She orders them each another drink. "So tell me," she says to Cynthia, leaning toward her, her chin in one upturned palm. "Speaking of Pennsylvania, do you miss Derek?"

"Miss him?" Cynthia swirls the ice cubes around in her glass.

"I sometimes wonder," Vicky says, looking dreamily at the twinkling colored lights over the bar, "how it would be if Handsome was gone. I don't want him to die or anything," she says to Cynthia, "but just if he was gone. He's just so much trouble. You know?"

Cynthia has found Harry, on the dance floor again, his smooth fair head bent over someone's dark waterfall of hair.

"Of course, Derek's not like Handsome, I can see that." Vicky grabs Cynthia's wrist. "He's an adult, you know what I mean? Ralph's such a kid I feel like Mom sometimes, you know?"

"He's very attractive," Cynthia says, her eyes on the dance floor.

"Oh—attractive." Vicky pokes her finger in her drink, pushing the ice cubes under the surface one at a time. "Hey, you, bar-maid," she calls, "we need another drink over here."

"I don't know," Cynthia says. She feels fine, more than fine, but some bit of drinking memory says that this is the drink that will do her in if she drinks it.

"Of course you don't," Vicky says. "Aren't I the one that's married to him?"

"They're playing another slow song," Cynthia says. "Do they want people to fall asleep?"

"You can dance with Handsome if you want to."

"Oh, no."

"Go on. It'll do him good to dance. He's dying to."

"I don't think so."

"He's a good dancer. Go on. I want to watch you two dance together. Ralph," she calls. "Get your butt over here."

"No," Cynthia says, but Vicky is taking her drink from her hand, and Ralph's hot hand is on her arm, pulling her toward the mass of dancers. Once on the floor, he swings her around and fits her against him in a workmanlike way. And they are dancing, she is dizzy with it, dancing with a man. It doesn't matter that it is Ralph, she barely remembers who it is that is holding her.

She lets her hand rest on his neck, feeling his shirt collar, his skin, his satiny hair, under her fingers. The other hand is clasped in his, and she rests against him, her body like a length of silk fluttering in the wind of the music. Cynthia's eyes are closed. She forgets to look for Harry.

When the music stops, she opens her eyes. Mrs. Gitlin's beautician is looking at her from a table a foot away. She winks and smirks.

"Thank you," Cynthia says.

"You're a pretty good dancer," Ralph says.

"Thank you," she says again.

"You want to go another one?"

Cynthia glances at Mrs. Gitlin's beautician. "I'd love to, but my ankle hurts a little. I've got weak ankles."

"Whatever." They start back to the bar. "Things look good for your cousin if this keeps up." Ralph indicates the crowd on the floor, at the tables.

"I guess so," Cynthia says. She can still feel the influence of the dance on the way she moves, more rhythmic, more graceful, she sways and darts between the customers.

"How about if I give you my card?"

"What?" she says, turning to look at him, bumping into a woman coming the other way.

He steadies her with a hand on her elbow. "My business card. For the band."

"Oh, right." Cynthia remembers it later, this walk back, as if she is descending through layers of smoke and sound, past the out-thrust arms and legs of people sitting at the bar. The grip of Ralph's hand on her arm is the pivot on which she revolves, nothing else is firm. She can't feel her feet, she is bodiless. Her clothes and hair seem to float around her as if a wind is blowing. The lights—the small ones inset in the ceiling, the sparkling string like a necklace over the bar, the laser of the band's red and blue spotlights cutting through the fog of cigarette smoke—they are solid, they are coming at her in waves.

"How much did you drink?" Harry asks her.

"What?"

"How many drinks did you have?"

She hears his voice, but she can't see him. She can only see the lights rushing at her, in lines, regularly, like the beat of music.

Streetlights. The truck. She puts her hand out to the dashboard, and turns to find Harry.

"How many drinks?" he says. He sounds angry.

"You never danced with me."

"I planned to," he says, looking out at the road ahead. "But by the time I got back to you, you were face down in your drink."

"I was not." Cynthia reaches up to touch her cheeks, her forehead. "I wasn't, was I?"

"Not in your drink, I guess." Harry's voice relaxes. "On the bar though. Vicky and her husband sort of propped you up."

"I don't remember that." Cynthia is afraid to ask what else she might not remember.

"You looked at me with your one eye and said you wanted to go home." Harry laughs. "You said, 'I'd like to go home now, Harry.' "

"What's so funny about that?"

"It was damn funny."

"I just got back from the doctor's." Cynthia shrugs herself out of her coat, the receiver snugged between her jaw and shoulder.

"I've been calling you for an hour and it's been busy," Vicky says.

Cynthia sits down at the dining-room table, and pushes her shoes off. "Maybe there's something wrong with the exchange." The house is full of still, hot, middle-of-August air. She turns the chair so that she can rest her feet on the cool wood floor.

"I just wanted to tell you that Vince wants you to come in half an hour early for a meeting."

"A meeting?"

"We're all supposed to. Lucky for him that I work today anyway. I wouldn't be coming in on my day off, I'll tell you that."

"What's it about?"

"Who knows." Vicky yawns. "Big changes, he says. Probably just the usual pep talk. So what's going on with you?"

"Nothing, really."

"What did the doctor say about your neck?"

"He said it was tension and bad posture." Cynthia realizes that she has the phone on her bad side, and she changes ears, holding the receiver in place with one hand, and massages her neck with the other.

"What about that pain in your jaw and the side of your head?"

"It's all the same thing, he says."

"Did you tell him what I read you about temporal mandibular joint disorder?"

"He says it's nothing like that. I'm supposed to do some exercises."

"Well," Vicky says. "That's good, I guess. How's Derek?"

"He's okay." Cynthia stops massaging her neck and places her hand on the table flexing and extending her knuckles, looking at her wedding ring. "He came up on Saturday."

"I know," Vicky says. "Vince told me you asked for the night off. How was it, seeing him?"

"It was fine," Cynthia says. "Listen, I've got to go. I have some things to do if I'm going to come in early."

She sits with the receiver in her hand, tapping her fingers against the table, unsatisfying thuds muffled by the protective pad and the tablecloth. She wants to see Harry, she hasn't seen him since he left for the bar on Saturday night. He spent the last two nights at the trailer, leaving the house to her and Derek. She had been going to stop in at the bar on the way to work, but if she has to go in early, he may not be there.

She replaces the receiver, picks it up again immediately, and dials. "Hello? May I speak to Harry?" She doesn't identify herself, but the barmaid recognizes her voice. "He's not there? Did he say when he'd be in? No?"

Cynthia clicks the receiver down, then picks it up and puts it on its side on the table, feeling as if she might cry. It's so hot, the air is pressing in on her. Harry will be home tonight, probably early since it's a Monday, but she can't wait that long. She wants to see him, tell him what Derek said.

"How's Harry?" Derek had asked her at the restaurant.

"The same," she'd said, holding her complicated knowledge back. She'd been relieved to feel friendly toward Derek. They sat across the table from one another, eating neatly, sitting up straight, untouchable. Everything had been fine. He had said nothing about her coming down, no questions, no reproaches. She asked about the hotel, about his brother, about Loretta. He asked about her job, about Vicky, about Harry's bar. He was watching her, she could see that, but she felt equal to it. He had told her some honeymoon jokes, trade jokes. They had laughed together about how he had brought his laundry home for her to do.

They ordered dessert, lemon meringue pie for both of them. The shimmering wedges were set before them, golden beads of caramelized sugar glistening on the white slopes of meringue, the quivering yellow base still showing the marks of the knife. Derek picked up his fork and paused. "I enrolled Joey in school," he said, and he brought the fork down sideways and cut off the point of the pie wedge.

Cynthia hadn't understood at first, believing that he meant he had gone to see the principal at Joey's school in Cleveland, old Sister Raphael. But it became clear that he was talking about the school in this hick town in Pennsylvania, not even a Catholic school. "How could you do that?" she said, her hands poised on the table as if she might spring across it. "It can't be legal," she made herself say reasonably, although her voice sounded thickened, rough.

"I'm his parent," Derek said, as reasonable as she. He cut another piece of pie and put it into his mouth.

Cynthia watched him chew, sickened by the thought of the lemon and the meringue turning to mush, to slime in his mouth, his large fleshy tongue, his square white teeth. She cut a piece of her own pie and pushed it to the side of the plate. She hadn't known what to say, had said stupid things. "I'm his mother," she said.

"Yes," Derek agreed. "And my wife."

"You can't do that without me."

"You have the option of being there."

"But he'll miss me."

"Not if you come down and live with us."

Cynthia shivers, remembering the calm evenness of his voice. Derek has made it clear. She can have the house and Harry, or she can have Joey. But there must be something she can do so that she will not have to make that choice.

They had argued all Sunday, shouting at each other, or speaking in cold logical tones. They had slammed doors, banged cups down on the table. She had wept many times, and once she had seen tears standing in his eyes. The two of them had moved through the house, dropping things, throwing things, leaving a trail of ruin behind them. She hadn't done the dishes or made the bed, had even forgotten to worry about the telephone, whether to leave it off the hook or not, but oddly enough, there were none of those phone calls while Derek was there.

Derek had left this morning before she got up. She lay, arms stiff at her sides, eyes shut, listening to him put his things in his duffel bag. She heard the rasp of the zipper closing, his footsteps bringing him to the side of the bed. When she opened her eyes, he was standing over her, face blank and tired. He said good-bye, and she echoed him. She heard the front door close. She hadn't done his laundry. She turned over on the bed and pressed her face into the pillow.

At the doctor's, she sat in the hard plastic chair in the waiting room, too tired to yawn, feeling a terrible ache all through her body from not having slept, as if she were being pressed between bars of iron. She was sure her blood pressure would be high, sure that the doctor would tell her something bad. Her pain, the twisting discomfort in her neck and shoulder—the warnings of a stroke? a heart attack? cancer? It was silly to think these things, she knew, but they were possible, people her age did get brain tumors, lived speechless and withered after a stroke. The stroke was the most likely thing. Her mother had died of a stroke, her aunt Louisa had had two.

When the doctor had run his hand over her neck, down her shoulder and her arm, she watched his face carefully for the twitch of the mouth, the widening of the eyes that would betray what he would feel it necessary to hide, or break gently. But he looked placid, slightly bored even, his round glasses slipping continually down. Each time he pushed them back, he ran his broad fleshy finger up the bridge of his nose in a loving way that made her want to do the same. When she was dressed, he looked at her from the other side of his desk and, still placid, asked if everything was all right otherwise, if there were any problems on her mind.

"Yes," she said, and waited to see what he would say.

"The usual sort of thing, I imagine," he said, looking into her eyes steadfastly. One of his fingers tapped a short rhythm on his desk blotter.

"Oh, you know," Cynthia said. "Too much to do, and so forth."

"You have a job," the doctor stated, "and a child. And then there is the house."

"Yes," she agreed.

"You must make some time for yourself," he said with great decision, his smile curving against his teeth.

Cynthia sat back, relieved and disappointed. She reached for her purse.

But the doctor was still tapping his little rhythm, now with a pencil. "Perhaps there are difficulties with the marriage," he said, not looking at her. "Perhaps sexual difficulties?"

Cynthia looked down at her hands lying on her purse. "Are you telling me that the pain is psychosomatic?"

"That term is often misused." He looked at her, waiting for her to answer his question.

Somehow Cynthia felt as if the doctor knew everything, knew

that Derek has been gone from home for months, that they have fought, that she has thoughts about Harry that she can't tell any-one. By running his hands over her body, the doctor had read her longings and her deprivations, knew that she hasn't been made love to all summer long. And she wanted to enter into the dialogue he was offering to initiate, she wanted very much to tell him that he was right, that she was miserable, twisted, that she hunched her shoulder and ducked her head to keep away all that was going wrong.

I have to see Harry, Cynthia thinks. She decides to go to the supermarket to delay a little, and by the time she gets to the bar, surely he will be there? She will go to the one on the way to the bar, to be more efficient. She runs upstairs, stopping to change her shirt. On the way out, she looks at the phone. Should she put it back on the hook, or leave it off? She won't be home, it won't matter, but she hates it when she walks into the house and it begins to ring. She puts the receiver back, takes it off, stands a minute looking at it, and then leaves it there.

In the car, she fumbles her seatbelt on as she drives, and smiles, thinking about Joey's views on safety. It is one of their things, one of the rituals of their days, that she is often in such a hurry she forgets her seatbelt, and he will scold her for it, and she will pull it over with one hand, steadying the wheel with the other while he snaps it into its lock. Right, she thinks, you're going to cry. She sniffs hard, pinches her nose to clear it.

At the first red light, Cynthia opens her purse to get a Kleenex, but she doesn't have any. She pinches her nose again, viciously. I have to call Joey, she thinks, sometime when I can talk to him while he's alone. She realizes she should have called him this morning, while Derek was still on the way to Pennsylvania. She pounds the steering wheel with the heel of her hand, stupid, how stupid she is.

But still, she can call when Derek's likely to be out. She tries to remember all the things he has said about what they are doing down there, what the schedule is like. Right after lunch might be a good time, when Derek will have started working, and Joey might be lingering before he goes out to play, eating cookies maybe, if Loretta wasn't too stingy to give them to him. She looks at her watch. Too late today, it will have to be tomorrow. When she looks back at the road, the car has drifted a little over the center line, and she jerks it back. Where is she going? The supermarket, right.

But when she gets there, it is closed, boarded up, scraps of paper and plastic cups blowing across the empty parking lot. She pulls in anyway and parks in a space marked by faded white lines. It seems to her that she was here just a little while ago, a few weeks, surely not earlier than the beginning of the summer. She used to come here when she was young enough to have to hold her mother's hand when they crossed the street, and she had cherished its dimness, its flickering old fluorescent lights, the wooden bins that held vegetables and fruit, the scarred black-and-white squares of the linoleum. The man behind the lunchmeat counter had given her, each trip, a limp pink slice of bologna which she nibbled all through the store. A weed has grown up in the space next to hers, emerging from a crack no more than an inch wide. It is monstrously big, it would be shoulder high if she got out of the car and measured herself against it.

She looks at her watch: only two o'clock, still too early to find Harry at the bar. Where is there a supermarket that is near enough? She begins to drive south, toward the bar, watching the sides of the street for signs. She passes Riverside Cemetery and feels the pull of it, sucking her toward her future, how many relatives does she have buried there? She remembers so clearly standing by the spiked iron fence waiting for the bus to go to school, to work downtown, and how her mind had been full of—what? Trivia, clothes, sharpened pencils, test papers, paperback romances to read at lunch hour. Had she ever thought then that she would be driving past it some twenty or thirty years ahead with no one to depend on, her child stolen from her? She remembers that she had expected, for a long while, that she was going away, pretty soon, to Europe, to

California, somewhere. She wasn't interested, wouldn't have believed in a future that consisted of events—trips to the store, to the houses of friends, to church—that would drift silently, lightly as dust, and accumulate in layers like stone, hard and grainy, with a false sparkle.

A Finast sign appears ahead, and she pulls sloppily into the right-hand lane and then into the parking lot. She gets out of the car and walks toward the entrance, feeling in her purse for her list. It isn't there. She walks back to the car, expecting to see it on the seat, but it isn't there, nor on the floor. She stoops, feeling under the seat, and then kneels down on the asphalt to extend her reach. Squeamishly, she runs her hand over the floor, feeling small unidentifiable objects under her fingers that slide away. Finally, she bends awkwardly, angling her head to look under the seat. She sees nothing. The pain in her neck makes her grunt, it is so sharp. She touches it gingerly, massaging, and then, feeling the grit on her fingers, curses.

Cynthia uses an old McDonald's napkin she finds in the glove compartment to wipe her fingers and neck; her knee has picked up a black smear of its own. She rubs it hard but it doesn't all come off. She tries to think what it is she needs to get at the store. Milk, as usual. Since Derek and Joey have left, the milk has gone sour more than once. Harry uses it only in coffee. But she is sure she remembers writing "milk," the second or third item on her list. She pulls a cart out, pushes it through fruits and vegetables. She has plums at home, and tomatoes and corn from her neighbor that she has to use up before they rot. There is almost no one in the store, a good time to shop, she notes automatically for future reference.

What else, what else? She can't remember, and she walks through the aisles putting cans and boxes into the cart at random, mayonnaise, oatmeal, strawberry jam, pork and beans—Derek is fond of pork and beans for lunch—margarine, the kind of cottage cheese that Joey loves with apple butter, refrigerator rolls, TV dinners—macaroni and cheese, spinach soufflé.

When she gets to the last aisle, her cart is half full, and she looks at the jumble of items with distaste. Does she need any of these things? She has a vision of her kitchen of the future—like in women's magazines, The Kitchen of the Future, all chrome and little robots—but hers will look just the same, the tired paint, the scarred wooden table and chairs, except that the cupboards will be full of things that are no longer eaten, cottage cheese turning moldy in its carton, Popsicles withering month by month in the freezer.

Bread, she is pretty sure she needs bread, and even if she doesn't she can freeze the new loaf. All right, bread, she says to herself, and turns the cart around. But she goes past the bread, all those rolls and loaves and muffins and croissants, rising, fertile, and yeasty, studded with raisins, brown and white and rich dark pumpernickel, miniature chocolate doughnuts, Hostess—Joey always begged for Hostess cream-filled cupcakes. It would be just like Loretta to buy them for him every day instead of for a special treat.

Ahead, the aisle is blocked by carts abandoned by women checking cartons of eggs. Odd, Cynthia thinks, that the whole rest of the store is empty, and here, like ants converging on a bit of dropped candy, a crowd is gathered.

She pulls her cart up and waits. Why would anyone wear a thing like that, she wonders, watching a woman in a shapeless, gaily flowered housedress running her fingers lovingly over the eggs, rocking each one in its oval cradle to check that it isn't stuck to the carton by its own ooze. All the women are doing the same thing. She counts—seven of them, old women, young women, the baggy red-flowered housedress next to a tight black spandex mini, gray hair, red hair, blond hair. Cynthia smiles, it's funny.

One of the old women has made her selection, and, breathing heavily, she starts trying to extricate her cart from those of the other women. Cynthia comes around obligingly to help. "Here, let me," she says.

"Thank you, dear," the woman says, and they struggle together with the jammed-up carts.

Easing the end of the cart past a display of English muffins,

Cynthia leans across at an angle that produces the pain in her neck again, and she straightens up suddenly. She sees one of the other women looking at her from across the metal tangle. Cynthia stares at her stupidly, massaging her neck, a young woman, blond. Pretty, she thinks, but too fat. No, pregnant. And then, like a door slamming, she recognizes her. It is Lucette.

Cynthia stares at her, at her blond hair pulled back in an elastic band, her fuller cheeks, at her belly—and she knows from the way Lucette is looking back at her that it is Harry's child. Tears spring to Cynthia's eyes and she blinks. She looks into Lucette's cart: two half gallons of milk, a bag of peaches, the carton of eggs she has just picked out.

And even as she sees this, Lucette is turning away. Oh no, Cynthia thinks. She pushes her own cart over to the side of the aisle, and grabs her purse. "Wait," she calls, "wait a minute." Cynthia catches up to her, and stands there, breathing fast. She grasps the handle of Lucette's cart, marking time.

"You remember me?" she asks finally.

Lucette nods, not looking at her.

"I heard you were gone."

"I'm back."

"I heard that, too." Cynthia settles her purse on her shoulder, smooths her hands down the front of her shirt. "How are you managing?"

"I'm doing fine," Lucette says.

"Are you back with your mother?"

Lucette turns her head toward Cynthia, her lips firmly set. She doesn't answer.

Cynthia looks at her in frustration. She wants to take Lucette's hand, to pull her hair sharply, to pinch some color into her cheeks. "Do you need anything?"

"No."

"What have you decided—" Cynthia begins, but Lucette gives her cart a push so that it rolls out a little into the aisle, and walks past it, down the aisle, away from Cynthia, who stands there pulling on the strap of her purse.

Cynthia follows her out of the store and watches her walking across the parking lot to a car with a man at the wheel. The car starts up with a low rumbling growl and they drive away. Cynthia walks to her own car and gets in. There is no hurry. She is sure that Lucette is staying with her mother. Where else would she go? The problem of who the man is occupies a small corner of her mind, but she can find that out. She turns the radio on, sits with her head back and her hands resting on the wheel. The radio sings "Brown-Eyed Girl" to her, a song she remembers from when she was in high school. She runs her fingers lightly over the bumps on the steering wheel, feeling her nerves jump and tingle, a buzz that travels up her arms and down through her body. Her thoughts run through her mind in a quickening spiral, eating up chaos. She has the whole picture in her head, she can see everything that ought to be done.

When the song is over, she turns off the radio and gets out. She goes back into the supermarket, back to the bread aisle. Someone has pushed her cart and Lucette's out of the way. She checks that the milk, the fruit, the eggs, are still in Lucette's cart, and pushes it to the checkout line. Outside in her car she thinks a minute, making sure she remembers the way to Lucette's mother's house. And then she starts the car and swings out of the parking lot.

Cynthia looks around one last time—does she have everything? She has a little time before work, but she wants to take a bundle of Joey's old baby clothes over to Lucette before she goes to the store. Hurrying out to the car, she combs at her snarled hair with her fingers. She drives down the street, angling the mirror toward her so that she can work on her hair with a brush, but there is too much traffic. She turns the radio on and sails along on a great wave of classical music, the notes sliding over each other, pouring out the windows.

When she gets to the house on Mapledale, she goes up the walk at a clip. The porch light is on, she notices, and makes a note to say something to Lucette about it. She knocks on the frame of the screen door and then opens it and goes in. In the front hall, she reaches out her free hand and turns off the outside light.

On the threshold of the inner door, Cynthia pauses. She can hear the murmur of the TV upstairs. She doesn't want to see Anna if she can help it. She has timed her visit so that Lucette will be home from work. "Lucette?" she calls, working her lips a little over the name.

There is no answer, but she hears footsteps, and Lucette appears in the arch between the front room and the dining room.

"I brought those clothes I told you I thought I had." Cynthia holds the bag out.

"I really don't need them," Lucette says. She keeps her eyes averted from Cynthia, makes no move to take the bag.

"They were packed away in the attic, just gathering dust. It's a shame not to put them to use. I kept them in case Joey had a little brother."

Lucette shrugs. "I might have a girl."

"Oh, that doesn't matter. A lot of them are just little sleepers and overalls and shirts—they'll do for either. Where should I put them?"

"Just anywhere," Lucette says.

Cynthia looks around, then drops the bag onto one of the shabby armchairs. "How was your visit to the doctor?"

"Fine," Lucette says. She leans against the wall.

"Did you remember to ask him about whether the baby might be breech?"

Lucette shakes her head.

"You have to remember that next time," Cynthia says. "They don't tell you everything if you forget to ask. You have to take some responsibility for your own health, yours and the baby's." She pauses, looking at Lucette, who is staring down at the floor.

Her light hair is lank against her cheeks and forehead, her arms hang down, hands open. "You look tired," Cynthia says. "Let me make you some iced tea."

"No," Lucette says sharply. She glances back toward the kitchen.

"It'll just take a minute," Cynthia says. She moves toward Lucette.

Lucette straightens up, partially blocking her way. "There's someone here," she says.

"Is it—" Cynthia pauses. "Ray?" She has met Ray here several times. She was happy to find out about Ray, but he makes her uncomfortable, how he is always touching Lucette, smoothing her hair, taking her hands, playing with her fingers.

Lucette shakes her head. She pauses, almost as if she is listening, and then moves aside. "You might as well come in."

Cynthia follows her into the kitchen where several months before she sat at the table for the first time, across from Lucette's mother. A man is sitting where Anna sat then, a huge man with cheerful pink cheeks. He is sitting poised with mouselike quietness, his hands folded, his eyes alert. When Cynthia comes in, he leaps up from his chair, inclining his head toward Lucette, waiting to be introduced.

"This is James Gandy," she says, and then gesturing toward Cynthia, "Mrs. Lynch."

"Ah," he says. "The cousin. Please, sit with us."

"I was going to make some iced tea," she says.

"Iced tea—how wonderful! We can have it with the zucchini bread I've brought. A gift from friends, although the vegetables were from my gardens. Helen and May Skrovan?" he says with a question in his voice, as if she might know them.

Cynthia turns on the gas under the tea kettle, her hands feeling big and clumsy. "You're a friend of Lucette's?"

"James was my landlord when I was living away from home," Lucette says in a small, tight voice.

"Lucette has told me that you work in a food store."

"Yes," Cynthia says. She counts the tea bags, one for each of them, one extra.

"I've often thought how much I'd like to work in some small retail establishment. The pay is bad, of course, but there would be the opportunities for conversation—those would be unmatched, I think."

"I'm not much of a talker," Cynthia says.

"Oh, better by far to be a listener, I agree," James Gandy says. "I'm sure I talk too much myself."

Lucette brings two ice-cube trays from the refrigerator and empties them into a pitcher. She begins to cut slices from the zucchini loaf, thick and dark. Then she cocks her head, listening, and the other two stop what they are doing and listen with her. There is a faint stir of movement from overhead and then a thread of sound that is repeated, louder.

Lucette lowers her head, puts down the knife, wipes her hands.

"Take her a slice of the bread," James Gandy says. "It's full of good things."

"She wouldn't eat it," Lucette says, but when James puts a slice on a plate, she takes it from him and goes out the back door of the kitchen. They hear her climbing the stairs slowly.

James sighs and examines his slice, prodding it with one of his large fingers. "Helen adds nuts and chopped apricot, I believe. It's very good."

He sighs again and is silent for so long that Cynthia turns to look at him. He is sitting very straight, chin pushed out, eyes on the cupboard behind her. "You're upset," he says.

"Oh, no," Cynthia says. She looks for something to do, but the tea is not ready to pour yet.

"You are," he states.

"Well," she says. "It was a lot to take in. But really, I'm not upset. I just keep my mind on what there is to be done."

"And your cousin?"

"Harry?" she asks, as if there might be some question about who was involved.

James Gandy shakes his head. He drops his eyes from the cupboard doors. "When I was a boy," he begins, "I used to get very upset about certain things—if my jacket got torn, if I spilled my milk, or spoiled something, got it dirty. You know how that is?" He turns to her for confirmation, and she nods.

"It's not only me," he says. "Other people feel it, too. When things are spilled, broken, in the wrong place, dirty—that is, with displaced matter on them. And how one wishes to order, organize, rearrange, paint, paper, fix, clean, move things from one place to another."

"There's nothing wrong with that," Cynthia says. Her fingers itch to do something, pour out tea, cut more bread.

"Not wrong," James says. "But all this is a constant battle against what's its name—entropy. You know entropy?"

Cynthia shakes her head. She picks up a few crumbs of cake from the table, rolling them between her fingers.

"In simple terms, it's a decrease in energy, the universe—everything in it flying away from its center, using up energy as it goes."

"I wasn't good in physics," Cynthia says.

"And we, we expend enormous amounts of energy fighting against this natural process." He sits back, sighing more happily now. He breaks off a corner of his bread and eats it. "After I was in the balloon"—he looks over at her to see her face when he says this, but does not pause—"I was sitting out in the front one day, just sitting, looking across the street, not at anything at first, but then after a few minutes, I realized I was seeing the house almost across from ours. No one had lived in it for a while, and everybody, my mother, the neighbors, thought of it as an eyesore. The family that lived there, they were a young couple, renting, and something happened. I believe the man killed his wife, and someone came to take the baby."

"How awful," Cynthia says. She strains her ears for sounds from above, but she hears nothing.

"No one else rented it, and the landlord stopped maintaining it. The brick porch steps cracked from the melting and freezing of the snow. The mailbox fell into the zinnia bed. And in the spring, vines and plants grew in the cracks of the steps, the porch roof sagged under the weight of water collected between the slates and the boards."

Cynthia feels cold, the picture of this house disintegrating before her.

James rubs his chin with his fingers, leaving a faint smear of zucchini bread. "In the summer, hollyhocks grew wild in all the flowerbeds—blood-red they were, pushing their tops among the porch rails, twining along the wires, hiding the face of the electric meter. And everybody looked at it and, you know, clicked their tongues. But I had the concept of entropy given to me from the balloon, and I was on the lookout for it. That house was approaching entropy, a picture of it, like a lesson for anyone to look at. That house left to itself."

"What does all that mean?" Cynthia says, pushing herself up out of her chair. The tea is ready, thank God, and she pours it, steaming, over the ice cubes.

"Just the unwinding of everything, everything happening on its own track. We're subject to it as well as that house, we're moving toward that time when everything will have flown out to the ends of the universe." He looks at her worriedly, wanting her to see what he sees. "It will be in place, finally, but not in a place of our choosing."

"You mean," she says, her voice trembling, "we ought to lie back and put up with it, that's what you mean?"

"That implies reluctance, the holding of a grudge." He moves his hand in a weaving motion. "Acceptance. Detachment. You showed up here, for instance. I am in acceptance."

Cynthia stands up, fists clenched at her sides. "You're crazy— that's not what life is like. You have to fight for what you want.

You can't just sit back and wait for it to be handed to you on a platter. You can't—" she starts to say, but she hears Lucette's step on the stairs, and they both turn toward the door.

"What's going on?" Lucette says.

"We are just conversing," James Gandy says. "Metaphysics, etymology, our environment." He flings his hands out, embracing the walls, the windows, the plates and cups. "How is your mother?"

"She says she might come down for dinner."

"I'll stay, then, and cook?" James asks.

Lucette doesn't answer. She pours herself a glass of iced tea. She drinks it standing up, sets it down on the table abruptly.

Cynthia feels that they are both waiting for her to go so that they can talk about something important. "Do you need any shopping done?" she asks.

"No," Lucette says. She rinses her glass under the tap and sets it upside down on the drainboard. "I don't need for you to come around any more."

Cynthia wants to grab her, to shake her, breach her swelling, rounded shape that is so firm, so self-contained. Lucette is like an egg that she can't get at, she wants to tap her, break her, crack her. She thinks with fear of how the baby may have something wrong with it, remembers in vivid color from a nature program some baby birds dead in their shells, born with their brain outside their skulls. "Don't worry," she says, "it's no trouble."

Above them there is the sound of dragging footsteps.

"I'd better get going," Cynthia says.

Driving to work, she strives to keep in mind her plans for the future, the neat paths down which she will travel, and oh, it will be difficult, she doesn't want to shirk difficulty, but the tasks to be accomplished will be as neat and separate as wrapped Christmas packages, dealt with one by one, and set aside. She tries, but there are other images rising in her mind. The baby birds, hardly risen into life before they fall back into a sort of slime. The dried-out husks of the seventeen-year locusts, hollow and complete, that she saw under the sycamore tree when she was young, numerous as grains of rice. Trees, bones stuck upright in the dirt of the cemetery where her mother was buried, graves open, holes to the past, where time travels through them with a whistle. And she moans with the effort of holding it all back.

"Hot for the end of September," the beer-delivery man says.

Harry nods, reaching for the clipboard held out to him.

"You need some more of the Lite? I got a few extra cases."

"I don't think so." Harry stands for a minute in the sun after the delivery man has driven away. He can't get used to the way it looks, this corner where the new bar sits. It's not the Maple Leaf, it looks wrong, foreign. The red brick of the side street crossed by the dull black asphalt of West Twenty-fifth. The rosebushes growing in the tall grass on the opposite corner. The used-car lot across the street, its line of plastic pennants slapping in the breeze. The secretive brick building where two young men dressed like Jehovah's Witnesses go in and out. He watches the traffic and the slow progress of a woman pushing a stroller in the street next to the curb. She should watch out for the kid, he thinks, checking the street for cars. But when she comes closer, he sees that the stroller has a bag of groceries in it instead of a child, and that the woman is old, her gray hair mostly hidden by the scarf around her head.

He is sweating, although it is only ten o'clock, but he stands a minute more. Outside, his thoughts rise and float away. That was the best thing about working construction, that so much of it was done outside. Working with the hammer, the saw, his actions mirrored by those of the men around him, sunk deep in the wind, the sun, the wet, his thoughts came and went, flew out into the air, harmless.

Inside the bar, he hears the phone begin to ring, and he half turns, waiting to see if he will be called to deal with it. He can hear Charlie's voice, and then the smacking ring when he hangs up.

Harry sighs, leans back against the brick façade of the building. He reaches for a cigarette, but his shirt pocket is flat. The pack is inside on the bar where he left it when the beer truck arrived. If he sticks his head inside the door, he could see it, lying on the dark old wood, next to the papers from the bank and the stack of bills he was adding up. He wants a cigarette, but he doesn't want to look at those papers.

The mailman drives up in his blue Skyhawk and parks in the bar's lot. Car must be fifteen years old, Harry thinks. The engine sounds good, a good V-6. It was the timing chain that went on those Skyhawks. Harry reaches into his pocket, fingering his change, feels the heavy metal circle of Al's ring. Al had a Skyhawk once, maybe the same year as this one, maybe from the year before. He remembers working on it when the chain went, under the car, knuckles bloody and stinging, bits of rust flaking off and falling in his eyes and mouth. He can see Al's anxious face stuck in under the hood.

"Harry." Charlie sticks his head out the door, then comes to stand teetering on the stone doorstep. "Hey, it's hot."

"What's on your mind?"

"Geneva, Mrs. Zaitchek, she's coming over. That was her on the phone."

"Okay." Harry shades his eyes to look at the sky.

"She didn't sound mad or anything."

"Got no cause to be."

"Well, you know, Geneva." Charlie scratches his chin. "She likes to stick her nose in."

"She's got a right."

Charlie rubs his hands nervously up and down his arms, as if he is cold. "Sure she does." He looks at Harry and then away, at the brick storefront with its drawn blinds. "She know I'm working here?"

"I saved it for a surprise," Harry says.

"Jesus, Harry, don't joke."

The phone rings again and Charlie goes to answer it. Harry watches, his eyes turned in the direction from which Geneva will come. A girl is walking toward him, all long denim legs and hair, a great pouf of it standing up from her head in front, nodding and dipping with every step she takes. Not bad, he thinks. She can see that he is looking. When she gets closer, she slides her eyes over at him apprehensively.

"Good morning," Harry says, nodding.

She half smiles, but doesn't answer, and she speeds up a little.

He's too old for her, Harry supposes. He tries to decide how he feels about this. Is he then an old man? Or about to be? How long does he have before no one will be interested in whether his chest is hairy or smooth? He shakes his head, thinking of how it was years ago, putting out his hand and all those smaller hands falling into it, their lips, their lowered eyes, the strands of their hair spread across the pillowcase.

A car turns the corner, Geneva's Chrysler LeBaron. He can see her haystack of hair—shorter, stiffer, redder since Al died—bobbing over the top of the wheel. She pulls up in front and parks on the street.

"Planning your retirement?" She comes around the car and stands with her back to the sun.

"Just taking a break," Harry says.

"Let's get in there and look at the figures."

Harry opens the door and holds it for her. They both stand a minute inside, their eyes adjusting to the dimness. Charlie is wiping the bar with quick inefficient jabs, his eyes down. Geneva snaps and unsnaps her purse, clearing her throat, and Harry waits. He knows that she and Al first came to look at this place together last year, in the fall, for Al had told him how Geneva had found fault with everything about it. "But that's her way," he had said. "You know her, Harry. Really, she liked it. She could see the possibilities."

Harry imagines Geneva remembering that time, Al at her side instead of Harry, standing just this one step into the cool, darkened air.

"What's he doing here?" Geneva takes off her dark glasses and points to Charlie with the earpiece.

Charlie pretends not to notice. He moves farther down the bar, his swipes with the cloth large and wild.

"Well?" She turns to Harry.

"Now, Geneva," Harry says, and stops, surprised to hear himself using Al's words, Al's tone.

"What is this long-haired screwup doing in"—she hesitates—"this bar?"

Harry has read her pause—she was going to say "my bar." "I've got the right to hire and fire," he says. "It's in the papers we drew up."

Geneva smiles in an almost kindly way. She stalks over to the bar and sits on a stool, slapping her purse down smartly. "So you do, so you do," she says. "But I also have some rights."

Harry shrugs, acknowledging this.

"And one of those rights is to see that you don't run this place into the ground with bad decisions. Hiring and firing!" She snorts. "Do you know how long I've been hiring and firing?"

Harry grins. "A long, long time?"

Geneva ignores this. "I've got an eye for who works out and who goes in the shitcan, and that"—she jerks her thumb at Charlie—"looks to me like the shitcan variety."

"He needed a job," Harry says, "and I needed an extra man to help with the heavy stuff. I can't ask Peg or Janet to sling cases of bottles around."

"*I've* done it," Geneva says fiercely, and she looks capable of doing it now, her body tense, the pale skin of her knuckles stretched tight.

Harry's eyes are drawn to her throat, which is working, the muscles tensing and jerking. "He hasn't done anything stupid yet."

"He hasn't had a chance." Geneva coughs again, clears her throat.

Harry turns his attention to a stack of cocktail napkins. He leans across the bar, takes them out of their holder and straightens them, squaring their edges with his hands. He hears Geneva's purse open and close, he hears her cough again, and then sigh. "You could give him a month," he suggests, still not looking at her.

"You. Come over here."

Charlie has retreated all the way to the door of the back room. "You mean me?" he says.

Geneva doesn't bother to answer. She sits looking at Charlie as he edges toward them. "What kind of experience do you have?"

"You mean work experience?"

"I don't want to hear about your filthy unsatisfying sex life." She pounds her fist on the counter. "Of *course* I mean work experience."

"I had a job at Discount Hi-Value."

"Doing what?"

"Pretty much everything," Charlie says. He is rolling and unrolling his apron. "I moved stock and mopped the floors and I rang up stuff sometimes if it was busy or if one of the girls was off. I did inventory once."

"Inventory?"

"I counted stuff on the shelves and another guy checked them off on a sheet."

Geneva turns to Harry. "In other words, he did anything that could be expected of a chimpanzee."

"Jeez," Charlie says.

Harry holds up his hands to indicate his impartiality.

"So why did you leave this miracle job?"

"It just wasn't my scene, the whole scene was getting like fried. The manager, Mr. B., was like this strung-out kind of guy."

"I see," Geneva says sweetly. She holds Charlie with her eyes. "You got fired?"

"Not to say fired," Charlie says. "A parting of the ways is what I call it."

Geneva taps a cigarette out of Harry's pack and holds it for Harry to light for her. "There must have been something that brought all this on," she states.

Charlie looks at his rolled-up apron.

She leans forward. "How about stealing?" she yells, and Charlie jumps back. "Was it stealing?"

"No," he shouts back. "I swear! I didn't steal anything. I mean it. Harry, you know I don't do that shit."

"Watch your language," Geneva says to him. "So what was it?"

"I kept coming in late, that's all. Not by much, either, but this Mr. B. had a real bug up his"—he looks at Geneva—"in his ear about being there right on time. Get here a couple of minutes early, he said, if you can believe it."

Geneva shakes her head and looks up. She sits there, immobile, takes a drag on her cigarette and blows the smoke at a spot on the ceiling that seems to interest her. Charlie looks at Harry. Harry shrugs. Geneva sighs. The three of them are still for a minute, watching the lazy spirals of smoke in the dark golden air.

"All right," Geneva says. "Get out of here. I want to talk to Harry."

"You mean get out of here," Charlie says, indicating the entire bar.

"Get out of my sight is what I mean. Go clean a toilet."

Harry jerks his head toward the back room, and Charlie picks up his rag and runs back there.

"He didn't even say 'thank you,' " Geneva says.

"Thanks for the inquisition?"

"Do you let him pour drinks?"

"Forget about Charlie. You wanted to look at the papers."

"Just let me see the sales figures."

Harry pulls out some of the papers and gives them to her.

"They're low during the week," she says.

"Business always drops during the week."

"When are you going to open up the other room? That ought to double your business."

"I'll get around to it. It needs some work."

"It's not just sentimentality," Geneva says. "You think I'm thinking about this being a memorial to Al?"

Harry looks at her, doesn't answer.

"I've got that quarter interest. I don't want to see it go down the drain."

"So you're a mercenary bitch, what's new?"

Geneva laughs. They hear Charlie break something in the back room. "All right. All right." She stabs out her cigarette. "So tell me, Harry, how's your cousin? Cynthia. How's Cynthia?"

"She's fine."

"You two getting along together?"

"Sure, we always get along."

"I see her driving around in my daughter's neighborhood. My daughter Barbara. Over by Riverside Cemetery."

"Probably shopping."

"She's always busy, isn't she?" Geneva gets up. "Her husband is still gone, I hear. And her son."

Harry opens the door for her.

"Good-bye, Harry." She turns and raises her voice. "I have the same feelings as Mr. B. about being on time."

"What?" Charlie calls. "What?"

"I'm going, Charlie," Harry says, after he has ushered Geneva to her car.

"You're going? Where?" Charlie emerges from the back room.

"I'll be back around seven-thirty if anyone calls."

"You going to have dinner and all with your cousin?" Charlie puts his rag down on the counter and then picks the phone up and wipes under it. "I heard Geneva was asking about her. Cynthia, Mrs. Lynch. Your cousin."

"Yeah?" Harry pauses by the door.

"Nothing wrong there?"

"What do you mean?"

"I just wondered why *she*"—he indicates the door through which Geneva disappeared—"was talking about her. Like if something was wrong."

"Nothing's wrong."

"I didn't mean anything by it," Charlie says. "She just seems like, you know, a pretty nice kind of woman. Not to say I know her or anything."

"Well, she's fine. I'll see you in a couple hours."

Later that afternoon, Harry sits slumped in his truck in front of the old house. He could go inside, he has a key, but the thought of the empty house depresses him. He could go and sit in the backyard, but he keeps telling himself that Cynthia will be here in a minute. It seems like too much trouble to open the garage door, unhook one of the lawn chairs, unfold it, set it up. Must be out shopping, he thinks, forgot something for dinner.

He sees one of the neighbors, a short dark woman, peering at him from behind her screen door. "You've only seen me a million times, bitch," he says to her, inaudibly. He feels as if he is picking up someone for a date, as if he is being stood up. He turns the radio on, flicks through the stations, but there is nothing on but talk—commercials, a washed-out rock star talking about how he wrote some forgotten hit song in 1973, a deep-voiced guy giving financial advice. Harry switches him off.

Bored, he opens up the glove compartment, and some maps fall out, along with a withered apple core and a flashlight which, he knows, has dead batteries.

It's Friday, he thinks. Friday, Friday. First day of the weekend, if you didn't start early on Thursday night. Long years of Fridays, feeling the quickening in the day. After lunch on Friday, the afternoon leveled out and dipped, a great sliding-board swoop toward the evening, faster and faster. Downing tools at five o'-clock, or maybe at a quarter to if the boss was gone or in a good mood, getting in the car, turning on the radio, stopping at the little store on the corner for a six-pack to start it off right. Showing up at the bar around nine-thirty or ten, going deeper and deeper into the evening, dropping into it, the leather of the bar stool firm under him, cooler intervals in the car if he decided to do some traveling, every bar an oasis of light, color, liquid, warm with the eyes and arms of women.

That was how it used to be. There were lights—the streetlights flicking past pale on their stalks—headlights slanting in front of them, his eyes blinking and dilating in the beams from other cars—the rush of reddish light and music when the heavy doors opened, letting him in to dance and drink—the secret blue-black dark of the interior of the car—hard unglamorous glare of a restaurant at 5:00 A.M.—the faded colors of the traffic lights seen against the almost-morning sky.

Harry wants a drink. He pokes under the seat where he used to keep a flask, but it is empty, he knew it would be. He would have laughed ten years ago if anyone had said to him that he was going to be owning a bar, even part of one. Good fucking deal, he would have said, what a way to go. He'd had some ideas then, or maybe he'd already given them up? He can't remember. Not about bars. Building things. Having his own company, a small one, along with a few guys whose work he liked.

But tonight is Friday, and he'll be there, watching the door, dealing with the pot-smoking musicians, settling fights before they start, soothing the feelings of the barmaids, cruising the bar from the other side, pouring drinks, running the register.

Christ, he thinks, where is Cynthia? And, as if that is all it takes to produce her, he sees her blue Nova turn onto the street from

Fulton Avenue. He sits in the truck, watching it come closer. She parks in front of him. He gets out and stands by the truck, watching her lock the car, switching the bag she is carrying from one arm to the other.

"I thought you forgot about me," he says.

"I'm sorry, Harry. Things were running late." She takes his arm, tugs him toward the house. "You're not mad, are you? Were you waiting long?"

"Not too long." He catches at her fingers, makes a move to take her bag, but she pushes his hand away.

"It's not heavy. What time is it?"

"Ten after six."

"Oh, Lord. I had no idea." She nudges Harry as they go up the front walk, and then waves at the neighbor, who is at her screen door again. "Get a life," Cynthia says, nodding and smiling.

Inside, she runs upstairs and comes down without the bag, her jacket off. "Do you want to eat outside? It's warm enough."

"Sure." Harry looks around the kitchen for evidence of dinner, but the table is bare, the surfaces of the counters flat and clean. He opens the refrigerator, but it's almost empty, just a half gallon of milk, a bottle of soda water, and some pudding cups standing in the glare of the inside light.

"Don't fuss around, Harry. Just give me a minute and I'll get stuff together. I though we could order pizza tonight since I was going to be late, and I'll make a salad. Okay?"

"Sure," Harry says.

"You call. I want pepperoni and add on anything you want. The number's by the phone."

While Harry calls the order in, he picks up a notebook by the phone with a list of times, some with a few words or a sentence by them. He carries it back to the kitchen, where Cynthia is slicing wedges of tomato on the cutting board by the sink.

"What's this?" he asks her.

"What?" She slides the tomatoes and some cucumber slices

from the board into a bowl, pushing them with her knife. She wipes her hands and takes it from him. "It's my telephone log." She looks at him, smiling.

"What do you mean?"

"Oh," she makes a gesture with her hands, a sweeping away. "I've been getting these phone calls."

"What kind of phone calls?"

"Obscene phone calls, or not exactly obscene, no bad language, but suggestive, sort of. You know."

"When did this start?" Harry clears his throat. He feels a dropping in his stomach.

"A while ago. I can't remember exactly."

"What does this guy say?"

"Just stupid stuff. Pretty harmless, probably. But I called the phone company anyway, and they said to keep a record. That's in case evidence is needed. And they put a tracer on my line. I had the idea that you had to keep the caller on for a certain amount of time, but apparently that's no longer the case, what with computer hookups. It's really simple."

Harry looks down at the log. " 'I'm waiting for you, babe,' " he reads. "He said this?"

Cynthia takes the notebook and puts it in a drawer. "They asked me if I recognized the voice. Can you believe it?"

"And you couldn't?"

"No." Cynthia scrapes some chopped green onions into the salad bowl. "I felt it was somebody who knows me." She looks at him. "I don't know why, though. I didn't tell them that."

"You don't seem worried," Harry says to her. He looks at her more carefully. She has a flush of color on her cheekbones, as if she has been out in the sun. Her eyes are glittering, her movements are quick, with a push of energy behind them.

She tests the tip of the knife against her fingertip. "I was spooked for a while."

"You never said anything."

Cynthia uses the potato peeler to reduce a carrot to a pile of curled shavings. "I'm all done," she says. "Let's sit down. How are things with you?"

"Fine," he says automatically. "I was over to see my mother." He picks a cucumber slice out of the salad, and she slaps his hand, puts a plate on top of the bowl, covering it.

"How is she?"

"They say she's the same. I think she's eating less."

"Old people don't need to eat as much, I've read that. She doesn't get any exercise, lying in that bed all day. How did she look?"

Harry wants to say she looked worse, but he isn't sure that this is true. If there are changes, they are small, subtle. Is the flesh covering her bones less thick? Does her hand move less often on the white blanket? Is the rise and fall of the sheet that covers her chest slower? He feels, when he goes to the nursing home, that each visit is laid on top of all the others, one more brightly colored translucent sheet, microscopically thin, the small differences as hard to see as the unfolding and decay of a rosebud. Trying to remember what she was like six months ago, two years ago, seems pointless. "She looked all right, I guess."

"She's tough. She's always been that way, the tough one in the family. I used to resent it that she outlived my mother." Cynthia laughs. "Wasn't that ridiculous?" She lifts the plate on top of the salad bowl and picks out a tomato wedge. "I'm so hungry," she says. "I didn't get much lunch."

"Did you have to go in to work?"

"Work?" She gets up to get a glass of water. "No." She drinks some, sets it down on the table. "How are things at the bar?"

"Geneva was by today. She was pissed off about Charlie working there."

"Oh, Geneva. Listen, Harry, did you tell them to deliver the pizza?"

"I told them."

She jumps up. "Let's go outside, we'll be able to hear the pizza guy there, don't you think?" She gives him the salad bowl to carry, and the salt and pepper, while she gathers plates, silverware, napkins.

Outside, Harry sets the bowl on one of the benches, and brushes the leaves from the top of the picnic table. It's still warm, but the upper branches of the tree are moving restlessly overhead. Cynthia sets out the plates, anchoring the napkins under them. She goes to get the salad dressing. Harry pulls up one of the lawn chairs and eases into it. His back hurts, a slow ache. He closes his eyes against the blue sky, the moving clouds.

When Cynthia comes back she has the pizza box. "I gave him a fifty-cent tip," she says. "He wasn't happy, but it was all I had." She puts the box down on the table and pushes it toward Harry. "So," she says, holding a piece of pizza with its point aimed at her mouth, "how was your day?" She bites the point off.

"Geneva came by," Harry stirs and lifts the bits of salad on his plate with his fork.

"That's what you said."

"She's worried about the profit margins."

"But everything's going fine, isn't it?"

"Well—" He spears a piece of lettuce. "I don't know. The money coming in seemed all right to me—"

"That's okay, then, right?" Cynthia takes another piece of pizza, carefully pulling apart the strands of cheese.

"How do I know?" Harry puts his fork down. All the years he spent helping Al out, he never dealt with money or licenses or employee relations, taxes, profit margins, breakage. He knows the things he can do with his hands—fixing, lifting, building—and with his voice and smile. "Al was crazy to think I could do this."

"I think you're worrying too much," Cynthia says. "Everything is going to be fine." She uses her fork to pry the crust away from her slice, and discards it. Harry remembers how their grandmother would scold when Cynthia did that to her good piecrust. He tries once more. "I'm in over my head," he says to her, and feels more in trouble as he says it.

"You worry too much," she says obstinately. "I know you can do it."

He watches her eat her pizza, her eyes traveling over the yard—the roses, the lawn, the white, peeling fence.

"Do you remember when we used to divide the yard so that I had one side of the path and you had the other?"

Harry nods. "I remember we used to fight over who had the half with the tree in it."

Cynthia laughs. "We were both so bossy, do you remember? Sometimes the other kids would leave because they couldn't stand us both trying to be number one." She sighs. "Maybe because we were both only children. Do you think that's bad for a kid?"

"It's not something I lose sleep over." Harry pushes the salad around his plate. He has eaten all the tomato wedges and cucumber slices. Only the lettuce is left, and the woody carrot shavings.

"I've thought sometimes about how it would be to have another baby." Cynthia laughs, covering her mouth with her hand. "I guess you think that's silly, at my age."

"You're talking like you're an old woman," Harry says. Is this what this is all about, a baby?

"Well." Cynthia leans her chin on her propped-up hands. "Not old, I guess, but it's late to be thinking about it."

"What's Derek say?"

"I didn't talk to him about it."

Harry thinks about this. Didn't talk to him about it?

"You're not eating," she says.

"I've got to go soon."

"You have to go? When?"

"Trying to get rid of me?"

"Harry, don't be silly. I was just asking." She shoves her empty plate away, puts her hands on the table.

Harry's stomach hurts. She is like a statue, like something behind glass. They are sitting as they have so many times—out in the yard, or inside at the kitchen table—facing each other. She smiles at him, but it is not the same. Something has turned slightly, like a globe, revealing a new country. Who can it be that is calling her?

"I haven't been around much," he says, searching. "I've been busy." But even as he says this, he realizes that, in fact, he has been here more often, not less. He lives here now, never stays at the trailer. He eats here almost every night, sees her every day.

"Of course," she says. "I know that."

She has this air of waiting, he thinks, her body held straight, alert. Her hands look poised, not idle, her eyes flitting about, not centered on him, as if she is not listening to what he says.

"Then again, maybe I've been around *too* much," he says, still probing, waiting to see when he hits on it, whatever it is.

"Don't be silly," she says again, but flatly, still with those bright watchful eyes, her head cocked—listening? He puts his hand to his back, on the sore place at the base of his spine. He would like to sit in one of the lawn chairs, but he doesn't get up, keeps his eyes on Cynthia, her eyes, her small movements, the twitching muscles of her face. She is still smiling at him, she seems unaware of his look.

"If you're going to go, help me take these in," she says.

Together they pick up the plates, the pizza box, the bottles and silverware. Going up the walk, Harry puts his free arm around her. "It's a nice evening," he says.

"Nice," she agrees. "Watch it, will you, I'm going to drop this stuff."

His arm falls and he lets her go up the steps in front of him. He watches the curve of her body as she bends to reach the door handle, the balancing movement in her hips, the suggestion of her spare flesh shifting. A woman's body.

He is putting the dishes in the sink, puzzling over the problem, moving around it, pushing at it—Cynthia, her difference, her eyes, the slick surface of her face, the movements of her hands, the phone calls, the pizza, her quick movements making salad—these things run like a movie. He lets the water stream over his hands, rubbing them to take away the stickiness, and listens to the sounds of Cynthia opening and closing the refrigerator, papery rustle of napkins, soft clunk of things thrown into the garbage. "What do you hear from Derek?" he says to her.

She pauses noticeably. "Nothing much," she says. "They're working hard, I guess."

Something here, he thinks. Derek? Trouble with Derek? And then the idea of a man presents itself. Cynthia. A man.

"You know when you're going to go out there?" he asks, not turning around.

"Go out there?" She rustles some more stuff, a plastic-bag sound, the snap of a rubber band. "We talked about some weekend next month. When I can get time off."

He turns around to watch her. "I mean when you're going to go out there and live. Sell the house and so on."

She puts down the plastic-wrapped package she is holding and stares at him. "I'm not," she says.

"Not?"

"Not going out there to live. Not selling the house." She smiles at him again, that smooth look on her face.

"You're not," he says stupidly.

"I was never going to go out there. I thought you knew. I was never going to go."

"Well." He dries his hands on the dish towel. "I see." The idea of the man looms larger. "You and Derek?"

Cynthia sits down at the kitchen table. She is composed. "We haven't had a fight or anything. We're not getting divorced. It's just a time in our lives when we're separate. That's all. He felt he had to be there, to help out"—she stumbles a little—"to be with his brother, this new opportunity. It was important to him. And," she goes on more confidently, "it was important to me that I stay here."

"He's your husband," Harry says.

"It's my life," she says. There is a change in her voice that Harry recognizes, a whiny edge that means she is defensive, holding on to what is hers. She sounded that way when she stood in front of him, seven years old, holding the toy they were fighting over to her chest with both arms. "My life is here. I realized that before it was too late. This house," she sweeps her arm around in a wide arc, "and, and everything. It's all here. You're here. That's all there is to it."

Harry feels cold. He looks at his watch, almost time to go. "I told Charlie I'd be back about now."

"That's okay," Cynthia says. "I've got some things to do." She gets up and hands him his jacket. "You're not worrying about me, are you?" She puts her hand on his arm. "I'm really happy, I'm fine."

He nods, puts on his jacket, but he lingers. "You could come to the bar with me," he says. "Have a drink before it gets crowded."

"I'd love to," Cynthia says. "Oh, I'd love to, Harry."

"Come on, then."

"But I can't, really I can't. I've got these things I have to do."

"What things?"

"I have to call Vince and talk about next week's schedule. I have to do some laundry."

Not Vince, he thinks, too old. But there's a son, what's his name? Too young. But maybe that's what she wants. He tries to imagine Cynthia with another man, unconsciously moving his shoulders, uncomfortable. "Well," he says, and they stand there looking at each other. She is finally looking him in the eye. The phone rings. "Might be Charlie for me."

"I'll get it." Cynthia flies into the dining room and picks up the receiver.

He follows her, leans against the doorjamb. She shakes her head at him, no, it's not for him, and then she moves so that her face is turned away, her shoulder and arm curving protectively around the phone. She carries the phone over to the window.

Harry moves back, just out of her sight if she should turn around. He can't hear much, a few words, long pauses.

"Who was it?" he asks when she comes back.

"Just one of the girls from the store." She tweaks at his jacket sleeve. "You'd better go before Charlie *does* call."

He moves toward the door. "What about Joey, though?" he asks, his hand on the knob.

"Go on, go," she says. Her voice is rough. "Never mind about Joey. Go on, I'll see you later."

Harry parks the truck and gathers up the grocery bag on the seat beside him. He gets out and stalls a minute, rolling up the window, glancing toward Barbara's house—Barbara, Al and Geneva's daughter. It is a neat brick box with cushions of flowers that are still blooming although it's the first of October, white shutters, a curving cement sidewalk, a dwarf fruit tree on the front lawn. A very married-looking house. He doesn't want to go into it. Geneva is inside, hampered by a two-day-old broken leg, but still to be reckoned with.

He had asked her when was a good time to come, that he didn't want to come when she was resting, and she had said he was to get his butt over there ASAP. Did he think she was taking naps, for Christ's sake? Her voice had been the same as always—loud, gravelly, demanding. He had somehow expected that her injury would have made it more like the voices of the old people at the nursing home, thinner and higher.

He goes up the front walk, holding the bag awkwardly in the crook of his arm. He raises his arm to knock, but before he can, Barbara opens the door. She reaches for the bag. "I hope it's the right stuff," he says.

Barbara peers into it. "Did they give you any trouble about the prescription?"

"No." He steps inside. It's a much cleaner place than he's used to. Cynthia's house always has a certain number of things lying around on the chairs and the floor, books and shoes and newspapers, that's what he's familiar with. This tiny front room, and the dining room that he can see part of from here, are as clean as rooms on TV, not even a speck of lint on the carpet, where a little girl is crawling.

"That's the baby," Barbara says to him. She picks her up and turns her around so that Harry can see her face. "Her name is Courtney." She jogs her up and down. "Say hi, say hi, say hi," she croons.

Courtney looks at him without interest, squirming to get out, down, away. Barbara offers her the receipt she took out of the bag, dancing it in front of her small grabbing hands. When Barbara has teased her too long, she screams, a short, sharp burst of sound that makes Harry jump.

"There now," says Barbara. She turns the baby over and props her on her hip. "She's got a real temper."

"Should have named her after Geneva."

"Oh, now." Barbara laughs. "It's so nice to see you, Harry," she says, pulling on the front of his jacket and letting it go. "You've never even been over here, have you?"

"No," he says. He looks around as if to check his memory against the gold carpet, the dark green sofa, the pictures of birds and flowers on the walls.

"Stop flirting with Harry and bring him in here."

Harry and Barbara both start, and then smile at each other. She puts Courtney down on the floor again and offers her a brightly colored toy. "Here baby, here you are."

"You've got to stop calling her that," Geneva says, still invisible. "She's got a name. As silly as it is."

Harry follows the sound of Geneva's voice into the dining room. She is propped sideways to the table, her right leg, white and thick in its cast, resting on a chair pulled up in front of her.

"She knows her name," Barbara says. "I'm going to get the coffee. You take cream, Harry? But no sugar."

Harry nods his head, wonders how she remembers things like that. Geneva is already studying the papers he has brought. He reaches in his pocket for the key ring to the Maple Leaf and pushes it across the table toward her.

"Okay, okay, this is bad. How much do they think they can get away with? Cheap band, if they'll show up." Geneva mutters to herself, shuffling through the pile. She looks up. "Where's the work schedule?"

"I just picked up the stuff on the desk and in the drawer," Harry says. "I didn't look at it."

"It was right there, on a clipboard, propped up against the wall."

"I didn't see it."

"Jesus!" Geneva pounds her fist on the table and takes a deep breath. "All right. All right," she repeats as Barbara comes in with cups of coffee. She holds one hand up, palm out, toward Harry. "All right," she says again.

Barbara sets the cups down. She places an orange-and-gray capsule next to Geneva's, smiles at Harry, and goes into the front room, where he can hear her talking to the little girl. He listens to her voice rising and falling, and then the answering word-sounds, mimicking, following her up and down the scale. He is tired, his back and shoulders ache. Yesterday he and Charlie had worked in the room Geneva wants him to open, tearing down a partition, working with crowbars. He's gone soft, he thinks, he's getting old. A year ago he would never have felt it the next day. He rubs the front of his thighs and feels the ache deep in the muscle.

"Get me some folders." Geneva points. "Over there, on that shelf. Now, look here." She writes rapidly. "This one to Evelyn." Evelyn is the senior barmaid. "This one is bills. I'll take care of these and Barbara can mail them. This one just goes back to be filed. Put them on the desk and I'll do them later, when I get back. You got it?" Geneva pushes the keys across the table toward him.

"I don't need these to get in, unless you've changed the locks."

"I know you've got a key to the door. But you'll need these others, to the office, the safe, the cooler."

Harry touches his knuckle to the lump of keys. "I will?"

Geneva picks up her coffee cup, touches it to her lips. "Cold, damn it. Barbara!" she yells, "I need a warm-up. What about you, Harry?"

He puts his hand over the top of his cup.

"All right," Geneva says. "This is it. I need you to go over there and keep an eye on things. Evelyn can take care of pretty much everything, she's got her head screwed on right. But they have to see that someone is around and think twice about starting trouble. Evelyn's no good for that, she looks wrong, too soft, too pretty." She closes her mouth tight after she says this, setting her lips, not looking at him.

Harry picks up the keys. "Fine," he says.

"Fine?"

"No problem."

"It has to be every night. For an hour, at least."

"Fine," he says, pocketing the keys.

"Well," Geneva says. She looks at him. "No smart talk? Just 'fine?' You feeling all right?" She takes out a cigarette, and smiles for the first time, tapping the filter end against the table. "How's your love life, Harry?"

"How's yours?" he says, before he thinks.

"Ha!" she says, her face an extraordinary mix of pain and triumph.

He says good-bye to Barbara, kissing her on the cheek. Courtney, pressed between them, catches at his coat, his ear, and he disentangles himself from her fingers.

When he is in the car he still feels those touches soft on his skin, the smooth brush of Barbara's face, round under his lips, the baby's fingers dabbling at his hand, the lobe of his ear. He rubs his face, thinking about women. How's his love life? Lousy. How long since he last screwed? He can't remember. When he first opened the bar, Hallie came to work for him and they had their old thing going for a while. But it hadn't been any good in such close quarters. Hallie was always trying to cook dinner for him, getting him to leave his clothes at her place. And it was awkward staying out nights, since he was living at Cynthia's full-time. Hallie had quit after a few weeks. She was working over at the Empire again, he heard, supposed to be back with her first husband. He misses waking up and seeing the unsleeping fish trailing back and forth in their tanks. Hallie, he thinks, remembering the paths of her hands on his legs, his back.

Barbara, nothing like Hallie. Like those girls in grade school who clapped the erasers, were chosen to crown the Blessed Virgin's statue with May flowers, to give the speech when the bishop came. Soft, rounded, clean faces. Quick, deft hands. Smooth bangs, small ears. Al had hoped Harry and Barbara might take to each other, though he had never said anything. Geneva hadn't taken any chances. "Touch her even once," she had said to Harry one night in the bar, how long ago now? Eight, nine years ago maybe, when Barbara was eighteen, and Harry just hitting thirty. "One look in her direction. You get me?" Harry had laughed, and she had said, her voice dropping lower, "I'll cut it off. You know me, I don't deal in figures of speech." But her speech hadn't been necessary, Barbara was untouchable to him. Al's daughter.

He approaches the corner, sees the neon sign he and Charlie put up, when was it? a few weeks ago. He counts—six weeks. He doesn't want to go back to the bar yet, the smooth dark surfaces, Charlie's anxious face. He drives past, tapping the accelerator, speeding up. Going over the West Twenty-fifth Street bridge, he glances to the left as he always has since he was young, when he thought he'd be able to see the zoo down there some place.

Once, a long time ago, his mother had taken him to the zoo. They had ridden the bus and then walked down the long curving brick road, past the many-windowed brick buildings, the coal yards. He had picked up clinkers to carry home in his pockets. He can't remember what the zoo was like that time, but he remembers the long walk, the sandwich picnic they had had on a stone bench in the small square bit of grass at the head of the brick road. He and his mother, chewing, carefully refolding the wax paper. She had wiped his face with a napkin wetted at the tiny water fountain. He had wished Cynthia was there, he remembers. Cynthia's mother had always taken both of them on visits and trips. His mother had usually refused.

Cynthia, his first girl. She used to like to remind him how they had been made to kiss each other for the camera, how the aunts had propped their fat baby bodies against each other on blankets, clapped their hands against each other for pat-a-cake. They had slept together upstairs at their grandmother's house, Cynthia's and his house now, barricaded with pillows in the center of the big double bed in their grandparents' room. Cynthia claims she remembers the iron bars of this bed stretching up toward the ceiling from where she was lying with her hairless head butted up against them, crying. Her first memory, she says. Harry remembers none of this.

He knows he ought to be turning around, going back to the bar, setting up a schedule so that he can keep an eye on both bars, get on with the renovation of the back room. He ought to find out what's wrong with Cynthia, what she plans to do about the house, her marriage, about Joey. Instead he drives further north on West Twenty-fifth, deeper into the city. He knows the name of every street he passes, the names of the bakeries, the thrift shops, even some of the trees are as familiar to him as the objects in his room at Cynthia's. He remembers where things that are gone used to be—the Smiling Dog Saloon, the decaying pink-shingled house where a dozen cats used to sun themselves on the porch and front steps, the blackened brick building that housed the Lion Knitting Mills. There was a girl he had screwed for a while who worked there on one of the specialty knitting machines, making scallops and rosettes and gilt-twisted braids of wool. He used to wait for her, parked illegally until she came running down the narrow steps, brushing brightly colored bits of fluff from her coat, combing it out of her hair. What color hair? He doesn't remember.

He passes the West Side Market, empty, plastic bags and bits of paper blowing through it, as ghostly as if it won't be filled with people and produce tomorrow. This is the route he takes when he goes on a binge. Up Twenty-fifth, down Detroit, circling back to certain unfashionable parts of the Flats, under the great bridges spanning the Cuyahoga River. He notes the bars he passes, the Sign Up, the Check It Out, Barney's Up River, the D and J, the B and R, the Why Not. He feels as if he knows them all, knows what they are like even if he hasn't been inside. He hasn't been out like that for a while, not since March.

The light ahead of him is hard and bright on the flat blue lake. He should turn back. He will, very soon, but for a while longer he drives, more slowly, weaving in and out of the maze of streets in the Flats. He remembers roaring around here with Lucette in his head. That was the last time. Never again one as young as that. It wasn't only her age, though. If it had been her friend, what was her name? she would have been a different thing altogether. A smart mouth, out for fun.

Lucette. Always waiting. Thinking. Holding things against him. Hot in bed. He believes he's forgotten her, but when he comes across something that reminds him, her face and the feel of her body are fresh in his head, the color of her hair, the taste of the inside of her mouth.

Ahead he sees the bridge he's driving toward rising in the air, the heavy counterweights falling, lights flashing. He pulls up, and then turns the car off. While he watches, leaning back, almost drowsing, an ore freighter passes in front of him, fitting snugly in the river, bigger than twenty houses. Far down the freighter, there is a man sitting on a lawn chair on a tiny, porchlike deck forty feet above Harry's head. The freighter is slow, like a dream stretching out.

Harry tilts his head so that he can see up into the metal web of the bridge. There is a sort of room grafted onto it, a control room, he guesses, that rides up and down with the bridge. He can see someone moving in it, just the shadow of a man, and Harry imagines what he might be doing—pulling levers? watching a wall of dials? He open the door of his car and gets out. Reaching into his pocket for a cigarette, he lights it as he walks toward the anchored part of the bridge. From here it seems that he could reach out and touch the scarred metal sides of the freighter, but he keeps his hands on the pebbled concrete of the railing.

The man in the lawn chair is getting closer as the freighter makes its slow progress downriver, and Harry feels himself suspended between the two of them—the man in the captain's hat, sitting in the sun, and the shadow man above in the web of the bridge, watching his dials, working his levers. In a minute the three of them will be in conjunction, like planets lined up with the sun.

The man on the lawn chair is suddenly alert. He roots behind the chair and holds up a white square, a card or piece of paper, possibly toward the man in the bridge. Harry squints—does it have writing on it? He can't tell. The man on the lawn chair unhurriedly holds up first one square and then another, as the freighter glides past at the same slow pace. Harry looks for someone he can ask questions of, but there is no one around, just the sliding piles of gravel and sand, the walls of the ship like great moving cliffs of iron, the slow roll of the river.

And then it is past, the man in the lawn chair has put his squares away and gone inside, the middle part of the bridge is creaking, getting ready to move downward, the river is rolling, swollen, toward the lake.

When the counterweights begin to slide up, Harry starts the car, but instead of waiting for the gate to go up, he reverses and drives back the way he came.

He finds Charlie sitting at the bar, an old *Playboy* spread out in front of him. "Come on," Harry says, "we've got work to do. I've got to keep an eye on the Maple Leaf while Geneva's laid up."

"Jeez." Charlie slides the magazine out of sight.

"You'll have to take care of things when I'm over there."

"I don't know," Charlie says.

"It's no big deal."

"Maybe you could get someone else." He swallows. "How about your cousin? Mrs. Lynch."

"Cynthia's got enough trouble." Harry starts taking glasses out, setting them upside down on the back counter.

"Trouble? What kind of trouble?"

"Oh," Harry says, and then stops, not wanting to talk about Derek, Joey, all that. "She's been getting phone calls," he says at last. "You know. From some pervert."

"Jeez," Charlie says. "That's, that's terrible. I mean to say. I hate to hear she's going through that stuff, that kind of thing."

"It's all right," Harry says. "She called the phone company, they're going to take care of it."

"That's good to hear," Charlie says. "A woman like that."

The trees are green on the side streets Harry is driving down, but they have a dusty look to them, they look old, crisped at their edges. It's Friday. The dashboard clock says it's almost six-thirty, later than he said he'd be. He was held up when the guy from the city came to look at the wiring, and then because of the last beer delivery. Often though, lately, Cynthia is behind schedule herself. "The later I get there, the more likely it is that dinner will be ready," he said to Geneva today.

"Ever occur to you to cook your own dinner, Harry?" she'd said.

He would cook his own dinner, or put something together anyway, he answers her now, turning the corner from Fulton, feeling the vibration in the steering wheel. Could be the U-joint, maybe one of the back tires. He doesn't ask Cynthia to cook for him, she wants to.

He listens to the noises the truck makes, separating out those that don't matter. There's a growling rumble, a hum almost below the threshold of his hearing, the U-joint for sure. Does she, though? The dinners she puts on the table now, and for a while back—pizza, leftover meatloaf, plastic containers of salad from the deli counter at the store—not like the old days, when she made biscuits, gravy, homemade dessert. He tries to remember when she stopped. He associates the change with summer, it was hot, she didn't like to use the stove. Coming up the street, he thinks with dislike of the possibly empty house, the dim rooms, the cold gray light coming through the kitchen windows, the dispiriting hum of the refrigerator. He misses Joey. And Derek. He never thought about liking or disliking Derek, but he misses having him around. He slows as he gets closer to the house, listening to the hum wind down, disappear. He'll just make a couple of sandwiches if Cynthia's not there, take them back to the bar.

But she's on the porch. She sees him and waves, coming down the steps as he gets out. "Harry," she calls as she runs toward him, "It's your mother."

He stops, his hand on the door of the truck. He has the silly idea that his mother has called, a feeling from the past when he used to go to Cynthia's house after school and had stayed too late, the short afternoons of fall cut shorter by homework and dinner, Louisa on the phone, her voice dry and knowing, unsurprised, come home, Harry, you're late again, come home. He stands by the truck, stuck in this feeling, the knowledge of all he has forgotten to do or left undone just beyond his reach. He'll remember it in a minute, what it is he ought to do.

Louisa, he thinks, the nursing home. "Not yet," he says to Cynthia. He wasn't ready.

"She's had another stroke. I called at the bar," she says. She has a funny look on her face. "I talked to that kid, Charlie. He said you were on your way home. I've been waiting for you."

She hugs herself, shivering, although it doesn't seem cold to Harry. His hands are burning on the cold metal of the truck.

"All right," he says. He opens the door again.

"Do you want me to come?" Cynthia says.

He shakes his head, gets in.

She comes closer, presses herself against the truck door, reaches up her hand to him. "I can come, this minute, I don't even need my purse."

Harry holds her hand, pulling a little on the fingers. He gives it back to her, and she backs away so he can pull out. "Call me," she yells as he starts off.

As soon as he is in his truck, hands on the steering wheel, he feels better. He drives fast, his foot hovering on the clutch. He stops at each stop light and sign, braking sensibly. Every time he comes to a corner the turn signal ticks like a clock, pushing his heartbeat faster.

She's only seventy-three, he says to himself. But then he's not sure that's right—is she seventy-two, is it next year she will be seventy-three? He tries to count back the years to her sixty-fifth birthday, the year there had been a big party at the house, the monstrous cake Cynthia had made, each of its tiny candles burning, no bigger than a finger. Seven years ago? Eight? He has come to think of that age, her age, as not very old, maybe only on the verge of being very old. Ninety is very old. But he realizes now that people die every day at seventy-two or seventy-three and no one is surprised.

Halfway there, he thinks as he goes through the intersection at Denison Avenue. He drives faster going over the bridge, but in his mind he is slowing down, he is holding back. He will never get there, he must get there. He thinks about the past, its disappointments, its failures. The truck barrels over the potholes, and his body bounces with a kind of manic glee, faster, faster.

He swings into the parking lot, jumps out, slams the door of the truck. Running across the asphalt, his feet feel light, he could run forever. He puts his back into opening the heavy glass door, and he is inside, breathing hard. The nurse in the lobby is rising, coming out from behind her walled-in desk to lead him to his mother's room. He takes this to be a bad sign.

He doesn't ask how his mother is, but the nurse tells him as they lope down the hall, his boots thumping beside her silent white feet. "She's being moved to the hospital," she says. "If you'd been a minute later, you'd have missed her. Just talk to her a bit, quickly. She can hear you."

How does she know? Harry wonders. The door to his mother's room is open. Her roommate is out in the hall, hunched in her wheelchair. He half raises his hand to her, but she doesn't acknowledge it. He wants to stop here for a minute, he would if he were by himself, but the nurse is shepherding him through, although she doesn't touch him.

It is so crowded, her room, it seems like another place. Two paramedics, their bags open on the chair and the bed, oxygen tanks, a heart monitor with its lights blinking. The bed, with Louisa on it, is the white, remote center of all this dark, snaking activity. As he comes in, they draw back from her, making a path for him, and he floats toward her, takes her hand.

"Her son," the nurse whispers behind him.

One of the paramedics grips his arm above the elbow and says, "Go on, you can say one thing to her before we haul ass out of here."

Her roommate's radio is on, a thread of Big Band music that jumps and bounces in his head. His mother. There is even less of her, the shapes of her seem flattened under the sheet. But there is still the bright star of her eye in her flat, ruined body. Her hand is lax, exhausted. She barely curls her fingers around his. When he raises his eyes to her face, her good eye is on him, patient, watching, as if there are no paramedics wheeling a stretcher up to her bed, no nurse hovering in the doorway. "Well," he says. He clears his throat.

Her lips move, but when he leans closer, she makes a face at him, the planes of her cheeks and forehead moving with surprising energy, and this youthful movement of her face takes him off balance, forces tears to his eyes. He holds himself rigid against them, tensing his muscles, gripping her hand more tightly. He turns his body away from the others. "Mother," he says, and then stops.

One of the paramedics moves forward, but Louisa makes a guttural, slurring noise, wrenched from her slack lips, and he hesitates. She pulls Harry's hand the slightest bit, and he moves closer to the bed, bends over her. "Hharrry," she says, drawing it out.

"What?" he says. The tears are sliding down his face, burning.

Louisa makes a motion with her hand that he recognizes, she wants him to do something.

"What?" he says, "what do you want me to do?"

Louisa struggles with her tongue, pushing her chin out so that the veins in her neck stand out, the skin falling away between them. But whatever it is she wants to say is too long, or too complicated. "Aaarrgh," she shakes her head in frustration.

"You can tell me later," Harry says. "Later. It'll be all right."

The paramedics draw closer again, but she drops Harry's hand and holds her own up, palm out, and they hesitate, held by the fierceness of her good eye. "Harry," she spits out, a chunk of sound. She reaches for him and he moves forward again as if she is pulling him on a string. She fumbles at his waist with her good hand.

"Money? You're worried about money?" Harry says, thinking she is reaching for his pocket. "The money is fine, it's no problem."

She bats his hand away, and turns her own over, curving her fingers. Before he can back off, she cups them around his balls, weighing them in her hand. "A mmaaann," she says to him, loud, and lets her hand fall back to the bed.

The paramedic at his elbow says in a loud voice, "Make a date with this guy at the hospital, Mom," and then to Harry, "Got to get moving, buddy."

Harry stands back and watches as they wheel her out. His balls have drawn up against his body as if against the cold, he can still feel her fingers. "Can I go in the ambulance with her?" he asks one of the paramedics.

"Better not, man."

The nurse is still there, and as he follows the stretcher down the hall she catches up with him. "I'm sure she'll be fine, Mr. Walker." She hesitates. "I'm sure it's only another little stroke."

He reads her name tag, Renfrew. Had she seen what his mother did? "Thank you," he says.

"I need you to sign some things." She gestures toward the front desk, and he follows her, glancing back at the ambulance. She lays the forms out in front of him on the chest-high wall around her desk. "I haven't seen you for a while," she says. "Not that you haven't been here, I'm sure, but I'm on a different schedule."

He signs his name over and over, and she slides each sheet away as he finishes it. "That's all," she says. "By the time you get there, they'll probably have her settled in. Say hello to your friend for me."

"My friend?"

"That nice man who used to come with you to see your mother."

"Al Zaitchek."

"Yes. He hasn't been around in a while."

"No." Harry puts his hand on the glass door and pushes. "He moved to Florida."

Harry uses his key in the back door of the house. He needs his jacket, and he had forgotten his wallet here when he left earlier, late for his appointment with the tax accountant. Now, his head still buzzing with figures, he is late to go and see Louisa at the hospital. She has been there for almost a week, is she getting better? He has to get after Charlie to see that the bar is in good shape before Geneva comes the next day. The house is dark. He crosses the kitchen to the dining room to look for the wallet on the sideboard. He has his hand on the switch when he sees that Cynthia is sitting at the dining-room table.

"I just came by to get my wallet, Cyn," he says.

"Fine." She doesn't look at him.

Her face is yellowy-white, washed blank. The telephone receiver is off, hanging by its wire over the side of the table. The bottle she usually saves for him is in front of her, its cap off, and a half-full glass beside it. He takes a step toward her. Come off it, he wants to say. Stop it. He is afraid to turn on the light.

"Go," she says. "You'll be late. You're late, aren't you?"

He sits down next to her. "You're drinking?"

"You want one?"

He takes her glass and drinks a swallow. It's straight. She takes the glass from him and holds it against her chest with both hands. "You should go," she says.

"What's wrong?" He has a sense that this has happened before, him sitting in a darkened room, asking what has gone wrong.

"Nothing."

He tries to gauge by her tone how bad it is. "Come on," he says. "What's going on?"

She takes another drink. "God. I can't even start."

He goes into the kitchen and gets a glass, pours an inch of whiskey into it. "Come on, Cyn." He looks at the phone dangling. "Was it that guy calling again?"

"No." She laughs. "Not him. Do you have a cigarette?" She takes it from him and holds it until he lights it. "He hasn't called for a while, not for a couple of days."

Harry remembers his speculations about a man, Cynthia involved with a man. It must have gone wrong, he has dumped her. He sees his wallet on the sideboard, across the room, lying beside the basket where Cynthia keeps letters and papers, but he doesn't go to get it. He sets himself to be patient. "What was it then?"

She sighs, a long breathy sound with a catch in it, a click in her throat. "Derek called," she says at last. "He wanted me to send Joey's things."

Harry feels the jump in his leg muscles, the beginning of the impulse to get up, get out, go. He brushes the table clumsily with his hand. "How did he find out?"

Cynthia ignores him. "I didn't realize," she says. "I just didn't think it through. I never thought he'd be so vindictive. I didn't see him that way. Did you? Did you, Harry?"

Harry shakes his head.

"I've been drinking. I know I've been drinking, but I'm not drunk. You have to let me tell you everything," she says. "I'll tell you everything, and you can say if I was wrong. Okay, Harry?"

"All right," he says, although he doesn't want to know, doesn't want to hear any more. He sees that her hands are shaking.

"All right," she echoes him. She takes a deep breath, it quivers in her throat. "I've been wrong about some things, I'd be the first to admit that. But now"—she takes another drink from her glass—"why now? I had everything under control." She turns toward Harry for a minute. "It was just a matter of seeing what was going on, facing up to it. You know?"

"Just tell me," Harry says. He reaches past her to put the telephone receiver back on its hook, but she pushes his hand away.

"Leave it alone. Let me tell you." She shoves her chair away from the table as if she needs more space. "I didn't know what to do. I was handling things wrong—this was in the spring, the summer too, a little. Things are different now that we're older, they've changed—I didn't realize it, did you, Harry?" She looks at him and then at her glass.

Harry nods, trying to fit this with the idea of another man.

"I always had an idea about us, you and me, Harry and Cynthia, that we would always—oh, this sounds so stupid—but we'd be together, we'd be solid for each other. We'd be each other's most important person. It's just like I was living in this box, this, this envelope, this—" she claws at the air to pull out of it the word she wants. "It's been years I've been thinking this."

Harry is terrified, his skin is cold. He puts his hand on her arm but again she pushes it away. She drains her glass and gives it to him, and he silently pours another inch of whiskey.

She sits for a minute, breathing in little ragged gasps. Then she turns to face him. "I've thought about us for so long. It didn't seem wrong to me. It didn't seem like it had anything to do with the rest of my life. And then—all this stuff, this spring—that girl, Lucette. Derek leaving. It started to get more important."

"I don't know what you mean," Harry says, but he does know, he feels it in his body, in his mouth. "What about Joey? What does this have to do with Joey?"

Cynthia shakes her head. "Derek was always jealous of you, always."

"He wasn't. You're wrong about that."

"He was—you must have seen it. You know he was."

"No," Harry says forcefully. "You're crazy."

"He was, he was. He'd lie in bed awake until I came upstairs if I stayed up talking to you. He'd watch me when you were there to see what I'd do, how I'd look."

Harry pulls her around to face him. "Cynthia, stop it, stop telling me all this. Just tell me what it is about Joey."

She rubs her nose with the back of her hand. "Derek says Joey is going to live with him in Pennsylvania. Live there with Loretta to look after him. He says he doesn't care if we get a divorce, but he means to have Joey. He says he's there already and there's not much I can do about it. He says if I try to do anything legal I'll be sorry." She lets her head fall against the back of the chair. "I don't know what he means by that—I'll be sorry—what does that mean?"

"I don't know," Harry says. He sits back, thinking, trying to see Derek in this new role.

"He says what I did—staying here, not coming to be with him—is the same thing as desertion, but that wasn't what I meant, it wasn't. I don't know what to do," she moans, "and I have so much to take care of, I don't know how I can handle all this."

"What do you have to do?" Harry asks. He looks at the dining room and out into the rest of the house, still and empty around them. "There's nothing that can't wait."

"There's so much," she says. "I can't tell you. I have all these things to arrange. God. I had everything planned out."

"I'll make you some coffee, Cyn, and something to eat. We can talk about this, about Joey, later." He starts to get up.

"You just want to leave, you want to get away from me, you know that's true. You know it."

"I have to go and see Louisa." He moves toward the kitchen.

Cynthia half raises herself in her chair. "Oh, *Louisa* needs you. I understand, of course you have to go if Louisa needs you, go on, sure. Go. You can't listen to me for a minute, you can't sit next to me for one minute."

"I'll be back. I'll come back before I go to the bar."

"That's safe enough. Everything will be different then, I won't want to talk anymore then." She walks across the room, leaning on the table, stumbling over the legs of the furniture. She grabs his arm and hangs on. "I'm telling you I had the hots for you, Harry. Can't you listen to that?"

Harry looks into her face. Her lower jaw is drawn down, her eyes screwed up small, her lips stretched tight.

"What are you talking about?"

"You heard me. I thought about you and me in *that* way. For a long time, Harry." She pushes closer to him. "And you knew it." She puts her hand up to his cheek, stroking it, smoothing the skin of his eyelid. "You knew it."

"I didn't," he says. But he remembers dancing with Cynthia, holding her in his arms. All in fun. But still, his hand on her back, the way she would look at him, he had liked to see that. He liked to come back to find her in this house, liked for her to be there in the bedroom across the hall.

"But that was all over," Cynthia says. "Everything was okay. That was all wrong, all out of proportion. I could see how it was supposed to be, that I should just be here for you. Just be here. There was a lot I figured I could do for you, I kept it to myself, I had to, for a while at least. So why now? Why all this now?"

"I don't know," Harry says. He pulls her hand away from his arm, and she sags against the door frame. "I don't know." He slams out the side door, down the sidewalk, into the truck.

"You look tired," Geneva says to Harry.

"Just my age," Harry says. His eyes feel inflamed and he resists the urge to rub them. His back hurts as he slides onto a bar stool, and he straightens up, moving his shoulders stiffly.

"Been getting enough sleep?"

"You worried about my morals?"

"I hear you've been sleeping at the trailer, the last week."

"Oh?" he says, clearing a spot on the bar to spread out the accounts. He motions for Charlie to give it the once-over with his rag. "Your spy network?"

"It's my property."

"So it is."

Geneva blows out some cigarette smoke and looks at him through it. "And anyway it was more like a conversation than any kind of reporting back."

"Tell Evelyn not to worry about me."

Geneva turns over the pages in the largest ledger, marking things occasionally with a pencil. "You and Cynthia have a fight?"

Harry doesn't answer. He pulls an ashtray over for Geneva's cigarette.

"None of my business, I suppose," Geneva says. "Although if you ask me—"

"But I do not," Harry says.

"Well, these look all right." She shuts the book. "How about the back room?"

"It's coming along."

"Let's take a look at it." She swings her crutches around and slides from her one-hipped perch on the bar stool. "Come on, don't be shy."

Harry accompanies her halting progress across the dance floor, Charlie following behind, nervously wiping his hands on his apron.

"Make yourself useful," Geneva says to Charlie, "get up there and open the door."

Charlie runs around them and swings the door open, fumbling for the light switch.

"Well," Geneva says. "My, my." She thrusts her crutches out and takes one more slow step inside.

The room is still dusty with plaster and littered with bits of wood. But the new walls are up, and the new lowered ceiling, the bar built in against the back wall.

"We got to paint yet," Charlie says, "and lay the carpet. That's all. The electric's done, and I put in the wet bar. There was this tricky bit where we had to look for the right place to make the water pipes connect. Harry got a book and also this guy he knows that's a plumber came in one day and—"

"Shut up, you idiot, and let me take a look around." Geneva advances, stopping to check where the drywall panels are joined, poking her crutch at the new outlets. "Did you have the city in to look at this yet?"

"They've been in. Not for the final inspection though."

"Hmmm." Geneva turns in a slow circle, ignoring Charlie, who is trying to stack the leftover two-by-fours against the wall. "So. Did you sign a pact with the devil? Get the elves in to help you?"

"Just me and Charlie." Harry leans against the wall. He is so tired that he feels high, the top of his head lifting a little when he takes a deep breath.

"Well." Geneva looks around again, unable to think of anything else to say.

"We'll be putting the games in by the end of next week."

"We got a list of the names," Charlie says. He pulls a grimy piece of paper out of his pocket. "Mostly video stuff, that's what the kids want. You want to take a look?"

Geneva waves the list away. "What do I care about what a bunch of suckers want to spend their money on? As long as you took the trouble to find out what's popular."

"Charlie's the expert," Harry says. He rubs his head against the wall, feeling the graininess through his hair.

"That relieves my mind, I'm sure." Geneva turns around. "I've got to give Barbara a call."

"I could run you back," Harry says.

"You look like you could use some sleep."

"Harry's been working like a maniac," Charlie says. "He's been here every night until four, five o'clock."

"My, my," Geneva says. "Well, let's get going."

She sits quiet in the car, watching Harry. He glances over at her a few times, but she says nothing until he pulls into her driveway. As he turns off the engine, she puts her hand on his arm. "What the hell's wrong with you, Harry?"

Harry, waiting for sleep, shakes himself. "Not a thing."

She snorts, but she lets go of him. As he walks around the car to open her door, he feels her eyes on him, burning through the windshield.

Driving back, he thinks of what he has left to do today. He has to get to the hospital to see Louisa, get back to check out the band that is auditioning at his bar, run over to the Maple Leaf to see that things are running smoothly. He won't be done until three A.M. or later, not until maybe four will he be lying in the bed at the trailer. This is what his life is like now: one thing after another that has to be done, taken care of, people to deal with, smooth down, deadlines. He meets with Geneva, keeps an eye on Charlie. It's a good thing, though. It tires him out. Sometimes he falls asleep before he can turn out the light, no time to think.

He imagines his head drifting toward the pillow, soft and white, the pale embroidery of the pillowcase rough under his palm, but no, there is no pillowcase like that at the trailer. Those are the pillowcases at Cynthia's, the embroidery done by his grandmother or one of his aunts, years ago. He thinks of that bed, those pillows, with some longing, their whiteness, their smoothness, the dim quiet of the old bedroom with its sleeping porch, the dark wood, the radiator with its heat rising. A wintertime picture.

He hasn't seen Cynthia for more than a week. He hasn't been back there to sleep, although he has gone during the day to pick up clothes. He doesn't go out of his way to avoid Cynthia, but she hasn't been there, the house cool and empty, the windows shut against the clear October air. He knows she hasn't gone, though, for she has left several messages for him at the bar. He knows he ought to call her, go and see her, but he's afraid to, he doesn't want to think about her or what she said. He doesn't want to think at all. He's not drinking much, he's afraid of that, too, afraid to slide down that dark gullet.

The sign in front of him says, "Toledo—97 miles," and he wishes he could keep on driving for those ninety-seven miles, and farther, just keep on going, the dark ribbon of the road unraveling in front of him.

The next day, when Harry opens the door to the bar, he sees with relief that it is almost empty. Charlie is at the far end, talking with a man from the neighborhood, a regular from when old Tomchek owned the place.

Charlie sees him and holds up his hand. "Geneva called, said she's coming over in fifteen minutes."

"Call her 'Mrs. Zaitchek' when she's here if you know what's good for you."

Charlie ducks his head eagerly, agreeing. "How was your mother doing yesterday?"

"My mother?" Harry says. "She was fine." He pauses, hand on the bar, watching Charlie set up. He had been struck by his mother's stillness on the hospital bed. Her body didn't seem any longer like the container of some terrible force, held back by the strength of her will. She had let him take her hand, she had listened to his voice, but she wasn't there in the same way she had been. Her good eye was dark as ever, as knowing, but it was sinking into her head, she was diving deeper into herself. "Did you check the stock?" he asks Charlie.

"I did part of it." Charlie pokes his head under the bar, comes up with cocktail napkins. "I found some of these with these what-they-call brain twisters on them. They're pretty cool."

"Fine," Harry says. He looks at the brain twister on the napkin that Charlie lays out before him, but he doesn't read it. Charlie is taking cherries out of a jar, helping them out with his fingers. One falls on the floor and he pops it in his mouth, looking around guiltily as if for his mother.

"And your cousin called, Mrs. Lynch. She wanted you to call her."

"I'll be in the back, in the office," Harry says. He makes his way through the clutter of tables and chairs. The office is dim even when he switches on the light, a long, bare, empty room sliced off the back of the dance floor. He sits down in the desk chair and is motionless for several minutes. Then he starts opening the drawers and piling the papers and files he takes from them on the top of the desk. When he has gone through all the drawers, he gets up to find a box in the unlit shadows at the other end of the room. He sets the box on the chair and loads the stack into it.

He tries to make his mind empty as he moves around the room, his feet shuffling up old dust, bits of paper, bent pop-tops. Someone has put the jukebox on in the bar. The bass chords boom through the wall, heavy and low, they penetrate the clatter of glasses and bottles, the ring of the cash register, the laughter, the raised voices. He has always found this sound comforting, could always hear it, wherever he was, whatever he was doing, could feel it even, thrumming in his breastbone, rising in his chest with the alcohol, reminding him that he felt good, for a while anyway. The words, the high fretful line of the melody would be lost, but he wasn't interested in those thin voices pleading for love.

He is thinking of them, all those bars where he sat, leaned against walls, bought and smoked cigarettes, found women, loved them, ate pretzels and popcorn from small napkin-lined baskets, and drank—tall glasses of beer cold in his hand, shots in chunky glasses. Those bars, the four walls of them closing in the yellow light, the ropes of smoke, the heat, the smiling faces, the warmth against the cold empty rooms where he slept, made money, faced his relatives.

There is a knock at the door, and Charlie sticks his head in. "She's here, with some other woman," he says, grimacing, his eyebrows raised out of sight under his long bangs. "It's maybe her daughter." He glances at the boxes on the desk and on the floor without interest. "You coming out?"

"In just a minute," Harry says.

"Don't be too long, okay? She gives me the shakes."

"I'll be coming right out."

There are a few people in the main room, although it is only a little past five. People in after work for a quick one, heavy drinkers just now getting ready for evening. Geneva is at one of the small tables by the dance floor that are usually set up only on the weekends. Charlie has overturned two of the chairs and she is sitting in one of them, her leg stretched out stiff in front of her.

The other chair is for Barbara, but she is over by the small stage, looking at the mike stands and the wires snaking around them. She makes a slow circuit of the room as Harry comes up to stand by Geneva. "This is so great, Harry," she calls. "Everything looks so nice."

"She doesn't get out enough," Geneva says to Harry, "if this place excites her."

Harry takes another chair and sits opposite her. "Can Charlie get you something?"

"If I want to drink I'll do it at home where I can fall down in my own bathroom. What's the story?"

Harry waits until Charlie has gone back to the bar. He glances over at Barbara. She is standing in front of a beer sign with a three-D moving waterfall. "No sense beating around the bush. I'm going to sell out."

"What the hell do you mean?"

"I'm going to sell the bar. I'll manage the Maple Leaf for you until your leg is better, but then I'm leaving."

"You shit. You're going to sell out. The great Harry Walker doing what he does best."

Harry looks down at his hands. "I've thought about it, and I have to do it. I'll give you half the profit of the sale."

"I guess it's cutting into your drinking time. Is that it? Not getting into your quota of beds?" Geneva leans toward him, spitting the words at him in a hissing whisper. "Once a loser, Harry, is that it?"

Harry shrugs, pulls out his cigarettes. "I've started packing the papers and files. They're in boxes in the office. I'm going to put it up for sale right away, next week."

Geneva laughs, and Charlie looks over from the bar uneasily. "That's what I like about you, Harry, you're a loser, but you're so neat, so thoughtful. What a relief it is to us all that you didn't just walk out with the files in a mess. Goddamn Al, goddamn his ass for being a sentimental fool."

Tears are running down her face. She looks around the bar. "That was his first idea when we came and looked at this place, that it would do for you. You shit. Barbara," she yells. "Get me out of here. Stop mooning over that fucking trash and bring the car around to the front. Get away," she says to Harry. "Get your screwup face away from me."

Harry gets up and stands by the bar. He looks stupidly at the clock. Five-fifteen. "Pour me a shot," he says to Charlie.

Charlie brings the bottle over. "I need to talk to you, Harry."

"Not now."

"No problem, sure." He puts the bottle down and retreats to the other side of the bar.

Harry sits down heavily on the bar stool. He is aware that someone has come to sit next to him, and he turns his body away so that he will not have to look at whoever it is. But this isn't good enough. He hears a throat being cleared, the click of long nails on the bar. He turns his head to see who is there, see if it is Barbara. But it's a girl, young, dark hair. He downs his shot, looking at her. Skinny, not bad. Does he need a woman right now? Does he want one?

"You're Harry Walker," she says to him, and he nods. "You don't remember me."

He shakes his head, gesturing to Charlie for another shot.

"You remember Lucette Harmon, I suppose." She comes down hard on the last word.

He looks at her more closely, as if she might be Lucette in disguise. "Yes," he says.

"Well, that's something." She sticks her hand out for him to shake. "Bev Archacki. I want to know if you know how Lucette is, how she's doing."

"What is all this?" Harry frowns. The whiskey is starting to work in him, the slow fire rising in his gut, and he wants to pay attention to it, he wants her to go away.

"You haven't seen her? You haven't heard anything about her?"

"Why should I?" he asks.

Bev gives a little flounce on the bar stool. "Buy me a drink, and I'll tell you why you should have."

Harry holds his hand up for Charlie. He turns his head slightly— Barbara hasn't come back with the car yet and Geneva is still there, her head cocked.

Bev takes a ladylike sip from her bottle of beer when it comes and sets it down square on the small napkin. She takes a breath and says, "Lucette is pregnant and it's your baby, *which* she's going to have in about a week." She holds up her hand. "Don't even say it might not be yours, because I know it is, but even if I didn't, there are these really accurate blood tests now and they can tell absolutely, so why would anyone lie? So just take my word for it, it's your baby. What I want to know is what are you going to do about it?"

"Do?" Harry is aware of Geneva behind him laughing.

"She's living at her mother's house and her mother's round the bend further than she ever was. Lucette's got to try to take care of her *and* herself. Plus your cousin is coming around all the time. Plus my stupid brother, who thinks he's going to be some kind of saint and marry her, for Christ's sake. And your cousin has been getting weirder and weirder. She called up there tonight drunk or something, moaning about the baby and her duty and so on. It was pretty scary."

"How do you know all this?" Harry says.

"My stupid brother called me, and I was tired of everyone being upset and no one doing anything. So here I am. And my thought is, what are you going to do?"

"A damn good question, Harry," Geneva says. "Honey," she says to Bev, "you sure know how to deliver the knockout punch. This has made my day. I really mean it." She lets loose a long peal of laughter, leaning against the wall by the door, propped up with her crutches.

"Don't laugh," Bev says to her. "It was your husband gave Lucette money to take care of herself. A handful right out of the cash register."

Geneva snorts, still laughing. "Stop, I can't take any more." She holds her side with her free hand.

"Don't you believe me?" Bev glares at her.

"Of course I believe you. It's just the sort of goodhearted dumb-ass thing he would do."

Barbara comes in and stops, looking in bewilderment at her mother laughing, at Harry paralyzed at the bar, at Charlie and the other customers, their mouths and eyes wide. "What—" she begins.

"Never mind," Geneva says. "Come on, get me out of here. You," she says to Harry, "wait for a week. I want to see if I can get up the necessary. I don't want the last thing Al did to go down the drain, even if you do." She pauses. "Are you sure you want to do this?"

Harry nods, his face stiff.

"You're out there with the garbage if you do. You're nothing."

Harry can hardly hear her, it is as if she is already gone, as if she is dead. He watches her slow-moving body recede into the brightness outside, and turns to the girl. "Cynthia knows about all this?"

"She was over there every damn day until Lucette told her to get out," Bev says. She pushes her beer back and forth, skating it

over the surface of the bar. "But she still wants Lucette to come
and live with her, and the baby too, when it gets here. She won't
give up on it. Listen," she says, "I just thought you ought to know.
No one has ever got around to telling you or whatever. I'm not
talking like you ought to be getting married or anything. I thought
maybe—" her voice trails off. "Well, I'm out of here. Hey, you,"
she says to Charlie as she passes him, "I see you got a real job."

"What?" Charlie says. "What?" He looks at Harry, who slumps
farther, leaning against the bar. "Harry?" He moves closer. "You
all right?"

"Fine," Harry says. "I'm fine."

"Well." Charlie wipes his hands. "Listen, Harry, mind if I ask
you something? That is, I mean to say, I got something to tell you,
ask your advice, kind of like. I know this is a bad time."

Harry reaches for the bottle and fills up his shot glass. He swirls
it, looking down into the amber spiral, seeing ahead of him the
cyclone of a binge swirling lazily with the whiskey. It is comforting, it is something he knows. He will go down into it and come
out the other side in some days or weeks and the world will have
changed.

"Harry?"

"Another time, Charlie." He picks up the shot and drains it,
pushes the glass away. "Charlie, Charlie."

"What?"

"Listen, Charlie, we'll talk about it later, whatever it is." He
laughs. "Later, believe me." He reaches behind the bar for his
jacket and, still laughing, goes out the door.

Driving, he follows the hot red and cool green of the traffic
lights. His eyes track the circle of numbers on the speedometer as
the pointer pushes up among them. His fingers move over the
wheel, feeling the familiar cracks and worn places. If he lifts his
hand to his nose, he will be able to smell the aftershave that has
been rubbed into the fake leather a thousand times, a thousand
nights out, a thousand times he has looked at his face in the mirror,
examining his freshly shaved cheeks.

He drives without thinking, going straight when the light is green, turning when he is in the right lane. But he cannot move randomly, not here where he knows every street, has seen every house. There is a map in his mind with all the bars on it, all the late-night breakfast places and all-night drugstores, all the stop signs, all the potholes. Any of these streets will take him to places that bring him pain—to Cynthia's, to the trailer, to Al's bar, to the house where he and his mother once lived, to the cemetery where his father is buried. The stores he passes are heavy with memory. His mother's hand pausing among the tomatos, feeling for flaws in the material of a shirt, opening the knobby metal clasp of her purse, receiving change. The parking lots where he parked to neck, the garage he used to smoke in back of, the places in high weeds where he prowled with his buddies, looking for treasure, dropped dimes, bottles to redeem, bits of twisted metal, motor parts.

He wishes it were dark so that he couldn't see every brick, every worn place in the sidewalk so clearly.

If he was younger . . . he imagines his younger self. Trouble was a sign to travel. He'd never gone far, just up along the line of the lake, to Toledo, to upstate New York, or south along the line of the freeway, maybe as far as Cincinnati, hop over the Ohio River to get his feet on the soil of a distant state. Why hadn't he gone farther? Why had he always come back?

Driving along the rim of the industrial flats, the great canyon of steel plants, he remembers when he'd gone as far as Chicago— couldn't even leave the Midwest, what a loser he'd always been. He'd driven west feeling fine—fuck the foreman, fuck that job— radio playing, a straight line into the sun. Ten years ago maybe, before he was thirty, anyway. Did he have plans about what he was going to do? He can't remember, only the straight ribbon of the turnpike he coasted along, beating time on the steering wheel of the truck, another truck, not this one.

He'd banged around Chicago for a couple of days, drinking in new bars, sliding his arms around new women, walking the streets by that unfamiliar lake, head tilted back to gaze at the new shiny-sided buildings. A lot of construction going on there then. He'd thought about that, he remembers. Lots of jobs, all those fancy apartments and office buildings going up along Lake Shore Drive. Money rolling in, workers in demand, no need to put up with the bad attitudes of management and crew foremen.

But when he'd been there a week, he'd started to lose momentum. To cheer himself up, he'd taken the elevator to the top of the tallest building in the world, as it was then. The Sears Tower. One brick on top of another, he thought to himself as the elevator swooshed silently upward, one more set of girders and one more again. The elevator was enormous. The highly polished metal walls stretched upward, twice, maybe three times as tall as Harry, the tallest man riding it. The ride seemed long. There was talking at first, giggling, children jumping and calling to each other. But as it went on, quiet descended, they found themselves riding in a silence so deep that they could hear the faint whispering of the cables, the metallic murmurs of the machinery that was propelling them upward.

At the top they all burst out, laughing and talking once more. Harry walked around, enjoying the light, the space. There it is, he thought, the city, Chicago. He liked the broken-edged curve of the lake, the silvery blue of the water, flat and smooth from up here. He tried to trace the streets he had walked, but from so high up it was hard to tell which was which. He moved from one side to another—north, west, south—dodging groups of children and young parents with baby strollers.

The sun was shining, it was a beautiful day, but he felt a sense of unease. The shape of the city was wrong, the lake was in the wrong place. He had never been to the top of the tallest building in Cleveland, the Terminal Tower, but if he had, the view could not have looked like this, so flat, so gray, so far away. He had no home here, no next of kin. If he passed out, there was no place anyone could take him, no one to pull his flopping head up and check if his eyes rolled back, no one to make a joke about his hangover the next day.

He wanted to leave, but he had become afraid to get back into the elevator. He walked past it several times, watching the older children in their pastel jackets, the women with baby backpacks, the men holding toddlers by the hand, crowding in through the tall doors, laughing, talking, jumping, crying, scolding, but he could not make himself follow them. He found himself sweating at the thought of seeing his face mirrored indistinctly in the bright metal walls, feeling the vibrations of the machinery in the bones of his feet. Not until he was almost alone could he persuade himself to get on, and then he rode down with his eyes half closed, promising himself a drink, visualizing it, a shot of Jack sitting on the familiar wood of the bar at Al's Maple Leaf. He turned his face away from the only other occupants of the elevator, an elderly couple who had waited for a quiet, childless ride, and thought hard about Cleveland, Al, the same streets he had known all his life, the streets he was navigating now, ten or more years later. He had come back, he is back, he had to come back.

Harry finds that he has driven in a great half-circle. He is near Louisa's nursing home, and he turns without thinking into the driveway. He pulls into a parking space and shuts off the engine, sits there thinking. He tries to figure out how many times he's been to visit Louisa: a thousand times? two thousand? He tries to figure out which is her window, tries to count from the end of the building, measuring in his head the remembered width of the rooms. But it all slides away from him and he can do no better than to say that it is one of three that are shaded by an old maple tree whose leaves are a deep fiery red, a ball of whispering light and color.

There is a different nurse at the desk, not the redhead. He feels relieved. This one is bent over the files, and quickly he slips through the door and across the lounge behind her back, his boots silent on the carpet. He stops to look at her from the safety of the hall. She is straightening up now, and her hair comes into view well before the rest of her, sculpted around her cap in a great pouf that overshadows her thin young face. She doesn't even glance over to where Harry is standing, and he grins.

But walking down the hall, putting his heels down carefully, his glee recedes. He can't think why he is here. But maybe there is something he can take to her at the hospital that will cheer her up, will bring her to herself. Surely he can find something on her dresser or in the drawer of her bedside table that he can take to her like a trophy.

Outside the door to her room, he hesitates, assembling his story in case her roommate is awake. Mrs.—what's her name? He knocks, pushing the door in at the same time. "Hello?" he says.

She is sitting on the edge of her bed, letting her legs dangle, kicking them a little so that her slippers flap against her old leathery feet. "Well, if it isn't Harry," she says. "I didn't think to see you."

"I just thought I'd come by to see if there was anything of my mother's she might want in the hospital," he says, nodding his head toward Louisa's half of the room, partitioned off now by a curtain.

"Oh, my, I don't know about that."

"I'll just take a look," he says, moving toward the curtain.

"Wait a minute now, honey," she says, "wait a minute," and when he keeps moving she struggles to drag herself to the end of the bed, to lay a hand on his arm.

But he is too quick for her, he pulls back the curtain. There is someone in his mother's bed, rolled away on her side, sleeping. For a minute, he is fooled into thinking that it is Louisa, that she has come back, another magic trick of his mother's, and why has no one told him? But even as he reaches out to touch her shoulder he sees that this is a much larger woman, her well-padded shoulder rises higher above the bed than Louisa's did, her legs under the blanket are enormous. Even her head, covered with uneven wisps of colorless hair, is huge.

Harry pulls his hand back in horror. She has not awakened, and he gasps with relief.

The roommate is behind him, slow but persistent. "I tried to tell you, honey," she says, pulling on his arm.

He follows her back around the curtain, breathing hard. "Who is that?" he says, keeping his voice low. "Why is there someone in my mother's bed?"

"They're overcrowded here, you know," she says, wagging her finger at him. "There's a waiting list. Now, you see, they've put her things that were left in a box. You have to ask the nurse. I don't know why they didn't tell you at the desk. Not that she had much. She didn't hold with clutter."

Harry sits down in the visitor's chair. "It doesn't make sense to have to move her"—he jerks his head toward the curtain—"around again when my mother gets back."

The roommate has pulled herself up on the bed and is sitting on it as if riding sidesaddle. "Well," she says. She casts her eyes down, wiggles her shoulders, flutters her lashes.

Harry stares at her. Is she flirting with him? He feels his face growing red. But then he sees that it is only that she is embarrassed.

He doesn't get it. Does she not want to have his mother back? Have they had an argument? His mother is difficult, he knows. Not everyone can get along with her. He says this to her, "My mother can be difficult to live with," he says.

"Oh, honey, she and I were like this." She holds her thin, twisted fingers together, trembling. "We never had a cross word. Not that she spoke all that much, but you know what I mean."

He waits for her to go on, but she has stopped. And finally it dawns on him what she means. "Oh, no," he says. She's not that old, he wants to say, only seventy-three. The hospital is temporary, like before, for she has been there before, and she has come back. But the look on her face silences him. It is sad and knowing. If I can face it, she seems to be saying, and I so much closer to it, why not you? Why not you?

On the way out, he strides quickly past the nurse at the desk. She looks at him in surprise, but says nothing. He needs a drink. How glad he is that he did not have to see her face, that monstrous woman in his mother's bed.

Where now? He knows that there is a liquor store in the little shopping center by the corner. He turns that way, driving slowly through the evening. The light is fading. He buys a pint of Black Jack, carries it back to the car. He takes a swallow of it like medicine and stands the bottle upright between his thighs. He does not want to drink in bars tonight, doesn't want the company of other men, his anonymous brothers, although that was the thing of it that he had liked—the silent expressive backs and shoulders of men hunched over the bar, communing, each of them, with a drink, or a parade of drinks, the only movement the circular swabbing motion of the bartender's arm on the bar or the arc and sparkle of beer coming from the tap.

He'd like to talk to someone, a woman. Or maybe not talk, but listen to her talking about something ordinary, about buying a dress, or what someone had said at work. Something he wasn't expected to respond to.

Hallie, maybe Hallie would be at home. It was early enough, she might not have gone to work yet, and he points the truck that way. Where is she working now? The Empire, that's right. Maybe her first husband won't be there, and if he is, well, that's fine, too. Surely he can visit an old friend. His fists clench on the steering wheel. He has never liked her first husband, a screwy bastard.

When he pulls up across the street from her house it is almost full dark. She lives in the top half of a duplex, and he peers up at the windows. They are lit, but he can't see any movement. Her car is in the driveway, perched at the end, almost overlapping the sidewalk, as if she is just about to leave. He gets out, carrying the bottle. At the door, he pauses. He has a key, Hallie has never asked to have it back, but he knocks anyway. He waits, and then takes a quick drink when he hears her coming down the stairs. "Hey, Hallie," he says.

She regards him, not speaking. She is ready for work except for her shoes and her hair, which is wet, hanging in little wisps around her face and on her shoulders. "Harry," she says finally. "What are you doing here?"

"Just dropping by," he says, smiling what feels like his old smile, and as he says it, he almost feels better, as if everything that has happened is far in the past. Another drink would make it even farther away, but he ought to wait at least until he is upstairs, sitting down.

She stands in the door, looking at him, pulling on one of the wisps of hair.

He looks past her, up the stairs. Was there a movement up there? He tenses, flexing his muscles. "Aren't you going to ask me up?"

"I don't think so."

"What's the problem?" He spreads his hands wide. "Just an old friend, coming by to talk."

"I just don't think so." She keeps her eyes on him gravely, tilting her chin up.

"Is he up there?" Harry can feel his jaw pushing out, an ugly fighting look, he knows. He tries to moderate it, but his body, his face, are growing and changing on him, intent on their own ideas.

"No," she says, "he's not."

"So, then? I just want to talk," he repeats. He watches her eyes, and he thinks she is beginning to soften, to waver. But she still bars the door. He thinks of reaching out, lifting her, just picking her up and carrying her upstairs. To talk. Or whatever.

But standing in the door she looks more obdurate than should be possible for such a small woman. Her crossed arms look solid, very much of a piece with her body. She is like a statue made of something heavy, one of the statues in the church, her draped clothing as heavy as stone.

"We could talk on the porch," he says. He glances around. There are no chairs, only the bare boards and a few empty clay pots.

"I have to go to work, Harry."

"Not for a while. It can't be more than eight."

"I'm sorry if you've got trouble." Hallie looks down at her bare feet. "But it's too late, too late for all that."

Harry is pretty sure that if he said to her, Hallie, I've just found out that I'm going to be a father, she would uncross her arms and welcome him in, hand him a beer, invite him to tell her about it. But he can't just come out with it like that. He can't say it standing on her front steps. So he leaves, goes to the truck. He looks back as he starts it up, hoping to see Hallie waving, but the door is shut. She has gone into the house.

Later, Harry sits in his truck parked in the lot behind the Maple Leaf. No one has noticed him, he is slumped down, and it's dark—the nearest streetlight is out. The trailer, where he spent so many nights with women, with Lucette, is empty. There is a light in one of the windows, but it's only the reflection from the light above the back door of the bar, moving and swinging in the wind. If he went over and looked in, he'd see nothing, no one. The trailer door is unhooked, it flaps when the wind gets up.

Harry rolls down the window. The air is cold and it smells like smoke, smoke and fallen leaves. The parking lot isn't quite real, it is some way between, a place where things are left, in transit. If he waits long enough it might get him to the place where the same good life goes on and on, where Al will come to the door and call out—can Harry give him a hand, does he want the keys to the trailer, does he want one for the road?

His lips work—he feels like he wants a drink, a slow ache in his gut, not just one drink, a long chain of them. Pretty soon he will go and get them, in a minute.

This has never happened to him before, a girl with a baby on the way. His sons and daughters have been aborted, maybe passed off as the children of other men by the married women he has known. He is four years older than his own father was when Harry was born, and this makes him feel as if he has been lucky, has pulled something off. How had she done it, Lucette? He tries to get a sense of her, of how she would be now, her belly big and rounded, but it's impossible. She was so thin, the bones of her wrists and ankles like straws. When he imagines her pregnant, she is grotesque, a swollen stick figure. He leans his head back against the padded headrest, feeling the torn place rub against his scalp.

No place to go for comfort or advice, those places are gone or used up. His eyes rest on the back door of the bar, a dark rectangle on the blank wall. It opens and two kids come out, stumbling over each other, laughing and calling to someone still in the bar, the bright smoky light spilling from inside, a pool of it lying on the weedy gravel. "Come on, let's party, let's party," one of them says, patting his pockets for his car keys, failing to find them, starting over again. "Come on," he says, "come on, you guys." His friend leans against the wall with his head down, taking deep breaths. "I'm okay," he says, "I'm okay, just wait a minute."

Harry slumps farther down, watching them. A car pulls in, narrowly missing a man on the sidewalk, an old man by his walk. He is slow, bent over, each careful step making his body lurch. It's Tase Penfield, going up to the Maple Leaf as he has done nearly every night of his life since Harry has known him—how many years? ten? fifteen? The happiest man I know, Al had said about him, half joking, he has everything he needs. Harry watches his slow progress past the kids. They don't look at him, he's invisible, too old to notice. Halfway across the parking lot he stumbles and stops to rest, one hand on the rusting fender of an old Dodge. Harry takes his keys out of the ignition. He gets out of the truck, closing the door noiselessly, and circles around behind the old man, breaking into a long, walking stride.

"That you, Tase?" he says, stopping short.

"Harry." He nods. "Where are you off to?"

"Out for a little air. You on your way in?"

"Might as well."

Harry takes his arm and they proceed slowly across the shifting gravel toward the back door. The old man's elbow is light, he feels it moving dryly in the sleeve of his jacket. He opens the door for him and holds it while he goes up the two steps.

"I thank you, Harry. Can I stand you a drink?"

Harry starts to say no, but why not start here, one drink is as good as another. "Well," he says, temporizing. He sticks his head in. Evelyn is behind the bar, no Geneva. No Al, of course. A great wave of sadness rolls over him, but what the hell, he thinks, what difference does it make? "Okay," he says, and follows the old man in.

Tase gets up onto his usual bar stool, Harry waiting behind him until he's settled. Tase holds up two fingers when Evelyn looks their way. "And a shot for Harry," he says when she brings the beer over.

Harry tries to slip the money to Evelyn, but Tase puts his hand on Harry's arm, holding him back, and gives her instead six wrinkled one-dollar bills. Harry drinks the shot quickly, holding it up first in salute to Tase. The bar is still quiet, an hour away from good times. The band is not here yet. All the glasses are clean, gleaming. The television is on but the sound is turned off. Evelyn is watching some kind of a nature show, long shots of birds floating on sheets of gleaming water, arcing and wheeling in the big television sky.

"Not the same with Al gone," Tase says.

"No. No, it's not." Harry turns his beer bottle around and around in front of him.

"Still, that's the way of the world."

"I guess it is." Harry catches Evelyn's eye. He wonders if Geneva would have called here and told what she knew about his business. When she comes over to wipe the bar near them, he looks at her carefully, but she seems the same, placid as always. "Did you ever knock someone up?" he says to Tase when she has gone back to her post by the television.

Tase turns to look at him. "No," he answers after a pause. "I've got no child, never have."

Harry is embarrassed, he ducks his head, picks up his glass and drinks to hide it. "I ought to be going," he says.

Tase stares straight in front, his hand cupped around his beer bottle. "That'd be the little blond girl." When Harry doesn't answer, he turns again to look at him, questioning.

Harry nods.

"Well, now. She was in here a while ago. I though she might be expecting. She had a look to her."

"When was that?"

Tase shakes his head. "In the spring? Might have been as late as June. It was warm, I do remember that."

Harry stares at him, thinking. "Was she looking for me?"

"Said she was looking for Geneva."

"Geneva?" Harry feels conspired against. Has Geneva known all this time?

"But I didn't think so, at the time. A nice little girl."

Harry holds his hand up to Evelyn. One more and he'll go.

"Pour one for me," Tase says to Evelyn when she comes. "We'll drink to Harry's child."

"Harry a father?" Evelyn says, laughing. "Finally got caught, did you?"

Harry puts his head in his hands, but Tase is going on, holding up his glass, shaking slightly. "It seems to me that Harry has been given a gift. A gift," he repeats firmly.

"An albatross, more like," Evelyn says.

A gift, Harry thinks. Well, that's one way to look at it. He has a picture of Lucette handing him a baby across a great gulf of space.

"I'm an old man," Tase says. "But I haven't forgotten that. How it is like a gift."

Harry looks at him, waiting for him to go on, but Tase stares ahead, his fingers trembling on the bar, silent. I'm out of here, Harry thinks. "I've got some places to go," he says. He takes some money out and leaves it on the bar for Evelyn. "I'll be seeing you, Tase."

The old man doesn't turn or speak, but when Harry gets up, he raises one hand in farewell. Harry goes out, letting the door fall shut behind him.

He crosses the parking lot quickly. The two kids have made it over to their car, or someone's. One of them is sitting on the hood fingering his keys. The other is squatting by the wheel, his head hanging down. "Have a good night, boys," Harry says.

He thinks he will drive over to the Briar Rose, or the Easy Over, or any place. Maybe he will drive down to the flats and drink from his flask in the shadow of the steel mills. There are miles of little roads down there, you can lose yourself among them, driving through the giant rusting machines that loom over your car like ghosts. Or he might go and have a look at the lake. Sitting by the lake in the dark was a pleasant thing, the sucking, splashing, the soft blackness of the water, the ruddy, city-lit sky.

But he is driving down Twenty-fifth, feels the tug of memory. Lucette's mother's house is down here, and he finds himself thinking about going by there, just driving by, slowly, to see . . . whatever. It can't do any harm, he thinks. It's dark, no one will know. He counts the streets going north from Denison Avenue, pleased that he remembers, can't be that old, memory not gone yet. He pauses at the traffic light by the fire station, and sees ahead the expansive darkness of Riverside Cemetery, deep with old trees, held back from the street by its black iron fence. He turns left by the great lit-up cliff of the Christian Science church.

He passes two side streets and slows down so that he can feel his way, lets his eyes slide over the houses—this one? this?—until the shape of one, its color under the streetlight, fits into the waiting slot in his brain. At the last minute, he stops and parks across the street. He gets out a cigarette and feels for matches. There are lights on in the house, the yellow glow from shaded lamps, a cold white fluorescent glare in the kitchen, the flickering blue from a television. He sits watching them, and smoking, shifting on the seat occasionally to relieve his cramped arms and legs.

After a while, there is a sense of movement in the house, the curtain across the front windows ripples and shifts. Harry keeps his eyes on the door, and in a minute or two he sees that someone is there. It is Lucette, he knows, she is on the front porch, a shadow against the railing. He gets out of the truck and goes up the front walk, stops at the foot of the steps, looking up. "I came by to see how you were doing," he says.

"I'm okay," her voice answers from the darkness of the porch.

"Mind if I come up?"

"There's no place to sit," she says. She moves forward a little, he can see the gleam of the streetlight on her hair.

He comes up and settles himself against the porch railing, lights a cigarette. "Have one?" he says to her, tapping the pack so that three cigarettes slide out neatly, each one a bit farther than the next.

"I can't smoke any more." She moves a little closer, so that he can see her better. She is leaning against the wall by the door, half turned away. He can see the great curve of her belly, its soft darkness, and how she is biting one of her fingers.

"I've got someone else," Lucette says to him. "In case you're interested."

"Well, well," he says. Out of the corner of his eye he sees that the curtain is twitching again. "I'm just here to talk."

"I thought you ought to know."

"That's all right." He draws deeply on his cigarette, blows the smoke out in a long, curling stream, flicks the butt over the railing. He puts his hands in his pockets, jingling his change. "You heard about Al, I guess?"

Lucette nods, he can see her hair flick with the movement of her head.

"Listen," he says. He moves toward Lucette. "We'll have to do some talking."

Lucette draws back a little, going farther into the shadows. "I'm not going to live with your cousin," she says. "I've made that clear to her."

"With this guy then?"

Lucette shrugs. "Probably not," she answers finally. "But I'm not waiting around for you to ask me," she adds quickly. "I was thinking Bev and I might get a place. If things work out."

"That's fine," Harry says. "I just thought I'd come over to the house, see how things were with you." He waits to see how Lucette takes this. Her head is down, he can't see her eyes.

"That was nice of you." She looks up, raising her eyebrows. "Finally."

"I didn't know," he begins.

"I was gone and you didn't even know it."

Harry doesn't have anything to say. He hadn't known, he hadn't asked. He starts to say that he is sorry, but she waves her hand, silencing him.

"That's all right," she says. She hesitates. "It's very nice to see you, Harry. It's nice that you came."

"Well," he says. "That's about it. I need to get back to the bar. Al left me a bar, did you hear that?"

She nods. "Bev told me. She used to come, when I was away, and I'd ask her what was going on and she'd tell me all the news."

He reaches into his pocket again, sliding his fingers among the coins, his fingers rolling Al's ring over and over between them. "Did you ask her about me?"

"Never. But she'd tell me anyway." Lucette laughs.

Behind her, the curtain is pulled across the window and he can see into the front room of her mother's house. A woman is standing there, holding the curtain back.

"That's my mother," Lucette says.

Harry nods. Without surprise, he sees that Cynthia is inside, too. He looks at her through the pane of glass, she is holding something that is clutched against her chest, her face is blank, amazed, her hair wild around her head. She doesn't move, and then the woman, Lucette's mother, lets the curtain fall.

Lucette moves forward and together they walk down the steps, down the front walk to his car. She stands on the grass while he opens the door, fumbles with the keys. He wants to kiss her, but he doesn't. He puts out his hand, holds it out until she extends her own, and they stand there a minute in the dark, the old maple tree creaking in the wind, its leaves silently drifting down. When he is driving back through the dark streets, this is what he remembers, Lucette's small cold fingers and the slow leaves falling.

ABOUT THE AUTHOR

MARY GRIMM was born in Cleveland, Ohio, where she has lived most of her life. She was managing editor of *The Gamut* at Cleveland State University before joining the faculty of Case Western Reserve University in 1989 to teach creative writing. Her fiction has been published in *Redbook, Story,* and *The New Yorker.* Her short story "We" won a National Magazine Award for *The New Yorker* in 1988 and was also selected by *Best American Short Stories* as one of the hundred most distinguished short stories of 1988.

ABOUT THE TYPE

This book was set in Bembo, a typeface based on an old-style Roman face that was used for Cardinal Bembo's tract *De Actua* in 1495. Bembo was cut by Francisco Griffo in the early sixteenth century. The Lanston Monotype Machine Company of Philadelphia brought the well-proportioned letter forms of Bembo to the United States in the 1930s.